THE SMARTING OF SELINA

'Phryne Wuldingdoune was right,' the matron said drily. 'She has delivered a prize cargo. I'm warned you three miscreants are especially wicked – let's hope your bums can stay clean of further stripes. I dare say you've had a lot of fun with those lustful redcoats, but that all has to stop. Chastity is part of smart training – Miss Kew, our discipline mistress, is very strict, and an expert with bare bottoms.'

'We're just pieces of meat, aren't we, Miss?' gushed Hardast. 'It is so exciting.'

By the same author:

MEMOIRS OF A CORNISH GOVERNESS
THE GOVERNESS AT ST AGATHA'S
THE GOVERNESS ABROAD
THE HOUSE OF MALDONA
THE ISLAND OF MALDONA
THE CASTLE OF MALDONA
PRIVATE MEMOIRS OF A KENTISH
    HEADMISTRESS
THE CORRECTION OF AN ESSEX MAID
THE SCHOOLING OF STELLA
MISS RATTAN'S LESSON
THE DISCIPLINE OF NURSE RIDING
THE SUBMISSION OF STELLA
THE TRAINING OF AN ENGLISH GENTLEMAN
CONFESSIONS OF AN ENGLISH SLAVE
SANDRA'S NEW SCHOOL
POLICE LADIES
PEEPING AT PAMELA
SOLDIER GIRLS
NURSES ENSLAVED
CAGED!
THE TAMING OF TRUDI
CHERRI CHASTISED
BELLE SUBMISSION
STRAPPING SUZETTE
THE ENGLISH VICE
GIRL GOVERNESS

THE SMARTING
OF SELINA

Yolanda Celbridge

This book is a work of fiction.
In real life, make sure you practise safe, sane and consensual sex.

First published in 2004 by
Nexus
Thames Wharf Studios
Rainville Road
London W6 9HA

www.nexus-books.co.uk

Typeset by TW Typesetting, Plymouth, Devon

Printed and bound by
Clays Ltd, St Ives PLC

ISBN 0 352 33872 5

Contents

1	Whopped Nude	1
2	Fur Undressed	18
3	Fit for the Cane	36
4	Prison Bound	53
5	Air Bare	70
6	Full Bung	85
7	Over the Knee	102
8	Twirlspank	119
9	Swanky Bum	136
10	Naked Squelching	152
11	Thwangs	166
12	Squirmbottom	180
13	Hot Weals	198
14	The Birch Bucket	215
15	Selina Smarting	232

You'll notice that we have introduced a set of symbols onto our book jackets, so that you can tell at a glance what fetishes each of our brand new novels contains. Here's the key – enjoy!

cp (traditional)

cp (modern)

spanking

restraint/bondage

rope bondage/hojojutsu

latex/rubber/leather/enclosure

fem dom

willing captivity

medical

period setting

uniforms

sex rituals

1

Whopped Nude

Selina Rawe climbed from her bath, onto the thick white carpet, and accepted a fluffy towel from her maidservant, who was sparkling in her French maid's uniform of black fishnet nylons, white apron over frilly black tutu, white blouse, her hard-swelling breasts braless underneath, spiked stiletto heels, and bonnet. As the girl waited with her bathrobe, Selina towelled herself, while swivelling to inspect her steaming nude body in the full-length mirrors flanking the tub: the high, full breasts dripping from the nipples; the flat, tan belly, narrowing to pencil thinness below her big whorled navel, then widening massively to the hips and haunches; the luxuriant forest of pubic fronds hanging wet and tangled, well below her pendant cooze flaps, between hard, rippling thighs; the swelling plums of her bare buttocks quivering softly as she passed the cloth between her legs; her tall, coltish body glowing gently golden, in an all-over bronzing, suffused with pink after her hot bath. She dropped her towel, without looking, and Jane caught it. Nude, she ignored the proffered bathrobe, and stepped on the weighing scale, where she licked her lips, nodding in satisfaction.

'A measurement, Miss?' said the maid.

'Well, I was forty, twenty-two, forty, only yesterday,' Selina drawled. 'Do you think I've put on weight?'

'Certainly not, Miss,' the maid replied, her accent as mellifluous as Selina's. 'Some muscle, perhaps.'

1

Selina tossed her head, allowing her long blonde mane to cascade over her back, and laughed, a smoky, fluted peal of bells from her throat.

'You flatterer, Jane,' she said. 'I suppose it's what I pay you for.'

'I try to give satisfaction, Miss,' said Jane, curtsying, with a slither of her shiny black stockings, and her own lustrous chestnut tresses bobbing in their pinned bun.

Selina accepted her yellow towelling bathrobe, and padded barefoot into the living room of her flat. Outside, it was a cheerfully sunny spring morning, and the traffic, muted by the heavy glazing, was dense on the nearby Fulham Road. She sat at her dining table, which was naped in fresh white linen, with daffodils in a vase. Noiselessly, Jane served her breakfast: two boiled eggs, pineapple juice, hot buttered toast with Seville marmalade, and coffee. As she ate, Jane stood beside her, hands folded over the apron covering her lap.

'Does Miss want the newspapers?' she asked.

Selina wrinkled her nose.

'Too, too yawn-making,' she said. 'I already know most of the rubbish, especially what the potwalloping hacks haven't dared include.'

'Very good, Miss,' said the maid. 'If Miss will pardon me, it must be awfully exciting to be in the newspapers. I'm rather envious.'

'Yet you've chosen to be a lady's maid, Jane. Writing a newspaper column is just a job, however exciting it may seem. I may be London's glammest agony aunt, and at the age of twenty-one, I jolly well should be, but I'm still on page five. With those looks, and that body, you could be in the papers yourself.'

'Miss is too kind,' said Jane, blushing, with an automatic curtsy. 'But I'd rather Miss didn't say things about my body, if it pleases. I'm too shy for that. I'm envious of Miss's body, too – why, I've an inch more at the waist, and an inch less up there, and down there.'

Selina paused to munch a mouthful of toast and eggs, then licked crumbs from her lips, dabbing them with her linen napkin. She sipped her coffee.

2

'You're a juicy package, gel,' she purred, 'and not so shy at school. In fact, you were a grimy oik, when I was a sixth form prefect, and a bit of a tomboy – the form monitors were always caning naughty little Jane Weels, of the remove, for mischief.'

'I'd prefer not to be reminded, if it please Miss,' Jane mumbled. 'It wasn't very nice, being caned on my bare bottom.'

'It was only a few years ago, gel,' Selina said. 'I wonder what made you choose to be a lady's maid. It can't be the pay, or the comfort. A maid's loft, with cold showers, and no boyfriends, isn't exactly sybaritic.'

'There are other rewards, Miss,' said Jane. 'A job well done, I mean,'

'Except when you don't do it well,' Selina murmured. 'You can be sloppy.'

'Oh, *Miss*,' blurted Jane, 'that's not fair, if it pleases. Miss knows I try to do my best.'

Selina waggled her little finger.

'Careful, Jane. I decide what's fair, round here.'

'Yes, Miss. Of course, Miss. Sorry, Miss.'

Selina pushed away her breakfast plate, opening her mouth in a yawn, which she covered with her stretched fingers. She strode into the secondary bathroom. It was carpetless, and occupied by a lavatory and washbasin. A number of brightly-coloured tubes and nozzles had been fitted above the sink. She doffed her robe, and handed it to Jane, who hung it on a peg, then waited, head lowered, as her mistress squatted naked on the lavatory seat. There was a hissing as Selina's pee spurted, wreathing her thighs in steam. Her nostrils flared, her eyes closed, and she breathed in deeply, as heavy dungs splashed, plopping loudly in the water beneath her buttocks.

'Ahh . . . yes . . .' she sighed.

After a few more moments, she rose, turned to the wall, with her legs wide apart, and spread her buttocks. Jane wiped her anus with two pieces of pink toilet tissue, which she dropped in the pan before flushing. Taking a long tube from the sink, she turned on a jet of water, and directed

3

the nozzle at Selina's anal pucker. The water squirted harshly all over her inner fesses and arse cleft, and Selina shivered.

'Golly, that's cold,' she exclaimed.

'Sorry, Miss,' blurted Jane. 'I'll warm it. Does Miss want deep or shallow lavage this morning?'

Selina pursed her lips.

'Deep, I think,' she replied. 'It feels better answering all my whingeing readers, with a nice clean bottom.'

Jane adjusted the tap, then pushed the nozzle within an inch of Selina's naked anus bud, so that the fierce jet of water pierced the wrinkled lips of the anus, directing the entire flow of water into Selina's anal passage and rectum. Selina's buttocks squirmed.

'Ouch!' she cried. 'That's freezing. You careless drab.'

'Oh, Miss, I'm sorry,' blurted Jane, adjusting the tap.

'No, leave it,' gasped Selina, knocking the girl's hand away. 'Mm . . . it's quite good, actually. A real bumfreezer. Ooh! It tickles so. Yes, push it all the way in, Jane, right into the rectum. Tickle my sigmoid colon . . . oh . . . yes . . .'

Jane thrust the tube deeper inside her mistress. Selina writhed, bent over, and clutching her thighs, with her buttocks jerking.

'And *écartez*, for a moment,' Selina gasped.

Jane pulled the tube from Selina's buttocks, and moved it aside, so that the water splashed on the ceiling, drenching her mistress.

'Oh! Bother!' Selina cried. 'You silly, silly, girl.'

'Sorry, Miss,' Jane stammered.

'Ahh . . .' Selina sighed, as a jet of slimy water spurted from her anus, soaking Jane's blouse, skirtlet and stockings.

'Again, Miss?' Jane asked.

'Yes,' panted her mistress. 'Colder, if you can. I wonder if I should give up hot lavage altogether.'

Jane thrust the tube into Selina's anus, slamming the sigmoid colon.

'Ouch!' Selina gasped. 'Bit hard, Jane.'

'I'm sorry, Miss,' Jane blurted. 'I seem to be all fingers and thumbs today.'

'Give me a good icy spurt, and perhaps I'll forgive you,' Selina said.

The water powered into her rectum, her buttocks wriggled violently, and she grunted, panting.

'Ooh! Ahh! That's good.'

After a few minutes of water filling her mistress's rectum, Jane withdrew the tube, and Selina's rectal contents squirted in a powerful jet all over the maid. Jane's blouse was soaked and transparent, revealing her hard bare breasts, naked under the flimsy cotton, with her nipples pink, erect plums. Panting hard, Selina instructed the maid to repeat the operation. After five repetitions, her long legs quivering, streaked with water, she pronounced herself sated.

'To your satisfaction, Miss?' Jane said.

'Yes. Yes, it *was* rather good,' answered Selina, rubbing her wet bare bottom. 'But I can't forget your appalling clumsiness.'

'No, Miss,' said the maid.

'And just look at your uniform! Quite a mess, you sloppy thing. You'd better strip, and put it in the laundry basket. You can do your housework in the nude today. I don't care if it's cold. I'm jolly cross with you.'

Jane began to unfasten the soggy straps of her skirt and pinny. Selina watched her, stony-faced, as the blushing girl stepped out of her shoes, rolled down her stockings and wet panties, revealing her massive, soaked pubic forest, and unpeeled her wet blouse, leaving her big bare bubbies quivering.

'Shall I fetch the slipper, Miss?' she whispered, when she was as naked as her mistress.

'You shouldn't need to ask, gel,' said Selina. 'I'm afraid that's *another* fault. You may dry, and warm up, then report back in the nude. *With* the slipper.'

In her bedroom, Selina inspected the array of costumes displayed on the bedspread, nodding her approval at the tidy symmetric arrangement: camel, dark blue, pink, green,

5

grey, black. She did not take long to select a suit of tight miniskirt and jacket, in shiny grey shantung silk; scalloped shell-pink bra, with matching thong panties; white blouse and sussies, with shiny white fifteen denier nylon stockings, the coarser weave giving a chunky sheen to her legs, as she slipped them over her smooth-shaven muscles. Bright sun shone through her bedroom window, and her body was clammy with sweat; she debated whether to go braless, and decided to fasten her forty-inch teats in their flimsy, unnecessary support, but looked long at the knickers, smiled impishly, and popped them in her handbag.

She selected a white waspie corset, laced it to nineteen inches across her flat belly, with a little wrinkle of her nose, as it *would* go tighter, then hooked her white sussie belt beneath it. She zipped her skirt, fastened her blouse across her pendulous bubbies – both garments a deliberate size too small – then snapped the garter straps in place, framing her massive blonde quim bush. She combed the tangled fleece for nearly a minute, until it shone sleek and glossy, with the tendrils dangling below her gash lips arrayed in rows, reaching several inches down her thighs. Sharp pink shoes, with heels that were not quite stilettos, completed her robing, as the obedient Jane knocked on the door. Bade enter, she tendered a slipper to her mistress, while shyly attempting to cover her breasts and quim hillock with her arms.

'My, you are a coy thing,' Selina said. 'And yet your nips are stiff.'

'I'm nervous, Miss,' Jane murmured, blushing. 'I always get nervous before a whopping.'

'You shouldn't earn whoppings, in that case,' Selina retorted. 'Let's have you, then. You know the drill.'

The maid parted her legs, and bent over, touching her toes, to present her bare buttocks for her slippering. The firm buttock meat was puffily scarred at waist and mid-fesse, by etched lines of panties elastic.

'Looks like your panties are a tight fit,' Selina said.

'You know they are, Miss. They're the ones you issued, and I told you they're a size too small, like my bras and corsets and skirts.'

'That's why you were braless this morning.'

'I . . . I suppose so. It's more comfortable to have bare breasts.'

'I don't pay my maids to be comfortable,' Selina snapped. 'I pay them to be correct. I should add whops for that, but let's get started, before your roster of crimes is too vast . . .'

She flexed the leather slipper, then raised her arm over the girl's bare bottom. *Whap!* The leather struck naked bumskin. Jane caught her breath, as her buttocks clenched, and her breasts wobbled. *Whap!* The slipper's imprint appeared pink on the bare flesh, and the maid gasped. Her titties quivered, the points of her nipples swaying erect, as her bottom and whole body shook, with her long legs trembling, beneath the glowing pink blossoms on her spanked cheeks. *Whap!*

'Oof!'

'Hurting?' said Selina.

'Gosh, yes, Miss.'

'Good. When did I last have to whop you?'

Whap!

'Ouch! It was a week ago, Miss. You find reason to spank me almost every week.'

Whap! Jane's bare bum quivered, as the flat of the slipper thwacked her reddened skin.

'I dare say it's unusual for maids to be spanked by their employers, and may seem rather harsh.'

Whap!

'Why, no Miss.'

Whap!

'You knew my requirements before you entered my employ.'

Whap!

'Ouch. Yes, Miss. I've no complaints.'

'You went to a proper school, that's why, and understand a lady expects good manners and deportment from her servants.'

Whap!

'Ooh . . .'

Jane's bare bottom was rosy with slap marks, and trembling incessantly, her cheeks clenching to a tight hairline.

'Above all, no sloppiness. A place for everything, and everything in its place. I believe in curing sloppiness with old-fashioned healthy English discipline, just as at school. There is far too much whingeing in today's England. You only have to see the pathetic complaints my readers send.'

Whap!

'You *have* been rather sloppy of late, Jane.'

Whap!

'There's really no excuse.'

Whap!

'Oof! No, Miss.'

Whap!

'I do think the slipper on bare clears the air between employer and servant, don't you?'

Whap!

'Ooh! Yes, Miss, I agree.'

Whap!

'Schools lay it on a bit thick, perhaps, with overuse of the cane.'

Whap!

'There is no need to go that far. I was too virtuous for the cane, myself, but I saw the marks my cane left on others, so perhaps I am a bit squeamish.'

Whap!

'Oof! Not at all, Miss.'

Whap!

'A slippering is much jollier. No hard feelings afterwards, and no horrid bruises on your bum. Well, not really.'

Jane's squirming bare buttocks were now well suffused in purple and crimson blotches.

Whap!

'Ooh! Ah! Y . . . yes Miss.'

'Some prefects, I know, actually took a delight in striping a girl's bare bottom, and making her cry. Personally I thought that was rather beastly.'

8

Whap!

'Ooh . . . uhh . . .'

Jane's naked bottom clenched tight, as her legs trembled, and her fingers were white, clutching her toes. Her titties shook, at each slap of the slipper to her bare nates.

Whap!

'*Ahh!*'

'I *am* hurting you, Jane. Perhaps your bottom's especially tender this morning.'

Whap!

'Ooh! Ooh!' Jane blubbed.

Though she held position, her bare bottom and titties shook uncontrollably.

'Yes, your cheeks are colouring up quite nicely. Should be a day before that fades, I'm afraid.'

Whap!

'Ooh!' Jane gasped, wriggling furiously.

The slipper continued to rise and fall for another minute, with Selina's own titties bouncing like jellies, trapped under her tight blouse, as she whopped the squirming maid's bare. Jane's naked buttocks glowed crimson, when Selina finally halted her beating. She stroked Jane's bruised bare bottom.

'My, you haven't changed since school,' she murmured. 'Feeling better?'

She reached for her handbag and jacket.

'Y-yes, Miss,' gasped Jane. 'It does smart a little.'

'Good. I reckon that was your usual fifty, wouldn't you say?'

'It felt like it, Miss. If it please, Miss, I was to remind you that Mr Addercop is coming tonight.'

'Ah, yes, dear Henry. I think we'll stay in for a little *souper à deux*. He always gets bally well pissed when we go out, and then he's a bore. You may prepare a nice *homard à l'armoricaine*. You'd better go to the fish market – after your whopping, you are excused from wearing knickers.'

'Thank you, Miss,' Jane said, kneeling, and ritually pressing her lips to Selina's toecaps.

'Now, throw on a frock, and scamper downstairs, to hail me a taxi.'

An hour later, Selina was sitting at her desk, in the bustling, open-plan newspaper office, sorting her post. Behind her, the partition wall was adorned with a giant enlargement of the photo that graced her daily column: Selina, sternly cross-legged, in dark woollen suiting, with a mid-thigh skirt, and her long legs well exposed in their shiny black nylons; fingers clasped, and lips pursed, like a schoolmistress about to deliver punishment. This effect was suggestively heightened by her dainty swagger stick, angled up from her lap, like a school cane. She wore a hat and sequinned veil, so that her features were recognisable to friends, but not to her public. 'Miss Etiquette' eschewed the computer, and insisted on a proper secretary, as well as properly written communications from her readers, on notepaper of acceptable quality, in fountain pen ink, and placed in a matching envelope, with the postage neatly affixed. That did not stop her frowning as she studied the dilemmas of her correspondents.

'Really,' she said to her secretary, Harriet Purse, a rangy, long-legged brunette from Sevenoaks, and of Selina's age, 'it doesn't get any better. Listen to this: "Dear Miss Etiquette, I'm engaged to be married to Darren in a few weeks, but I know he's been giving a portion to Leanne, who is to be one of my bridesmaids. I'm really gutted as you can imagine, and I wonder if I should teach him a lesson by snogging his mate Kev, who is to be our best man. I know Kev fancies me something rotten and I wouldn't half mind going all the way with him, especially as he gave one to my best friend Wendy on a holiday in Ibiza, and she was over the moon. Trouble is, I really fancy Kev, and don't think I could stop seeing him after I married Darren, especially as it would take Wendy down a peg, who is a stuck-up madam if you ask me, and I know Darren used to go with her before. I used to go with Wendy's current boyfriend Wayne – we met in Corfu – and Darren is jealous, because Wayne is on the rebound from Leanne, and wants me and him to be an item again, though I don't know if Wendy suspects. What should I do? Yours in confusion, Cherilene, Basildon". Really, Harriet, the mind has ceased boggling, but it still comes jolly close to boggling.'

'Yah,' said Harriet. 'Do you want to answer that one?'

'I suppose so. Here goes. "Dear Cherilene, I am obliged to you for informing me that humans can be gutted as well as fish. Otherwise, perhaps it is you who needs to be taught a lesson. What you should do is take a very cold shower, or several, before having a frank discussion with Darren. If he is a real man, he will put you over his knee, take your panties down, and give you a sound spanking on your bare bottom, which is something any red-blooded man would have given you long ago. Failing that, you could move away from Basildon and its complications. I am sure you will find adequate romantic opportunies in Brentwood, or Billericay. Yours sympathetically, Miss Etiquette." Got that?'

'Yah,' said Harriet. 'Here's one from a filly in Edinburgh, worried because her boyfriend likes to paint her in blue woad, and lick it off. Something to do with potassium permanganate.'

'Yuk! Messy. Send it to the science editor,' said Selina, already frowning over the next letter. 'This one looks a bit more serious: "Dear Miss Etiquette, This is a very difficult letter for me to write, but I feel you will understand. I am a reasonably fit and attractive housewife, age thirty, and I live in Berkshire, in a lovely house valued at nearly a million. My husband works in London, in a merchant bank, and we have always been very happy, until the other day when, after we'd had a few drinks, and were feeling amorous, he asked me to spank his bare bottom. I've heard of such things and imagine they are practised by perverts, so naturally I refused, which rather dampened our evening. Since then, I notice he has been very coy about undressing or lovemaking, which he will only do in the dark, although he is very brutal in penetration, as if he wants to punish me, which actually I rather like. I have felt his bottom sometimes when he is on top, and it feels hard and leathery, as if bruised by beating. I suspect he is visiting some house of shame to enjoy the filthy pleasures I refuse

11

him. What should I do? Yours, Valerie, confused in Pangbourne." Well, that's easy.'

'Yah, I'd think so,' said Harriet. 'Take a riding crop to the whelp.'

'Perhaps not so dramatic, Harriet,' said Selina. ' "Dear Valerie, I suggest you pull yourself together and stop feeling sorry for yourself. A British stiff upper lip is called for. In your kitchen, you will undoubtedly find some long soup spoons or similar. Tell your husband he is a vile pervert [he won't deny it] then order him to remove his clothing. Give him a sound thrashing on his bare behind with your chosen implement, until his buttocks are crimson, and he is whimpering. They must be crimson – such a *satisfying* colour. Tell him he can expect the same, whenever you have reason to be displeased with him, and make sure he displeases you often. You will find a vast improvement in the quality of your marriage. Don't try and fathom why, but men need to be disciplined, to stop them being beastly. The same goes for women, so don't whinge if your reinvigorated hubby takes his strap, puts you over his knee, and gives you some of your own medicine. It will do you a power of good, and who knows, you might enjoy it. You don't want to lose a house worth a million, do you? Yours encouragingly, Miss Etiquette."

Selina answered several more letters in similar vein, before the approach of noon indicated lunchtime, and a general exodus of women, eager to secure their places in the Bunch of Grapes wine bar, a cavernous Victorian pub, from which dockhands and Irish labourers had been politely ejected, to make way for soup, quiche, and the rustling of designer skirts. Selina perched on a banquette between Harriet and Claire Boosey, the crime editor.

'Jolly good advice, Selina,' Harriet said, munching through her smoked salmon sandwich, 'that gel in Berkshire. Give hubby the spanking he wants, though personally, I'd advise *him* to thrash *her* bottom, the self-pitying cow. Gels need a good school, and sound whipping, to teach them manners.'

Claire sipped white wine, blushed, and, with a nervous smile, nodded assent.

12

'I'm not sure I don't rather agree,' mused Selina. 'You know, when I joined the paper, I thought I'd be a real reporter. Sometimes I wonder if I'm not fed up solving witless people's problems. If only I had an *assignment* – going undercover, to spy on people like the Berkshire gel, to see how my advice works out in practice.'

'I dare say you wouldn't want to go to Basildon.'

'Well, not that, no.'

'You could spy on me,' Harriet said, impishly. 'My boyfriend spanks me.'

'Really? With what?'

'Just his hand, usually. On the bare bottom, mind. Puts me *wonderfully* in my place. It really stings, and then we *do sex*, and it's absolutely topping.'

'Just spanking?' murmured Selina.

'Well . . . he sometimes whips me with a riding crop.'

'Bare bum?' blurted Claire.

'*Completely starkers*,' Harriet whispered theatrically, pausing, for a sharp intake of breath. 'That *really* hurts, but it's *yummy*.'

Eyes shining, she took a triumphant bite of her sandwich.

'Weren't you ever spanked, Selina?' she drawled.

'Only at school,' said Selina, sipping her white wine. 'Slipper and strap, you know. Hurt like the dickens.'

'On the bare?'

'Of course.'

'Yes, it would hurt. But it's fun, afterwards. You were never caned? That's something else again. A good caning on the bare . . .'

Harriet shivered, pleasurably.

'Ugh!' replied Selina. 'Not caned. As a prefect, I had to cane gels, on the bare. Yuk! It leaves horrid marks, quite apart from the smarting. Of course, that might be good, in a real punishment caning, for minor delinquents, of the grimier classes. For domestic corporal punishment – which Miss Etiquette recommends – bare-bottom spanking, or slippering, is quite enough.'

'Yes, of course,' Harriet drawled, 'but admit caning fascinates you, as it does every girl – baring up to a brute

13

with a rod is *too* shiver-making. You give all this super pukka advice – cold showers and spanking and get a grip on yourself – as if toying with the idea of *real* corporal punishment. You must have *some* experience, apart from school.'

Selina smiled, blushing slightly.

'There's one place where you can observe real corporal punishment,' Claire said. 'Or could, if the authorities would let you. Ever heard of Auchterhuish?'

Selina shook her head.

'I seem to recall the name from school geog,' Harriet said. 'It's a geological quirk, in the Hebrides, a hot spring, or geyser, like Iceland.'

'Well,' Claire continued, 'today it's an experimental tough prison for wayward girls. Only minor miscreants – truants, dole fraud, that kind of thing. They get a short, sharp shock, called 'smart training', with corporal punishment on the buttocks, as part of the programme. If only I could sneak in an investigative reporter, undercover, to observe this barbaric regime at first hand! She'd have to *experience* it, too. But there's no way to do it, other than bending a judge, to make it look legit, and no judge would touch it, coming from a newspaper.'

Selina's eyes sparkled.

'If I could find a way to get myself in,' she said, 'you'd back me?'

'Of course,' said Claire. 'That would be terrific, if you're sure you can take, you know . . . corporal punishment. Of course we'd have a backup system, a code word to get you out, if you found it too rough.'

'Corporal punishment is easy to take, if a gel has the right attitude,' drawled Harriet.

Selina blushed, smiling coyly.

'It's not as if we all haven't been to proper schools,' she murmured.

Claire made a moue, pretending to rub a sore bottom.

'I could write some columns in advance,' Selina continued, 'and I'm sure Harriet wouldn't mind answering the new input. If I stayed there, say, a month, I'm sure I'd have enough copy for a super exposé.'

14

'You'd be incommunicado for at least a month, then,' Claire said, licking her lips, 'unless you can find some way of smuggling a letter past the prison censors, without revealing yourself. Of course, your piece couldn't be ongoing, or your cover would be blown. You'd have to make plenty of notes, and secrete them, for your articles, after you get out. What a yummy scoop!'

'I'll find a way. You see, a friend of mine is something rather grand in the Home Office. Is it a deal, Claire?'

'Deal, Selina.'

'Right, ladies,' Selina said, rising, 'I have an afternoon's shopping to do. Important date this evening.'

She winked.

'Is he going to spank you?' Harriet asked, impishly.

'Gracious, no,' Selina replied.

As the doorbell rang, Selina was putting the finishing touches to her evening costume: her little black number, a skimpy silken mini-dress, held to her bare shoulders by two gossamer straps, and clinging like liquid to her haunches, bottom and breasts, with her scarlet thong panties and strapless satin sheen bra clearly outlined beneath; black sussies, with seamed stockings of eight denier nylon, atop patent leather stilettos, very high; a rose in her hair, and an amethyst brooch clipped, though apparently pinned, to the naked skin of her left breast, just above the nipple, which was only just concealed by the plunging cleavage of her dress. She walked carefully into the sitting room, with her spike heels occasionally catching in the pile carpet, and made herself easy in her leather armchair, hoisting her dress up almost to her waist, so that the narrow string of her thong peeped above its hem, biting between the full red lips of her quim, amid the abundant blonde foliage of her gash forest. She listened to Henry divesting himself of hat, umbrella and gloves, in the hallways, and his boisterous 'Jane, you tempting little minx', spoken loudly enough for Selina to hear. She smiled, licking her teeth, and pressed her thighs almost together, but left an inch of bare skin visible, including her mound, scantily veiled by her shiny scarlet panties gusset, and her befurred gash, almost fully exposed.

'Mr Addercop, Miss,' said Jane, her face flushed.

She curtsied, revealing tight black knickers, under a frilly tutu, as she showed Henry in. His tall, slim, bulk filled the doorway, youthful sandy hair billowing over his brow, and his fleshy lips creased in a smile. He was dressed for dinner, with a black silk bow tie. His jaw dropped, as his eyes lit on Selina's gash, in the split second before she smoothly crossed her legs, with a slither of nylon.

'Henry, it's been simply ages,' drawled Selina, motioning him to a seat beside her. 'You must be feeling awfully fruity, to be flirting with my maid.'

Henry blushed.

'Oh, you know . . .' he mumbled.

'Not getting much, these days?' she purred. 'Too busy at grand intrigues at the Home Office?'

'I say, Selina, that's jolly unfair,' he blurted defiantly. 'I've more totty than I know what to do with.'

Listening, in the corner, Jane blushed.

'Liar,' said Selina. 'You wouldn't have been peeking up my dress, if that were so, you mucky pup.'

'You are a tease, Selina. I say, I love that brooch on your, ah, bosom. Isn't it a bit painful, having it pinned?'

'Yes, a bit,' said Selina. 'That's part of the fun.'

'Gosh. You modern gels . . .'

'I'm not a modern gel,' Selina retorted. 'I'm an old-fashioned English gel, as you should know, if you read my column.'

'But I do. I love reading you, Selina. You're so horribly cruel. You're a young fogey, like me. A fogeyess, perhaps.'

'Are you sure you don't mean "ogress"?' she purred, baring her teeth. 'I'm not sure I wouldn't prefer it.'

Selina toyed with her flute of champagne, while Henry put away three glasses of calvados. Their gossip continued when they went to table, where Jane deftly served the lobster, with a good chilled chablis to accompany. Henry tucked in.

'Anyone would think you hadn't eaten for days,' Selina said.

'Jane's cooking is so bally marvellous,' he replied. 'Well, what's new in the scandal sheet?'

Selina murmured some unpublishable trivia, about minor royals and celebrities surprised at venery with partners not their own, sometimes of the opposite sex. Henry licked his lips.

'And you?' he said. 'Not tired of being the nation's favourite agony aunt?'

'I am, rather,' she said, and recounted her conversations at the office, including that with the crime editor.

'So you see,' she concluded, 'I'd need a few rules to be bent – a compliant judge, to sneak me into this programme. You being a Home Office mandarin . . .'

She crossed her thighs, with a slither of nylons.

'It would be rather cold, up there in the Hebrides,' Henry said.

'I can take it. Heavens, I went to boarding school, and can put up with anything. I gather the place is a hot spring, geyser thingummy, so it shouldn't be too cold.'

Henry smiled.

'If you can beat me at cards, I'll do it.'

'Deal,' said Selina.

After pudding, they took their balloons of cognac to the leather sofa, and sat, relaxed, but not touching, with Henry puffing on a cigar. Noiselessly, Jane cleared away the dinner things, polished the table, and replaced the linen nape with a green baize cloth, upon which she placed a pack of cards, and two piles of coloured wooden chips.

'Ready, Henry?' Selina said, rising, and uncrossing her legs as she did so, to flash a sliver of pubic bush at her companion.

'Rather,' he said.

2

Fur Undressed

Selina's nylons slithered, as she strutted to the table.

'You know how I hate this,' she drawled, as Jane pulled back her chair, and she sat down at the card table, letting her skirt ride up over her thighs. 'I always lose.'

While Henry took his seat, she studied the bulge at his groin, and licked her teeth.

'You wouldn't like it if I cheated, to let you win,' he rejoined, through a cloud of fragrant cigar smoke.

'That's true. And I've a reason to beat you tonight.'

'Shall I sit, Miss?' said Jane, her own eyes on Henry's swollen crotch, and with a blush on her cheeks.

'Of course,' Selina said. 'You deal, as usual.'

Jane dealt the cards, and both players studied their hands.

'Three cards,' said Selina.

Jane exchanged her three cards, while Henry took one.

'Just to let you think I'm bluffing,' he said lazily.

'In that case, I'll bet you fifty,' Selina said, pushing chips to the centre of the cloth.

'Your fifty, and raise you a hundred,' countered Henry.

Selina bit her lip.

'Rotter,' she said.

'Want to fold?'

'No. Your hundred, and another hundred.'

'That's a lot of money,' Henry said. 'The gutter press must be paying well.'

'I refuse to be baited. Are you in or out?'

'I'll see you,' said Henry, matching her chips.

'You sure?'

'Don't bluff, Selina, it doesn't suit your ethereal beauty.'

'You *are* a cad.'

'And, caddishly, I'm seeing you. Show what you've got.'

Pursing her lips, Selina slowly unfolded her hand, and placed one queen on the baize, then another, and another.

'Just the three ladies?' Henry said.

'Wait. I haven't finished. You'll pay a price for being impetuous.'

She continued, laying two threes on the table.

'Full house, queens on threes,' she said impishly.

Po-faced, Henry displayed his hand: a knave, and four fours.

'Seems I scoop the pot,' he said, 'unless you want to invoke lady's privilege.'

'You know I do, damn you,' Selina said.

'Well, lose a garment, then. Your choice which, though I see you haven't many garments on.'

'You're worse than a cad,' Selina murmured. 'Will you accept a strap of my dress as one garment?'

Henry guffawed.

'*That's* a new one,' he said. 'Certainly not. You'll take off the whole dress.'

'Oh, go on, Henry,' she pleaded. 'Be a sport. Last time we played it was winter, and I had oodles of things on.'

'Let the dealer decide,' said Henry.

'Well, Jane?' Selina demanded.

Jane blushed.

'I think . . . *two* straps might count as one garment,' she blurted.

Selina glowered at her.

'Very well,' she said. 'Undo me, Jane.'

The maid fumbled with Selina's straps, until, abruptly, the front of her dress peeled from her breasts, and fell to her lap. Henry whistled softly; Selina's bubbies were revealed, almost naked, by her strapless scarlet bra, through which her nipple mounds poked high.

'They've grown,' he chortled.

19

'You absolute beast,' purred Selina, retrieving her wagered chips. 'Deal again, Jane.'

The next round was also unsuccessful for Selina. After heavy play, in which the pot rose high, she was obliged to show she had only two pairs, fives and sevens, which Henry beat with three tens.

'Lady's privilege again?' he smirked.

'Of course,' she said. 'Will you accept the rose in my hair as a garment?'

'No.'

'How about my bubby brooch?'

'Not that either.'

'Oh, Henry, you are beastly.' She pouted.

'I don't see what you're complaining about,' he drawled. 'In this game, I stand to lose money, but you lose only modesty. And now I'll have to do you some beastly favour, too. Let's have that dress off.'

'What does the dealer say?' Selina asked.

'If it please, Miss, begging your pardon, the dealer must side with Mr Addercop,' Jane blurted.

'Very well,' hissed Selina, glowering. 'Peel me, maid.'

She rose slightly on her haunches, allowing Jane to slip the dress up from her buttocks, over her breasts and belly, until it came free. Selina sat, with a feigned shiver, in only her bra, thong panties, sussies and stockings. She shook her head in disdain, sending her blonde tresses cascading over her bare back and breasts, heaving under their tight fastening of translucent scarlet satin. Henry inclined his head, roguishly eyeing her thighs, and pretending to peep at her panties, and half-exposed quim lips, although they were concealed by the folds of green baize. Automatically, she crossed her legs, and shot him a baleful look.

'Beast,' she said.

'You still have your shoes and stockings,' he said mildly. 'Not to mention your unmentionables. I suppose you never thought of taking *those* off.'

'Why, I ... I wouldn't feel dressed without them,' she retorted.

'At this rate, you'll be undressed one way or the other, won't you?' he said. 'Would the lovely Jane like to deal?'

Jane blushed again, with a pleased smile, and dealt. Selina looked at her cards, pouted, and asked for four replacement cards, while Henry took none. Her run of bad luck did not mend, and each beaten hand obliged her to lose a garment. Each shoe came off, followed by her sussie belt, then the left and right stockings, peeled from her bare legs as slowly and tantalisingly as possible. At last, Selina sat in only her bra and panties, and smiled impishly, as she revealed a straight flush; then bit her lip, as Henry nonchalantly displayed four sevens.

'Now we'll see your priorities, Selina,' he said. 'Which is it to be, bra or panties?'

'I don't suppose you'd accept one bra cup as a whole garment?' she said.

Jane tittered.

'In an ideal world, the size of your bubbies would qualify each as a separate structure,' Henry pronounced, 'but we live in a cruel one, so it's all off.'

Trembling, Selina allowed Jane to unhook her brassiere, and peel it from her skin. Her huge teats quivered, naked, with the nipples stiff and engorged. Henry licked his lips. Lazily leaning back, he parted his thighs to scratch, making no attempt to conceal the massive erection in his trousers. Jane peeked at the cock bulge, her lips pursed.

'Would the beauteous Jane deal what, I fear, must be the *coup de grâce?*' he purred, and Jane blushed.

She dealt, and play ended with Henry showing a pair of twos, while Selina had nothing but a nine.

'Seems I scoop the pot,' he said.

'I suppose you want me to stand, so you can look,' Selina said.

'Yes, please.'

She stood, and let her maid peel off her panties, lowering them to her ankles; with a moue, Selina stepped out of the panties, and stood in the nude. Henry gasped, looking at her pubic fur, and the pendant gash flaps beneath, sparkling with moisture. She approached him, twirling her

21

naked breasts, rubbing the bare flans of her arse, and stroking her cunt fleece, swaying inches from his mouth. He did not attempt to touch her, but sat still, gasping heavily, and his face red.

'You never even trim it,' he murmured. 'My, it is so lush. Fur undressed! A chap could feast in there forever.'

'I'm not sure I like your tone,' Selina said. 'Perhaps it's time you had your lesson. Jane, would you please help Mr Addercop off with his clothing?'

Henry panted hoarsely, as the maid stripped him. He stood, hands in front of his balls, vainly trying to conceal the massively erect cock, risen almost to his navel.

'The implement, please, Jane,' Selina ordered.

Blushing, and gazing at the erect tool, Jane handed Selina a copper soup ladle. Selina delivered a smart tap to the helmet of Henry's cock, and he winced.

'Down on your knees, Sir,' she hissed.

Henry crouched on all fours, while Selina mounted him, her cunt pressed to the small of his back, across which a shiny smear of fluid seeped from her gash. The ladle slapped his bare arse.

'Ooh, Miss,' he groaned.

Whap! Whap!

'Ooh!'

'Giddy-up, Sir,' Selina rasped. 'I'll have to ride you till that disgraceful erection wilts.'

Henry began to hobble back and forth across the carpet, then round the room, whinnying hoarsely, as the ladle spanked his buttocks. Selina was jolted up and down, her naked breasts bouncing heavily, as she thrashed him.

Whap! Whap! Whap!

'Ouch!'

'Trot, you lazy beast.'

Whap! Whap! Whap!

'Ooh, Miss, you are terribly cruel,' Henry gasped, speeding to a trot.

Selina's buttocks slithered on his back, in a wide pool of shiny fluid, oozing from her gash.

'Yes,' she hissed. 'I'm an ogress.'

22

Whap! Whap! Whap!

'Ouch! Ooh!'

She reached under his belly, and pressed the ladle to his balls.

'Ooh . . . no . . .'

Whap!

She struck smartly on the helmet of his cock.

'Ooh! That does it.'

He reared up, sending Selina sliding from his back, slimed by her come. Nude, she faced him, her hands darting to cover her gaping mouth, as she gazed, wide-eyed, at his quivering stiff cock.

'Oh, Sir,' she bleated, 'what do you mean to do with me?'

'*You* know, madam,' he snarled, grasping her left nipple, and pinching it, to lead her, whimpering, to the leather sofa, where he thrust her down on her back, parting her thighs with his knee.

Selina offered no resistance, but spread her legs as wide as they would go, with her feet rigid, and toes pointing to the ceiling. Her cunt was revealed, swollen and dripping come, amid the glazed forest of cunt hairs.

'Yes . . .' she gasped.

Her hand sped to her quim, and began to frot the extruded clitoris, gleaming with come.

'Yes, do me Sir, do me, I'm yours . . .' she whimpered.

His glans played at the entrance to her gushing slit, riding up and down amid the cunt folds, and tickling her clitty.

'Oh, Sir, don't tease a poor wench . . .' she moaned. 'Do me hard.'

'You asked for it, hussy,' he panted, and thrust his cock between her gash flaps, cleaving the pouch in one slamming movement, with his tool disappearing up to his balls inside her wet cunt.

'Ahh . . . yes . . .' Selina moaned, her thighs and buttocks rising from the come-slimed leather, to buck vigorously, as he began to fuck her, with hard brutal strokes.

He fucked for over two minutes, while Jane watched coyly, her hands hovering at her lap, and her nyloned thighs pressed together, with a hint of moisture in her stockings, peeping below her tutu. She watched Selina's legs, locked tightly around Henry's pumping buttocks, and touched herself between the legs.

'That's better,' gasped Selina, still masturbating her clitty, as Henry poked her. 'I needed a good pounding. You may be a prime rotter, Henry, but I can't resist that horrid tool thing of yours. Are you enjoying yourself?'

'Can't you bally well tell?' Henry panted. 'You've the juiciest, tightest slit of all, and you know it, Selina. I say, why not do it doggy fashion?'

'Ooh! Henry,' squealed Selina, as he withdrew, flipped her over, and reinserted.

'Gosh, yes, that's good.'

'Even tighter,' grunted Henry, his belly pounding against her raised buttocks.

He caught Jane's eye; the maid reddened, and lowered her head, swiftly removing her hand from her crotch.

'I say, Selina . . .'

'Yes, Henry? Oh, harder, harder, yes, ram me to pieces, you awful beast. I haven't been this wet for simply ages.'

'The maid gel, she usually waits outside . . .'

'Is she still here? Oh, yes – well, let her watch, she's only a drudge, you know.'

'I think she's been frigging, watching me bone you.'

'Really? How awfully quaint. Then let her frig, though I suppose I'll have to spank her for it later. Ooh, yes, Henry, that's *so* good. You're in fine form, you rampant stud. Can't you feel my cunny squeezing your cock? I want to milk every last drop of your spunk.'

His hips slapped against her sweating bare buttocks, as his cock withdrew, come-slimed, from her dripping pouch, and pounded deep inside her at each new stroke. So copious was her come, that his cock made a splashing, squelchy sound, at each thrust. Drool dripped from Selina's slack lips, as her fingers masturbated her stiff wet clitty, and she wriggled, groaning, under the fucking. Jane's lips were slack and drooling also, and the maid had her hand under her raised skirt, and inside her panties, where she caressed her naked cunt.

'It's terrific, Selina. Nobody fucks like you. So tight, like a wet velvet purse. Come to think of it, you've another purse, even tighter, and I mean to try it.'

'What? No, wait, Henry, don't stop fucking, I'm almost going to spend . . .'

Henry withdrew his dripping tool, with a loud, squelching plop, from her cunt, and nuzzled the tip against her writhing anal pucker.

'No! I beg you, Henry, not there.'

'Nothing wrong with a spot of bumming, gel. Don't tell me you haven't been done in the bumhole before.'

'Henry, don't be gross. No, as a matter of fact, I haven't.'

'Then this is your first time.'

'No! That's grubby. It's the sort of thing guttersnipes and serving wenches do.'

'Oh, go on, Selina, be a sport. It won't hurt, at least, not much. You'll like it.'

'I absolutely won't be a sport. It's horrid. Oh, go on, make me come in my cunny. I'll have to wank off, otherwise.'

Henry glanced at Jane's red face, the girl's jaw drooping, glazed with spittle, and her eyes heavy-lidded. She masturbated inside her panties, with oozed come staining her tutu and stockings.

'Serving wenches, eh?' he drawled. 'Well, I know of one serving wench . . .'

He beckoned Jane with a crooked finger.

'Oh, yes, Sir,' she panted. 'It's all right. You, as a master, have your needs. Yes, please do my bottom hole.'

'Jane!' squealed Selina. 'You wouldn't.'

'I would, Miss, if you please, begging your pardon. I've longed to feel Sir's member inside me, ever since he's been servicing you, Miss, and especially, in my . . . you know where. It's a super thrill, begging your pardon, Miss.'

She pulled down her panties and crouched on the carpet, beneath the sofa, with her skirtlet up, bare buttocks high and spread, so that her come-soaked anus and perineum winked at Henry, above her dense tangle of pubic fronds.

He plunged into her gaping anus bud, while straddling her, with his weight on her arched back.

'Ahh . . .' Henry gasped.

In a single thrust to Jane's proffered anus, his cock penetrated her rectum, with his balls squeezed in her arse cleft. He began to bugger the maid, whose hips shook, as her buttocks slapped his balls, meeting his every thrust with a squirming embrace of her bum cheeks.

'Yes, that's tight,' he panted. 'I haven't had such a tight juicy hole in ages. And what a lovely spanked arse. You've whopped her recently, haven't you, Selina? There's nothing so sweet as a good whopped arse. Is mine bruised? It feels jolly stingy.'

'Yes, it is, actually,' said Selina. 'So, technically, I *have* beaten you, Henry, and you owe me one.'

'I suppose so,' he panted. 'But you *always* beat me.'

'That's why you come,' she purred.

'*Touché.* I know a compliant judge down at Saltdean, near Brighton. She'll fix things. Leave it with me.'

'You are an angel, Henry. There remains the problem of my empty quim, while you tup my maid. I suppose I'll just have to frig myself.'

'Yes, do.'

She watched Henry's cock ramming Jane's bum, his massive shaft shining with come and arse grease, and mewled, as her fingers rubbed her erect clitoris. Come seeped from her cunt, down her twitching bare thighs, to wet the sofa.

'Oh, yes, Henry, give the slut a bumming . . .' she cried hoarsely, as she masturbated.

'Ooh! Ooh!' gasped Jane, as her bare arse melons quivered. 'Oh, that hurts, Sir. It hurts so much! It's so good. Do me harder . . . harder . . .'

'I like watching the gel squirm,' said Selina. 'I'm having a super wank, at any rate. And you *will* keep some spunk for my cunny, won't you, Henry?'

'You know me,' he panted. 'They call me the dairy man.'

'Boaster,' moaned Selina. 'Ooh, what a lovely wank. I'm going to come . . .'

26

'Please do. I like one troll frigging while I fuck another. My, her bumhole's greasy.'

'Buggery's a dreadful thought,' Selina gasped, masturbating vigorously, 'but rather exciting to watch. It must hurt her awfully. Ooh, yes, I'm going to explode soon. What about you?'

'Yes, my load's on its way, up this tight little arse. But it's elastic enough, the slut – she's no stranger to cock in her bumhole. The gel's wanking too. Just look at the minx.'

Jane's entire body shuddered under Henry's arse-pounding, as her fingers jabbed her come-slopped cunt, with her juices dripping onto the carpet.

'Uhh . . . uhh . . .' she moaned, her belly fluttering, as her wanking fingers tweaked her stiff clitty. 'Oh, bugger me, Sir, harder, bugger my hole . . . oh, yes, I'm coming . . . Ooh!'

Her body shook in spasm, as Selina effortlessly wanked off to climax, with a series of high, shrill gasps; Henry, grunting, filled the maid's anus with his spunk, spurting so powerfully, that it bubbled over the lips of her anus. From Jane's shaking bodice, a pack of cards dropped to the floor, spilling all over the carpet, to be drenched in the come squirting from her cunt.

'Why, the minx!' Selina squealed. 'Extra cards – so that's why I lost. She was cheating . . .'

'Please forgive me, Miss,' Jane whimpered. 'I wanted Sir's cock so much . . .'

'Lustful slut,' snarled Selina. 'Now you're really for it.'

'A proper thrashing?' said Henry.

'I should say so. She's had the slipper today, but cheating merits something tastier.'

'She might wriggle, she's a powerful wench. Best bind her first.'

'Right-ho.'

'Do you have some sticky tape, ropes, rubber cords, that kind of thing?'

'Possibly, in the downstairs broom cupboard. Jane would know. Jane, dear, would you go and fetch whatever's suitable?'

'Yes, Miss. Shall I put my knickers on, Miss? I haven't washed, and my bottom's all squishy.'

'No, don't do that. Better strip completely, and go downstairs in the nude. Take a cloth for your cunny, so you don't drip on the carpet. We'll want you in the nude, I expect, for your thrashing.'

'Very good, Miss.'

Jane curtsied, then, beetroot red in the face, stripped off her maid's costume, folding the garments neatly, with her shoes, sussies and stockings on top of her bodice, apron, blouse and tutu. Naked, she padded from the room, rubbing her bottom. Henry licked his lips. His softened cock swelled, as he watched Jane's buttocks swaying.

'Splendid filly,' he said, rubbing his hands. 'Almost as fine a croup as yours, Selina. Golly, that was a good bumming.'

'Well, you can keep that sort of filthy stuff for the servant girls,' Selina said.

She clasped the swelling helmet of his cock.

'I expect you're going to get all hard, as we bind the poor girl.'

'Rather. A girl, naked and tied up, is rather stiff-making.'

'You can keep your stiff cock for me,' she said, tapping him. 'Next poke, your cream's for my cunny, or else I'll *really* thrash your bum.'

'You might get *really* thrashed yourself, at this Auchter-huish place,' said Henry.

'How do you know?' she said.

'Home Office secret, gel.'

The maid entered, with an armful of ropes, straps, packing tape and kitchen wrap.

'I do hope it won't hurt very much, if you please, Miss.'

'Oh, I expect it shall, Jane,' answered Selina. 'You must be prepared for that. But we'll make you nice and cosy.'

Jane blushed, espying Henry's naked cock, risen again to full erection. On his instruction, she lay face down on the carpet, after being told to part her legs, and clamp both hands between her thighs, with four fingers of one hand

28

inserted into her cunt. She obeyed, the fingernails brushing her luxuriant gash fleece, then nervously stroking the fleshy, moist lips, before plunging deep into the pouch; she lay, grimacing, with her spine slightly arched. Spunk and come dribbled from her bottom. Henry bound her arms and legs with layers of adhesive tape, leaving her buttocks and teats naked. Next, he wrapped her tethered limbs in transparent cling film, very tightly, with layers of film trapping her hand inside her cunt, and snaking up her bum cleft, leaving buttocks and teats bare. Jane began to sob, her face wrinkled, and spittle drooling from the corners of her mouth.

'What is to happen to me, Miss?' Jane whimpered. 'Another slippering?'

'A little bit more than that, I suppose,' Selina replied.

'Is that why my bubbies are bare, as well as my bottom?' Jane asked.

Selina flushed.

'Well, I . . .' she started, then looked at Henry, who merely smiled, licking his teeth.

'Yah,' she said.

Jane shuddered.

'I *was* naughty,' she said faintly. 'But I *so* wanted bumming from Sir's cock.'

Over her sheath of cling film, Henry began to wind rubber cords around her body, knotting them severely, until she was cocooned in rubber.

'I'm a little surprised at you, Jane,' Selina said. 'Whence this extraordinary taste for, ah, bumming?'

'Oh . . . well, as you know Miss, I was in service with Mr Gawain Breasted, before I came to you.'

'Old "Double" Breasted!' whooped Henry. 'I was at Reppingham with him. So he's been up your damson jampot too.'

'Henry, don't be crude,' said Selina, watching, as the rubber cords swathed Jane's quivering body. 'Was Mr Breasted such a monster?'

'He was a good employer,' Jane blurted, 'but a strict disciplinarian, though he could be very sweet. I couldn't

29

resist him, especially after he'd given me a hand-spanking on the bare bottom, usually about a hundred spanks, which made me awfully hot and wet. He knew I was wet, because my cunny bush and lips were all squelchy on his thigh, and he said he wouldn't do me in the cunny, though I obviously wanted it, but he didn't mind bumming me. He was awfully . . . big, down there, and I needed him inside me, any fashion. So I let him bum me, that first time, bending over the sofa, with my face in the cushions, while he took me from the rear. I'd already been spanked by that time, and my bottom really smarted. Also, my cunny was flowing, and he took some of my come to lubricate his organ. I'll never forget his fingers prising my cheeks apart, and then the hot tip of his organ, quite monstrous, nuzzling against my pucker, and then the dreadful pain as he penetrated me. My bottom resisted, however much I tried to relax, and then, at the third or fourth thrust, I gasped in shock, as my whole inside bottom just opened up, and he slid into me with no trouble at all, right to my hard bit.'

'Filling your rectum,' Selina said.

'Oh, yes. Well, he started to shaft me, and my bottom squirmed, and thrust up to meet him, and it was just lovely, though painful at the same time. Like being full to bursting. I was in the nude, and was absolutely lathered in sweat, with my bubbies bouncing below me like two big custards, and I just thrilled, as I felt his hot cream spurting in my . . . my rectum, and I was so shivery and tingly, I just exploded with come, and I was dripping all down my thighs. After that, he bummed me pretty much every time he spanked me, which I got him to do, with little mistakes on purpose. He never poked me in the cunny, out of respect, only in the bottom. So, if it please you, Miss, my taste for *that* isn't really my fault.'

Jane's body was fully swathed in close-knotted rubber cord.

'I say,' she whimpered, 'it is awfully tight, and very hot. I'm really sweating.'

'That's part of your punishment, Jane,' Henry said. 'Now to hang you.'

He wound two long rubber straps into a cable, and slipped them across the top of her breasts, underneath her armpits. Hoisting her to her feet, he looped the cable over the door jamb leading to the kitchen, and pulled, until her feet dangled well above the floor. With the cable tied above the makeshift gibbet, Jane swayed helplessly in the air. Two firebricks were roped to her ankles, stretching her trussed body, with the bricks dangling an inch from the floor. His cock rigid, Henry rummaged in the kitchen for a paper shopping bag, and popped it over her head.

'Oh . . .' Jane moaned.

'I'll take the slipper,' Henry said, 'while you may use this, Selina. Very handy for the occasional chastisement.'

He handed her his thick, silver-studded belt.

'I expect you'd like to mark those naughty buttocks quite vividly,' he said, 'so you thrash her bottom, while I give her a titty-whopping.'

'Oh! No, please . . .' moaned Jane, the paper bag rustling at her anguished gasp.

Selina curled the belt around her fist, and raised it, studs out. Her hand checked her quim, and came away slimy with her cunt ooze. She bared her teeth, and, nostrils flaring, lashed the naked buttocks of the hung girl.

Opposite her, Henry slippered Jane's naked breasts, with backhand and forehand strokes, in rapid succession. Jane wriggled, her body held by the bricks weighting her ankles.

'Ooh . . . uhhh . . .' she whimpered.

Whap!

'Ah!'

Vap-vap-vap!

'Ooh! No, please stop!'

Whap!

'Ahh . . . ohh . . .'

Vap-vap-vap!

'Ouch! No! Oh, my bubbies!'

'Be quiet, you beastly girl,' Selina hissed. 'Take that!'

Whap!

'Ouch!'

'And that.'

31

Whap!

'Ooh!'

'And that . . .'

Whap!

'*Ahh* . . .'

Jane's buttocks, reddening under the strap, jerked and clenched in a frenzied squirm. Panting, Henry held his slipper aloft, and whipped her firmly on the nipples.

'*Oh! Ohh!*'

Selina wiped the sweat from her brow, and let her hand fall across her bare, heaving titties, stroking the hardened points of her nipples, to her wet pubic forest, and the swollen lips of her cunt, with the erect clitoris standing extruded from the lushness of the gash folds. Her thumb brushed her clitty, and she gasped, her spine stiffening.

'Ooh!' whimpered the writhing girl.

Jane's hand, trapped in her cunt, moved jerkily inside her wet pouch, and the clear plastic cling film swathing her pubes was sloppy with liquid, oozing from her gash. Breathing hoarsely, Selina touched her clitty, flicking and rubbing it, and began to masturbate, as she whipped the girl's blotched crimson bum flans. As her come flowed over her wanking fingers, she flogged the helpless naked buttocks faster and faster.

'Ooh! Gosh, no, please, Miss, I can't take it . . . oh!' squealed Jane, her paper bag soaked dark in her drool.

Henry's slipper spanked the bouncing bare teats, darkened with crimson bruises.

'Oh! My titties . . .' moaned Jane.

'Silence, bitch,' hissed Selina, sweat stinging her blurred eyes, and her hand slopped in the come, spurting from her cunt. 'Take what's coming to you without blubbing.'

Whap! Whap! Whap!

'Ooh! Ah! Oh!'

There was a loud hissing sound, and Jane's plastic cunt pouch swelled, filling with golden fluid, as she pissed herself.

'Ooh . . .' she wailed. 'Oh, I'm so ashamed . . .'

'Why, you filthy beast,' Selina snarled.

32

Her whipping continued, harder and harder, with the girl's body shuddering under the double lashes to bare breasts and buttocks. Jane's bottom was profoundly welted, with the imprint of the belt's silver studs clearly imprinted amidst weals of dark crimson and purple. Not an inch of her bumskin was free of the mottled blotch of weals, puffing to hard ridges. Selina masturbated vigorously as she flogged, drool sliming her chin, and come spurting from her pulsing cunt, to stream in glistening rivulets down her rippling bare thighs. The smacking of Henry's slipper on the maid's naked teats, and her wails of distress, were blurred by the pounding in Selina's ears, as she wanked herself closer and closer to come. Suddenly, she yelped, as Henry pulled her hair, and she dropped the belt. Twisting Selina's mane, he forced her, whimpering, to kneel before his stiff cock. He ripped the bag from Jane's head; the maid was scarlet in the face, her eyes hooded, and her mouth glazed with drool. Her trapped hand feverishly fingered her clitty, stabbing her cunt, still dribbling drops of piss, which sprayed from fissures in her cling film.

'Yes,' hissed Henry, 'she's wanking, just like you. See how girls can get carried away? Maybe you both need a spell of smart training at Auchterhuish. Jane can watch as you suck me off, Selina.'

'Oh, Henry! No . . .'

'Do it, while you wank. You can't be just *half* a slut, Selina.'

'Oh . . . oh . . .' Selina wailed, as Henry pushed his swollen glans between her lips. 'Urghh . . . mm . . .'

She began to tongue the helmet vigorously, while still masturbating her clitoris. Henry wrenched her hair sharply, forcing her mouth down over his shaft, until she engorged his cock with her lips right on his balls, and his glans filling the back of her throat. She bobbed her head up and down, sliding her lips all the way up his cock, to press his glans, with her tongue flickering on his peehole, before plunging, to fully engorge the cockshaft once more. Henry resumed Jane's tit-whipping.

'Ooh . . .' the girl moaned, wanking off hard, and her

33

plastic pouch filling with oozed come, as her bare breasts, glowing with bruises, bounced and slapped together.

'Like it, bitch?' Henry grunted. 'Like the taste of Jane's arse grease?'

'Mm . . . mm . . .' gasped Selina.

Her fingers slid into her pouch, and began to pound her wombneck, with her thumb pressing her clitty, as she fingerfucked.

'Then you can swallow my whole load,' panted Henry. 'My, you suck well, Selina. I'm going to spurt in a jiffy. Oh, yah . . . yah!'

Selina gulped, as the hot flood of cream filled her throat, so powerfully, that it bubbled from her lips, down her chin. She swallowed most of the load, watching Jane wank herself to climax, as Henry dropped the slipper and squeezed the maid's swollen nipples with his fingers, trembling slightly, as Selina sucked sperm. Selina tweaked her throbbing clitty as the hot cream flowed into her belly, and whimpered, as orgasm washed over her. As Henry's cock discharged the last hot spurt of spunk, she continued to suck the softening flesh, licking his peehole, until he was fully detumescent. She slid her lips from his cock, and nibbled his balls.

'Good, Henry?' she panted. 'Gosh, what a monster you've got. It must have hurt poor little Jane dreadfully, up her bum.'

'Yah . . . good for you?'

'Yah.'

Jane whimpered, snuffling and sobbing, as they relased her from her bonds. Selina stroked the raw welts of her belted bare arse.

'I don't know my own strength,' she murmured, 'but you can't say you didn't deserve it. Now, Jane, it wasn't that awful, was it? And you did manage a come.'

'It wasn't awful, Miss. I got all hot and wet, and . . . you know. You flogged my bum much better with Sir's belt than with the slipper, and my bottom smarted so much! I hope that isn't what you must expect at smart training, Miss, for I'd cry if I thought your bottom was mistreated,

34

or you were strapped and bagged or things like that. Mr Addercop hurt my titties so much, I thought I couldn't bear it, then I started to like the pain, horrid though it was, and it is sort of thrilling to know my bubbies will be all bruised and sore for ages. But it's not that, Miss. I let the side down, by peeing, and I'm just scared you're going to fire me for being so naughty,' Jane sobbed.

Selina cradled her, and stroked her bare breasts. She tweaked the big strawberry nipples, making Jane shiver.

'Why, Jane, you're a gem,' she cooed, 'absolutely the best maid I've ever had. Why ever should I want to fire you?'

3

Fit For The Cane

'You must be Selina Rawe,' rang a deep, melodious girl's voice.

The name was muffled by the hubbub. Selina toyed with her lemon juice, in the gloomy pub, deep in the labyrinth of Brighton's Lanes quarter, and did not look up, until she was entirely shaded by the tall, ripely curving body of a girl in a tight black leather miniskirt, matching military blouson, and black nylons, leading to shiny rubber boots. At her belt dangled handcuffs, a truncheon, and a small rubber quirt, about one foot long, with four thongs, that could have passed for an elaborate keyring. Her miniskirt was of the thinnest leather, clinging to her ripe buttocks, and suggesting she wore no knickers: only the outline of sussies and stockings showed. The blouson also clung to her skin, the big bubbies jutting high, without any mark of a bra strap. In the eclectic culture of The Lanes, she was not quite remarkable.

'Are you addressing me?' Selina said, squinting up at the newcomer's massive breasts, jutting tightly under black leather; the blonde locks ironed flat, over wide, sensuous lips, and big eyes, in an angelic baby face, belying her stern apparel.

Selina's own hair bobbed an inch shorter than usual, her long tresses trimmed, in a frivolous pretence at disguise. The girl sat down at the tiny wooden table, wet with beer slops, and made a moue. She carried a bottle of lager, and placed it in front of her, then lit an unfiltered cigarette.

36

'Of course I am,' she said. 'There's no one else to match your description. The size of your tits and bum alone identify you.'

'Well, really . . .' Selina began.

'I'm prison officer Celia Cockle,' she said. 'Prisoner Rawe, you address me as Miss Cockle, or plain officer. I'm your escort to the special parole board at Saltdean.'

'Prisoner Rawe . . . oh, yah, that's me,' Selina blurted.

'Funny place to collect a prisoner,' the blonde girl said, puffing aromatic smoke. 'Still, it takes all sorts. You're not the first unorthodox I've had to deal with, Rawe. Smoke?'

'Gracious, no, thank you. I'm not really a prisoner, you understand,' Selina said eagerly. 'It has all been fixed up with Miss Parkhurst, of the parole board. She knows my friend Henry, of the Home Office – I'm to get into smart training, and I've special code words to use, if it's too horrid, and I want out, but I can only use them once, so of course I can't tell you what they are . . .'

She stopped, uncertainly.

'All slags have some bollocks story. It makes no difference to me,' Celia said, shrugging, and taking a swig of her beer.

Her cigarette drooped from the corner of her mouth, and she managed to inhale and blow smoke, without removing it. She picked up Selina's leather holdall, and shook it.

'I say, wait a minute,' Selina protested.

'What's this?' said Celia, curling her lip.

'Why, my things – clothes, you know. A good suit, some nighties and blouses and underthings –'

'You won't want that, where you're going,' the guard sneered. 'Prison drab for you, slag.'

'But if the parole board don't accept me for smart training?' Selina retorted.

'Then it's back to the regular nick. But they'll accept you, all right. I can see the size of your arse.'

'I really don't think you should talk that way,' Selina blurted.

Celia reached forward, and slapped her with casual nonchalance on the cheek.

37

'Ouch!' Selina cried. 'How dare you?'

The guard slapped her twice more. Selina wiped a mist of tears from her eyes, and sat, crimson-faced and trembling.

'You're a prisoner, missy, a common, banged-up slag, and I talk any way I please. Now, get up, and let's be having you. It's a fair bus ride to Saltdean, and you won't give any trouble, or else I'll have to cuff you and call a wagon, and you'll have to pay for it, out of your prison stipend.'

'No,' said Selina, blushing, as the tall girl grasped her arm, to lead her into the bright sunlight, 'I won't give any trouble. I mean, I'm here by choice.'

'Sure you are, missy,' leered the blonde guard.

They walked up towards the bus terminal, by the rail station, turning heads as they went: two striking blondes, one evidently dominating the other. There were wolf whistles.

'Ignore them,' snapped Celia. 'Brighton's like that. Pretty depraved sort of place, all kinds of mischief and beastliness going on. Sexual things, you know. That's why the parole board meets out at Saltdean, in Miss Parkhurst's villa. Air's cleaner out there.'

She spat on the footpath, and lit another cigarette. After twenty minutes of waiting, and two more smokes, Celia pushed Selina up the stairs of the bus, and they sat in silence, as the vehicle chugged along the gleaming white splendour of Brighton's promenade, then the straggling outer suburbs, neat and clean under the bright sky, with the turbid waters of the Channel gleaming beside them. Selina gazed at the green English grass, breathing the sea-fresh air, and thinking that it was her last taste of freedom for a while. In the picture-postcard village of Saltdean, they descended, and walked for several minutes through pretty seaside villas, until they entered a deserted avenue, where the houses were grander and spaced apart. At the end of the cul-de-sac, they entered the driveway of a white villa, decked with honeysuckle, in a spacious garden of apple and pear trees, and luxurious rose bushes.

Celia led her round to the back, explaining that slags did not use the front door. She produced a key, and unlocked the door of an outhouse, a few feet from the back door of the house proper. Inside, there was a bench, cupboard, and bare floorboards, with feeble illumination from a tiny window.

Celia Cockle locked the door behind them, and lifted her mobile phone. After a brief report, she turned to Selina, who stood shivering, despite the heat in the small room, and clutching her holdall.

'Strip,' she ordered.

'What?'

'You're to appear in prison drab, missy. Girls in their own kit can have an attitude, and you do look a stuck-up bitch.'

'Now see here, Miss Cockle, I've had quite enough of this,' Selina blurted. 'Take me to Miss Parkhurst at once.'

Celia struck her twice on the cheek, very hard.

'Ouch!' Selina howled, rubbing her cheek, and wiping away a sudden tear. 'You beast! You're awful!'

'Get real, bitch,' said Celia. 'You're a slag. You have no rights, and make no demands. You'll leave here, one way or the other, in a prison van, and if you're smart, you'll be nice to me, for I can have you shackled and gagged. Furthermore, I know all the strappers up at Auchterhuish, and as well as Miss Parkhurst's report, they'll expect mine, over the grapevine, like. Now, strip.'

She opened the cupboard, and withdrew a shapeless sacklike dress, a pair of frayed knickers, and some scuffed tennis shoes.

'You'll put this lot on,' she drawled, 'but you can strip slowly, for I like to watch a girl shamed.'

Selina hesitated, biting her lip. Celia played with her truncheon.

'By law, I'm not allowed to mark you, or even touch you,' she spat, 'but there's plenty I can do that won't leave a mark.'

She made obscene gestures, indicating penetration of Selina's bottom with her truncheon, and then her hand made as if to squeeze hard on Selina's cunt. Selina shuddered, flinching.

'All right, Miss, all right,' she cried. 'I'm quite aware I must obey. After all, that's why I'm here.'

Trembling, she began to undress. Celia lolled on the bench, ogling her, and with one leg up, thighs parted, and her miniskirt riding high, almost to her spread crotch. Selina removed her navy blue velvet jacket, folded it neatly on the bench, and placed her handbag on top. Beneath her pale blue satin blouse, the outline of her scalloped brassiere showed clearly, thrusting her breasts very high. Celia licked her lips.

'I wonder what colour your bra is?' she purred. 'I rarely wear one myself. I like the feel of leather on my nipples. Well, we'll soon see. Show your titties, gel.'

Blushing, Selina began to unbutton her blouse, noticing that Celia was doing the same, opening the top of her leather blouson, to reveal several inches of bare flesh, the cleft of her breasts, almost to the nipples. One hand slipped beneath the leather, and began to caress her naked breasts. Selina undid her last button, and, shivering, slipped off her blouse, standing with her bubbies shivering in their skimpy powder blue bra.

'Very nice,' said Celia. 'And colour coordinated – I bet a snotty bitch like you has sussies the same. The bra off, please. Nice and slowly. Let those juicy big bubs spring out one at a time.'

Selina reached behind her, and unhooked her bra, her free hand crushing the cups to her titties, then releasing the left one, which sprang bare over the bra fabric. She attempted a smile at her captress.

'Like what you see?' she murmured.

Celia licked her bared teeth.

'Now the other,' she ordered.

Selina dropped her bra to her waist, and stood as the guard ogled her naked teats.

'Those nips are stiff,' said Celia, with a leer. 'You get off on stripping, eh? Bit of a tomboy?'

Selina blushed hotly.

'No,' she said. 'It's just . . .'

Doesn't the gel realise I'm in disguise?

'Just what? You like being shamed and ogled?' rasped Celia. 'Lots of gels do, you know. Skirt off, please.'

Selina unzipped and removed her skirt, leaving her standing in her high heels, navy nylons, and powder blue sussies.

'As I thought,' said Celia. 'Stockings next. And turn round, so I can watch your bum. It's a lovely big peach, forty inches, I'd guess.'

Shivering, Selina obeyed. She kicked off her shoes, and rolled down her nylons, aware of Celia's eyes on the rolling globes of her bottom, in its tight panties.

'I like the knickers,' Celia said. 'Nice high cut, scarcely more than a string. Why bother at all, with such a skimpy thong? I don't. It must chafe, between your quim lips. Maybe gels like you enjoy that.'

'Yes . . . I suppose it *is* for my own pleasure,' Selina murmured. 'Aren't all gels' undies?'

'Do you wear a corset?'

'Why, yes. Quite often, as a matter of fact.'

'Thought so. That slim little waist of yours, I imagine you can get it down to seventeen inches. Must hurt.'

'Well, it does, actually, but I sort of like –'

Selina halted in mid-phrase, and whirled round.

'Now look here, Miss. Do you think I'm some kind of kinky pervert? Or a . . . a lesbo?' she blurted, then gasped, as she saw Celia's blouson open, and her full naked breasts jutting from the leather, with the big strawberry nips high and stiff.

Her leather skirtlet was rolled up over her pubes, with the cunt naked, and Celia's fingers playing inside the fleshy red lips of her wet glistening slit. The girl's cunt hillock gleamed white, fully shaved of hairs.

'Let's have the sussies off,' drawled Celia, 'then the panties. What's wrong, Rawe? Never seen a shaven cunny? You'll see plenty where you're going, including your own.'

Her fingers danced in and out of her open gash, penetrating deeper at each thrust, with her thumb tweaking her erect shiny clitty. Selina blushed fiery red.

41

'It's not that . . .' she blurted.

'Come on, gel, you must wank off all the time,' said Celia. 'I expect you do it looking at yourself in the mirror. I do. Or whenever I get gels' juicy bums to look at. It's something you get used to in the prison service, whatever side of the cage you're on. You'll have plenty of frigging on Auchterhuish, and the better you are at it, the happier you'll be. Especially with a shaven cunny. It improves the sensation no end.'

'I . . . I don't understand,' Selina mumbled, unfastening her sussie belt.

'Why, healthy gels wank each other, don't they? Don't tell me you haven't done *that*.'

'Girls did it at school,' Selina stammered, 'but I wouldn't join in.'

'So you wanked off alone.'

'Yes, of course. I wanked off quite a lot. I mean, not because I wanted to, but because I was fruity, I mean, I *did* want to, but – oh, I don't know what I mean!'

Celia laughed, not unkindly.

'I *love* wanking off,' she said. 'I've always masturbated, especially watching gels caned bare-arse, at my snobby boarding school. It was a good reason to join the prison service.'

Selina stood, bare titties wobbling, wearing just her high thong panties, the powder blue satin clinging to her cunt hillock, with copious hairs of her lush pubic mane spilling over the gusset. Celia drew her breath. Her fingers wanked off faster, at her dripping cunt.

'*What* a forest,' she breathed. 'Panties off, gel.'

Biting her lip, Selina rolled down the panties, the sticky gusset making a plopping sound as she unpeeled it from her wet cunt lips. She was nude.

'Juicing, eh?' cried Celia. 'You *are* an exhibitionist. Well, we've five minutes to wank off, before you're due. They're doing another girl now, a right troll, I believe, and you'll ride up to Auchterhuish together – if you pass.'

'I don't want to masturbate,' blurted Selina. 'This is too, too shame-making.'

'You're a liar, as well as a whore,' said Celia.

42

Sprawling, she kicked Selina's garments onto the floor, and drew her thighs up onto her belly, exposing her wet frigged gash.

'Kneel down, bitch,' she purred.

'I don't understand.'

'Yes, you do. Kneel, and tongue me.'

'I'll do no such thing.'

'Missy, do you want the strappers at Auchterhuish to greet you with the *special welcome*? They can do things with seashells and thistles that teach you pain you've never dreamed of. And I can make it happen.'

'Oh, gosh,' wailed Selina.

'You've had boyfriends who licked your cunny?'

'Yes . . .'

'Then you know how to do it. Kneel, and do me, bitch.'

Selina's fingers touched her cunt, and came away glistening wet.

'Oh . . .' she gasped.

She knelt before Celia's naked thighs; tongue out, her face approached the girl's shaven, come-slimed gash. Her tongue touched Celia's erect clitty.

'Mm . . .' the sweating blonde girl gasped.

Selina's lips pressed the lips of Celia's cunt. Warm, oily come seeped into her mouth, as she increased the pressure, and began to flick her tongue on the clitty, while chewing the swollen cunt flaps.

'Suck, bitch,' moaned Celia, her cunt basin writhing, and her hands clasping Selina's hair.

Selina began to suck on the pulsing cunt, feeling the clitty inside her mouth, and her tongue basting it, as Celia's come poured into her throat. She applied her teeth to the stiff nubbin, biting gently, and Celia howled.

'*Urrgh!* Mm! Oh, yes, that's good . . .'

Her come dripped over Selina's bare titties. Moaning, Selina's fingers stroked her own bare bottom, feeling the goosefleshed nates quivering, then descended, across her anal pucker, to the wet, pulsing lips of her quim. She inserted two, then three fingers into her slit, finding her clitty with her thumb, and, as she gamahuched the writhing blonde, her hand, snaking backwards across the small of her back, and through her spread arse cleft, masturbated her own cunt. Her cunt gushed come, all over her wrist and wanking fingers. Faster and faster, she licked and sucked Celia's streaming gash, with come filling her mouth, and dribbling down her chin, onto her breasts, as if bathing them in hot milk. The girl's nyloned thighs locked Selina's head, squelching, as her thighs pumped, and pushing Selina's face firmly into her vulva. Her freshly-washed cunt smelled like flowers. As she masturbated, Selina's free hand cupped Celia's bare buttocks, to the blonde's moans of excitement, and kneaded the taut arse flesh, while getting a finger inside the girl's anus.

'Ooh! Oh, that's good,' gasped Celia, as Selina waggled her finger inside the arse-greased anal hole. 'Oh, yes, I'm going to come . . .'

Selina sucked and tongued faster, her naked breasts waggling, and her own cunt pouring with come, as she vigorously masturbated.

'Oh, yes, do me!' Celia yelped. 'It's the best come ever, you beastly fucking lesbo. Oh, yes . . . yes . . . *Ahh* . . .'

As the blonde guard heaved in climax, Selina's fingers masturbated her own cunt to climax, and her breasts and belly fluttered, as oily come poured from her quivering gash, and she moaned, wracked in her own orgasm. She lay, lathered in sweat, for a minute, her face still smothered by Celia's dripping cunt, and lapping her oozing come, before the guard ordered her to don her prisoner's garb. Selina did so, head low and face blushing, not looking the blonde girl in the eye. She fidgeted, scratching, in the sack dress and coarse panties. As Celia led her to the courtroom, she murmured:

'I don't normally . . . I mean, I don't know what came over me. Please understand! I'm not a lesbian, Miss.'

Celia smiled, reached under her sack dress, and patted her on the panties.

'All cons say that,' she said. 'Especially ones with gorgeous bums. You're a slut, missy, and you can't be *half* a slut.'

* * *

44

'Next prisoner, Selina Rawe. You must understand, prisoner Rawe, that although you have not yet served any time, this is a parole board hearing, not a courtroom, hence you are without benefit of counsel. You have already been sentenced by a court, and despite our revulsion at your vile crime of benefit fraud, we are not here to pass further judgement, rather, to examine your fitness for an exceptional disciplinary regime, with a view to your more rapid redemption.'

Selina shivered. Henry's friend, the pert and pretty Miss Pippa Parkhurst, looked absurdly young for a judge; as instructed, Selina neither gave nor received any nod of recognition. Miss Parkhurst gave her a brief, charmless smile, not to her, not about her, as though judging a microbe on a slide. The room was stripped bare, with white emulsioned walls, and polished brown wooden floor-boards; the only gaiety was a pot of mixed flowers, marigolds and pansies, on the judge's desk. The uniformed Celia Cockle stood immobile, by the door.

'Through counsel, you have requested transfer to the smart training programme,' she said, 'with a corresponding reduction in time served.'

Selina nodded.

'Yes, ma'am,' she said.

'It is a wise move,' she said, with the ghost of a smile. 'Smart training is not for every street slut, but only for those gels who possess a remnant of moral fibre, to be toughened by shock treatment. Think of it as the army. I sincerely hope we may pronounce you fit.'

'Thank you, ma'am,' Selina murmured, head lowered.

'Fit for the punishment by the cane, on your bare buttocks,' Pippa said slowly, baring her teeth, and Selina paled, buckling at the knees.

She must surely know who I am, but not the others. So she must go through this charade.

Pippa sat between two other board members: Miss Leofra Wolliman, and, to her rather anxious surprise, Mr Gawain Breasted. Selina was sure no one would recognise the veiled Selina Rawe of her newspaper photo – especially not in prison garb. Pippa was a thirtyish, full-figured ash blonde, her pert breasts and generous bottom tightly swathed in sombre black skirt and blue blouse; Miss Wolliman, a brunette, slightly older, with glasses perched on her Roman nose, and a figure no less ripe than Pippa's, yet, under her stern white blouse, a crimson bra showed clearly, cupping large titties. Mr Breasted was a rather less innocent version of Henry, with black hair slicked back, and a nasty leer, as he unashamedly ogled her body.

Just the sort of cad who would do . . . those things, to poor Jane.

Her eyes fell on his crotch, where there was a rather monstrous bulge, just like Henry's; she blushed, and looked away, as his eyes twinkled, catching her glance. She lowered her head, hands meekly clasped at her groin. Surely judges weren't supposed to be sexually aroused? Her costume didn't help – no bra, and horrid prison knickers, two sizes too small, that chafed and itched, as though made of hemp, and, worse, had stains at the gusset from the girl who had previously worn them; on top, the shift of coarse fabric, far too small, and very thin, clung to every curve and crevice of her body, outlining her breasts and bottom, and the swelling of her pubic hillock, before sheathing the rippling muscles of her thighs, and ending several inches above her bare knees. Pippa rapped her gavel on the desk.

'You may remove your garments, prisoner,' she ordered.

'I . . . I beg your pardon?' Selina blurted.

Pippa stared at her malevolently.

'We haven't much time, Miss Rawe,' she rapped. 'You, depraved gel, of all people, should be untrammelled by modesty. Strip, and be quick about it. We are required to examine your body, and test your suitability for the strict discipline on Auchterhuish.'

She leered at both her companions, who leered in turn at Selina.

'That is something you are already quite familiar with.'

'I . . . I'm afraid I don't understand,' Selina stammered.

The leers turned to cold frowns.

'The slut has amnesia?' drawled Miss Wolliman.

'You are ordered to strip, Miss Rawe,' said Gawain Breasted, licking his teeth. 'Best be quick about it, for your own good.'

Gulping, Selina grasped the hem of her beastly garment, and pulled it over her head, letting her naked breasts wobble, as she shook them free.

'And the panties,' said Mr Breasted.

Her face wrinkled in a blush, Selina rolled down the panties, and stepped out of them, leaving her nude, but for the scuffed prison issue tennis shoes. Automatically, she cupped her hands over her abundant pubic forest.

'There is no need for that. You may turn round,' Pippa ordered. 'Bend over the back of your chair, with your legs parted, and your buttocks spread and displayed. You may grasp the seat of the chair for support, but I want your feet well back and to the side.'

Selina gaped at Pippa's face, mutely pleading for a sign of confidence, but saw none.

'Come, Miss Rawe,' snapped Leofra Wolliman, 'you are surely aware of the requirements for admission to smart training. We are obliged to examine your buttocks, in the event – the very *likely* event – that corporal punishment shall be deemed advisable. You, of all people, should understand.'

Helplessly, Selina bent down as ordered, and felt the chair back bite into her navel, as she lowered herself forward, spreading her legs, with an eddy of warm air fluttering the dangling hairs of her cunt fleece against her quivering bare thighs.

'Bottom higher, and wider,' said Pippa.

Selina obeyed.

'That's better. Well, now you know what it feels like, as if you didn't before.'

'What *what* feels like, ma'am?' quavered Selina.

Mr Breasted tittered.

'Why, baring up below,' said Leofra, also chuckling.

'Your dossier reveals you as quite a scamp,' Pippa said. 'A vicious trollop, as your sentencing justice pronounced,

47

when he sent you down for two years. You were signing on for benefit in three different east London boroughs, and all the time, every newsagent in Stratford, Forest Gate and Manor Park carried your obscene postcards – "Miss Whippham, toff blonde model, gives naughty gents lessons in good behaviour". Now the boot, as it were, is on the other foot.'

'Oh . . .' Selina moaned.

'Heavens, Miss Rawe, didn't your counsel explain matters to you?'

'No,' Selina blurted. 'I mean, yes, yes . . .'

Henry said nothing about this. What sort of wicked stories has he told? I've never even been to east London . . .

'You surely don't deny it?'

'No, ma'am,' she whimpered.

'The hussy is certainly a good actress,' said Mr Breasted. 'She speaks just like a normal gel. I suppose her true gutter accents will slip out, when we test her.'

'Undoubtedly,' said Leofra.

'To make sure you understand clearly,' said Pippa, 'the regime at Auchterhuish is one of strict physical discipline, corresponding to imprisonment at hard labour of former times. The discipline includes short, sharp physical shocks for misbehaviour, that is, corporal punishment with the cane, whip or tawse – items with which *Miss Whippham* is undoubtedly familiar.'

Her voice dripped scorn.

'Oh . . . yes, I suppose so,' Selina gasped.

'So, you are no stranger to corporal punishment.'

'Why, no,' Selina said, 'I mean, at boarding school, I was spanked on the bottom quite a lot.'

'My dear Miss Rawe,' said Mr Breasted, 'we are not your sordid customers in Manor Park or the like. There is no need to put on an act.'

'I'm sorry,' Selina said.

A cabinet door creaked open.

'We are not here to punish you,' said Pippa. 'Your punishment shall take place during smart training. We are here to test you *fit* for punishment.'

'Oh!' Selina gasped, looking round, to see her judges inspecting an assortment of disciplinary intruments – canes and straps – arrayed in the cabinet.

'Keep your eyes front and head down!' snapped Pippa.

Trembling, Selina obeyed, yet raised her head slightly, to see their reflection in the French windows, looking out onto the lawn.

'Surely . . . you don't mean to beat me?' she whimpered.

'Certainly,' said Pippa drily. 'It is one of your fitness tests. A light beating, to make sure you can take it. Heavens, gel, as Miss Whippham, part of the depraved world of . . . of whipping and spanking *for pleasure*, you've undoubtedly been bare-beaten yourself.'

'Only spanked, ma'am, honestly!' Selina cried. 'At school. Sometimes on the bare, I admit, but usually on the knickers, drawn up tight.'

There was laughter.

'Those lying ways *will* be beaten from you, if we approve your entry to Auchterhuish,' Leofra said. 'We at this board have dealt with many cases of lying sluts who cheat the social security, many, who sell their bodies for vile profit, but rarely one mired in this incomprehensible world of corporal punishment for pleasure.'

She shuddered.

'How can any gel even think of such a thing?' said Leofra, smirking, and brushing an errant lock from her brow.

Her breasts quivered under her tight blouse.

'I swear I've never been caned . . .' Selina began, before her voice tailed off.

Her naked breasts shivered violently, as her whole body shuddered, erupting in prickly gooseflesh.

'The common hussy expects us to believe she attended an English girls' boarding school, and was never caned bare-bum?' Mr Breasted guffawed.

'Sir, I was a prefect,' Selina insisted. 'I caned girls – on the bare bottom – but I was a good gel, and was never caned myself.'

Mr Breasted rose, flexing a whippy little cane, and his crotch bulging; the two ladies followed, Leofra with a thick

49

leather tawse, in two tongues, and Pippa trailing a rubber quirt, with four vicious-looking thongs, two feet in length.

'All that is about to change,' Pippa said. 'You shall be tested with three implements, of ascending degrees of severity, and typical of those applied to inmates' bare bottoms during smart training. There are *thwangs*, the traditional Scots tawse, of forked leather tongues, used normally to beat errant schoolgirls on the naked bottom; the rubber quirt, carried by prison guards, for summary punishments in the field; for more formal chastisement, the traditional English wooden school cane, the birch being of course outlawed. But of course *Miss Whippham* is familiar with them, even the birch.'

'Oh, please, ma'am,' Selina moaned.

'What a hypocrite,' exclaimed Mr Breasted. 'She admits, or pretends, that, as a schoolgirl, she caned girls on the bare, without tenderness, as she watched their naked buttocks squirm and redden, and no heed to their whimpers for mercy. Then, as a vixen of the cane, she flogged beastly perverts, who paid for their sleazy pleasures. And she pretends to be frightened of a simple six of the best. It is well known that perverts, who take pleasure in beating girls on the bare, frequently enjoy the cane on their own bottoms. As long as the nates wriggle and redden, small matter whose they are. I suggest we make the test harder – say, a dozen.'

'Oh, no sir, please,' wailed Selina.

Her bare bottom shook, and she started, as hot wet drips sprayed from her cooze, onto her quivering inner thighs.

'A dozen might be appropriate,' mused Leofra, her nylons slithering, as she rubbed her thighs together.

Selina began to sob.

'Do you want to be accepted for smart training, or not?' spat Pippa.

'Yes . . . oh, yes . . .'

'Then, not another word from you. As a convicted prisoner, you must take everything you get, without blubbing or whining. Understood?'

Her eyes brimming with tears, Selina nodded. She flinched, gulping, but without protest, as several hands began to paw her naked bottom, kneading and stroking the flesh.

'I think we can dispense with measurements,' Pippa said, 'as Miss Gurdell's nurses can take care of that. This figure is quite outstanding. The bottom must be a good thirty-nine, perhaps forty. And see how perfectly pear-shaped the buttocks are, riding so high, and merging so flawlessly into the spine, with those delicious dimples. Yes, I'd say forty. The waist, too, is an achievement – the slut must wear a corset, to achieve such slimness.'

'Mm . . .' murmured Mr Breasted. 'Good firm English rump.'

'One of the best arses I've felt,' added Leofra. 'Well fit for the cane. And those titties – I guess at least forty, and certainly a C cup, perhaps a D.'

Selina panted hoarsely, as delicate fingers clasped her gash flaps, pressing them together, and rubbing them up and down.

'I like the quim,' said Pippa. 'And the forest adds lustre. I've never seen a hillock so bushy, and just look how the hairs dangle down over her cooze, between her thighs.'

'It *is* pretty,' said Mr Breasted. 'A hairy minge is always acceptable. Too bad she must be shorn, but then, a gel's shaven slice has its charms, and she shall grow back twice the jungle. Do you wish to test inside the pouch?'

'Let me,' said Leofra.

'Lady's privilege, my dear.'

Selina shuddered, as Leofra's fingers entered her slit, penetrating almost to the wombneck, and roiling the soft wet gash meat. Tears of shame sprang to her eyes.

'She's very tight,' Leofra said.

She fingered Selina's cunt for nearly a minute, before withdrawing her fingers.

'I think the slut is wetter than normal,' she drawled, 'as if her shame is exciting her.'

'Shame is the currency of perverts,' said Pippa. 'But to the essential – have we the anal speculum?'

'No need, I think,' said Mr Breasted.

'Uh . . .'

Selina gasped, with a jerk of her bum, as his finger poked into her anus. It waggled in the tight aperture, and then she bit her lip, stifling a wail, as the finger prodded deeper into her channel, plunging through her arse-greased tube, into her rectum, until it touched the root of her sigmoid colon. Mr Breasted reamed the slimy walls of her rectum, making Selina grimace and bite her lip, with her bottom wriggling, and her anal sphincter involuntarily clutching his penetrating finger.

'My, she is tight,' said Mr Breasted. 'An anal virgin, I think. Deliciously spacious rectum, yet beautifully elastic and prehensile. She'll be very popular on Auchterhuish.'

'Governess Gurdell does like anal virgins,' said Leofra. 'Especially ones with large mammaries, like this specimen. I'll just check the teats, if I may?'

'Of course,' said Mr Breasted.

4

Prison Bound

Selina's eyes were tight shut, her red face wrinkled in discomfort, as Miss Wolliman squeezed her breasts together, tweaking and pinching the nipples, until, despite Selina's expression of shame, the big plums stood stiffly erect. Mr Breasted's finger continued to probe her anus and rectum, now wetting with copiously flowing arse grease, so that the digit slid easily in and out, despite the tightness of her channel, and the squirming of her bared buttocks. Mr Breasted breathed heavily. Pippa applied her fingers to Selina's gash flaps, poking a couple of inches inside her slit, and gasped.

'Why, I believe she is juicing,' she exclaimed. 'She does have a lovely tight gash, I'll admit. No virgin, but, I imagine, highly selective about frequency of partners.'

Selina blushed deeply.

'Juicing, eh?' rasped Mr Breasted, his finger pummelling Selina's anus, as her buttocks twitched and clenched. 'Then it has to be a dozen. Shame to mark those gorgeous globes, but stroke her less than a dozen, and I warrant the pervert won't even feel it.'

'We could make it eighteen,' said Leofra, pawing Selina's naked titties. 'Half a dozen each with tawse, cane and quirt.'

'Oh,' Pippa cried, withdrawing her hand from Selina's cunt. 'When you said that, Miss Wolliman, her slit fairly poured juice.'

She wiped her come-slimed hand on Selina's pubic hair.

'Eighteen it is, then,' she pronounced.

Selina's buttocks wriggled, as the finger slid from her anus. Her blushing face was wrinkled in shame.

'Oh, no, please,' she moaned. 'Haven't I been humiliated enough?'

'Ouch!' she cried, as Pippa smacked her hard on the naked breasts.

'Not *one more* word out of you, harlot,' she hissed, 'or you can forget about smart training. Why, a mere eighteen is *nothing*. Agreed?'

Sobbing, Selina nodded.

'Now,' said Pippa. 'Miss Wolliman, I'd like you to warm her up with a tawsing – then, I shall increase the pain with my flogger – finally, Mr Breasted may apply the cane.'

'Ohh . . .' Selina gasped, as her bladder gave way, and a powerful jet of golden piss steamed from her gash, down her quivering thighs, to pool the floor beneath her.

'Beastly!' said Leofra.

'She is only seeking attention,' snapped Pippa. 'We may ignore her deliberate foulness, and continue with our test. I take it she has passed the physical examination?'

The others warmly agreed that Selina was a prime specimen of girl meat. Pippa placed the pot of flowers on Selina's head, instructing her to keep it balanced at all times throughout her test, as a measure of her correct deportment. She raised her hand, to Leofra's tawse. Selina watched her reflection in the windows, as the gleaming leather thongs were poised high above her naked bottom. She saw her own face, glistening with tears, under the pretty flowers in their pot, and winced. Her heart pounded, with her breath coming in harsh gasps. Leofra Wolliman raised her arm high, making her big titties jiggle under the crimson bra. Selina's nipples tingled, and her cooze and clitty throbbed, as come dripped from her gash flaps onto her quivering bare thighs. Her bottom, too, seemed to tingle, its every pore sensitive to the air and light, as it awaited the kiss of the strap. The dreadful prospect of a bare thrashing made her nude body fully alive. The garden, hazy through the French windows, shimmered before her eyes: trees, bristling with twigs, prickly shrubs, flowers swaying on long stems – how many rods she saw, as though the whole of nature conspired in the punishment of a girl's naked bottom! What would it be like? So often she had watched girls' bums redden at school, under her cane – or Jane's bottom reddening and squirming under the slipper.

How well I know the feel of whopping, the easy flow of the strokes, the pride in a job well done. Well, Miss Rawe, this is the moment of truth. An English girl must bare up and take her medicine. They'll see I'm tough enough for smart training, but they'll be laughing on the other side of their faces, when my scoop hits the headlines. Meanwhile, grin and bear it. But that tawse looks so menacing. What will it feel like, stroking my naked bottom, without even the small protection of panties? This isn't the slipper, or strap. I'm scared. Can I take it? My cunny, dribbling so abominably with my juice, and my nips rock-hard in excitement. How shame-making! Please hurry, Miss, don't make me wait, get it over with. I am so frightened of the lash . . . giving is one thing, taking is quite another. Did I flog those girls to exorcise my own terror?

The tawse whistled. *Whap!* Red fire streaked Selina's bare buttocks, as the twin tongues of the tawse jolted her, and her gorge rose. Her nates automatically clenched, trying to dissipate the fearful smarting, as the tawse whistled again. The flowerpot teetered, but Selina's straight neck kept it balanced on her head. *Whap!* The cut took her on top buttock, stinging hideously, and tears leapt to her eyes. *Whap!* Selina's bare arse began to squirm, the soft tan globes churning madly – anything, anything, to make the dreadful pain fade! Yet, it was useless. Her whole bottom was on fire. *Whap!* Her breath came in rasping pants of agony. *Whap!* The tongues stroked her in the backs of her thighs, in the crease below her stretched buttocks, and she clenched her teeth, to avoid crying out. She clung to the chair, which rattled, as her body shuddered. *Whap!* The six were complete, and Miss Wolliman lowered her tawse. Through blurred eyes, Selina saw her in the glass; she, too, was flushed and panting, and her nyloned thighs squelched, as she pressed and rubbed them together. Selina's tawsed buttocks continued to wriggle, after the beating had stopped, as the smarting continued to throb in her wealed bumflesh. Her gasping and choked sobs gradually ebbed.

'A little too much theatrical squirming,' Pippa said, 'but on the whole, she hasn't taken it too badly. However, you've left her haunches unmarked, Leofra. Never forget the tender haunches. Strokes there *really* hurt.'

'Are you suggesting I don't know how to flog a girl's bottom?' snapped Leofra.

'Of course not. It's just that, in this case, attention to the haunches is . . . never mind. I'll put matters right.'

Aren't they going to ask how I feel? When I caned a schoolgirl, I was always nice to her . . .

Pippa stood well back from Selina's bottom, and raised her arm. *Whap!* The thongs of the rubber quirt wrapped Selina's bare left haunch, with a fourfold smart.

'Oh!' she squealed, gasping furiously.

White fire seared her haunch, with the thong tips striking her lower belly. The quirt's pain made her long for the tawse to return. Her bottom shook, squirming and clenching, yet the smarting would not go away. Her skin pulsed, as though being stripped from its meat. *Whap!* Her right haunch jolted, under the tongues, and the pain was so great, Selina had to bite her lip to stifle a scream, as her gorge rose in fear and agony. She fought to right the flowerpot, trembling on her mane.

Oh, no . . . this is worse than anything I'd ever dreamed. What must poor Jane have felt, as I thrashed her bare bum? It smarts so awfully! And I've already been flogged once! I don't dare think what must the cane be like. I can't take it, truly I can't, but I mustn't speak out. I must take it.

'Jolly good, Miss Parkhurst,' said Mr Breasted. 'Strong delivery, and the fesses already well bruised. It is most important, is it not, that a thrashing be given on the *naked* bottom – none of your namby-pamby knickers or nighties – for maximum shame to the miscreant, and maximum visual appeal to witnesses.'

56

'*Most* of the bruises come from my tawse,' said Leofra.

'Quite so,' replied Mr Breasted. 'But the lovely dark weals on the haunches complete the painting, eh? I know that Miss Parkhurst is particularly adept at teat-whipping – the quirt, with its wide spread, is admirably suited for flogging bare bulbs, especially titties as big as this gel's – and I wonder if we shouldn't add a mammary flagellation to the gel's test.'

Oh, no! Whipping a girl's bare breasts . . . It can't be, the very idea is unspeakable. I can't believe it.

Whap! The quirt spread its tongues across the full expanse of Selina's bare buttocks, now squirming and clenching in rapid rhythm. *Whap!* Selina gasped, her breath rasping fast, and her eyes screwed tight shut, in her red face, wrinkled with pain. *Whap!*

'Ooh . . .' Selina groaned.

'Quiet, gel!' snapped Pippa.

If only I'd known . . . so many times I've watched a girl's bare bum wriggle under my whopping, and I admit, I liked the power, the excitement. Now I'm getting excited, despite the fearful pain. My cunny's dripping, and my clitty's all stiff and tingly. How dare I get a terrible thrill from being beaten? They'll see! But that's part of the dreadful humiliance, knowing that their eyes are fixed on my bare, dancing and squirming, and reddening I'm sure, with the most horrid welts – I'm the centre of attention, and it's my bum they're ogling. That Gawain Breasted, he makes me shiver, with that insolent cock so stiff, as he looks at my bare bum flogged. Would he . . . could he? No, it's too horrible to think on. Yet that lustful Jane takes it up her bum, and likes it . . . craves it. Me, fucked in the anus? That hard tool, thicker than any finger, ripping my bumhole, and spurting his hot cream in my rectum? It's unthinkable. How sore my bare bum is! And there's the cane still to come. How I long to touch my clitty, to masturbate. Oh, I'm bound to pee myself again, under the cane on bare . . . if I don't come first. There, I've thought it.

Whap!

'*Ooh!*'

Selina shrilled, as Pippa delivered a vertical stroke to the vertical, with the tongues catching Selina squarely in her taut arse cleft, the leather nipping her anus bud, and the pendant lips of her gash. Gasping hard, Pippa lowered her quirt.

'I say, jolly good, Pippa,' Mr Breasted enthused. 'That last stroke was masterly. I don't suppose we should test her with a quim-thrashing?'

'Miss Gurdell might think we've exceeded our responsibilities,' panted Pippa. 'She doesn't like to receive damaged meat. And anyway, the slut will have her fill of the subtler treatments, once Miss Gurdell's guards get hold of her.'

Quim-thrashing? I can't believe what I hear. They sound so casual. A whipping on the naked cunny? Oh, no . . .

Fingers stroked her flaming bare bum, tracing the weals, now puffed into hard ridges, agonising to the touch. Selina shuddered, sobbing gently.

'A splendid bottom,' said Mr Breasted, parting the buttocks wide, to finger the anus pucker, inflamed and swollen from its quirt stroke. 'So ripe, and begging for penetration. Such full, golden orbs, bright and juicy as a June morning – and an all-over suntan. You'll be shy of showing your welts, on some continental nude beach, after Miss Gurdell has processed you, my dear. Or perhaps you won't – perhaps your weals will attract beastly foreigners, ready to poke your bumhole, in public. That's what foreigners and perverts like.'

'Now, Gawain,' said Pippa sternly, 'we are to test the gel's bum for CP, nothing further. Your turn with the cane.'

'Right-ho, Pippa,' said Mr Breasted.

His blurred reflection in the glass lifted the cane high over Selina's smarting buttocks. He bared his teeth, licking them.

'You think you've been tanned, Miss Rawe,' he murmured, 'but the cane will teach you what tanning really is. Of course, as Miss Whippham, you'd know all about that. Flogging the arses of squirming perverts – ugh! Now it's your turn to squirm.'

I didn't! I wasn't! I'm not Miss Whippham! Don't they know? Oh, what's the use . . .

'Mind you keep your head erect, and don't spill the flowerpot,' said Mr Breasted.

Selina jerked, as Pippa's fingers poked her slit, penetrating the gash to a couple of inches, and rolling the nails around her pouch meat.

'I say, she's well juicing,' she exclaimed. 'And look at her thighs, wet with come. She *is* a pervert. Better cane hard, Mr Breasted. The official Home Office policy on perverts is to weal so deeply, they no longer crave flagellation.'

'I've only the six,' grumbled Mr Breasted.

'Make them stingers, then,' replied Pippa.

The cane whistled.

'Urrgh!' shrieked Selina, as the white-hot pain of the stroke lanced her full, fleshy mid-fesse.

Her body jerked, the spine and legs rigid, as her flogged buttocks wriggled.

'Jolly good stroke,' said Leofra.

'A lovely weal,' added Pippa.

The second caught Selina on top buttock.

'Oh! Oh, no!' she shrieked, her fesses clenching and squirming.

'*Will* you be silent, gel?' snapped Pippa.

Mr Breasted took her on the thigh backs, below the pumping bare buttocks. Her body jolted, with her dangling titties wobbling, nipples erect. Shiny come squirted from her slit lips, sliming her quivering thighs.

'Oh . . . ooh . . .' Selina moaned.

Her rubber soles stamped the floor, as her thighs and buttocks churned, wriggling and clenching.

'She's incorrigible,' said Leofra.

'To Miss Gurdell, no one is incorrigible,' said Pippa. 'Especially a gel with mouthwatering buttocks.'

Through her tears, Selina saw the two females move closer, slightly behind and to the right of her caner. Ogling her naked bottom, each delicately slipped her hand under the other's skirt.

'Three to go,' panted Leofra.

Her knuckles moved at Pippa's cunt, while Pippa massaged hers. Selina gasped, as a fresh surge of come spewed from her slit: the two parole judges were wanking off, as they watched her caned.

Vip!

'Ahh!' Selina screamed, without any rebuke this time, for Mr Breasted's cane took her in a vertical slice to the perineum and bum cleft, the cane's shaft smacking her anus bud, and the tip whipping her right between the gash flaps.

'Oh, yes,' moaned Pippa, frotting Leofra faster, as Leofra's fingers stabbed her dripping quim.

'Mm . . . harder,' murmured Leofra, her cunt writhing as she was wanked.

Their nylon stockings glistened with come, seeping from their soaked panties.

'I say, Mr Breasted, what a magnificent bulge you are sporting,' Leofra whinnied. 'This gel *must* be something special, to excite you so.'

'Rather,' grunted Mr Breasted.

Vip! The fifth stroke took Selina again in the bum cleft, now bruised flaming crimson, and the cane tip squelched in the come, spuming from her twitching cunt lips, while the full force of the stroke landed on her anal pucker, bruised raw, and vividly swollen.

'Ahh! Ooh . . . ooh . . . oh, my bummy! Oh, you beast!' drooled Selina, her flogged thighs and buttocks wriggling in a frenzy, but her shuddering spine and neck still managing to stay straight, balancing her flowerpot.

Leofra and Pippa had their skirts up, showing their sodden panties, with come spewing down their garter straps and stockings, as they mutually masturbated.

'Cheeky slut,' drawled Mr Breasted. 'You deserve a teat-flogging for that.'

'No, please!' Selina wailed. 'Oh! I can't bear it.'

'I advise you not to say that, Miss Rawe,' panted Leofra, 'otherwise the board cannot recommend you for smart training. Oh, yes, Pippa, just there . . . touch me . . . oh, yes . . . yes . . .

'Only one to go, more's the pity,' hissed Mr Breasted.

Vip! The cane lashed Selina in full mid-fesse, the stroke aslant, and forming a cross weal.

'Ahh . . .' groaned the wanked Pippa. 'Yes . . . *yes . . .!*'

'Oh! Ohh . . .' sobbed Selina, her crimson bare buttocks continuing to squirm, clenching, after Mr Breasted lowered his cane.

'What do you mean by this, ladies?' he growled, turning to the two masturbating females, each trembling in ebbing orgasm. 'What? Wanking off? Haven't I warned you before about overstimulation?'

'Y . . . yes, Mr Breasted,' mumbled Pippa.

'Then you know what to expect,' he drawled, loosening his belt buckle.

'Here, Mr Breasted?' whispered Pippa. 'I admit we deserve it, but . . . in front of the slag, and her guard? Shouldn't we wait for the prison van, so that Miss Cockle can remove her?'

'The troll's looking out the window,' said Mr Breasted jovially, 'and Celia's a loyal Home Office employee. Usual punishment – who's first up, gels?'

'She'll see our *bottoms*, Mr Breasted,' hissed Leofra.

'I can't wait,' Mr Breasted drawled. 'For some reason – the sea air, a gel's well-thrashed bottom – I'm incredibly fruity today. Saltdean means the sweet swish of discipline – before going up to Cambridge, I had a cramming tutor here, Auntie Jen. Splendid figure of a woman, used to discipline us on the bare, in front of the whole class, if we got our Latin verbs wrong, and by golly, could her cane sting. We were all frightfully in awe of her. Funny thing, the harder she flogged, the more I adored her. "So little time, and so many bottoms to whop," she used to say, as she caned me starkers. A real lady's thrashing makes a man, and a gel, I dare say. Let's put that to the test, on *your* naughty bottoms, gels, this sunny Saltdean day.'

'I'm rather shy in front of Miss Cockle,' said Pippa, although she was already unfastening her garters and sussie belt, with her skirt dropped to the floor.

'Celia went to a good school,' drawled Mr Breasted, 'so that settles the matter.'

'See nothing, hear nothing, Sir!' snapped Celia, clicking her heels, and saluting.

Mr Breasted had his naked cock unsheathed; Selina gazed at the misty reflection in the glass, gulping, as her cunt recommenced juicing. The organ was massive – almost as big as Henry's. Two naked croups shone like four moons, bending over the judge's desk.

'They *are* juicy bums,' murmured Mr Breasted.

He raised his silver-studded leather belt, folded in two, with the studs outward, and began to thrash each bottom in turn. *Vap! Vap! Vap!* The chamber echoed to the strokes, and the little gasps and cries of the two flogged judges, as their bare bums squirmed and reddened under Mr Breasted's vigorous thrashing. By the fiftieth stroke, each bottom was crimson with ugly blotched welts, and the girls were snuffling in distress. Mr Breasted stroked the flogged bottoms with his naked stiff cock.

'Mm . . .' sighed Pippa. 'That was awfully hard, Mr Breasted. You are so strong. My bum's quite on fire.'

'I'm quite helpless,' gasped Leofra.

Mr Breasted spread Pippa's crimson arse cheeks, pressed his glans to her anal pucker, and suddenly, he was tupping her in the bumhole. Selina gasped, as copious come spewed from her own cunt lips. She saw his massive tool slide, gleaming with Pippa's arse grease, in and out of Pippa's squirming anus, saw her body writhing and thumping on the desktop as he buggered her, and heard little mewling gasps as the tool slammed between her pert, wriggling buttocks. Leofra masturbated, watching her colleague's torment. Selina trembled, the flowerpot precarious on her head. Her cunt tingled, gushing come, as she watched the buggery. After Mr Breasted had buggered Pippa for several minutes, he whipped his greasy cock from her anus, and plunged it forthwith into the bumhole of her colleague.

Pippa and Leofra, sworn justices of the Crown, were two buggered females on heat, bare arses writhing under a master's tool. Pippa maintained her pleasure by a vigorous frig, her fingers squelching in her come-slimed cunt, while her partner squirmed and threshed under Mr Breasted's powerful penetration of her anus. The floorboards shook, at his pounding. After several minutes, his cock plopped from Leofra's anus, and reentered Pippa's, whereupon Leofra set to a vigorous wank of her come-spuming cunt. Pippa was buggered for several more minutes, and then it was once more the wanking Leofra's turn; and so on, until both girls had been buggered four or five times, orgasming frequently, whether fucked or wanked, and Mr Breasted's grunts indicated that he was ready to spurt in Pippa's arse.

He slammed the writhing naked girl with all his brute force, with the desk clattering, and vibrations shaking the floorboards. The room echoed to the slaps of flesh on flesh, as Mr Breasted's hips smacked his victim's squirming bare buttocks. Selina's chair trembled under her belly. It was Pippa's anus which took the full force of his ejaculation; a creamy froth of spunk bubbled at her anus lips, as he drove into her rectum, his spurt so powerful that it overflowed the anal channel, and the bubbling mess slimed her twitching thighs and arse. Pippa was unable to restrain her yelps of orgasm, as she climaxed, under the buggered spurt, and Leofra masturbated herself to further spasm, eyes glued to the master's balls, and his spunk-slimed cock in her friend's anus. Mr Breasted groaned, grasping Pippa by the hips, and wrenching her from the desk, to pull her buttocks against him like some rag doll's, so furiously did he seek to impale her rectum with his tool, still pumping, sunk to her arse root. Pippa gurgled, mewling and wincing, as the stiff cock poked her remorselessly.

'Urrgh . . . ahh . . .' she groaned.

Mr Breasted's face was twisted in a rictus of fierce delight, as the girl sank, under his thrusts; when his spurt had ebbed, he pulled her writhing body from his cock, and cast her aside. Pippa flopped to the floor, face scarlet, and spunk and come drooling from her buggered anus.

'Ohh . . . yes . . .' she gasped, 'ooh . . .'

She rolled over, striking Selina's foot; Selina jumped, and the flowerpot toppled, crashing to the floor, and spattering earth over Pippa's come-slimed quim and raw, fucked anus.

'Why, you . . .' she began, when a klaxon hooted outside.

Selina saw the gloomy white bulk of a prison van.

'Beg pardon, ma'am, the van's here to collect the miscreant,' Celia announced.

Pippa clawed at her slimed cunt and bottom, trying to wipe off the sticky mess from the flowerpot. Pansies and marigolds were plastered, in a slime of spunk and arse grease, all over her bum cleft.

'My bum's filthy,' she hissed. 'It's her fault. I want to punish the slut.'

'Beg pardon, ma'am, but the prison van can't wait. I'm sure Miss Gurdell will take care of matters,' said Celia.

Pippa leered.

'I *know* she will,' she said.

'Wait,' said Leofra. 'Has the prisoner passed fit?'

'Of course,' said Pippa. 'I did the paperwork in advance. The Home Office doesn't test a gel unless she is *already* fit for smart training.'

Celia wrenched Selina's hair, and marched the whimpering girl to the back door. Selina clutched her prison smock, covering her breasts and belly, and tried to shield her welted bottom with her hand.

'You won't be needing that rag,' Celia said. 'Smart training prisoners travel undraped. That's what the regulations say.'

'You mean I'm to go all the way to Scotland in the nude?' Selina blurted, squirming, as her mane was wrenched by the roots.

'Only to Gatwick airport. You'll be flown to Scotland, in custody of the Auchterhuish strappers. What they'll do to you, I can only imagine.'

She pushed Selina into the back of the van. Before she entered the gloom, Selina turned back, to look at the placid seaside villa. A middle-aged man in a city suit was being greeted at the front door by Pippa.

'Miss Parkhurst?' he said. 'I'm sorry I'm a bit late for my appointment.'

'Sorry?' snapped Pippa. 'You'll be sorrier still, worm, when I cane your bare arse.'

'Yes, indeed, mistress,' the man said, gratefully, as he entered.

Celia released Selina's hair, and smiled, as she locked them inside the prison wagon. Immediately, the van revved up, and set off.

'Some folk pay for their disciplinary hearings,' she said. 'Yours was free.'

Adjusting her hair, Selina blinked, adjusting her eyes to the gloom; the only light came from the grille, separating them from the driver, another prison officer, with her hair perched in a bun, in the same uniform as Celia. The passenger box had a bench on either side, with sets of leg-irons at intervals along each bench. Above the seats, handcuffs and metal branks were bolted to the wall, and rubber cords dangled from fastenings on the ceiling. Selina gaped, aghast.

'Some bitches get unruly,' Celia said, laconically. 'Like this one.'

In shadow under the grille, Selina saw a girl, sitting bolt upright on the bench. She was nude, save for a horrid cluster of bindings, that kept her immobile. Her ankles were hobbled, and her arms raised fully stretched above her, with the wrists locked in cuffs on the wall. Her head was enclosed in a metal cage, a brank, with a tongue-depressor filling her mouth, preventing her from speech. Her back arched against a metal post, to which a sheath of two-inch thick rubber cords fastened her belly, and upper breast, the cords biting her flesh so tightly that the skin puffed in ridges all round her bonds. The thighs were forced open, and her cunt prominently displayed, by a set of clothes-pegs, pinning the very lips of her gash, with the juicy wet meat of her slit glistening pink and exposed. Between the layers of rubber cords, her large bare breasts shone with rich purple bruises, clustered round her big plum nipples, that could only have come from a whip. The nipples themselves were distorted, the buds squeezed pale, clamped in two mousetraps, dangling beneath the teats. The mousetraps and cunt clamps were fastened to strings, bunched by the door, and the guard's seat. Celia tugged the string of each mousetrap in turn, drawing a gurgle of pain from the strapped girl, then the clothes-pegs on each cunt flap, which made her squeal, with her bare bottom writhing on the harsh wooden bench.

'You're not going to give trouble, are you, Rawe?' said Celia.

'N-no, miss.'

'Then you can get away with minimum restraint. It's only an hour or so to the airport, then you'll be released into the custody of the strappers. I dare say they'll want to gag this one again – wouldn't stay still, back in Hove, and we're short of staff, so with no one to guard her, they had to truss the slut.'

Celia lit up a cigarette, blew smoke over Selina, then opened a locker, snapped open a can of lager, and swigged heartily.

'Ahh . . .' she said, wiping her lips on a hank of Selina's hair.

At her order, Selina sat opposite the trussed girl, whose eyes met her in a wide, dreamy gaze. She did not seem at all frightened or ashamed, and, as Celia fastened Selina's ankles in a two-foot wooden ankle hobble, there was a faint smile on the girl's branked lips. The girl was perhaps nineteen, with a rich shock of auburn hair, massive, well-formed teats, and thick thighs, rippling with whipcord muscle, leading to big, firm buttocks, on which the brank's position obliged her to perch, almost lifted from her seat. The girl's eyes lowered, to stare at Selina's gash, and Selina blushed, for now the girl's eyes twinkled, and she did smile – her own auburn forest of pubic curls rivalled Selina's massive cunt growth. In contrast to Selina's satin-shaved armpits, the girl carried mammoth tufts of auburn hair beneath her arms. Celia followed their eyes.

'Hairy bitches,' she growled. 'That will come off, and you'll be bare as newborn lambs, with the chill wind slicing your slits. Bumholes, too. Bet you've never had those downy hairs round your bumhole shaved, eh, slut?'

She forced Selina's wrists behind her back, and bound them, pressed to her buttocks, with two rubber cords, winding the rubber several times around her wrists. Selina gasped, but did not speak in protest, until Celia produced two mousetraps.

66

'Please, Miss Cockle,' gasped Selina, 'for pity's sake . . .'

'Silence, unless you want your cunny clamped, and your slit stopped up with gum,' snapped Celia.

The trussed girl giggled.

'Oh, no, not my titties –' Selina moaned.

Whap! Whap! Whap! Whap!

'Ooh! Ouch!'

Celia slapped Selina's bare breasts, leaving the quivering titties flushed an angry pink. Selina sobbed, wincing and screwing her eyes shut, as Celia fastened the two mouse-traps to her nipples.

'Oh . . . oh . . .' Selina gasped.

Her nipples were squeezed to bulging envelopes of pale flesh, the traps linked to Celia's wrist by their fastening string. Celia sat in the corner of the van, and jerked each of Selina's nipple strings.

'Ooh! Please, stop!' she squealed.

'Just see you behave, eh?' said Celia.

Selina gazed at her trussed companion, making a rueful, sympathetic face. The girl's eyes were glazed and hooded, and her nostrils flared; her lips creased in a smile, over the hideous tongue flap, and at her tousled cunt hairs, a trickle of come seeped from her gash flaps, where her abnormally large clitoris shone stiff and extruded between the folds. Celia swallowed her beer, puffed smoke, and chuckled.

'She's wet, the bitch,' she said. 'Likes the look of you, Rawe. Those big bubs and that hairy minge turn her on. Dying for a wank, she is. Well, I suggest you oblige her. I can assure you, darling, Miss Selina Rawe here is an excellent licker. She loves to wank off as she licks a tasty slit.'

Selina began to shake her head from side to side, her eyes closed. *No, no, this can't be happening.*

'Ooh . . .'

A jerk on her breast-string made her squeal.

'On your knees, miss. Put on a show. Lick her out. Suck that big fat clitty. She wants it.'

The seep of come at the girl's cunt increased to a shiny trickle.

'No, Miss Cockle, no . . .' Selina moaned. 'What happened between us was one thing, but not in public . . . it's too degrading. I can't. I won't. I mustn't.'

Snarling, Celia stuck her cigarette in the corner of her mouth, and pulled both Selina's nipple strings, until the mousetraps stretched her teats to monstrous balloons. Tears streamed down Selina's cheeks. Celia took her small rubber quirt from her belt. *Whap!*

'Ooh!' Selina screamed, as the thongs whipped her bare breasts.

Whap! Whap! Whap!

'Oh . . . oh . . .'

Whap! Whap! Whap!

'*Ahh!* Oh, it hurts!'

Her teats quivered under the flogging, with Celia working the tongues around the stretched breasts, and covering the upper and lower portions equally, and at every third stroke, lashing the clamped nipples right on their buds. The flogged nipples turned deep bruised purple, while Selina's naked breasts were pocked with little clustered welts. Selina shuddered, gasping and moaning, with her face glazed with tears.

'On your knees, bitch,' rasped Celia, lighting another cigarette.

She placed the stub of the old one just below the trussed girl's cunt lips, and it sizzled to extinction in the drip of liquid from her slit.

'Mm . . .' the trussed girl moaned, as her bare bum slithered on the bench, slimed by her copious come.

Selina's titties were flaming red, the nipples raw and purple. She slid, sobbing, from her bench, and, with a clank of her ankle hobble, knelt before the trussed girl's open cunt. She had to raise her buttocks high to fit in the narrow space between the benches, and Celia placed her boot tip in Selina's quim. She rolled up her skirt, revealing her shaven pubes, the gash flaps swollen and glistening with juice, then put three fingers inside her pouch. Smiling, Celia masturbated, flicking her clitty, and jabbing her fingers into her wet slit. With a moan, Selina extruded her

68

tongue, pressed her lips to the girl's hairy cooze, and began to tongue her clitty. Come spurted from Selina's gash, wetting her thighs.

'*That's* better,' said Celia. 'You don't mind if I wank off, watching your delicious whipped arse, Selina?'

'No, Miss,' whispered Selina. 'I don't mind.'

5

Air Bare

The trussed girl's cunt was wet. Selina shut her eyes, as she licked the swollen gash lips, getting her tongue inches inside the slit, while her nose rubbed the girl's massively extruded clitty; then, opening them, she watched the labial folds dilate and quiver, under her sucking pressure. The girl's cunt basin trembled and strained at her bonds, as though she wanted to crush Selina with her thighs; her cunt juiced copiously, sliming Selina's lips, nose and chin with oily come. Selina moaned at the intrusion of Celia's steel toecap into her own slit, viciously stretching the pouch, until the toecap found her wombneck, and began to ream its hard knob.

Their bodies shook, as the van's engine rumbled beneath them. Celia began a rhythmic footfucking of Selina's cunt, her come-oiled leather sliding easily in and out of Selina's gash, with a flick to Selina's stiff clitty at each penetration. Selina gasped, as her gash juiced, while Celia's footfuck quickened her tonguing of the trussed girl, who moaned and writhed, wrenching at her bonds, and making her metal head brank clatter. Drool dripped from Selina's slack lips onto her quivering teats, pinched almost white by their nipple traps.

The bitch Celia . . . she saw that I needed a wank after my beating. Why, oh, why, did those cruel lashes on my bare bum excite me so? And a flogging on my bare titties . . . the shame and pain made me wet. I want to come . . . I need to come. A girl is helpless when she needs to come.

'Yes . . .' moaned Celia, masturbating vigorously; her uniform jacket was open, baring her big quivering titties, crusted by ash from the cigarette smouldering at the corner of her lips. 'Yes . . .'

Selina sucked hungrily at the girl's cunt, making her shiver. She gulped, swallowing the come which poured from the jerking slit lips, her face now a lake of the girl's cunt juice. Her bare buttocks thrust upward, parted, with the perineum and anus bud exposed in their taut trench, towards the toecap penetrating her own oozing slit.

'That's it, Selina,' drawled Celia. 'Show your bum cleft. You want another lathering on those lovely red cheeks, don't you?'

No . . . not another whopping, oh please . . .

Whap!

'Urrgh!' Selina shrieked, sending vibrations through the girl's cunt, as Celia's rubber quirt descended on her smarting bare.

The girl shuddered, and moaned in pleasure. *Whap! Whap!* Liquid fire streaked Selina's raw buttocks, and they clenched, squirming, as her shrieks were absorbed by the tongued vulva, becoming a deep groan, like the noise of blowing into a seashell.

'Mm . . . mm . . .' squeaked the branked girl, writhing and wriggling, under her gamahuche. Her cunt gushed come; Selina knew it would not be long before she brought the girl off.

'Mnnh . . .' she trumpeted, biting the girl's cunt flaps in her agony; the girl jerked, whimpering, and come spurted from her gash, flooding Selina's nose and throat, as she began to shake in her climax.

Selina fought to swallow the torrent of come, spewed by the girl's jerking cunt, as the girl whinnied and brayed, belly convulsing, in her orgasm. Selina's nipples were rock stiff in their traps, and her own come sluiced her quivering thighs, as the quirt thongs bit into her bare bottom, like slithering, vicious serpents, chewing her flesh with white-hot teeth. The pain flooded her, bringing a rush of tears to her eyes, and she swallowed the girl's come avidly, to prevent her gorge rising in agony. Her bare bottom was on

71

fire; the guard's boot continued to fuck her dripping cunt, spewing come, and Selina felt her own belly flutter. The orgasming girl still moaned and whimpered, as the rush of sweetness in her own loins overtook Selina, and her breasts and belly began to heave. The strokes took her on the tenderest portion of her top buttocks, with the thong tips licking the spinal nubbin, and at the same time, Celia's boot pressed her clitty hard.

'Ahh . . . ahh . . . *yes* . . .' Selina gasped, as her body shook in a shuddering, quaking orgasm, that had her cunt spewing juice over her thighs, calves and hobbled ankles.

Celia's boot withdrew from Selina's fucked cunt; withdrawing her face with a squelching plop from the girl's cunt, Selina burst into tears.

'What's the matter, bitch?' snarled Celia, still masturbating, as Selina turned her head to see the guard's parted thighs, and her wrist plunged into her gash.

Her back curved, and belly squeezed, Celia had her whole hand inside her slit.

'I came . . . when you whipped me!' Selina sobbed. 'How beastly, how shameful!'

'You *wanted* to come, when the judges were testing you,' Celia drawled. 'I know the signs, you rotten pervert. You were longing for a wank, as they flayed your arse! Admit it.'

Whap! Whap!

The tongues streaked fire across Selina's bare, throbbing fesses.

'*Ahh!*' she squealed. 'All right, I admit it. I don't know why . . . I'm no pervert!'

She gazed at Celia's fist, penetrating her come-slopped gash.

'Like what you see?' said Celia, mimicking Selina's words of not long before. 'Do the same to her, slut.'

'Oh . . .' mumbled Selina. 'That's rude . . . I can't.'

Whap! Whap! Selina's whipped nates convulsed.

'Ahh! Ohh!'

'Do it, bitch. Fist her,' Celia ordered. 'One come isn't enough for perves like you two. Get all your fingers into her pouch, then ball them in a fist, and fist her.'

72

'Very well, Miss,' Selina blurted. 'Just please don't whip me any more. It smarts so dreadfully!'

Selina wiped the tears from her eyes. Kneeling, she extended her fingers in a gun, and poked them into the girl's slit. The girl's eyes followed her, with her trapped teats heaving, and her ribcage rising and falling under the tight rubber cords. Selina got her fingertips into the hot wet slit, pushed further, as the girl's cunt basin jerked, and her buttocks began to writhe in their come pool. She thrust, until her fingertips touched the hardness of the wombneck; squeezed her thumb in, until all five fingers were inside the girl's cunt elastic. Selina formed her fingers into a fist, filling the wet slimy pouch, as the girl whimpered and moaned.

'I'm hurting her,' Selina gasped.

'I'll hurt your arse with my whip, if you don't obey. Now punch hard.'

She raised her quirt in menace. Selina jabbed her fist against the wombneck, making the girl shudder; again, harder, and again, until her wrist was sliding in and out of the clinging oiled gash flaps, like a piston, as her knuckles pummelled the girl's deep cunt. Celia withdrew her fist from her own slit, and recommenced clitty-masturbating, with strong flicks and tweaks of her distended red nubbin. She licked her teeth, as she watched Selina fist her victim.

'Ooh! Ow!' the girl squealed, writhing in obvious pain, as Selina's punches grew harder.

'Wank off, Selina,' ordered Celia. 'You want another frig, don't you?'

Her face scarlet, Selina moaned, as she obeyed, her fingers probing her own wet cunt. She grasped her stiff clitty, and began to tweak the distended nubbin between the finger and thumb of her free hand, while continuing to fistfuck the squirming, wriggling girl, her body pouring with sweat and come, and gurgles of agony trilling in her throat, as her head rocked in its clattering cage.

'Uhh ...' Selina whimpered, as tongues of pleasure licked her spine and belly. 'I ... I've never wanked off so much, before, Miss.'

'Sure,' panted Celia, fingering her clit, with the muscles of her bare belly beginning to ripple. 'A fucking tart like you – Miss Whippham, eh?'

'No!' gasped Selina, masturbating vigorously, and with sweat pouring from her naked body, as she pounded the girl's squirming vulva with her come-slimed fist. 'I didn't . . . I wasn't –'

'Suit yourself,' grunted Celia. 'I suppose you're one of these glacial whores, who only gets off wanking over her naked body in the mirror. Definitely lesbo – well, you'll get plenty of diddling practice up in Auchterhuish, especially if Miss Gurdell accepts you as one of her sapphic sisterhood. She likes big-bummed gels. *Then* you'll know what wanking and lesbianism are all about.'

Celia groaned.

'Oh, yes, I'm almost there. How's your wank, Selina? Better than the whip?'

'As if a gel could climax from a whipping,' Selina retorted, blushing.

'You did, didn't you?' drawled Celia. 'Under smart treatment, you won't know any other way.'

'No!' Selina cried. 'That's horrible.'

'Plenty of sluts leave for the island,' panted Celia, masturbating hard, 'but precious few return.'

'Uhh . . . uhh . . .' drooled the trussed girl, her buttocks jerking up and down, as Selina fisted her, while the girl's cunt flaps engorged Selina's come-slimed forearm to half its length.

'I know your sort,' said Celia. 'You love the whack of a strap on bare bum, and the sight of a stiff cock poking a bitch, with her wriggling and shrieking in pain, but you pretend you're above it all, a voyeur. You're just a slut like the rest of us, thirsty for wanks and cock and a spanked bottom. That's all girls are, and all they'll ever be.'

'Urrgh . . . urrgh!' gurgled the fisted girl, titties and fesses bouncing madly, as her come soaked Selina's forearm, and she wriggled and shook in new orgasm.

Selina flicked her clitty, then withdrew her hand from her gash, and stroked the ridged, puffy weals of her bare bottom. She winced, as her fingers traced the weals of cane, tawse and whip, then she groaned, as she slapped herself. Her palm rose and fell, spanking her own naked smarting buttocks, as tears flooded her eyes.

'Oh, no,' she moaned, 'please, no . . .'

Smack! Smack! Smack! Her squirming bare arse cheeks darkened to deep crimson blotches, overlaying the vicious weals of her thrashings.

'It can't be. Surely, I'm not . . .' she panted hoarsely.

Her forearm rose and fell like a scythe, slicing her naked buttocks.

'That's what I like to see,' crooned Celia. 'Spank yourself harder, bitch. Nothing like a spanking, as you frig. How raw your bum is! I'm nearly there . . . ooh, yes, what a super come . . . yes!'

Smack! Smack! Smack! Selina's bare buttocks jerked and clenched, under her own spanking.

'Oh, no . . .' she moaned, 'I can't believe this . . . yes . . . yes, I'm coming . . . *oh!*'

Come spewed from her gash, as her fingers frantically twitched at her throbbing stiff clitty. The van filled with the gasps and sighs of orgasming females, over the growling of the engine, which slowed, changed gear, and abruptly came to a stop.

'Ah,' gasped Celia. 'Gatwick.'

She rose, smoothed down her uniform, then freed Selina, save for her ankle hobble. Trembling, Selina began to put on her rough prison smock, until Celia struck panties and smock from her hand, and ordered her to carry them.

'You won't need them,' she snapped, as she unfastened the fisted girl from her bonds.

The rubber cords flew off her bruised flesh; the opened brank slid on its hinges from her face, and the girl's arms were freed from their high cuffs. The pegs came off her cunt lips, and the mousetraps from her nipples, which bounced back into high crimson prominence. Nude, but for her ankle hobble, the girl rubbed her raw, bruised cunt, making a moue at Selina.

'Look, I'm sorry,' Selina said. 'I didn't mean . . . that is, I was ordered . . . I've never fisted a girl before . . .'

Celia took the girl by the nipples, and lifted her up; there was a squelching plop, as her anus slid free of a gnarled metal bum plug, inches thick, and a foot long, bolted to the seat beneath her. It was slightly curved, with a bulb at the tip, like a replica of a cock, thickly shining with the girl's arse grease. Selina gaped. All the time, the girl had been anally impaled by that terrible thing! Selina gazed at her nude body, rounded with full, ripe titty flesh, big plum nipples perching cheekily erect, and massively swelling arse flans; yet the coltish thighs, back, shoulders and flat belly rippled with whipcord muscle. The bare breasts wore a tapestry of quirt scars, like those wealing Selina's own bubbies; the buttocks also bore long streaks of thrashed skin, etched in a crisscross of puffed welts. The girl had not long ago taken frightful punishment on the bare bottom.

'Thank you,' the girl whispered to Selina. 'That was *super*. And –' she turned to Celia, and rubbed herself, with a pout of pursed lips, at the bruised anal pucker '– thank *you*, Miss, for a super bondage.'

'You're not finished yet,' said Celia. 'That beer's gone right through me, and I need to pee. Get down and open your mouth.'

'Oh, Miss, must I?' said the girl, with a moue.

Selina gasped, as the naked girl did a somersault, and lay down on the floor, face up, and mouth open. Celia lifted her skirt, and squatted, with her cunt positioned over the girl's mouth. A powerful jet of piss spurted from Celia's gash flaps, directly into the mouth of the girl, whose throat bobbed, as she swallowed the piss. Some of it bubbled from her lips, and drooled down her chin, but she absorbed almost the whole splash of piss, which lasted about ten seconds. She rose, licking her lips.

'What's wrong?' she said to the gaping Selina. 'Don't you like playing pee games?'

'No . . . certainly not,' Selina gasped.

'It's awfully good fun. Pee has oodles of good things in it – very healthy. I'm Hardast Bratt, by the way. I shouldn't really be here, but I'm the victim of a dreadful misunderstanding. It's beastly unfair – I was absolutely fitted up!'

'Selina Rawe,' Selina blurted. 'Actually, I'm not what you think. I mean, I shouldn't really be here, either. There was a misunderstanding, you see ...'

'There always is,' said Hardast. 'I do hope we're going to be friends, Selina. You're so lovely. That was an absolutely *terrific* fisting you gave me. You must have an awful lot of practice. I was so *wet*! We could play peeing games, I'm sure you'll like it. Or,' she giggled, 'spanking games, if you prefer. You've such a fabulous bottom.'

'Of course we'll be friends, Hardast,' Selina said guardedly. 'Your bottom is super, too.'

'You think so?' squealed Hardast. 'Oh, *thank* you! I could just kiss you for that.'

'Enough lip, you sluts,' drawled Celia. 'Form up.'

'Please, Miss, you're not going to make us walk through the airport in the nude?' said Selina.

Her reward was a slap on the nipples, making her breasts wobble, as she winced.

'We're on the tarmac, right by the plane,' Celia said. 'I'll leave your hands free, till you're on board, then the strappers of Miss Gurdell's flight will place you in appropriate restraint for the journey.'

'Restraint ...?' Selina gasped, clutching her bruised breasts. 'Oh ... no ...'

Smack! Celia laid another spank on her naked teats, her fingernails clawing at the nipples. Grimacing, Selina bit her lip, her face flushed and wrinkled in pain and anger. The girl bared her teeth, licking them, as Celia opened the door.

'Prisoners, at the double!' she cried.

Selina needed both arms to steady herself, as she descended from the prison van, her ankle hobble clattering against its bumper, while Hardast flexed her knees, and sprang down, breasts bouncing, to land like a cat. Both girls shuffled across a few feet of tarmac, to the steps of a small executive jet, and hobbled up the steps. At the top waited a guard in an air hostess uniform of pillar box red: a very tight miniskirt, scarcely covering her full buttocks, or even her panties; red bumfreezer jacket, and white satin blouse, flounced at the neck. A short, crook-handled cane, of gleaming yellow wood, dangled from her belt. Her shoes were red, over sparkling high-denier sheen nylons, a sultry reddish bronze colour, with a dark red seam. Under a jaunty box cap, perched on her flowing ash-blonde tresses, she smiled, with dazzling white teeth, as the two captives arrived at the hatch door. Celia bounded up the steps after her charges, and handed a paper for the girl to sign, which she did with a gold fountain pen.

'They are dirty, fighting sluts,' she said to the guard, as she returned down the steps, 'so you'll probably need to bind them.'

'Heavens,' exclaimed the guard, 'I shouldn't think it will come to that! They look like well-bred gels.'

Celia shrugged, as she climbed into the cab of the prison van.

'You aren't going to misbehave, are you, girls?' the guard said. 'Miss Gurdell insists no girl, however miscreant, is irredeemable. Celia does exaggerate – you must think we're brutes!'

'Then you aren't going to put us in bondage?' Hardast murmured.

'We carry all means of restraint, since you *are* felons, but won't use them unless you're *awfully* naughty. You'll have to travel in the nude, of course – those are the Home Office regulations, and we are naturally empowered to punish any mutiny on board – I'm afraid the prescribed punishments are jolly severe. I'm strapper Jasmine Wadd, and my colleagues and I are your flight attendants. Come, I'll show you to your seats.'

Inside, leather armchairs stood around glass-topped coffee tables; there were potted ferns and palms, sofas, a dining table, a large video screen, and, in the stern, a bathroom and kitchen. The doorless bathroom contained a squatter commode, restraining straps hanging at its side, with a small shower cubicle, equally festooned. Three other strappers stood in attendance, wearing the same red skirts as Jasmine, but with their jackets off; their translucent blouses, rather too tight for their prominent bubbies, showed the teats naked under the cloth, supported only by

skimpy red scalloped bras, underslung, to revealed prominent bare nipples. Like Jasmine, they wore canes at their
belts. She introduced them as strappers Avril Pflock, Kim
Rumbelow, and Tuppy Knightley. Each nodded to the new
prisoners, with a little tap to her cane, causing her nyloned
thigh to ripple. Like their blouses, their short skirts clung
tightly to their feline bodies. Jasmine followed Selina's
gaze, and smiled.

'Yes, we are all chosen for our bottoms,' she said. 'Like
you, Miss Rawe. Both of you have superb croups, as does
Bethany Knowte, our third miscreant on board. Unfortu-
nately, she has been rather naughty. I dare say you have
too, Miss Rawe. What lovely bruises you have on your
fesses! Bubby stripes, as well!' She tapped each of Selina's
nipples. 'Miss Gurdell will mend your manners.'

Selina's eyes fell on a third nude prisoner, obviously the
naughty Bethany, sitting on the floor. She sat on her
bottom, with her arms stretched before her, the hands
pressed to her feet. Wrists and ankles were locked in
double ankle-cuffs, the right wrist to left ankle, and vice
versa. From the cuffs, a pole extended between her raised
thighs, ending at the naked lips of her gash, which were
tightly pressed by a large clamp, so that the cunt flesh
protruded, pale and distended, from its fangs. The girl's
eyes were twisted in pain; her mouth was wide open,
gagged by a steel band, fastened at her nape, under a thick
hazel mane. Her haunches and thighs bore fresh cane
weals, a latticework of delicate red stripes, puffing above
the hard pale skin. She sat on a towel, with a wide moist
stain under her clamped gash flaps, glazed with a seep of
fluid. The elfin captive's coltish body was slim, lean, and
tautly muscled, but with teats and buttocks that sprang in
full, massive firmness from her svelte frame, and a waist
strikingly slender under her jutting ribcage. Her big, satin
teats were almost perfectly round, like hard melons, with
domed nipples, whose soft brown skin stood in whorls
above the creamy breast flesh. The waist narrowed like the
point of a triangle, so slim, it suggested severe corsing.
Below, clustered around her clamped cunt lips, a huge

pubic forest glistened with sweat and seeped juice, its curls lapping her anus, and extending up her belly, almost to her navel. Tufts, equally lush, sprouted from her armpits.

'Yes, she is hairy, isn't she?' said Jasmine, casually. 'Almost as ripely tufted as you, Selina. You don't mind if I call you Selina? Your quim lawn is absolutely divine! Pity it'll all have to come off, when we get home. Still, those are Home Office regulations. Actually, some of us strappers shave, too, in sympathy with you poor slags. And a bare quim is quite yummy, really.'

Selina and Hardast sat on the sofa, facing the crouched Bethany, who glared at the newcomers sullenly. Their hobbles clanked as they sat, thighs spread, with their bare cunts at Beth's eye level. She stared unabashed at their naked cunt folds – both Selina's and Hardast's were gleaming with dribbled fluid – and a gleam came into the girl's eyes. The strappers abruptly sprang to attention, as the cabin door opened, and a tall, unsmiling girl sauntered out, her blonde hair cascading over bare shoulders, and below her big conic nipples. She was nude, and barefoot, save for a peaked red cap, the same shade as her shiny painted toenails, which were trimmed to sharp points. In addition, a loose rubber cord encircled her hips, with a rubber quirt dangling over her thighs, its thongs lapping her hard bare skin. Her massive bare bubs peeked through the mane of shiny hair, their nipples big as plums, with a pink, soft sheen, while her swelling cunt hillock, curved like a sickle, gleamed as bare-shaven as Celia Cockle's. She wore nipple rings: each of her fleshy cones was pierced, and from the taut bud hung a golden hoop, four inches in diameter. As her teats rose and fell over her slender ribcage, the nipple rings swayed, lapping against her naked flesh. Inspecting the three captives with a lazy eye, she caressed her rubber quirt, like the one Selina had felt on her bare, at Saltdean, and Selina blanched.

'Ready for take-off?' she drawled. 'Get the meat strapped in.'

'Yes, captain,' blurted Jasmine.

The strappers fastened the three prisoners in harnesses of webbing, pinned through buckles in the floor. The plane's engines whined, as the strappers took their seats, and fastened their safety belts. Each girl's skirt rode up, revealing thin thongs of shiny red knickers, and red garter straps, over bare thigh flesh; the knickers scarcely covered their gleaming, shaven cunt hillocks. The aircraft began to shudder, as it taxied. Suddenly, Selina and Hardast were pinned to the sofa, as the engines screamed, and the plane sped to take-off. Smoothly, it lifted to the sky, and there was a thump, as the undercarriage retracted. The hazy green land of the home counties became a quilt of fields, towns and roadways, drawing further and further away, as the aircraft climbed steeply, until they sailed, humming, above fluffy white clouds, with the sky a brilliant azure, illumined by a harsh yellow sun.

Jasmine and her strappers undid their seat belts, and rose, their skirts still flounced up, with a good portion of bare buttock revealed, scarcely covered by the thin string of the panties, biting quite deeply between their firm, fleshy bare fesses. Their nylons made squishy noises, as they bent over to unfasten their prisoners, and Selina could smell Jasmine's perfume, as the girl's hair brushed her naked breasts. She had a clear view down the front of her uniform jacket, to the tight satin blouse, where the strapper's huge bare bubbies swayed silkily in their undercup bra. After some discussion among the strappers, Bethany was released from her restraint apparel, with her cunt lips springing back to shape, making a loud squelching noise, and emitting a little spurt of cunt juice. A plastic hobble, applied to her ankles, kept her svelte, muscular thighs wide, and she was made to sit in the armchair facing Selina and Hardast, with her bare quim gaping amid its jungle of moist cunt hairs. The towel, placed beneath her buttocks, quickly became stained with seeped gash fluid. Upright, her bare breasts showed in their true, massive roundness, perfect spheroids, like enormous melons. Finally, her steel gagging band was removed, and she clapped her mouth shut, making a sullen rosebud of her lips. She wiped tears from her eyes, while massaging her huge teats, and patting her big domed nipples.

'Everyone always picks on me,' she grumbled. '*I'm* always in the wrong. It's jolly well not fair.'

The loudspeaker crackled.

'This is Captain Phryne Wuldingdoune speaking. Welcome to Miss Gurdell's flight, with our flying time to HMP Auchterhuish approximately two hours. The prison staff will do everything to make your journey comfortable, and you'd better enjoy it, for it's the last comfort you worthless slags shall have, for many a month. You shan't be allowed clothing, and, if it's any consolation, know that your captain prefers to fly in the nude, for comfort. Our governess, Miss Gurdell, *prefers* gels in the nude, to monitor the perfection of their bottoms. We call this flight "Air Bare". In-flight entertainment is provided, but remember that you are prisoners, and it is not voluntary. No talking from the prisoners without permission.'

After a dry laugh the message ended. Jasmine wiped her beaded brow, and removed her bumfreezer jacket; her blouse was translucent, like her colleagues', and her naked bubbies jutted starkly under the thin fabric.

'Better we don't take your hobbles off, for the moment, if you don't mind,' Jasmine said. 'Now, I expect you'd like a nice cup of tea. Do you prefer Darjeeling or Lapsang Souchong?'

Selina opted for China tea, Hardast for Indian, while Bethany was to receive only water, 'for being naughty'. Having taken their orders, Jasmine strutted to the galley, her firm teats bouncing only slightly, under her clinging blouse. Returning, she blushed slightly, seeing Selina and Hardast ogling her large titties.

'Captain Wuldingdoune favours in-flight nudity,' she explained, 'because she thinks our authority over prisoners is strengthened by being as bare as they are. That's Miss Gurdell's philosophy. Some of us, however, believe in the power of our uniforms. So we compromise.'

Soon, the girls were munching on custard creams – Bethany got only a dry water-biscuit – and sipping fragrant tea, with plenty of sugar, brewed by Avril in the galley.

'Miss?' said Selina, to Jasmine. 'May I ask – what did the captain mean by in-flight entertainment?'

Avril, Kim and Tuppy smiled.

'Well – you've nearly finished your tea, so I suppose it's all right – you each have a towel under your privates. That's to absorb, you know, gooey stuff from your cunnies. You can begin by having a jolly good wank. Well, all gels like to masturbate, don't they? We have to observe you, to decide how depraved you are.'

The TV screen flickered, and came to life. Selina gasped.

They were in the middle of a porn film: two naked males, with monstrous erections, pleasured a compliant nude girl, her anguished face half obscured by her tousle of swaying hair, as she was fucked in the anus, while sucking the other's cock right to the balls. Her drool slimed the cock shaft, as her head bobbed up and down, sucking and tonguing the stiff cockmeat, with her jaws spread wide.

'Mm . . .' said Hardast, licking her teeth.

Bethany's tongue lolled from slack lips, dripping drool, as she tweaked her nipples. Behind them, at the toilet door, was a slither of moist nylons from the cooing strappers. Selina's fingers followed Hardast's and Bethany's, in sliding down her belly to her quim, and beginning a vigorous clitty-frig. She gasped, as her seep of fluid turned to a stream, and her fingers squelched in the flooding lips of her slit, causing her to jerk rigid, at each twitch to her throbbing clit. Come gushed from Selina's cunt, soaking her bottom towel. On screen, the action changed: the buggering male drew his cock from the girl's anus, without spurting, and grasped her hair. He pulled her, squealing, to his loins, and obliged her to suck his cock, slimed with her own arse grease, while his companion lifted a tawse, and began to lash the girl's naked buttocks.

The crack of the whipping echoed above the aircraft's whine. Avril, Kim and Tuppy watched, licking their lips, with eyes shining. The two nude males were brutal young studs, with monstrous tools. The whipped girl shook, with tears visibly streaming from her eyes, as she sucked cock, while her bare buttocks reddened and squirmed under the savage tawsing, and her big bubbies shivered like jellies at each crack of the instrument. Selina wanked off harder, her

83

fingers a blur at her streaming cunt, while her two friends jabbed and pummelled their bare, writhing slits – Hardast moaning, and Bethany emitting savage little growls. Jabbing, tweaking – *my pouch so hot and wet, my nubbin so stiff* – Selina whimpered, as her belly fluttered.

Beside her, Hardast drooled, panting, her fingers inside her sluicing cunt, and pounding her pouch, while she pinched her nipples. Bethany's palm rubbed her extruded, glistening clitty, while she clawed her big quivering teats together, scratching and jerking at the erect nips. The two girls whined, with their cunts gushing come, as their bellies pulsed and contracted. At her moment of spasm, Bethany gave a last raking claw to her bruised teats, then squeezed her waist, with her fingers almost touching, and her thumbs pressed to her spinal nubbin. Her knuckles were white, squeezing her pencil waist tighter than any corset, and making her gasp in pain, while her pressed thighs mashed her clitty, provoking her to rasping groans of climax. Simultaneously, Hardast's frigged cunt spurted come, as she gasped in her spasm.

Selina masturbated faster and faster, slapping her cunt lips and clit, with her titties wobbling, and spittle sliming her chin, to drip onto her quivering bare bubbies. Her fingers in her cunt made a loud slopping noise, as oily come spurted from the lips of her slit, drenching her inner thighs, pubic bush and arse cleft, before soaking into the wet towel beneath her clenching bare bum. She began to slap herself on her stiff nipples, the smacks resounding inside the narrow aircraft, then pinched and tweaked her nipples until they were blue and raw. The filmed girl's head was suddenly revealed, streaked with tears, and wrinkled in anguish. Selina shuddered, as orgasm flooded her: the whipped and buggered fellatrix was her maid, Jane.

'The in-flight entertainment is for us, really,' said Jasmine, panting slightly. 'Although you should take advantage, and enjoy yourselves. These are the last wanks you'll have for a while, I'm afraid. Miss Gurdell takes a jolly dim view of prisoners caught masturbating.'

6

Full Bung

Giggling, the strappers took their skirts off. Their thong panties glistened, soaked in gash fluids, which dripped down their garter straps to their reddish-bronze nylons. Then, the girls removed their blouses. Their teats sprang unfettered into view, big and quivering in their nudity. They kicked off their shoes and, clad only in panties, nylons, sussies and suspenders, each lifted her rubber quirt.

Jasmine smiled at Selina.

'See, Selina?' she purred. 'We compromise – only strip after take-off.'

Bare breasts swaying, they advanced on the masturbating Bethany. *Thwap!*

'Take that, you slut,' Jasmine hissed.

'Ooh!' Bethany squealed, as Jasmine's quirt lashed her across the naked breasts. 'Oh, Miss, what have I done now? Why is it always me?'

'Questions, you bold wench?' snarled Tuppy.

Her quirt whipped Bethany's naked thighs.

'Ouch! Ooh!' wailed the girl, without interrupting her wank.

Kim lashed her shoulders.

'Wanking off, you slag?' she hissed.

Avril's quirt streaked Bethany's belly.

'Ooh! Ouch!'

Tears streaming down her cheeks, Bethany writhed, tongue lolling from her drooling mouth, as she wanked off harder and harder.

'She *is* a slut,' Jasmine sneered. 'No mercy, gels.'

She dragged Bethany from her seat, by the hair, and draped her body over the chair back, with her bottom exposed. In turn, the strappers whipped the girl's bare buttocks, the tips of their quirts curling around her haunches, to lay dark crimson blotches on the skin. Bethany squirmed, as Jasmine held her down, with her hair firmly wrenched. The bare-beating continued fiercely, with Jasmine pausing to lift Bethany up, exposing her torso, so that the whips could lash the big, wealed orbs of her naked breasts. Selina gaped: Bethany was still masturbating.

'You sluts may continue your diddling,' Jasmine gasped, turning to Selina.

Jasmine's face was flushed, and her nipples erect, with a lake of come sliming her bare-shaven pubes, beside her narrow groin thong, with drips of come from the gusset of the panties, shining on her quivering bare thigh tops. Soaked in come, the thong had shrunk to a string, passing between her cunt lips. Selina blushed, looking at Hardast, whose tongue was between her teeth, as she eyed the squirming Bethany's lashed bottom, and masturbated her clitty, with loud squelching gurgles, from her fingers deep in her slit.

'Uhh . . .' Selina sighed, closing her eyes briefly, as her fingers frotted her erect nubbin.

Opening them, she focused on Bethany's squirming croup, streaked with weals, with the arse globes clenching frantically. The flogged girl writhed and gasped, her face glazed with tears and wrinkled in pain, with her hand, pinioned between her thighs, continuing to frig her come-slimed clit.

'Our turn next, I hope,' panted Hardast, frotting vigorously. 'Look at the bitch squirm! What a sweet thrashing! Oh . . . yes . . . oh, that's good . . .'

'Our turn?' gulped Selina. 'How can you say such a thing? The poor girl, what pain must she feel –'

'She's *feeling*,' cried Hardast, hard-frigging her gushing slit. 'Isn't that the best thing? Look at her wank off.'

Selina gazed at Bethany's bum globes, their tapestry of red weals writhing, and felt her cunt sluice hot oily come, all over her masturbating fingers.

'Oh . . . yes . . .' she gasped.

Around the whipped girl, the nude titties of the strappers danced, bouncing like big balls, as they flogged her naked flesh. Their own bare bottoms, hidden merely by the strings of their thongs, pressed between pulsing buttocks, squirmed and clenched in their exertion, to mimic the agony of their victim. As she masturbated, panting and drooling, Selina's bottom slithered, squelching, on her towel, slopped with her exuded come. The strappers leered at her.

Only at me, why not Hardast? Do they know who I really am? A good girl, not a slut, like the others . . .?

'Selina's one of the best friggers I've seen,' panted Tuppy.

'*The* best,' added Avril.

The tongues of the rubber quirts mercilessly streaked Bethany's wriggling bare flesh: the buttocks, breasts, belly, and cunt, with quirts snaking between her thighs, to whip her right between the buttocks, on the anus and gash flaps, where her thumb tweaked her erect clitty. Bethany wailed, drooling and snuffling, with tears running down her cheeks, splattering her bouncing bubbies, as come sprayed from her wanked cunt, over the rippling hard muscles of her whipped thighs. The strappers whirled, bare bodies glistening with sweat, as they lashed their victim's helpless wealed flesh, its very helplessness seeming to fuel their flagellant rage. Selina moaned, tweaking her stiff nipples, and pressing her bubbies tightly together, as she wanked her cunt.

'Yes . . . I'm coming . . .' panted Hardast.

'Me, too,' answered Selina, her voice a harsh rasp. 'Oh, yes, yes, what a lovely come . . . *yes!*'

The two masturbatresses writhed, come spurting from their twitching cunts, as their bellies convulsed in orgasm.

'Excellent, inmates,' said Jasmine. 'Miss Gurdell will be pleased with you.'

'But, Miss,' Selina said, 'you said that inmates weren't allowed to masturbate.'

'I didn't say exactly that,' responded Jasmine. 'Nothing can stop gels wanking off – we all know that. I said that

87

Miss Gurdell takes a dim view of it. She likes an excuse to discipline naughty bare bottoms.'

Her hand slipped to Selina's left upper thigh, following the haunch round to the soft curves of the bare buttock. She licked her lips.

'Like yours, Selina,' she said. 'We are all chosen for our bottoms, but yours is outstanding. And an all-over suntan! You are quite the peaches and cream, my gel. In fact, I'd love to lick cream from your peach.'

She leaned closer, still caressing Selina's bare fesses.

'To be honest, these meat flights – as Phryne calls them – give us a chance to let our hair down.'

She giggled, removed her hand from Selina's bum, and pressed it to her lips.

'We like wanking off as much as any inmate,' she blurted. 'Away from home, we can be naughty gels.'

She cupped Selina's breasts with both palms, rubbing her erect nipples in a circular motion. Selina gasped, licking her lips, and continued to masturbate her flowing cunt.

'Do I excite you, Selina?' murmured Jasmine.

She touched Selina's clitoris, and was rewarded with a convulsion of Selina's belly, and a moan of pleasure.

'Oh! It seems I do . . . yet, we strappers must eschew love. Nevertheless . . .'

Jasmine's fingers parted the thong of her panties from her shaven hillock, to show Selina the rich ruby lips of her own gash, pulsing and dripping come. She placed her finger at her clitoris, and began to caress herself. Kim, Avril and Tuppy had Bethany dancing, suspended from her wrenched hair, as the quirts lashed her all over her body, with Tuppy leering, as she sliced the rubber tongues repeatly between the girl's legs. Hands tightly clasped around her narrow waist, so that her thumbs massaged her spinal nubbin, Bethany howled, at each lash to her naked cunt, leaving the gash and perineum wealed crimson. She made no attempt to close her thighs, and, between lashes, continued a hard frigging of her bruised clitty.

'Doesn't it excite you, to see a girl flogged in the nude?' said Jasmine, kneeling, with her face at Selina's quaking belly. 'Especially with the delicious fear that one day soon, it will be *your* body shivering under cruel whips?'

'No!' gasped Selina. 'That's awful.'

'Yet, you're wanking off.'

'Oh . . . I can't help it,' Selina wailed.

'It is normal. All girls like to do it, as much as possible,' Jasmine replied, her hand pumping at her slit. 'But we must eschew too much of a good thing, or our moral fibre will suffer, as Miss Gurdell teaches.'

'I'm frightened of smart training,' moaned Selina.

'You all *asked* to be accepted,' said Jasmine. 'Miss Gurdell's regime is strict but fair. Why, there are gels who avoid whopping altogether.'

She grasped Selina's hand, and transferred it from her slit to Jasmine's own, while placing her fingers inside Selina's pouch.

'Yes,' she breathed, 'their bare bottoms remain pure and virgin of canestrokes . . . those luscious naked orbs, swaying and shivering in the Scots breeze, without a mark of tawse, cane or whip . . . nothing but healthy spanking.'

She laughed. Come poured from her cunt, as Selina masturbated her, poking hard into the strapper's writhing cunt basin.

'Ooh, ooh, that's so good,' gasped Jasmine. 'You *are* an accomplished wanker. I'm afraid it'll have to go in your dossier. Yes . . . *ooh!* Tweak my nubbin harder . . . jings, that's good. How many times a day is your norm?'

'Oh, Miss, that's cruel,' Selina blurted. 'I don't . . . I mean, I do, but I don't keep count. It would be awfully rude.'

'Boyfriends, then?'

'Yes . . . of course.'

'Do they spank you? Outside your professional duties, as Miss Whippham. It must be wonderful, to whip a beastly male on his bare arse, make him squirm and blub. But males can't do without spanking gels.'

'I *have* been spanked,' Selina blurted, 'at school, I mean. Most girls have, haven't they? But bare whipping – it's horrid. I can't imagine how Bethany seems to relish . . .'

89

They glanced at the girl, squirming under whipstrokes; then at Hardast, entranced by the flagellant spectacle, her thighs parted as wide as her hobble would permit, and her knuckles pounding inside her come-slopped cunt.

'Or Hardast,' Selina panted.

'Most girls do relish being spanked,' Jasmine said firmly. 'So, on Auchterhuish, we make corporal punishment pain, not pleasure, to wean them from their depraved habit. Are my fingers pleasuring you, Selina?'

'Oh ... oh ...' Selina gasped, 'can't you tell? I'm so awfully wet.'

'Me too,' panted her masturbatress. 'Let's come together, shall we? That's the super thing about being a girl. We can wank off, and come, as often as we please.'

She pushed her quivering bare breasts into Selina's face, and Selina began to lick and chew the taut nipple plums, getting each in turn into her mouth, then biting, licking and sucking the erect buds. Jasmine gasped in pleasure.

'Are there no men on Auchterhuish?' Selina asked, her voice muffled by Jasmine's huge teats.

Jasmine slapped Selina's bare titties hard.

'Ouch!' Selina cried. 'I didn't mean any harm.'

'You must put men from your mind,' said Jasmine. 'So many of our gels are in trouble because of males, and smart training teaches them to do without those cock-proud potvaliants. Isn't this good, gel? Who needs males, when loving women have each other?'

She tweaked Selina's throbbing clitty between finger and thumb, until Selina yelped, her cunt flowing with hot oily come.

'Oh ... oh ... I'm so wet, you're bringing me off, Miss ...' moaned Selina.

'Yes,' hissed Jasmine. 'Do me, slut, do me hard, fingers right in my cunny, pound me, hurt me, oh, yes, yes ...'

Bethany's body still quivered with whipcracks; drooling and snuffling, she knelt, tonguing Tuppy's gash, while Kim and Avril masturbated openly, thongs draped at their quivering thighs, and all the strappers sluicing come from their gleaming, shaven cunts. Their nylons glistened with cunt juice. Avril suddenly knelt, parted Bethany's buttocks, and began to lick her anus bud. Kim continued to whip Bethany, on the back and shoulders, and inserted her stockinged toe into Avril's own anus, making the girl moan; Avril's fingers slipped between her thighs, and she began to wank off, licking Bethany's anus pucker, while Kim got her big toe inches inside Avril's bumhole. Tuppy pressed Bethany's head to her quim, while tweaking and pinching her own bare nipples, until they stood erect, red and bruised. Her come flowed over Bethany's face, dripping down the prisoner's naked breast melons.

'Oh . . . yes . . .' gasped Selina, 'oh . . . I'm coming. I've never come so much . . . *ooh!*'

She convulsed in orgasm, spraying copious come over Jasmine's wrist, while Jasmine herself drooled, as her belly fluttered, and her cunt gushed, in her own climax. Beside Selina, Hardast slapped her own bare titties raw, while frigging her gash, until she too groaned in climax, spurting come all over her thighs and bottom towel. Kim and Avril masturbated hard, with the rubber quirts striping Bethany's bare back, and the gamahuched Tuppy wrenched Bethany's hair to the roots, as her come poured over the girl's lapping face. Bethany wailed; a powerful stream of piss jetted from her crack, puddling the floor beneath her, as her fingers danced at her quim, slopped with pee and come, and she quivered in orgasm. The strappers gasped and cooed, as they writhed in their own spasms. Suddenly, the cabin door was flung open, and the captain appeared, smiling grimly.

'I thought so,' she hissed.

The strappers disengaged themselves, and sprang to attention.

'We were obliged to discipline the prisoners, for insolence, captain,' said Jasmine, 'according to Home Office regulations.'

'Good thinking. Let's sweat them, shall we?'

Selina gaped, tongue hanging out, as the nude captain strapped a rubber belt to her waist. From it sprouted an enormous false cock, of black rubber, gnarled and striated, and over a foot long.

'Never seen a *godemiché*, miss?' sneered Phryne. 'You *do* have a lot to learn about discipline.'

She stroked herself on her full bare arse globes, turning slightly, as if to preen, then pulled on each of her nipple rings, stretching the nipple domes, and making the teats bounce back, with a quiver of breast flesh. Winding a hank of her long blonde mane through each nipple ring, she pulled the tresses up, wrenching her breasts high, with the nipple rings stretching her red conic nips to pale envelopes. She suddenly let go of her hair, so that her breasts sprang back to their normal jutting state, quivering, and the nipple rings jangling. She licked her teeth.

'From the looks of things, Jasmine,' she drawled, 'these wretched sluts were masturbating.'

'Like all slags, they are addicted to frigging, Miss Phryne,' Jasmine blurted.

'We had to thrash the prisoner Bethany Knowte,' said Kim. 'She is the ringleader.'

'Commendable,' said Phryne Wuldingdoune, stroking her giant rubber strap-on. 'However, I fear you steward-esses are too kind-hearted. Jasmine, will you oil my shaft of discipline?'

Jasmine cupped a palmful of Selina's come, and rubbed it into the dildo, until the striated rubber glistened. Phryne thanked her, with a pat to her nude bottom. She strutted aft, to the quivering body of Bethany Knowte.

'The ringleader, eh?' she said. 'You've given her a good skinning, by her marks, but the bitch has pissed herself.'

She whipped Bethany's bare breasts with her quirt. The girl shuddered, her face wrinkling in pain.

'At the crouch, slut, and give me bare,' Phryne ordered.

Bethany obeyed, kneeling, with her bare buttocks high and spread. Phryne's whip cracked across the girl's naked fesses, glowing with jagged weals.

'*Oh!* Why me?' Bethany gasped, snuffling, as tears came to her eyes.

'Why not? Lick up your mess.'

Her face to the floor, Bethany's tongue began to slurp and swallow her own piss. Phryne squatted slightly, behind the girl's buttocks, with the tip of her strap-on level with the anus bud. She grasped Bethany's hips, and placed the helmet of the rubber cock an inch inside the anus bud; then, with a single, savage thrust of her loins, she plunged the dildo to the full depth of Bethany's bumhole. Bethany trembled, and groaned, as Phryne began to bugger her with her strap-on, but continued to lap up her piss. As the rubber shaft slid in and out of the girl's squirming anus, Selina saw that it had an attachment: a stubby rubber prong, inserted between Phryne's swollen cunt lips, and jerking against the captain's erect clitty, at each plunge to her victim's rectum. Phryne's nipple rings jangled, her bare conic breasts trembling, as she buggered the sobbing girl. A seep of shiny come appeared at her gash flaps, beginning its slow trickle down her rippling bare thighs.

'Hurt much?' she drawled.

'Yes, Miss,' gasped Bethany, through piss-drooled lips. 'My bumhole aches horribly. People like to hurt me . . .'

'Excellent,' said Phryne.

The big melons of Bethany's breasts quivered with each thrust of the dildo, and she whined, as the tool rammed her deep rectum. Beside Selina, Hardast began to masturbate again.

'Hardast,' Selina hissed. 'We mustn't.'

'Oh, hang it,' panted Hardast. 'I never could resist a good wank. Isn't the captain dishy? I hope she does *me*.'

'How can you say such things?' gasped Selina.

'Don't you want her to fuck you in the bum?'

'No!'

'Only boys, then?'

'No . . . no . . . I don't want . . .' Selina whimpered.

'Yes, you do. All gels like a bumming.'

Hardast licked her lips.

'It can't be so,' Selina moaned.

'You know it is,' said Hardast.

Selina's cunt was juicing, as she watched the hard black dildo penetrate the girl's wriggling bottom. The shaft shone with Bethany's copious arse grease, and made a dreadful sucking plop, at each entry and withdrawal, as Bethany's anal shaft sucked the prong into her rectum.

93

'Look at Bethany,' hissed Hardast. 'See her erect nips, and the come pouring from her cunt, as that tool splits her arsehole. Every gel loves full bung.'

Bethany swallowed the last of her pooled piss, and Phryne put her foot on her shoulders, squashing her teats to the floor, as she continued to bugger her squirming arse.

'Ooh ... ooh, Miss ...' Bethany gurgled. 'Ooh, it's fierce, it hurts me so much, you'll split my bumhole in two, Miss, please ...'

'Please what, you scum?' snarled the buggering Phryne.

'Please ... bugger me, Mistress,' gasped the squirming girl. 'Give me what I deserve. Flog me, shaft me, split my hole ... I *must* be a bad gel, to be hurt so, though I can't think why. Am I allowed to come, under punishment?'

'What a sauce!' giggled Avril, openly wanking Tuppy's clit.

'You filthy slut,' snarled Phryne. 'Strappers, the prisoner has incurred further chastisement, for insolence.'

Come poured from Bethany's cunt, as she writhed under the monstrous black shaft ramming her anus.

'Ooh,' she squealed. 'I can't help it, Miss. I'm going to ... come! Oh ... oh ... *yes.*'

A sluicing jet of come spurted copiously from her flapping gash, as she shuddered and yelped in fierce orgasm. Panting, eyes blurred with sweat, Selina wanked her own clitty, in time with Hardast beside her. She felt Hardast's fingers on her nubbin, and responded, grasping her friend's rock-hard clitty, and stroking it, with little squeals of delight from Hardast. Selina quivered, as pleasure from the girl's probing fingers engulfed her, with electric thrills darting from the nubbin of her spine. Jasmine and Kim masturbated each other, as Phryne's tool emerged with a plop from Bethany's buggered bumhole. The strappers cooed, their nylons slopped with come from their gushing cunts, as they wanked each other's clitties. Panting, Phryne turned to the come-slopped nude bodies of Selina and Hardast, each writhing, with her fingers aslither in the other's pouch.

'As for these filthy little beasts ...' she drawled. 'You want in-flight entertainment, gels?'

Selina wailed, as the strappers grasped her and Hardast by the hair, and slung them to the deck, beside Bethany, who lay, moaning and sobbing, and rubbing her bruised bottom. Hardast panted, but did not cry out.

'Let's see you love each other, then,' spat Phryne.

Her quirt lashed Selina on the open cunt.

'Ooh!' Selina howled.

The pain! Such agony, and dreadful shame. How can any gel whip another's naked cunny?

'Better obey,' gasped Hardast.

'No . . . no . . . I can't . . .' Selina moaned.

The quirt took her on the bare titties.

'Ahh!' she sobbed.

Whimpering, she allowed the laughing strappers to position Hardast on top of her; Hardast's cunt basin was pressed to Selina's face, while Hardast's own lips touched Selina's quim.

'Let's see you squelch,' drawled Phryne.

'No, please, Miss,' Selina begged, her voice muffled by Hardast's buttocks and cunt hairs. 'I've never . . . ooh!'

The quirt whipped her on the naked soles of her feet; her buttocks thumped the floor, as she shuddered.

'Uhh . . . no . . .' she moaned, gasping at the touch of Hardast's tongue on her throbbing clitty.

She fastened her mouth on the swollen lips of Hardast's gash, and began to chew and suck, as copious fluid from the girl's cunt spurted to her throat. She gagged, swallowing the girl's hot oily come. Hardast writhed on Selina, her nude body slippery with sweat, and her belly heaving against Selina's bare breasts. Selina's bruised nipples were squashed by the girl's taut belly muscles, yet sprang to full erection, at the teasing, tickling pressure. Hardast's pubic jungle tickled her chin, as Selina tongued the girl's clitty, getting it between her teeth, and biting, with a yelp and a jerk from Hardast. Panting, her breath stopped by the writhing cunt in her face, Selina sucked hard on the gash flaps, while chewing the clitty between tongue and lower teeth. She wriggled, feeling Hardast's tongue on her own clitty, and moaned, as her spine tingled, with come flowing from her cunt into Hardast's eagerly lapping mouth, then bit hard on the girl's swollen nubbin.

'Mm! Mm! Mm!' Hardast gasped, her thighs thudding on Selina's shoulders.

Selina kept her teeth on Hardast's clitty, while ramming her nose into the oily squirting slit.

'Urrgh . . .' Hardast gurgled, her own lips sucking Selina's cunt juice with loud squelching slurps.

Selina's hips bucked under the gamahuching, and she gasped for breath, as a flood of Hardast's come engulfed her face.

'Mm . . .' she whimpered. 'Yes . . . yes . . .'

'Eek!' squealed Hardast, as a trio of quirts lashed her writhing bare bottom.

The strappers laughed as they flogged her. After whipping Hardast's buttocks for several minutes, the masturbating strappers grasped the pair of tribadists, flipping Selina on top. Air cooled her bare bum, and she screwed her eyes shut, without ceasing her cunnilungus of the writhing, slippery girl beneath her. Her own cunt, uppermost, gushed come into Hardast's slurping mouth, as her clitty tingled under hard sucking and chewing. She heard the whistle of rubber, and her buttocks clenched. Three thongs lashed her bare bottom, their tongues slicing her skin like white-hot knives, and she shuddered, buttocks squirming and clenching, with her cunt slamming against Hardast's face.

'Ooh! Urrgh!' Selina squealed, her cries vibrating through Hardast's come-soaked pubic jungle.

Tears sprang to her eyes. She looked up, face contorted in agony, to see Kim, Avril and Tuppy standing over her, hands inside their dripping slits, and quirts raised; behind them, Phryne straddled the crouching Jasmine, with her rubber tool plunged in the strapper's anus. Jasmine whimpered softly, as she was buggered, her face wrinkled in pain. Avril rubbed her bottom, grimacing, as she whipped Selina with Tuppy and Kim, who looked apprehensively at the glistening oily tool penetrating the bumhole of the quivering Jasmine. Phryne's face was split in a rictus of dominance, her cunt dripping come over the rubber tool, and the clitty-tickler pounding her swollen nubbin, at each thrust into Jasmine's quivering anus.

'Go on, bitches, suck till you come,' she sneered at Selina and Hardast. 'Redden that gel's fesses, ladies, until it's your turn for a bumming.

'Urrgh!' Selina screamed, as the tongues lashed her naked bumskin, raising glowing welts. She plunged her face deeper between Hardast's wriggling wet thighs, and bit savagely on the clitty.

'Ooh! Mm!' Hardast squealed; a gush of come spurted to wash Selina's nose and mouth, as the gamahuched girl began to buck in orgasm.

The hard rubber tongues again streaked Selina's defenceless bare; her eyes awash with tears, she shrieked, as the climaxing Hardast fastened her teeth on Selina's clitty, and bit strongly. Selina wiggled her bottom, to escape the lashes on her bare, and Hardast's biting embrace. The quirt cuts, wealing her threshing bare buttocks, drove her cunt smacking and slithering on Hardast's come-slimed face.

'Oh, must I, Miss?' whimpered Tuppy, to be rewarded with a slap to the titties from the captain.

Selina glanced, to see the strapper crouching in Jasmine's stead, and the buggered Jasmine, eyes streaked with tears, rising, to take her place above Selina's buttocks.

'Ahh!' Selina screamed, as Jasmine's quirt lashed her again.

'Wanking off with a slag, you promiscuous bitch?' Jasmine snarled, through her tears of buggered pain.

'Ohh . . .' whimpered Tuppy, crouching and wriggling, as the giant black rubber tool penetrated her bottom. 'Ooh, it hurts, Miss . . .'

Phryne laughed, her hips slapping Tuppy's bare bottom, as she buggered the moaning girl. Jasmine's quirt lashed Selina three times on the tender top buttocks, and Selina yelped, sobbing. The pain flooded her, blending with the sweet pressure of Hardast's teeth on her throbbing nubbin, until the two seemed one: the fiery strokes to her whipped

97

bare buttocks melding with the flood of electric pleasure from the girl's mouth on her cunt.

'Faithless lesbian slut,' hissed Jasmine.

The two tribadists writhed in a bath of sweat and come, licking and sucking each other's raw, drooling cunts. As the rubber thongs continued to whip her writhing bare, Selina sobbed into Hardast's gash, her tears mingling with the girl's copious come. Tuppy was buggered to whimpering orgasm, and then it was Kim's turn for the captain's tool in the anus. She submitted in silence, save for the occasional passionate gasp, or mewling whimper. Come streamed down her quivering nylon thighs, as she was penetrated by the monstrous tool, until she yelped in climax. Selina could not reach her spasm, although Hardast, whimpering beneath her, climaxed repeatedly under Selina's passionate gamahuching. Selina gasped, as fingers prised her buttocks apart.

'What a juicy portion,' Phryne panted. 'Best of the lot. A good forty inches, I'm sure. That luscious meat squirms well under whip, let's see how she wriggles under tool.'

No! No! Should I use my code word? No, that would be cissy. Besides, who would even listen?

The hot rubber tool, slimed with girls' arse grease, nuzzled Selina's anus pucker. Her lips sucked harder at Hardast's cunt, swallowing the come which flooded from the lips. She clutched Hardast's slippery nude body, like a protective charm.

'Full bung for you, bitch,' hissed Phryne.

No, no, please, not that . . .

Her buttocks spread, involuntarily, baring her whole perineum, with her pucker throbbing naked in the taut, quivering arse cleft. The tip of the tool penetrated her anus bud, to the depth of an inch, making her catch her breath, at its sweet tickling pressure.

Oh! It's just like dunging. Please, let this be enough, please don't split my bum with that dreadful thing, please, a million times please . . .

'Ahh!' Selina screamed, as the ruthless blonde penetrated her anus, then lodged in the tightly constricted anal elastic, pushing gently.

Her wealed bottom wriggled helplessly, at once clutching and trying to expel the invading shaft. Her breath came in great shuddering heaves, bubbling in the bath of come, spurting from Hardast's licked cunt. Phryne thrust, sending shockwaves of agony through Selina's belly, but the shaft seemed jammed halfway into her bottom.

Oh, please, no further. I can't take it.

Phryne poked again, and Selina wailed, as her bumhole gave way, of its own accord, and the rubber tool slid smoothly, right to her rectum, filling her, splitting her. The tool withdrew, sliding in its bath of Selina's arse grease, then plunged again, ramming the anal root. Phryne's bare hips slapped Selina's buttocks, as she bum-fucked her.

Oh! Ooh! It went in so easily! I've done it! Like an achievement, so curious, it hurts terribly, but it's sort of a good hurt. I'm full, and whole, and my belly's longing for that lovely hard pressure. Just like a delicious big dung, only coming back, again and again, filling me up. Wait! No! Oh! Whatever am I thinking? I'm buggered!

Phryne's massive conic breasts bounced vigorously, sometimes squelching on her victim's bare back, as she bent low, straddling Selina's writhing body in her powerful buggery. Her nipple rings clashed like cymbals, biting Selina's flesh when her bugger pressed close. Selina's face slapped Hardast's flowing cunt, her tongue lapping the copious come that spewed from the slit lips, while Hardast gamahuched Selina, her face just below Phryne's jerking bare quim, which showered Hardast's face in droplets of cunt juice.

'Yes, Miss, give her full bung,' cried Tuppy, wanking hard.

Jasmine, Avril and Kim also had hands twitching at their wet quims. The giant rubber tool, slimed with Selina's arse grease, pounded her squirming anus, while Selina wriggled, writhing, on top of Hardast's nude body, with her face twisted in a scarlet grimace of pain, and her eyes tight shut. Her cunt gushed come, into Hardast's open mouth.

Tool in my bumhole feels so good, yet it's wrong . . . why do I love it?

The horrid penetration of her anus went on, until Selina thought she could bear it no more; yet her quim spurted juice, and her buttocks thrust to meet the buggering tool, with her anal elastic clutching the shaft, clenching her sphincter to embrace the engine filling her belly. Selina squirmed and whimpered for a whole minute – two – then several.

'You *are* a beastly lesbo,' panted Phryne. 'Look how wet her cunny is, gels.'

No . . . no . . . I'm going to come . . . I'm filled, burst, split, I want to be buggered forever . . . oh, yes, I'm spurting, I'm coming . . .

'Mm . . . mm . . .' Selina groaned. 'Oh . . . urrgh . . . *yes!*'

Phryne's rubber tool slammed her arse root, again and again, until Selina's body convulsed in orgasm, that drenched Hardast's face in come.

'Ah . . . yes . . . *yes* . . .' grunted the buggering blonde girl, knees buckling, as her own belly heaved.

Her titties quivering, with a jangle of her nipple rings, she jerked her hips, plopping the giant tool from Selina's bumhole, then slapped Selina's bum with the flat of her hand, once backhand, once forehand. Selina lay, panting and quivering, on top of Hardast, while Phryne swivelled, to grasp the crouching Bethany Knowte, by her hair.

'Ooh . . .' moaned Bethany, as, wrenching her hair by the roots, Phryne dragged her to the flight cabin.

'The slut has earned further punishment,' she snarled.

The door closed behind the two girls, and, after moments, Selina heard a rhythmic tap-tap-tap from the flight deck. Before each crack, the awful sound of a whip on bare flesh, was a whistling noise, and after, a girl's piteous whimper. Selina grimaced, tears streaking her cheeks, as she rubbed her bruised, buggered bumhole, and wiped her cunt of still-dribbling come. She had nowhere to wipe her slimed fingers but her pube hair and, when that was soaked, she smeared come on her mane, which soon glistened with the shiny cooze juice. The strappers donned their uniforms once more, and pulled the two nude girls apart, fastening them into their safety harnesses.

'We shall be landing soon,' said Jasmine. 'Remember that any further beastliness – wanking off, cunny-sucking, and dreadful bum practices, all the things common trollops are addicted to – shall incur the *strictest* punishment, once you are in Miss Gurdell's charge. Even speaking of your vileness aboard this aircraft shall be chastised.'

She fetched two juice drinks, and carried them to the captain's cabin. The door opened briefly, permitting Selina to observe the flight deck. Phryne stood on tiptoe, her bare bottom facing the door, and behind her, Bethany Knowte, vigorously flogging the naked fesses with Phryne's own rubber quirt. Phryne's massive bare nates were vividly striped with welts, and shook convulsively, squirming and clenching at each whipstroke. She could not escape her chastisement, for two taut rubber cords attached her nipple rings to the ceiling, pulling her breasts up, and obliging her long, coltish legs to strain on tiptoe. Her hands were locked, white-knuckled, on top of her quivering blonde mane. Streams of come glistened on her rippling thighs. Bethany took the drinks, and poured them over Phryne's croup. *Whap!* The quirt's tongues kissed her naked wet buttocks, and Phryne shuddered.

'Ah! That's better,' she gasped. 'A good licking on the wet bare puts meat in a gel's titties. Harder, you slut!'

'Ooh, why is it always *me* . . .?' Bethany moaned.

7

Over The Knee

Miss Gwendoline Gurdell rubbed the last smears of avocado fudge from the nipples of her thirty-nine inch breasts, using her fingertip to polish the golden hoops which pierced her nipple plums. Then, she thrashed her naked body with a sheaf of birch twigs for five minutes, standing, to tickle her thighs, buttocks and breasts, and stepped, dripping with sweat, from her private sauna, to immerse herself in the ice-cold plunge pool. She wriggled, head under water, and her long tresses floating like golden lily pads behind her. When she emerged, goose-fleshed, her waiting maid enfolded her in a giant bath towel, and massaged her vigorously. Gwendoline raised her arms, so that the girl, perspiring in her black costume of short, frilly skirt, tight flounced blouse, fishnet nylons and high shoes, could dry her armpits, shaven to smooth pearl. She parted her legs, for the girl to towel her hard on the buttocks and perineum, padding the neat trim of her pubic bush, its lush fronds growing exuberantly between Miss Gurdell's rippling thighs, until it ended in a cut as severe as any ornamental hedgerow, leaving an inch of bare pube-hillock on either side of its triangle. Gwendoline lowered her arms, and held her arse cheeks open, the croup pouting, for the maid to towel the wrinkled pucker of her anus, completely shorn of any hairs. Balancing on a single leg, she lifted each foot in turn, to be dried between her toes. Her proffered leg shone straight and shaven smooth, its muscles quivering, as the maid frotted her toes and, although the massive ammonite whorls of her naked gash were exposed, the girl did not look up from her task.

'And no tickling, Susan,' Miss Gurdell admonished, in a cool, purring voice. 'You are quite a new gel, but you know how I hate to be tickled.'

'Yes, Mistress, I do,' Susan murmured, head low.

'Oh! You are a sweet maid, but you mustn't tease,' Gwendoline exclaimed. 'I simply cannot bear teasing from one of my dear gels.'

Her bath completed, Gwendoline padded nude into her dressing room, where Susan opened her armoire, and began to lay out a selection of underthings. Gwendoline seated herself at her looking glass, applied a dab of perfume to her earlobes, then smeared puce lipstick on her mouth, with a dab to each nipple. Rising, she inspected her nude body in the glass, turning, to caress her bare buttocks, jutting teats, and the flat, muscular slab of her narrow belly, swelling to wide hips and generous, hard-fleshed thighs. She stroked the firm, ripe pears of her naked buttocks, and licked her lips.

'How old would you say I look, Susan?' she murmured.

'Why, Mistress, that's not for me to say,' Susan replied. 'Girls get the thwangs for less, if Miss Kew overhears such talk.'

'No, go on. I absolve you.'

'Not a day over twenty, Mistress,' piped Susan.

'Flattery can get you thwangs, too, gel.'

'Twenty-one, perhaps.'

Gwendoline sighed.

'All of twenty-four!' she cried.

'But you are the youngest prison governess in Britain, with respect, Mistress.'

Gwendoline shuddered, her bare teats bouncing, as she pouted in a theatrical moue.

'Such harsh words,' she sighed. 'I prefer guide – helper – perhaps mistress of ceremonies. Even here, in the outer isles, where it is so important to maintain a modicum of culture amid the bleakness. Your own age, Susan?'

'Nineteen, Mistress.'

'Ah! How young and happy you are. I shall write a melancholic ode, to the passing of youth. Perhaps I shall have Arioma or Kristel set it to the music of the lyre, and sing it in the nude at sunset, with the solar chariot illumining her body. For the moment – decisions, decisions! – the green sussies, I think. Lemon panties, and the lemon stockings. Yes, I feel green and yellow today, green for the trees and lemon for the fruit thereof. The goddess Demeter murmurs to me. It shall make me feel youthful, for Miss Kew tells me I have a rather beastly duty to perform, this morning.'

'And your corset, Mistress?'

'Lemon also. Rather tighter than usual, I fear. A number three. I must have my wits about me. I'm rather dreading it. It is so distressing, when unpleasantness invades our graceful arbour.'

'A . . . a chastisement, Mistress?' said Susan.

Her nostrils flared, and her thighs shivered, pressing together under her skirtlet, with a little slither of nylon.

'I fear it will come to that. Miss Kew will undoubtedly give me such details as appropriate. But you ask a question, gel? Would *you* merit chastisement?'

'Oh, I hope not, Mistress,' Susan blurted. 'My bottom is pure, and has been since you were gracious enough to elevate me to your service.'

'You are a good gel, Susan. Superbly submissive and feminine, though the two mean the same thing. Two gels are to appear before me, who appear to have forgotten their femininity. Gels dear to me, who might soon have been in sight of their nipple rings. It is most distressing.'

'I suppose you will have to spank them, Mistress.'

'If Miss Kew says so, I suppose I must.'

'On their bare bottoms, no doubt.'

Gwendoline brushed her lips with a fingernail.

'I imagine so,' she drawled. 'Then, Phryne Wuldingdoune is flying in a new batch of inmates, and I shall have to interview them, fearing they may prove as incalcitrant as the last intake – even though they come with the warmest commendations of bottom beauty. The last lot had croups to dream of, yet turned out low girls, fit for hard labour and thwangs. I shall appraise their bottoms, on their welcome spanking, before seeking dear Miss Kew's advice.'

'I'd be awfully privileged to watch, if my mistress felt generous.'

Inspecting the array of bras, knickers and corsets, laid in a rainbow of colours on the bed, from which Susan had extracted the garments demanded, Gwendoline turned, making her big bare breasts sway, with their nipple rings clashing.

'You are a forward gel,' she purred, flashing her teeth, and placing her hand beneath the maid's frilly skirt, to caress the globes of her bottom, almost completely bared by her narrow thong panties. 'I'm not sure I don't rather like you for it.'

Sitting on her bed, she extended a leg, and Susan began to roll the lemon yellow nylon stocking up her satin flesh. When Gwendoline's leg was sheathed in smooth lemon, the maid tapped out the crinkles, pulled it up further, within four inches of her mistress's cunt flaps, and snapped the floral top on the rippling thigh skin. Gwendoline flexed her leg, lowered it, and raised the other, for Susan to repeat the procedure. The gleaming pastel stockings shone garishly against her alabaster skin. As the second lustrous nylon crept up her flesh, she toyed with her lush pubic hairs.

'You don't think my lawn needs a trim, Susan?' she drawled.

Susan glanced up at her mistress's gash, the pink folds swollen and moist in their whorls, with the pert forest of pubic tresses jutting above the upthrust hillock.

'I think it suits you quite well like that, Mistress. The edges are trim enough.'

'I feel *bushy*. It's rather naughty.'

Susan snapped the second stocking in place, and Gwendoline rose, still rubbing her pubic tresses.

'The corset, now,' she said.

Susan picked up a lemon nylon corset, ribbed with steel rods, at the top of which were two bra cups, splayed upwards. Gwendoline lifted her arms, stretching her belly, while the maid positioned the corset, then fastened it at the back with two eyes, and began to lace up the smaller eyelets. The eyelets were positioned in three ranks of a dozen, inches from each other, and Gwendoline ordered her to choose the tightest.

'Are you sure, Mistress?' said Susan.

'Of course. I must get down to nineteen – I'm sure I can.'

Susan's arm muscles knotted, as she pulled the corset tighter and tighter across her mistress's belly, while the cups, snug in place at the underside of the teats, thrust her jutting bare bubbies to full prominence, the nipples pointing upwards from her ribcage. At last, every inner eyelet was fastened, with the tails of the corse lapping on the tops of Gwendoline's swelling bare buttocks, and the waist pinched a third lower than its normal girth, with the naked breasts trembling like jellies in their bra cups, thrust up by the hard bone frames. Gwendoline lowered her arms, breathing in deeply, and patting her hourglass belly. Her nipple rings swayed back and forth, brushing the stiff corset, as her breasts shivered. Swiftly, Susan girdled Gwendoline's tummy in the suspender belt, hooked tightly, and fastened the green garter straps to her stocking tops.

'That's better,' she gasped. 'How it hurts! Are you sure that's nineteen inches?'

'Even less, Mistress,' murmured Susan.

'Flattery again?' cried Gwendoline, beaming, as she swivelled, to inspect her corsed waist in the glass.

'I shouldn't dare, Mistress,' Susan replied. 'The panties, now?'

Gwendoline stroked her pubic tuft, framed naked by stocking tops, straps and suspender belt. The triangle of lawn came to a neat point, just above the topmost whorl of her cunt flaps, a naked outcrop against her smooth flesh, with the large clitoral bud extruded at the apex of the gash.

'Yes. Oh, what a bother, to wear panties. It is the burden of rank,' she said.

'All inmates must, Mistress, except during chastisement,' Susan murmured.

'You, Susan, are one of my gels, and I don't think of my gels as inmates. Are you wearing panties?'

Susan blushed.

'Why, of course, Mistress. It's a hard habit to break. Couldn't you feel them, when you touched my bottom?'

'No, I couldn't. That's what made touching your fesses such a pleasure. They must be very *small* panties.'

'A string, Mistress, slightly skimpier than a thong. It is standard issue for maids. Miss Kew's prescription.'

'Show me,' Gwendoline ordered. 'I am *perfectly* aware of what Miss Kew prescribes, but I should like to see how they look on you, Susan.'

Her face red, Susan flicked up her skirtlet, to reveal her naked cunt basin, the slice of her hillock scarcely sheathed by a narrow strip of pink satin, supported by a string, so thin as to be almost invisible, looped around her waist. Black garter straps connected her nylons to their plain black satin suspender belt. Gwendoline's fingertips reached out, to trace the rear string, as it decended into her bum cleft, to be completely enfolded by the ripely protruding cheeks of the girl's bottom.

'Pink! How fetching,' Gwendoline said. 'But it looks tight. Doesn't it hurt your pouch?'

'Yes, Mistress, a little,' Susan answered. 'It passes between my cunny lips, with some discomfort. Miss Kew says it ensures correct posture.'

Gwendoline clapped her hands.

'I've a ripping idea,' she cried. 'I'll try on your panties, Susan. You don't mind, do you?'

'It's not my place to mind, Mistress,' the maid answered.

She unsnapped her garter straps, then rolled the string from her hips, where a harsh red imprint was left by the thong, and stripped the gusset from her hillock and gash lips, with the slender fabric making a wet sound as it peeled off the bare cooze. She handed the string to Gwendoline, who wrinkled her nose, as her fingers slipped on the oily gusset.

'You are rather wet this morning, Susan.'

'I'm sorry, Mistress,' Susan blurted, blushing, 'but your talk of bare-bottom spanking must have excited me.'

'As a lower gel, Susan, you had your share of discipline,' Gwendoline said, with a slight shudder. 'I am surprised that the thought of, ah, *bare-bottom spanking* moistens your pouch.'

'It is the idea of watching another gel spanked, Mistress,' Susan mumured.

'Scarcely kind,' chided Gwendoline. 'Be careful *you* don't earn a spanking, for boldness.'

'If you chose to spank me, Mistress, I should take it with good grace,' the maid replied.

'But you shouldn't like it.'

'I should learn to like it, Mistress.'

Gwendoline gazed at Susan's bottom.

'Take off your sussies,' she ordered. 'They spoil my view.'

Susan obeyed, baring her belly and hillock; Gwendoline placed her hand on Susan's naked bottom, stroking the quivering melons, and coming to rest on her bare cunny, its hillock shining, shaven smooth.

'My, you *are* wet,' she breathed. 'And your nubbin – anyone can see it's shamefully stiff.'

'Being nude down there is rather thrilling, Mistress,' said Susan.

'Then we'd better get you pantied again quick,' said Gwendoline, with a smile. 'You put on *my* panties.'

'Mistress?' blurted Susan. 'But that's improper . . .'

'I am the governess of Auchterhuish,' rapped Gwendoline, 'and I decide what is improper. I want to see those lovely buttocks of yours sheathed in a governess's panties. It is my whim.'

As the maid slipped, shivering, into Gwendoline's high-cut thong panties, in frilly lemon yellow satin, Gwendoline flicked open her garter straps, then struggled to roll Susan's string over her own bottom.

'My, these are fearfully tight,' she gasped.

'I'm a size smaller than you, Mistress, I think,' Susan said, 'although Miss Kew insists we wear panties two sizes too small.'

'My panties suit you,' Gwendoline pronounced. 'I'm rather jealous.'

Her cunt lawn, and ripely swelling cooze flaps, protruded well beyond the pink sliver of the maid's string, with the binding cord a taut line between the flaps, pressing the very mouth of her slit. She made a moue.

'Ouch,' she said. 'You'd better refasten my garter straps.'

'You're going to keep my panties, Mistress?' gasped Susan, as she knelt to obey.

'They are divinely uncomfortable,' Gwendoline replied. 'Pink suits my lady's place. Yes, I shall keep them, and you may wear mine.'

'Wearing panties of distinction? It's a spanking offence, if Miss Kew finds out,' the maid blurted.

Gwendoline's lips were slack, with a trickle of drool at the corner of her mouth, as Susan fastened the last of her mistress's garter straps, the maid's face inches from Gwendoline's cunt. Shiny streams of come trickled from the tight pink gusset of the string, now stained dark, and glazing Gwendoline's protruding cooze flaps and naked thighs with come, already moistening the lemon stocking tops to a damp yellow.

'Pull your panties up to their tightest,' Gwendoline ordered, her hand trembling a little, as her fingers brushed her moist quim lips, protruding from her tight thong. 'No need for sussies, just yet.'

She sat on the bed, and watched, as the girl obeyed, wrenching the thong and waistband, until the gusset bit between her cunt lips, and only the bottom cord, clasped in her bum cleft, marred the purity of her naked fesses. Gwendoline blushed hotly, wiping her brow of sweat. She panted harshly, watching the girl's smooth bare buttocks. Briefly, she shut her eyes, gulping hard, as she drew her hand from its oily nest between her quim flaps, leaving a smear of come on her heaving corset. Wearing only her stockings and sussies, with the lemon corset thrusting up her bare, quivering titties, Gwendoline patted her thigh.

'Over the knee, gel. Your tummy here, hands on the floor, and your bottom raised,' she panted.

'Mistress? I beg your pardon?' Susan stammered.

109

'You are guilty of a spanking offence, are you not?' Gwendoline blurted, licking her teeth, and her eyes bright.

She caressed her naked breasts, pinching each nipple between finger and thumb, until the plums stood quivering and erect.

'Y-yes, Mistress, but –'

'Obey, you minx, or it shall go worse for you.'

Trembling, Susan assumed submissive posture, crouching over her mistress's thighs, with her bared buttocks upthrust.

'In order to save you from Miss Kew, I am going to spank you first,' Gwendoline said, squeezing Susan's buttocks with her left hand. 'A dozen slaps on that naughty bare bottom.'

'A dozen? Oh, Mistress.'

'It's as hard for me as it is for you, gel. How I hate to mar the purity of a gel's naked bottom! But sometimes . . . it must be done.'

Slap! Gwendoline's first spank cracked on Susan's bare arse, leaving a glowing red handprint.

'Ouch! Oh . . .' the girl wailed, clenching her naked fesses with nervous little jerks.

'Silence, minx,' Gwendoline hissed. '*It's what you want.*'

Susan's naked buttocks writhed, dancing and clenching under the hard bare-bum spanking, with her frilly skirtlet bouncing above her beaten fesses, at each slap from her mistress's spread palm. The buttocks reddened quickly, with each palm print embedding itself on top of the last, until the croup was a blotched mass of crimson skin. *Slap!*

'Ouch! Oh, Mistress!' wailed the spanked girl.

Gwendoline paused.

'Hurt, eh?' she panted.

'Oh, yes, Mistress. My bum's smarting like the dickens.'

'Good. It's not a pleasant duty, you understand, but it's for your own good. And it shall warm me up for spanking *two* naughty bare bums. Miss Kew mustn't think her governess is soft on miscreants.'

Slap! Slap! Slap! Gwendoline's firm bare titties quivered, as she spanked Susan.

110

'Ouch! Ooh!'

A smear of come oozed from the girl's wriggling cunt, sliming her spanker's nylons, while from Gwendoline's own cooze, the come increased from a seep to a flow, drenching the sliver of pink guarding her pubes, and glazing her cunt lips with an oily sheen, as her hot liquid dripped onto her thighs and moist stocking tops.

'Part your buttocks,' Gwendoline gasped. 'Wider. I want a good view of . . . in there.'

Susan spread her bottom cheeks, until her full gash and bumhole were on view, the shaven perineum taut and shiny. Gwendoline completed the dozen, with three spanks hard in the cleft, her palm catching Susan's squirming arse pucker, and the lower cunt flaps, as well as the inner buttock walls, which reddened like the rest of the crimson croup..

'Ooh! Oh, gosh,' the wriggling girl sobbed.

Gwendoline began to stroke the hot bare, caressing the crimson bum flesh with one soft palm, while her free hand delved into the pink soaking sliver of her panties. She gasped, as her fingers connected to her stiff clitty, and she began to rub herself.

'There, there, it's over now,' she panted. 'My, how hot your bottom is, Susan.'

'You're a corking spanker, Mistress,' Susan gasped.

'How kind. Do you want some cold porage for your bottom?'

'Thank you, no, Mistress, I'll be all right, I mean, it's not as if I've taken thwangs. It's sort of nice and hot and throbby.'

With a tiny giggle, she wiggled her buttocks, under Gwendoline's caress, but made no move to rise from her submissive posture. Gwendoline gasped, as she masturbated faster and faster. Her hand slipped between Susan's thighs, and made a sticky wet noise.

'My,' she exclaimed, 'you're all wet, Susan. Does a bare-bottom spanking really excite you?'

'Bare-bum spanking excites any gel, Mistress,' Susan murmured. 'It's hardly fair to blame me.'

111

'I'm not blaming you, gel,' gasped Gwendoline, brushing aside the soaking gusset of the maid's panties, and allowing her fingers to play inside Susan's cooze, while she frotted her own clitty. 'But I suppose you'll want to be off to the lavatory, to diddle yourself?'

'Oh, Mistress, what a soft touch you have,' moaned Susan, her spanked bottom writhing anew, pressing her nubbin and slopped cunt onto her spanker's knuckles. 'I can hardly say yes, can I? It would be a crime.'

'Wanting is not the same as doing,' panted Gwendoline. 'I don't like to see a gel tense, especially a maid, as it interferes with her work. What if I gave you *ex cathedra* permission to diddle yourself here and now?'

'I'd thank you, Mistress.'

'I'd have to watch, of course, to ensure your frotting was decorous.'

'I quite understand, Mistress.'

'You may squat, doggy fashion, Susan, and masturbate while I observe you from behind. Spread your buttocks nice and wide, so that I can monitor your slit.'

Face red, Susan slipped from her position, and crouched on the floor, skirt up, and arse cheeks well spread.

'You may lower the panties, or take them right off,' Gwendoline said.

Susan slid the panties to her knees, affording her mistress a view of her nates and furrow, completely exposed, the whole naked bum cleft glistening with her seeped come. Gwendoline looped a forefinger between her nipple rings and tugged hard, blanching the wrenched nipple flesh. She gave a little groan of pain, as her fingernail sliced her stiff clitty.

'You may masturbate,' she panted.

Susan's fingers slid up from her thighs, and began to poke inside her dripping slit, pulling the lips apart, to show the glistening pink cunt meat. Her fingers danced inside her come-slimed pouch, with her thumb tweaking and jabbing the stiffly extruded clitoris.

'Uhh . . .' she moaned, frigging hard, with her knuckles squelching inside her slit.

112

'Is that good?' said Gwendoline, masturbating her slopped cunt, with her thighs now spread wide, and fingers pinching her erect nipples, as she frotted her swollen clitty.

'Oh . . . yes . . . so good . . .' Susan gasped.

'You must diddle a lot,' said Gwendoline. 'Don't be frightened, Susan, you aren't under smart training just now. Governess's lodge is outside Miss Kew's regime.'

'Well, yes, I do, Mistress. All wenches do.'

'Despite the penalties?'

'Oh! We know it's thwangs on the bare, if we get caught by Miss Kew's purity patrol, but maids can't help wanking off, Mistress, can they?'

Susan's fingers were a blur at her pulsing wet cunt, as she masturbated, with long, sure strokes.

'Smart training,' Gwendoline said, 'is to reinstil the spiritual virtues my gels have been tempted to abandon. Masturbation is an unspiritual habit.'

'But, Mistress, can such a sweet pleasure be totally wrong?'

'It's not a question of wrong. Virtue resides in the perfection of the naked female bottom, and pleasure distracts from chaste contemplation of the fesses, either still, or spanked. Do you sometimes masturbate together, with other girls?'

'Sometimes we wank off in pairs. Kristel Gummi and Arioma Clique are my best wanking chums.'

'So, a gel's nude body excites you?'

Susan blushed.

'Beauty excites all of us, surely, Mistress?'

'Including *male* beauty?' Gwendoline drawled, frotting her come-slimed cunt. 'I am tempted to allow that bare male buttocks may attain a level of harmony, though lower than the female's. When spanked, they have a certain artistic value, however crude.'

'Well, Miss,' Susan gasped, as she wanked, 'sometimes I dream of a piping hot male, young and smooth and muscly, with a big . . . you know, a big stiff tool, filling me up, in my lady's place, or – I suppose this is awfully naughty, but please forgive me my dreams, mistress – swiving me really hard, in . . . in the bumhole.'

'Really?' gasped Gwendoline, frigging vigorously, as she gazed at the wanking girl's agile fingers, squelching inside the intricate, mushy whorls of her naked gash. 'Kristel and Arioma ... two of my most virtuous gels, masturbating with you, a maid, Susan?'

'Oh, gosh, I hope I haven't got anyone into trouble,' Susan panted, not pausing in her wank.

'No, gel. And do you frot in front of each other? Does it stimulate you to look at another girl masturbating?'

'Oh, yes, Mistress. We often wank off in pairs, or even threesomes, that is, diddling each other's clitties, and pinching bubbies, but sometimes it's just as much fun to diddle your own, and watch your friend wank hers. It's like watching yourself in a living mirror. We have diddle races, to see who can come first. Sometimes we draw lots, for a gel to get caught on purpose, wanking off in dorm, after lights out, and then the duty strapper makes her take off her pyjama bottoms, or lift her nightie, and touch her toes, then thrashes her bare, and we all have a jolly good wank as we watch her bum redden.'

'Hmm ...' Gwendoline said, 'I wonder if mutual masturbation, by spiritually *advanced* gels, might not, itself, be spiritual? Exploring fantasies – males, indeed! – to ensure that such fantasies remain safely where they belong.'

There was a slithering snap, as Gwendoline pushed her sodden panties right down, revealing her bare cunt basin, buttocks and thighs, gleaming with her spurted come.

'What are you fantasising at this moment, Susan?' she gasped.

'Oh, Mistress, I don't like to say ...'

'No harm shall come, I promise.'

'A huge hot male, a young nude man, all smooth and rippling with muscle, with a huge tool and big tight balls, full of cream ... it's been so long, in prison, since I had – *you* know, Mistress – well, he's strapping me with his belt, laying it on really hard, striping my bare bum, and I'm wriggling naked, in shame and pain, and then, when my bum's as hot and smarting as can be, he pulls my hair, and

114

I have to put my lips on his monstrous, throbbing tool, and suck and suck . . .'

'And swallow his sperm?' panted Gwendoline, her hand squelching loudly, as she wanked her come-slimed cunt. 'Take his hot spunk into your throat and belly?'

Susan's fingers parted the lips of her cunt, and four fingers penetrated the slit, jabbing deep into her drooling pouch, while her thumb pounded her stiff pink clitty.

'Uh . . . uh . . . no, Mistress, that's the bittersweet part. He wants to spunk in a gel's hole, of course, so he penetrates with his huge stiff tool, and swives and swives in a wet soft cunt, all squelchy and slimy, as her bum pumps against his balls, and his balls are slapping on her wet buttocks, and then he whips his tool from her cunny, and slams it so hard into her nether hole, her bumhole, and begins to poke her frightfully hard, and he is so big, it hurts so awfully much, and she squirms and squirms, as he spanks her bare haunches while he bumswives her, and the come can't stop running down her thighs as she's pinioned under his buggery, for it's been so awfully long since she's had a man, and she'll submit to anything, he takes his belt and whips her wet thighs, making her howl in agony, and squeezes her big bouncy titties, pinching her nips and tugging her nip rings till she squeals, and pushes his cock deeper and deeper into her bumhole, till she just comes and comes, and then his spunk erupts inside her, filling her bum and sploshing all over her legs and bum, and still he's whipping her thighs, all wet with come and spunk, and she can't stop coming . . . ooh, Mistress . . . ooh . . . yes . . . yes!'

'You see yourself as "she"?' gasped Gwendoline, her belly heaving under its tight corset.

'No, Mistress . . . oh . . . oh . . . uhh! In my fantasy, it's *you* I see bumswived . . . yes . . . *ahh!*'

Come spurted from Susan's cunt, as she exploded in orgasm.

'Me . . .? You cheeky minx,' gasped Gwendoline. 'I should spank your bare for that . . . ooh . . . ooh . . . *yes!*'

Pinching her nipples to whiteness, buttocks squirming, and her fingers a blur at her wanked cunt, Gwendoline, too, sprayed oily come from her cooze flaps, as she moaned in her come-drenched spasm.

'*Me* . . .' she panted. '*Me* . . .'

There was a knock on the chamber door, and almost at once it slid open, as Susan stumbled to her feet, smoothing down her skirtlet, and kicking aside the come-soaked lemon panties.

'Ah, Miss Kew,' blurted Gwendoline, reddening. 'I was in the process of robing myself.'

The entrant smiled lazily at her governess's exposed cunt, then at the maid shivering in wet stockings.

Miss Kew's lustrous auburn tresses framed wide, strong lips and high cheekbones, her face, like her bare arms, suntanned a golden brown; her tall body and long, coltish legs encased in a tight black uniform of cotton shirt and woollen skirt, both immaculately pressed, with black nylons leading to kneeboots, buckled and spurred at the ankles. Her shirt was open-collared, with narrow lapels, the cleavage reaching deep into her suntanned breastflesh, revealing a good portion of her massive breasts, bunched together by a scalloped undercup brassiere. Her skirt clung tightly to her buttocks, with no panty line marring the perfection of the smooth arse globes. Her only adornment was a golden badge, pinned at her left breast; at her black leather belt dangled handcuffs, a rubber baton, coiled leather whip, and an ashplant cane, two feet long. She eyed Gwendoline's pink thong, as she hastily slid it up over her buttocks and pubes.

'Maid's panties, miss?' she said. 'I must be mistaken.'

'Yes, Miss Kew, I am afraid your eyes deceive you,' blurted Gwendoline. 'I had to administer a light bare-bottom spanking to my maid – for a trifle, you know – and she . . . she mixed up her panties, the silly goose. No harm done. The, ah, purpose of your rather abrupt visit?'

'I did knock, miss,' said Miss Kew, curtsying. 'I thought you might have forgotten your appointment with Dawn and Janet, the two miscreants. I have been waiting with them in your anteroom, if it please you, and am anxious to get their chastisement done, so that they may return to hard labour in the peat bog.'

116

Gwendoline grimaced.

'Please, Miss Kew. You know you have a free hand with the lower gels, but I prefer to be spared the details.'

'Very good, miss,' purred Miss Kew. 'I know your mind is on higher things. May I remind the governess to put on her dress, before appearing?'

'Why, yes – you interrupted us,' blurted Gwendoline, blushing. 'Susan, the . . . the . . .'

'May I suggest the green silk?' said Miss Kew. 'It is nice and tight, clings well to waist, thighs and croup, and will show off your corse to perfection. Bare arms, for ease of disciplining the miscreants' bottoms.'

'Why, yes. Just what I was going to . . . Susan, if you please?' Gwendoline said.

'Perhaps not the pink thong, miss,' drawled Miss Kew. 'I see you were thinking of the lemon pair – more appropriate, I suggest.'

'Why, yes . . . I was simply trying . . . you know . . . a mix-up,' gasped Gwendoline, blushing.

She turned her back to Miss Kew, and ordered Susan to divest her of the thong panties, replacing them with the high-cut lemon pair; she winced, as the girl rolled them over her bottom, and the gusset, soaked in the maid's come, touched her bare cooze. She made sure her sussies and stockings were trim, then wriggled into the clinging tube of dark green silk, held to her bare shoulders by thin straps, and extending to a hem halfway up her lemon-stockinged thighs. The silk moulded her ripe croup and heavy, jutting teats, straining high over the corset cups, with her nipple rings presenting twin circles, starkly symmetrical under the silk. She straightened, smoothing her belly flat, and scrutinised herself in the glass, before letting the crouching Susan slip a pair of bottle green calfskin stilettos over her stockinged toes, strapping the buckle tight, just above the ankles.

'Very well,' she said, breathing deeply. 'I trust all is prepared for my interview with the, ah, miscreants?'

Miss Kew snapped smartly to attention, clicking her heels, and saluted.

'Prisoners ready and waiting for discipline, governess,' she rapped. 'Shall I dismiss the maid?'

Gwendoline glanced at Susan's eager face.

'Why, no,' she blurted. 'I have decided she is to attend me.'

'Has this lower gel virtue enough to witness chastisement?' purred Miss Kew.

'Assuredly, Miss Kew,' retorted Gwendoline. 'Look at that croup – the swell, harmony, size, heaviness, curve – are not such tasty fesses virtue?'

With a smirk, she strutted to her drawing room. Miss Kew eyed Gwendoline's skirted buttocks, swaying sensuously, and stroked her sleek waist cane.

'Yours too, governess,' she murmured. 'A most spiritual bum, and ripe for *my* virtue.'

8

Twirlspank

Gwendoline gazed through the window of her eyrie high up in Auchterhuish Castle: the froth-capped grey sea, stretching to other islands, misted in the distance; the beaches, strewn with seaweed and pebbles, and the collectors, working in the nude, for security, scavenging for the precious *Fucus aromaticus*, the fragrant pods of bladdered seaweed, draped on rocks and sand, at low tide; the granite bulk of the guesthouse, by the jetty, with the service boats bobbing in the tiny harbour; wisps of steam, from the fumaroles, amid rolling green slopes, sheathed in heather, moss and bracken, with myriad wild flowers, and the work parties of girls roped together, under the whips of their strappers, digging turf from the peat bogs; the rows of prisoners' huts beside the parade ground, with the gaunt silhouettes of pillory and whipping-post. The nude body of a miscreant dangled limp in the pillory, her bottom striped with weals; cawing seagulls swooped, to bite on her exposed body, with the prisoner's moans borne faintly by the sea breeze. Gwendoline turned away, with a shudder.

She remained seated at her desk, with Susan, hands at her lap, standing demurely by the window, as Miss Kew introduced the two miscreants. Gwendoline glanced at their charge sheets, laid on her leather-framed blotter, then looked up, pressing her gold fountain pen to her lips, as the two girls stood, trembling, before her.

'Dawn Tregarsh,' she intoned.

'Yes, Miss.'

'Janet Pummer.'

'Miss.'

The two nineteen-year-olds curtsied, short skirts bobbing. Each wore brown pleated gym skirt, white ankle socks, and runners, with a tight tan, short-sleeved blouse sheathing their braless breasts. They were bare-legged, the skin of face, arms and legs golden with an outdoor work tan, and each had her short hair cut in a bob, the tresses scooping her cheeks and bare nape. Each had big, thrusting titties, straining at the thin, drab of her work blouse; ripe, muscled croup and thighs, the long legs toned by hard labour. They stood sullenly, legs apart, and hands clasped at the spinal nubbin.

'Well, Dawn and Janet,' Gwendoline said. 'I would like to hear confession, in your own words.'

The girls bit their lips, and remained silent.

'Silence will be taken as admission of guilt,' Gwendoline snapped. 'Miss Kew – the evidence, please?'

Miss Kew opened a canvas bag, and, with tongs, removed a half-empty packet of potato crisps. The girls' eyes widened with fear.

'How are we to explain these . . . things?' said Gwendoline with a moue of distaste.

'Potato crisps, governess,' said Miss Kew. 'A snack food. The prisoners were caught fighting over them.'

'They were hers, Miss,' blurted Dawn.

'No, Miss, hers!' squealed Janet.

'These slags are also suspected of mutual masturbation, governess,' said Miss Kew drily, 'although we've never caught them in flagrante.'

Dawn and Janet blushed deep crimson.

'These are two serious offences,' Gwendoline said. 'Possession of an illicit item, and fighting over it. The gel in possession of the item must have been attacked by the gel desiring it, hence you are both guilty.'

'The duty strapper was alerted by noises, at three a.m., in dorm, governess,' said Miss Kew. 'She suspected illicit masturbation, but found the two miscreants naked, and wrestling on the floor, each striving for possession of the item. Prisoner Tregarsh had her mouth flecked with fragments of the illicit foodstuff contained therein.'

'Then Janet was the assailant,' Gwendoline mused. 'I am interested to know how you obtained this disgusting thing, Dawn.'

Dawn Tregarsh bit her lip, but said nothing. Her eyes were moist with tears.

'You both realise that a spanking must be administered,' Gwendoline said, 'and on your bare bottoms. The tariff depends on your willingness to cooperate. So far, I hear nothing to save you from a *severe* spanking.'

The two girls looked warily at each other.

'Please, Miss, I found it on the beach,' mumbled Dawn. 'I was fucus-picking, and . . . it must have been washed up in the tide. I couldn't resist temptation . . . they were sour cream and chives flavour, Miss.'

Gwendoline grimaced.

'What was for tea, yesterday, Miss Kew?' she asked.

'Bashed neeps, porage, and boiled mutton, governess,' said Miss Kew. 'Complete nutrition, by Home Office regulations.'

'Fucus-pickers work in the nude, to prevent pilferage,' Gwendoline said. 'So how did you slip the offending item past the strappers?'

'Please, Miss,' said Dawn, blushing fiercely, 'I secreted it in my lady's place.'

'Do they not check there?' demanded Gwendoline.

'Normally, they just sniff, Miss,' blurted the blushing girl.

'I scarcely think the things would be edible, after immersion in seawater,' said Gwendoline. 'And as for immersion in a gel's pouch . . . I don't believe a word, Dawn, and you've earned deeper chastisement with this farrago of lies. *Who* gave you this forbidden item?'

Tears dribbled on the girls' faces, and both swallowed convulsively, but said nothing.

'They are villainous London hussies, governess,' snarled Miss Kew, 'and their code of honour forbids *grassing up*, in their thieves' argot. I suggest we discipline them for the known offences, pending further interrogation.'

121

'I agree,' Gwendoline said, sucking the head of her fountain pen. 'One other thing – when discovered fighting, they were both in the nude. Were you *masturbating*, gels? Were the crisps payment for vile favours?'

The girls blushed deeply, but were silent.

'Bah!' snorted Gwendoline. 'Spank them, Miss Kew. Over your knee, in the spanking chair. Janet first.'

Miss Kew sat on the satin cushion of the high-backed spanking chair, drew her skirt up almost to her crotch, and motioned Janet Pummer to take her place, over her nyloned knee. Trembling, the girl obeyed, bending over Miss Kew's knee, with her hands on the floor, with her buttocks high and spread. Her skirt flounced up over her pantied croup, and, with a smart tug, Miss Kew pulled the high-cut brown panties from the buttocks, exposing the naked fesses, with deep red strap marks, as the panties stretched, quivering, across the back of the girl's knees. The panties gusset bore stains of dried fluid. Miss Kew rolled up the blouse and, delving under the girl's tummy, knotted the ends below her breasts, fully baring the buttocks, thighs and lower back. She raised her arm.

'Please, mum,' blurted Janet, 'surely it isn't fair that Susan should watch?'

Susan's tongue lolled from her parted lips, as she gazed at Janet's bare bottom, and her hands clutched her crotch, with her frilly skirt inched up over her thighs.

'Cheeky slut,' hissed Miss Kew. 'Nothing is fair, in smart training.'

'Two dozen is their tariff,' Gwendoline said.

'Oh, Miss! Two dozen?' wailed Dawn.

'Now it is three dozen,' replied Gwendoline, primly, licking her pen, with a slither of nylon, as she crossed and uncrossed her thighs, her eyes on Janet's bare croup.

'Bitch,' Janet hissed at Dawn.

Miss Kew held Janet's head down, by the neck.

'Begin the spanking,' ordered Gwendoline, crossing her legs, beneath her desk.

Miss Kew's palm slapped the bare buttocks full on mid-fesse, leaving a pink imprint on the girl's quivering flesh, which clenched tight, after the spank. Two rapid slaps deepened the imprint to scarlet. There was a slithering sound, as the girl's bare-shaven cunt writhed on her spanker's nylons.

'Ooh . . .' Janet gasped.

Smack! Smack!

'Ooh! Ouch!' whimpered the writhing girl, her spanked bare bum clenching and wriggling on Miss Kew's nylon stockings.

'Stop this girly blubbing,' Gwendoline ordered.

Janet's bare buttocks darkened to a blotchy mass of crimson bruises, as Miss Kew expertly spanked the entire, quivering expanse of bum flesh, from the upper thighs to top buttock, right up to the spinal nubbin. Janet gasped, sobbing, but did not cry out, her breath rasping from her heaving breast, in short sharp pants. Her face, bright red, was a wrinkled mask of pain. At each spank, her bum cleft tightened to a hairline, while her long bare legs shot rigid behind her.

'Ooh! Oh, Miss, it's too much,' she blurted. 'I'll talk, honestly, I'll own up –'

Smack! Smack!

'*Ahh!*'

The girl's spanked bare bottom squirmed frantically.

'A little late, I fear,' said Gwendoline. 'The tariffs are set, for both of you. Continue the spanking, Miss Kew, while we hear the gel. It may mollify her further chastisement.'

'Oh! Ohh . . .' sobbed Janet. 'It wasn't my fault, Miss. Dawn asked me to wank her off, and she would share her crisps with me, and we diddled in the nude, and then she said I could only have one scoop, and grabbed the bag from me, and hit me on the titties, so I hit her back. It was self-defence, Miss.'

'Spank her the full three dozen,' sniffed Gwendoline, 'and then Dawn may take hers. Perhaps we shall hear another side.'

'Oh, Miss . . .' wailed Janet.

Miss Kew spanked on, until the sobbing, shivering girl had taken thirty-six spanks, and her puffy bottom was bruised crimson. Susan watched, eyes hooded, and drool seeping from the corner of her slack lips, as her hands twitched at her crotch, with her skirt ridden up almost to her stocking tops. The spanker wrenched her victim's hair, pulling her to her feet; Janet stood, legs quivering, as she fumbled to draw her panties up over her glowing bare bum. When her panties were drawn tight, she rubbed her hands round and round the spanked bare bum flesh, moaning and crooning, with little gasps, her face wrinkled in pain, and tears seeping from her eyes.

Miss Kew slapped her thighs, nodding at Dawn to replace the spanked girl. The surface of Miss Kew's nylons glistened with fluid, where Janet's naked gash had writhed. Dawn took position, with a glance of hatred at Janet, now standing with her head lowered, hands at top buttock, and tears trickling down her cheeks. After knotting her blouse at her ribcage, Miss Kew ripped down her panties, to expose her bare. Roughly pushing the girl's head down, she lifted her spanking arm.

'Mayn't I speak, Miss?' gasped Dawn. 'She grassed me up, the cow, but it wasn't like that.'

'You may speak, while your bottom reddens, gel,' snapped Gwendoline.

She nodded at Miss Kew, who brought her hand down on the girl's bare. The buttocks pinked instantly, with the raw imprint of Miss Kew's palm on the gasping girl's firm, meaty arse globes. The spanks rained on Dawn's bare, while her face suffused with red, and tears glazed her cheeks. Her buttocks squirmed and clenched, as Miss Kew's spanks darkened her wriggling bare bumskin.

'Ooh . . . uh . . .' the girl panted.

'Ahh! Oh, I'll tell, Miss. It was Janet who got the crisps. *She* wanted to wank. It's true! She came to my bed, and let me smell the crisps, then took off her pyjama bottoms, and began to wank herself off, saying that if I'd wank her, she'd share them. Her cunny was spurting juice, all over her thighs, and I got all hot and wet myself, and couldn't resist. We got naked, and I wanked her with my fingers, while she did me the same. We never tongued, Miss, honestly.'

Clenching and jerking, Dawn's bare buttocks glowed with spanks, in a mottled crimson lattice of fingermarks.

'To think I once considered Dawn and Janet as possible disciples,' said Gwendoline, rather faintly, and pressed her nyloned thighs together, with a light squishy sound. 'Their bottoms so nearly perfect! Dawn's bare so meaty, dusky and taut, with Janet's a rosy aureate hue, full and smooth, like globes of porcelain. Go on, Dawn.'

Dawn's bare jolted under another spank. Gwendoline slipped a hand under her dress, checking to see that her sussies were securely fastened; fiddling with one strap that seemed loose, she snapped it back in place, with a loud click. Her green tube dress rode up to her stocking tops, and she allowed it to remain, with her fingers still brushing her naked thigh, between stockings and panties. Gwendoline gazed at the girl's bare bum spanked red, her fingers toying with the gusset of her panties.

'Ouch! Then, Miss, I stripped off, and she wanted to tongue me, but I wouldn't, so we wanked each other off with our hands. We had orgasms, then she popped a crisp into her wet slit, and said, if I wanted any, I'd have to eat them from her pouch. So I knelt down and sucked at her slit, until the crisp came out, all wet and soggy, but the sour cream and chives flavour was sort of tasty, with her girly juices. She let me have another one, and another, and her clitty was all big and swollen, and I had to suck that, to get the crisp out, and swallow all her juices too, for she was flowing with wetness, Miss. I was wanking myself at this time, and as I washed down the crisp with a mouthful of her come, I brought myself off with my thumb and finger. I sucked her quim till she had another orgasm, then she only let me have one scoop of crisps from the packet, and slapped my nipples, and said I was a silly goose, and would never have my nipple rings. So I got the hump a bit, and slapped her on the quim. It was all wet and squishy, and made a big ploppy noise, and –'

Smack!

'Ooh!' she gasped. 'Oh, that really, really hurts, Miss. Well, then we set to it, wrestling, and I thought it was only in fun, but I got a terrible pounding, with the cow kneeing me in the slit, and biting my nips, which hurt horribly, so I got my fist up her gash, and began to scratch, then I clawed her bum, and . . . well, it was self-defence, Miss.'

Smack! Smack!

'Ooh! Cripes, how it smarts. Ooh . . .'

Dawn's bare bum squirmed, rubbing her quim on Miss Kew's glistening nyloned thighs. Gwendoline's fingers crept inside the band of her panties, and found her quim, throbbing wet and oozing oily come. Belly heaving and aflutter inside its tight, restraining corset, she shuddered, as her fingertips brushed her swollen clitoris.

'Beastly gel. Then what?'

'Then the strapper caught us, Miss, and ordered us to report to Miss Kew, for grave offence.'

'The stories aren't good enough,' Gwendoline gasped, fingers inside her gushing slit, and beginning to wank off quite powerfully. 'Spank her the tariff, Miss Kew, and we may find out *how* the illicit foodstuff came from the mainland, and who acts as tuck mistress.'

Miss Kew continued the spanking, and the girl's naked arse globes rose and fell in the rhythm of the slaps, both fesses squirming, and blotched red. Gwendoline's stockings slithered wetly, as she masturbated. Susan had her skirt up, and blatantly rubbed her crotch, licking her teeth, as her eyes fastened on the spanked girl's threshing bare buttocks. Miss Kew's teats heaved, like her victim's bottom, straining against her black blouse, their bare portions squeezed like clenched fesses. The chastised girl sobbed and snivelled, gasping, her face red and streaming with tears, as the spanking drew to its close. At the thirty-sixth stroke, Miss Kew released her, and the trembling girl fumbled to pull her panties over her glowing red bum, while pausing to rub her buttocks, with little cries of pain, and hopping up and down, her braless titties bouncing in their blouse. Their dancing nipples were hardened to stiff little cakes.

'Oh! Oh, what a hard spanking,' she wailed. 'Oh, Miss, my bum smarts ever so much, like it was caned. I never knew just a spanking could hurt so.'

'*As if it had been* caned, Dawn,' murmured Gwendoline.

'I'd rather thwangs any day, Miss, honestly,' Dawn sobbed. 'Miss Kew is *such* a hard spanker. Thwangs are sort of impersonal, but when her hand spanks bare, you *feel* hurt.'

Knickers up, Dawn joined Janet in submissive stance, before Gwendoline's desk. Gwendoline removed her hand from her sopping quim, and wiped it on her lemon nylons, before clasping both hands beneath her chin, and eyeing the penitent girls, both snuffling, as they cringed. Susan's hands rested decorously at her lap, on her smoothed and straightened skirtlet. Miss Kew rose, stretching herself, before snapping to attention, with a click of her heels. Her uniform skirt neatly covered her nyloned thighs, glistening with the come oozed from the spanked girls' cunts.

'The truth must come out,' purred Gwendoline. 'It's time for the spanking glove. *Who* is the tuck mistress? This time, a spanking without tariff, until one of you confesses. Susan, if you please?'

Susan opened a cupboard, and withdrew a large leather glove, the inside padded, and the palm and fingers covered in leather strips, bolstered by steel rods at each finger, and a steel disc sewn into the palm. With a curtsy, she handed it to Miss Kew, who put it on. The two penitents gazed, wide-eyed, as Miss Kew flexed her fingers.

'You don't think thwangs would be appropriate, governess?' she said.

Gwendoline blanched.

'Not at this stage, Miss Kew. I hope, not at any stage. I must approve necessary harshness to rude lower gels, but in my domain, more sympathetic discipline shall always hold sway. Heavens, a spanking on the bare should be quite fearful enough to quell the boldest wench.'

'I beg to differ, governess,' answered Miss Kew. 'In fact, I suggest increasing the general tariffs, both for spanks and thwangs. Caning on the bare should also, I respectfully submit, be of unlimited tariff. There is no reason why a persistent miscreant cannot take a hundred canestrokes in one set. These are undisciplined times.'

127

'A hundred canestrokes on the bare!' Gwendoline gasped, pressing her hand to her crotch, suddenly spurting with fresh come. 'I cannot approve chastisement which I myself could not endure.'

'Today,' Miss Kew continued, 'Phryne Wuldingdoune delivered three of the most shameless drabs I have ever encountered: Hardast Bratt, Bethany Knowte, and, worst of all, a depraved pervert named Selina Rawe. I propose introducing them at once to profound discipline, since mere spanking shall scarcely tickle such toughened bottoms.'

'You shall let me judge that, Miss Kew,' Gwendoline replied frostily. 'I shall interview the new gels, and apply an introductory spanking, as is my custom. Now, to the matter. I have a super idea to make these gels confess. We shall let them spank the truth from each other. Each gel will wish to make the *other* guilty of "grassing".'

'Admirable, governess,' Miss Kew replied, licking her teeth. 'A girl spanked without tariff is sure to blab. With the spanking glove, their bottoms will really smart.'

'Yes,' blurted Gwendoline, blushing, 'I am aware.'

Gwendoline decreed that Dawn would first spank Janet. Dawn donned the spanking glove with a gleam in her eyes, while Janet sullenly bent over and touched her toes, her buttocks bared to Dawn's waist height. Dawn ripped down her panties, and the well-spanked arse glowed fully naked. Gwendoline rose, and stepped forward from her desk, smoothing her green tube dress firmly over her breasts, stocking tops and panties. Arms folded, she stood over Janet's quivering bare bottom.

'This spanking is without tariff, Janet,' she said. 'It will go on until you have told us the truth. Then, you will spank the truth from Dawn. Spanks to be delivered with straight arm, not raised above the shoulder.'

Dawn smiled knowingly. She raised her stiff, straight spanking arm to shoulder height, then placed her left foot on her right knee, balancing on the one foot. With a sudden motion, she whirled, making her skirt flutter up, to show her bruised red bum in its skimpy knickers, pirouetted in a full turn, and slapped her spanking hand on Janet's bare. *Crack!*

'Oh,' Janet gasped, her buttocks clenching, as a vivid red bruise appeared over the blotch of her previous spanking. 'Ooh . . .'

Dawn whirled again. *Crack!*

'Uhh . . .' Janet squealed, her face red, and tears springing to her eyes, as her naked arse melons squirmed frantically. 'Gosh, mum, that's tight.'

Crack!

'Ouch.'

Crack!

'Ahh . . .'

'Speak up, you cow,' hissed Dawn, pirouetting once more.

Crack!

'Oh! Oh!'

'A novel way of spanking, yet effective,' Gwendoline said.

'A Scots custom, governess,' Miss Kew said drily, called "twirlspanking", performed at certain highland games, where males ceremonially spank females, with their canes strapped to the erect sex organs.'

Gwendoline blushed. Dawn's whirling gloved hand smacked the quivering bare nates of her victim, squealing and sobbing.

'Uhh . . . ooh . . .' Janet groaned.

Her croup flamed with bruises, the bare arse melons clenching and quivering, with her fingers shuddering on her toes. Gwendoline gasped, watching the spanker's thighs ripple, her poise perfect, as she slapped the helpless bare fesses beneath her. Gwendoline pressed her thighs tightly together, with a wet squelching noise; Susan, by the window, leered, fingers twitching at her crotch, and her skirtlet well up, showing her stocking tops and wet panties gusset. Miss Kew stood at ease, hands behind her back, smiling tightly at the squirming naked buttocks. *Crack!*

'Ooh! Ahh! I can't take any more, Miss, please,' Janet whimpered.

'Then you had better talk,' Gwendoline replied.

'Ooh! Oh, I don't know, I'm sure!' wailed the spanked girl.

'How about the time you wanked off Miss Wadd, in return for some Edinburgh shortbread?' Dawn hissed.

'It's not true. I never –'

Crack!

'Ahh! Ooh!'

'Or your nude swims at midnight, when the Oban fishing boats are in?'

'That's a lie! It is you and Kristel Gummi who –'

Crack!

'Ahh! Stop,' gasped Janet, her spanked bare quivering like two red jellies.

'The crisps, Janet?' murmured Gwendoline.

Gwendoline's face was bright red, her stockings slithering audibly, as their tops moistened, with trickles of fluid staining the nylons, on her quivering thighs.

'I don't know ... ask Dawn.' Janet sobbed. 'Let me spank her, and I'll get the truth.'

'You bitch,' hissed Dawn. '*You* said to Miss Wapping, you'd take fellows *up the bum,* if she'd take you into the guesthouse.'

Crack!

'Oh! I never! I mean, she refused ...'

The set continued to over forty spanks, with Dawn's body dripping with sweat, her blouse drenched, and its fabric clinging to her titties, as they bounced and shook with each twirl. Her bare thighs, revealed by her fluttering skirt, were moist with glistening streams from her cunt lips, swollen under their skimpy stained panties. Janet gulped her denials, until her naked bottom was fiery with hard crimson bruises, and she slobbered, whimpering, as the spanking glove slapped the trembling bare jellies of her arse. *Crack!* The fiftieth spank resounded in the chamber.

'Ahh! My bottom! It stings awfully! Oh, please stop.'

'It was *Hamish* who got you the crisps, eh?' snarled Dawn.

Crack!

'Ooh! Ohh!' Janet shrieked. 'You rotten fucking bitch, he's *your* boyfriend. And it's *your* bumhole that takes Nurse Cream's biggest clyster . . .'

Gwendoline paled, gasping, and her face wrinkling in rage. She called a halt.

'I believe Janet is telling part of the truth,' she said to the panting spanker. 'But further chastisement is futile, when it elicits only foolish, wicked fantasies. Boyfriends, indeed! And the very idea of . . . of perverted anal penetration! On *my* island!'

Dawn lowered her spanking hand, her prison uniform soaked in sweat, and with come gleaming on her rippling bare thighs. Janet rose, snuffling, face grimacing in pain, and her bare buttocks unconsciously clenching. Gwendoline's nostrils flared, as she observed the fluid trickling from the girl's cunt. Janet's thighs, too, were streaked with seeped come.

'I don't know what I said, Miss,' Janet blurted. 'My mind was far away. It's like that when a girl is spanked on the bare.'

'Yes, I know,' said Gwendoline, 'it's so – anyway, let's see what you get from Dawn, when she's far away in . . . in excitement.'

Dawn's panting subsided to a sullen grunting, as Miss Kew ordered her to bend over and bare her bum. Janet was permitted to rise, sobbing, and rubbing her flaming red buttocks. With her skirtlet bouncing over her wrists, her hands kneaded her bruised flesh, squeezing and caressing, as if her caress could diminish the puffy red welts of her spanking. Her tears dried when Gwendoline proffered the spanking glove. Janet licked her teeth, savagely gleaming, as she ripped down Dawn's panties, and exposed the bare bum entire.

'Twirlspank, mum?' she asked.

'It seems only fair,' Gwendoline replied.

Janet's skirtlet fluttered, as she whirled. *Crack!*

'Mm!'

The spank crimsoned Dawn's bare, with a livid palm-print. *Crack!*

'Ah! Bitch!' Dawn gasped.

Her naked fesses began to churn, squirming, and clenching to a hair line. Janet twirled a full circle, smacking the buttocks with forehand and backhand strokes.

'Oh! It hurts!' shrieked Dawn, her spanked bare writhing, and her face creased in anguish.

At each twirl, sweating and panting, Janet laid an artful spanking, taking care to mark the haunches and thigh backs and underfesses, as well as top buttock, an inch from Dawn's twitching spinal nubbin.

'Ouch! Oh!' squealed Dawn, red bare fesses writhing.

'It was *you* who got the crisps,' Janet snarled, 'if not from Hamish, from *one* of the service boys.'

'No! I swear!'

Crack!

'Ooh! Ahh . . .'

'Roddy, perhaps. Or Denis . . .'

Crack!

'Ooh! Please . . . oh, stop, Janet. How it hurts!'

'It's meant to hurt, you bitch,' Janet hissed.

Crack!

'Uhh . . . uhh . . .' the spanked girl sobbed.

Dawn's bare bum, livid with spankmarks, desperately wriggled, as though the pain could dissipate down her rigidly tensed legs. She rocked on the balls of her feet, gripping her twitching toecaps, as Janet's gloved palm raised wide, puffy blotches over the whole expanse of her nates. The spanking went to fifteen smacks, then thirty, with Dawn's breath rasping, as she squealed and sobbed. Each spank jiggled her teat globes, soaked in sweat, against the thin restraint of her blouse.

'And it's *you* who wanted into the guesthouse,' panted Janet. 'I saw you store some fucus weed up your slit, when you thought the strappers were off guard, to bribe Miss Wapping.'

Crack!

'Ahh . . .' Dawn groaned, as her naked arse squirmed. 'You're mad. I wouldn't risk the pillory, and you can't bribe Miss Wapping.'

'But the crisps,' murmured Gwendoline.

Her legs trembled, with thighs pressed tight, and a darkening smear of liquid staining the nylons, seeping down from her vulva. The maid Susan gazed, drooling, at Dawn's spanked bare bum; her hands dabbled openly within her panties, as if to scratch herself, but the gusset was drenched in her come, which trickled copiously down her rippling nyloned thighs. Each movement of her hand lasted longer, with her knuckles clenching, as she thumbed her gash and clitoris. Her face was bright red.

'Even if you *did* find the crisps by accident, you should have handed them in to a strapper,' Janet gasped. 'Arioma Clique told me you gave *her* some for a wank, before you even thought of me. Bitch!'

Crack! Crack!

'Oww!' Dawn howled, as a backhand and forehand slapped her trembling arse melons.

'But I think you got them from a boy,' Janet insisted.

Suddenly, she slapped Dawn's bottom with her ungloved palm, and did not remove her hand from the spank. She extended her forefinger, and poked into the wrinkled anus bud.

'Ouch! Stop,' squealed Dawn.

Janet rammed her finger, penetrating the girl's bumhole right to the knuckle, then began to ream her finger round and round in the anal elastic.

'Oh! Stop! Mum, tell her to stop,' Dawn blurted. 'That isn't spanking. It hurts.'

'It *is* part of spanking,' intoned Miss Kew.

Janet removed her finger, slimed with Dawn's arse grease, with a loud plop. Her face was twisted in anger.

'You *have* had a boy up you,' she hissed. 'Your bumhole's stretched wider than by any nurse's clyster. And a *big* boy . . . it could only be Hamish.'

'No!' cried Gwendoline. 'It's impossible. Miss Kew, I despair of these lying hussies. A spanked gel, in her frenzy of pain, can only spew the most outrageous untruths.'

'Shall we desist, and reward them with a spell in the pillory, governess?' purred Miss Kew.

133

Janet and Dawn paled, gasping.

'I . . . I'm not sure,' blurted Gwendoline. 'They *have* been spanked soundly, after all.'

'For such a serious offence . . .' Miss Kew murmured. 'I repeat that mere spanking makes little impression on the modern hardcore slut.'

Gwendoline bit her lip.

'Yes . . . yes, I suppose you're right. They are but lower gels, more's the pity. Such beautiful bare bottoms, even – *especially* – when spanked. Perhaps *one* day, I may welcome them to the ranks of my disciples.'

'I suggest they be hobbled, governess, and your maid Susan may escort them to the undressing room. You and I have business to conclude.'

Gwendoline went pale.

'Oh . . . are you sure, Miss Kew?'

'Quite sure, governess. By your own guidelines.'

'Yes . . . yes, I suppose so. Susan, open the punishment cabinet, please, and apply two hobbles to Dawn and Janet.'

Susan opened a rosewood cupboard, in which whips, canes, and tawses hung in gleaming rows, with an array of branks, braces and hobbles beneath them. Selecting two wooden hobbles, two feet in length, Susan squatted, and expertly clamped each girl's ankles in her hobble. Dawn and Janet stood trembling and glowering, each with her skirt up, and rubbing her spanked bottom, with grimaces of pain, as they shuffled helplessly in the hobble clamps. Miss Kew ordered Susan to take the prisoners to Miss Cream, for undressing, and certification as fit for punishment, then to await her by the pillory. Susan curtsied to Gwendoline and Miss Kew, and led the hobbled girls outside. She escorted their clumsy feet along the stone corridor, to the steep flight of stairs, where she halted.

'Rough luck, gels,' she murmured. 'There's something I must do. Shan't be a tick.'

She lifted each girl's skirtlet, to reveal her spanked bare bottom, then, licking her teeth, fully raised her own. Her panties were soaked in come; Susan thrust three fingers inside her wet pouch, and pressed her clitty with her thumb, wanking herself off with only a few strokes, to a profound, fluttering orgasm.

'Uhh . . . uhh . . . *oh*,' she gasped. 'Oh, *yes*. That's better, gels. The sight of your lovely spanked bums had me really fruity, in there, and I was dying for a wank.'

From Gwendoline's apartment came a rhythmic tap-tap-tap, of bare hand on bare skin, and the faint moaning of a girl in pain.

'Ah! Yes, Miss Kew, harder . . .' Gwendoline whimpered. 'I deserve it. I must pay for my pleasure at marking the divine bottoms of those gels . . . ah! Harder, spank harder, I beg you. Gosh, it stings. Higher, on the soft skin . . . ouch! Yes . . . now my haunches . . . you'll be careful to leave an even blush, Miss Kew? Ouch! Ooh! You spank so divinely. Oh! My thighs . . . yes, if you must. Spank me for desiring to masturbate at a gel's red bottom. Ah! Ooh . . . spank me for my beastly thoughts, make my bottom blush. Hamish – surely not dear Hamish – ooh!'

Her nipple rings jangled, as she was spanked. Susan smiled, and thrust her hand right inside her come-soaked gash, from which she extracted a packet of salt and vinegar flavoured crisps. She handed it to Dawn.

'Split these, gels,' she said. 'I've plenty. I am blessed with an extra-big pouch.'

The girls fell ravenously on the forbidden foodstuff.

'And an extra-tight bumhole,' purred Susan. 'Ask Hamish . . .'

9

Swanky Bum

'My, you've a big pair of heavers,' drawled Nurse Belinda Cream. 'Perfectly round, like beach balls, and with positively outsized nips! Yum! There was a gel with roundies at Cheltenham, as I recall, and we used to twit her something rotten, but she wasn't as big or firm as you, Miss Knowte.'

The young nurse licked her lips, her teeth flashing, perfect white pearls, in her lustrous African face.

Bethany Knowte blushed, sullenly. She stood in the nude beside Selina and Hardast, in the nurse's surgery. Miss Cream peered at her nipples, then set to pinching and rubbing the breast flesh; Bethany grimaced, but said nothing, her mouth slack and fearful. The three girls bore vivid red marks of the ankle hobbles, waist chains and handcuffs which had recently bound them, the implements now in the custody of two unsmiling, jackbooted strappers in tight black uniforms with shiny black nylons, who stood by the surgery door, canes at the ready, and glossy peaked caps snug over their eyes. The nurse's gaze passed to Selina, who trembled, head hung low.

'Now these,' Miss Cream cried, 'these are even more splendid! Such bubbies! Firm and big and ripe, and . . . well, sheer anatomical perfection.'

Selina winced, as the nurse felt her titties with hard fingers.

'And the arse! Turn round, gel – let me look – mm! Oh, *yes* . . .'

She massaged the firm meat of Selina's bare, and Selina

shut her eyes, brow creased in a frown, as her fingers caressed the puffed slits and ridges of her bum welts.

'You've all taken some basting,' Miss Cream said thoughtfully. 'Especially this one, Miss Bratt – let's see – lovely ripe bottom and bubs, also. Quite a crop from Air Bare.'

'Don't you want to feel, Miss?' lisped Hardast, parting her legs, and thrusting up her bare titties, while licking her lips sluttishly.

The matron obliged, kneading her breasts and buttocks, and poking her finger into Hardast's moist pink slit.

'We're just pieces of meat, aren't we, Miss?' gushed Hardast. 'It is so exciting.'

'Phryne Wuldingdoune was right,' the matron said drily. 'She has delivered a prize cargo. I'm warned you three miscreants are especially wicked – let's hope your bums can stay clean of further stripes. I dare say you've had plenty of airborne wanks, with those lustful redcoats, but that all has to stop. Chastity is part of smart training – Miss Kew, our discipline mistress, is very strict, and an expert with bare bottoms.'

Her eyes twinkled.

'My department is the innards, not the outers, you'll be glad to hear,' she said. 'Let's get you shaven, then cleaned up inside. My, what awfully big bushes you gels have.'

She pointed to a doorway, where gurgling and hissing of water and steam announced a bathing facility.

'The stews,' she said. 'There are showers and steam baths, of course, but as new bums, you are for shaving – quim, anus and perineum must be totally smooth – and full bum-sluicing, or colonic irrigation.'

She saw Selina make a moue.

'Never had an enema before, miss?' she demanded.

'Of course I have,' said Selina. 'Rather fun, actually – *you* know – and normally called *lavage,* in polite circles. It's part of a proper gel's kit.'

'Proper gels!' Miss Cream sneered. 'All slags arriving are "new bums" until they've been broken. The governess insists on a friendly approach to the slags, but any lip, and it's bare-bum thrashing, or worse. You passed Dawn and

137

Janet in their pillories, on your way here, I expect. Didn't you see the lashes on their bare bottoms, and the agony in their faces? And their offence was relatively trifling.'

'We did see two girls, Miss,' blurted Selina. 'They were being caned on the bare. The girls were crying, and squirming dreadfully, and I had to look away. The pillory seems awfully cruel.'

The nurse caressed Selina's arse cleft, with tickling fingers, and Selina shivered.

'So behave yourselves,' said Miss Cream. 'Heavens, Miss Gurdell doesn't *want* gels to wear stripes. Lucky gels with porcelain bottoms may become her disciples, or else serve in the guesthouse. All gels are chosen for smart training by the excellence of their bottoms, as you are aware. Miss Gurdell teaches that only a gel with excellence of fesse may attain *moral* excellence.'

She swivelled, and patted her own massive buttocks, which trembled delicately at her touch.

'Staff, too,' she murmured, coquettishly.

In the stews, the three nude newcomers were greeted by blinding clouds of steam, and droplets of sweat appeared immediately on their skins, as the wave of heat struck them. The vast theatrical chamber held a terrace of wooden sauna cabins, rows of Turkish toilets without partitions, where several girls squatted, dunging, beside each other; shower baths, a swimming pool, and a pit filled with hot, bubbling mud, in which several naked girls sat, bound in rubber corsets, and their muddy faces wrinkled in discomfort. A strapper stood above them, cracking her whip at intervals, whereupon the girls dived fully into the mud, until, after a long interval, the strapper whipped the mud's surface, and they reemerged, gasping and spluttering. Apart from her peaked cap, the strapper wore only a black one-piece swimsuit in shiny nylon, and was barefoot on the slippery bathroom tiles. As Selina gazed around the hall she saw other strappers, costumed alike, and each waving whip or cane over their charges. She heard a groan from one of the sauna cabins, guarded by a swimsuited strapper; looking in, she saw a girl clad entirely in rubber, like a diver, with a rubber mask and goggles entirely misted by sweat. She lay on the bench, writhing and shivering, as sweat poured from the fastenings at her ankles. Selina jumped back – the door of the cabin was scorching to the touch. The swish of the strapper's whip drew Selina back to her comrades, huddled and appehensive.

Miss Cream, now stripped to a clinging white nylon swimsuit, appeared from the steam. She was tall, with coltish, muscular bare legs, and her sensuous Nilotic features brooded with sombre, almost ancient Egyptian royalty. The shiny swimsuit glowed like a pearl against her lustrous, chocolate-brown skin, smooth as a tulip petal, and emitting a perfume of mingled flowers, incense and salt sea. Her swimsuit was strapless, clinging to her ripe curves like the skin of a grape, with her massive bubbies upthrust, scarcely covered by the thin fabric, and the big plum nipples visible, only just covered by the swimsuit's low breast. Her buttocks, likewise, were almost completely exposed by the very high-cut swimsuit thigh line; the thong, a mere ribbon snaking across the swelling naked hillock of her mons, shaven satin smooth, dipped below the folds of her vulva, into the creamy dark perineum, then appeared as a sliver of white shiny fabric from her bum cleft, to climb between the bare buttocks, until it widened suddenly, to cover the upper fesses and spinal nubbin, while clinging to her pencil-thin waist. Her thighs and buttocks rippled, as she padded towards the perspiring girls, though her firm breasts shivered only slightly; her gait was tall and imperious, with the skin beaded by droplets of sweat, not flowing. Her thick black tresses were swept back in gleaming, gentle curls, bound at her neck with a white ribbon, baring a high, regal forehead, high cheekbones, and wide, sensuous lips, curled in a sneer. She held a long yellow cane, curving, with a crook handle.

'Follow me, gels,' she said, disdainfully swishing her cane inches from Selina's buttocks, with a malicious glint of her teeth.

She turned, and led them, without looking back, until they reached an alcove. Inside it were a number of metal surgical tables, festooned with straps, cords, chains and nozzles, with varied apparatus of taps and pipes covering the walls. Selina gaped.

'Frightened of a proper, hard enema, miss swanky bum?' said the nurse. 'Lovely liquid, swelling your belly, and sluicing your colon, till you're sparkling clean, inside and out?'

'A hard enema. Isn't this a bit over the top?' Selina blurted.

'People pay to have an Auchterhuish enema, and always have done,' said Belinda. 'That's why we have the guest-house, with its own separate geyser. The prison is built on a hot spring, a geyser, like those in Iceland, which is not far away. Auchterhuish has been an important centre of culture since neolithic times, although culture's beyond beastly oiks like you.'

She swished her cane again, this time catching Selina on the left thigh. Selina winced, looking at her with pleading eyes, and was rewarded by Belinda's shiny pink tongue licking slowly across her snowy teeth, with a gleam in her eyes.

'Up on the tables, face down, and legs apart,' she commanded.

When the three girls were in position, she ordered them to spread their bum cheeks, and raise their hips. This done, she inserted a rubber cushion under each girl's cunt.

'Comfortable, swanky bum?' she drawled to Selina.

'Yes, Miss,' Selina stammered, shifting and quivering, as the hard metal struts bit into her teats and belly.

Belinda laughed.

'Enjoy it while it lasts. I'll have to strap you down, for the number one enema will have you wriggling like blazes. This is no pint and a half for Chelsea twits, but a high colonic. A gel's bumhole can take up to six litres of fluid, you know, and when you're full, your tummies will swell up in absolutely yummy lumps, like a horror flick.'

She giggled.

'You'll take only a weedy two litres now, so if I hear any girly blubbing and squealing, then I'll use *this* on your bares.'

140

She swished her cane, with a loud whistle.

'Strokes in surgery don't count as judicial punishments, and are without tariff,' she drawled. 'So I can send you back to house whipped raw, with no questions asked. This cane has a long history. It belonged to my English daddy, a captain in the Foreign Legion, and he left it to me, advising me it needed constant exercise. *He* used it on my Somalian mummy, as well as whipping the serving maids when they were lazy. They had to work in the nude, and it was a cause of great pride for a maid's naked buttocks to be freshly wealed, for then she got to wear a flower inserted in her anus. Mummy was a princess, but was proud to go nude, apart from her gold and jewels, with a flower in her bottom. She told me her secret of contentment, that Daddy caned her bare bottom every Sunday, and that bare-bottom caning keeps a gel virtuous. Which is why they sent *me* to an English boarding school.'

She touched each girl's buttocks in turn with the tip of her cane, drawing it down the bum cleft.

'Such lovely croups,' she breathed. 'I'd like to make them virtuous. And those hairy quims will be so much prettier when I've shaved them silky smooth, like mine.'

Selina winced, as a thick rubber strap, six inches wide, bit into the small of her back, pinioning her to the table. Belinda drawled that it was a flogging girdle, to keep the buttocks still, during a table-whipping, with a similar girdle normally restraining the upper thighs, but that it was also a useful restraint during colonic irrigations. Smaller cords fastened her ankles and wrists to struts, jutting from the table corners. Cross-splayed on the table, she was just able to twist her head, to observe Bethany and Hardast in the same position. Hardast's eyes gleamed, and she licked her teeth, with little throaty growls of pleasure at her bondage. Bethany's teat melons were squashed flat under her ribcage, the discs of pale flesh cupping her torso. Selina's own breasts were painfully squashed, with her nipples grating on the sharp metal. There was a loud hissing, with jets of steam shrouding the tethered girls. Miss Cream's fingers dabbed unguent on Selina's anus bud, her finger well inside, poking and tweaking the anal elastic, as she smeared it with the lubricant. Water gurgled from myriad pipes.

'Ooh,' Selina gasped, her buttocks clenching, as a hard rubber tube poked an inch inside her anal channel.

Belinda giggled, as Selina wailed.

'Ouch! Oh!'

The tube pushed right to her rectum, its hard nozzle thudding against her colon. Selina began to squirm.

'Oh, it hurts, Miss,' she whimpered.

'Quiet, or you'll take the tube right to the caecum,' said Belinda.

Selina craned her head, to see gleaming rubber tubes snaking from each girl's bottom, towards the battery of taps on the wall.

'This is to make you clean,' purred Belinda. 'Don't fight it – let the fluid inside, and you are not to squirt until I give permission. Any unauthorised release will earn heavy punishment. I mean my cane on the bare, gels.'

She adjusted several taps, and the alcove filled with a gurgling whoosh, drowning Selina's yelp of pain, as a load of hot fluid spurted into her anus, filling her belly with a monstrous, swelling ache.

'Oh . . . oh . . . oh . . .' she gasped, gagging.

Her raised buttocks quivered on their rubber cushion, as more and more fluid pumped into her anus.

'Miss, I'm going to burst,' she whimpered.

Vip!

'Ooh!'

Belinda's cane lashed Selina's bare buttocks, quite hard across full mid-fesse, making her gorge rise, and her tears spring.

'I warned you,' murmured Belinda, 'no blubbing.'

Selina's body twitched uselessly at the rubber cords, cutting into her flesh. The gurgle of the pipes rose to a whine, with the anal tubes juddering, and writhing snake-like from the girls' squirming bottoms. Selina tried to shift, to ease the ache in her belly, but to no avail; the hot fluid continued to fill her, and she gasped, tears flooding her eyes, and her body wracked by twitching spasms of agony. At last, the gurgles and hisses ceased. Selina quivered, as the tube slithered from her anus, tickling her, like a big hard dung.

'Hold it in, gels,' warned Belinda, 'until I give permission to evacuate. I'm going to restrain you only four minutes. You've only had a couple of litres each, so I don't think you need stoppers – they are exquisitely uncomfortable – but I shall insert them, if necessary.'

Two litres of water in my bum! If it is only water . . . it feels all oily and squishy. Selina panted, suppressing her groans. Her skin poured with sweat. She was prisoner of the liquid, a monstrous presence in her anus and belly, threatening to burst out at any moment, and requiring the tightest pressure of her anal sphincter to hold in her fluid load. She could feel her tummy horribly swollen, rubbing on the table, and had to arch her spine, to avoid putting pressure on her inflated belly.

'Think of it as a big stiff cock up your bumhole,' said Belinda, 'filling you up with lovely hot spunk. All gels like anal fucking, don't they, and that lovely feeling of full bung, when a stud is pounding your bumhole?'

Selina blushed.

'Some slags demand deep colonic penetration,' Belinda drawled. 'Three feet of tubing into the lower colon, and an oil and vinegar lavage. The silly tarts think that a really clean bumhole won't destroy the perfume of *Fucus aromaticus* . . . so that they can smuggle it from the beach, and sell it for a fortune. But they're wrong. Anyway, staff get their bumholes laved too. There is nothing you slags endure that we cannot. Even Miss Gurdell.'

Her hand slipped under Selina's swollen belly, and began to caress her; Selina gasped, as her fingers traced hard bumpy swellings, where her colonic tubing trapped fluid.

What must I look like?

'You've lovely lumps, miss,' said Belinda.

Selina's eye caught a flash of red, outside the door. A posse of girls in red one-piece swimsuits scampered towards the swimming pool, with shrieks and splashes, as they dived in. One girl was nude, save for crimson panties, with golden nipple rings dangling from her breasts. The generously cut panties covered most of her croup, but did not conceal the purple weal ends from Bethany's quirt, aboard Air Bare.

'That's Phryne and her air gels,' Belinda said. 'Phryne likes to show off her rings, so she does everything bare balcony, when possible. Jammy cow.'

The alcove filled with the gasps and groans of the three laved girls, wriggling in their bonds. Selina wrinkled her face in distress, the splashes and whoops of the carefree girls in the pool shrilling, over the thumping of her heart. *Four minutes of torture! I'm going to burst, I know it ...* Belinda padded catlike around the heaving nude bodies, hands on her hips, alternately gazing at their pain-wracked faces, and stroking clenched buttocks, or swollen, lumpy bellies, grotesquely distended by the fluid. The seconds, then the minutes, ticked by, as the breath of three girls rasped harshly.

'Ooh ...'

'Uhh ...'

'Nngh ...'

Groaning and gasping, the nude bodies writhed in their rubber bonds. Belinda stood with her ripely rounded cunt hillock, under her clinging swimsuit crotch, swaying before Selina's tear-blurred eyes. The black girl reached to her breast, and hooked thumbs into the swimsuit fabric. She pulled, and the swimsuit slipped off her breasts. The satin black teats sprang to jutting melons, topped with brown nipple domes whose soft flesh tensed, stiffening under Selina's gaze, until the nipples were as big as ripe plums, shiny, succulent and hard of skin. The chocolate teat flesh globes swayed, quivering slightly, but their perfect balls thrusting without need of support, as Belinda slowly drew the swimsuit down over her flat, muscled belly.

'I expect you gels to be messy,' she drawled, 'and I don't want to spoil my swimsuit.'

Selina gazed, as the white nylon slithered over the dark brown belly, approaching Belinda's pubes; it slid over the swelling cunt mound, revealing the top of a gleaming mons, shaven smooth. The denuding continued, the swimsuit gusset peeling from Belinda's cunt lips with a sticky plop, until the swimsuit dangled at her thighs, and she kicked it off, draping it on a hissing geyser tap. Smiling, she stood in the nude before Selina and the groaning enemees. Her cunt hillock and lips were massive, the hillock curving like a chocolate pear into the lustrous dark folds of her gash. Belinda parted her slit flaps between finger and thumb, revealing the pink meat inside, gleaming with cunt juice; after an instant's exposure, smiling impishly, she pressed her slit shut again. She licked her lips, stroking her shaven brown mons, its glossy skin entirely depilated, and shining, as though polished with wax. Her entire body shone with the same hairless gleam, its firm, creamy dark flesh glinting with tiny beads of sweat.

'See how lovely a hairless slice is?' she said coyly. 'You'll be like me, when you're shaved, after your cleansing. Now, you may evacuate, one at a time, when I give the word. You first, swanky bum. On the count of three, press your stomach muscles hard, and relax your anal sphincter. One ... two ...'

At 'three', Selina groaned in relief, as her tensed belly shot a violent stream of fluid from her anus. It splattered all over Belinda Cream's nude body; the nurse stood, until she was drenched with Selina's anal fluid.

'Ooh ... ahh ... yes ...' Selina gasped, her whole body wriggling, with tears streaming down her face.

'Ahh ...' Belinda sighed, licking her lips. 'Not a bad spurt. Next, Hardast, then Bethany.'

The process was repeated by the others, each squirting her jet of liquid from her anus, to spray the black girl's body.

'Mucky pups,' Belinda said, smiling, with liquid dripping from her nude body.

She turned on a brisk shower head, and rinsed the arse fluids from her body, rubbing her breasts, and tweaking the stiff nipples between her fingers, with loud slaps to the dark bare melons of her bottom. Selina watched, as

Belinda parted her buttocks, showing her hairless crack, and massaged the chocolate wrinkle of her abnormally extruded anal pucker. Her naked arse globes bore faint mauve palm prints, where she had slapped herself.

'We'll go again,' she said.

Selina sobbed, as the tube crept into her anus. This time the enema was hotter, and she gasped, as its probing streak of heat penetrated her rectum and colon, flooding her belly with searing liquid. Her tummy swelled painfully, as her buttocks squirmed over the invading tube; once more, the bursting girls had to hold for four minutes. They panted, sobbing, with Belinda repeating her threat of a bum stopper, for any laxity. The swellings on Selina's belly were huge, hard and lumpy.

Will my tummy ever be flat again . . .?

This time, it was Hardast who squirted first, with a powerful jet of mucky liquid splashing all over Belinda's naked body. Then it was Bethany's turn; she spurted a clearer jet, and when, at last, Selina was called to evacuate, she sprayed a torrent of clear liquid, drenching the nude black girl, who stood before her, her bare cunt inches from Selina's eyes, licking her lips, with her fingers cupping her chocolate gash.

'And again,' murmured Belinda.

'Oh, Miss . . .' groaned Hardast.

Belinda grabbed her cane, raised her arm over her head, and, back muscles rippling, lashed Hardast's buttocks. Her fesses clenched, and her breasts jiggled, very slightly, as the cane landed on the girl's naked flesh. The heavy cane struck the naked buttocks with a sonorous *thwack*, seeming to cling to the weal it instantly raised, before sliding across the bare bottom, into the air.

'Ooh . . .' Hardast squealed, her caned buttocks clenching hard.

'Quiet, bitch,' snarled the black girl.

Rapid forehand and backhand strokes deepened the livid weals on Hardast's bare. Her buttocks shook, but she did not cry out, subsiding into a choked, sobbing gasp.

'Uh . . . uh . . . uh . . .' Hardast whimpered.

'Anyone else?' demanded the nurse. 'You won't always have such soft treatment. You'll be in Miss Kew's domain – she'll break you with fucus picking, drill, ditch digging, route marches, and punishment parade, where you must watch your friend's bare bum lashed, and be glad it's not yours. You have a long time ahead of you, slags.'

Without protest, the girls accepted the long, slinky tubes, penetrating anus, rectum, and deep bellies.

'Prepare for a shock,' Belinda said, turning the tap. There was a rush of water, and the three girls jerked stiff on their tables, buttocks clenching, and legs wriggling, rigid against their straps.

'Ooh!'

'Ahh!'

'Oh! Oh! Oh!' Selina gasped, as the jet of ice-cold water penetrated her.

The glacial fluid pumped inside her belly, bursting her with its icy, stabbing fingers. *I can't bear any more of this . . .* For over a minute, the sluicing continued, until all three girls had teeth chattering, and slack lips drooling, as their nude bodies wriggled helplessly, wrenching at their bonds.

'Can't bear it, eh? You shall. Hold for a full five,' said Belinda laconically. 'If I see any spurts or dribbles, it's the stopper, *and* the cane, while you strain.'

Thighs spread, she stood before Selina. Belinda's fingers parted her quim lips once more, but this time, she did not press the flaps shut, holding them wide, so that Selina could glimpse the seep of shiny come sliming the swollen cunt flaps, and dripping onto the rippling black thighs. Her erect pink clitoris was extruded from the gash folds, and Belinda placed her fingertip upon it. She licked her lips, then began to rub herself. Then, her soft fingertips caressed Selina's buttocks, tickling the squirming arse cleft. A hard bare sole clamped the small of Selina's back, above her flogging girdle.

'Are you in pain, my sweetums?' cooed Belinda. 'How your poor bum squirms! Pain is so cleansing for a gel.'

Selina jumped, as hot oily droplets began to splatter her bare bottom. Atop her, the black girl was masturbating.

Her powerful thighs parted wide, her lovely black bum all silky and writhing, that juicy pink slit wide gaping open . . . oh, I need a wank . . .

Selina's cunt began to ooze come, as the black girl's sole throbbed on her back. Hot droplets of Selina's cunt juice slimed her gash flaps and upper thighs. The nurse's come trickled from Selina's arse globes into her cleft, running down in hot, oily rivulets, to seep into her slit, and mingle with her own gash ooze. Selina rubbed her stiffening clitty against the hard metal table, gasping, as her spine and cunt basin thrilled. The flow of Belinda's come grew faster, as her long, slender toes began to claw at the flesh of Selina's back. Selina reamed her cunt basin against the table, whimpering, at each jab to her swollen stiff clitty. Suddenly, the masturbating black girl gasped repeatedly, and the splatter of her come on Selina's buttocks became a torrent. Belinda exhaled once more, then removed her foot from Selina's body.

'Uhh . . .' Selina gasped, frotting her clitty hard against the table rim.

Her cunt gushed come.

'You may all evacuate, on the count of three,' ordered Belinda. 'One, two . . .'

At 'three', the enemees shrieked, sobbing, as three jets of clear fluid drenched the nude black nurse. Her icy bumload spurted from Selina's anus, splashing, as it sprayed the naked black flesh of the masturbatress. As her load squirted from her anus, Selina rubbed her clit, with frantic jerks of her cunt basin, and gasped loudly, as come poured from her pulsing gash, and her tortured belly convulsed in a spine-jarring orgasm.

'Excellent, maids,' purred Belinda. 'Your arse loads are all clear . . . except for one gel, whose liquid was rather oily with quim juice. It is not unknown for gels to be sexually excited by a sluicing, but be aware that masturbation, unchaste wetting or other beastliness are whopping offences, and if I find out who it was –' her cane tip tapped each girl in the bum cleft, with Selina the last, and the cane lingering, to poke inside her pouch '– she'll be rubbing a *very* sore bottom.'

148

'Did I hear "sore bottom", Miss Cream?'

There was a jangle of nipple rings, as Phryne Wulding-doune poked her head into the geyser alcove. Water dripped from her naked breasts, and her thin crimson bikini panties were sodden from the swimming pool, clinging like paint to her bottom and cunt hillock. Behind her clustered Jasmine, and her colleagues, all with dripping crimson swimsuits, and laughing eagerly.

'A figure of speech, captain,' drawled Belinda. 'But if your gels are at a loose end, there are coozes to be shorn.'

The air crew clustered around the groaning enemees, unfastening their bonds, and flipping them onto their backs.

'Gosh, Selina,' said Jasmine, cupping Selina's buttocks to position her for shaving, with her thighs spread wide, and cunt basin exposed, 'what a glorious bush! I . . . I've been thinking of your bottom, and fleece. Shame it must go, but I just know your bare slice will be ever so . . . you know, wank-making.'

Jasmine was blushing, as Belinda pushed her away from Selina.

'The swanky bum's mine,' she said tersely.

Jasmine made a moue, and joined her colleagues at Hardast's and Bethany's cunt forests. Belinda distributed strops, cut-throat blades, and tweezers. Holding tweezers and a five-inch razor, she bent over Selina, with her naked black breasts almost in Selina's mouth. She stroked Selina's exposed cunt basin, lower buttocks and thigh tops, her fingers playing with the downy hairs of the perineum, before moving up the slit, to caress Selina's fleece.

'I can't wait to touch that bare quim skin,' she whispered. 'Will it be pale, against that golden all-over tan?'

'I expect so, Miss,' said Selina. 'My tan comes – *came* – from nudist beaches in Provence, or the Greek islands.'

'Rather posh, for a mere slag,' said the black girl, lifting her tweezers.

'Ouch!' moaned Selina, her bum jerking.

Belinda held up her tweezers, clamping a tuft of long golden hairs.

'These were hanging way down below your cooze lips, gel,' she said.

Her tweezers delved between Selina's arse collops.

'Ahh!' cried Selina.

Hardast looked round, and giggled; both she and Bethany had their cunt hillocks lathered in foam, with the girls in red scraping decorously with their blades.

'You'll have to be quiet,' ordered Belinda, frowning.

'Ooh!'

Selina could not help crying out, as tears sprang to her eyes, and Belinda held up a further clump of hairs, from her anal perineum.

'I warned you,' Belinda said, and stuffed the hairs into Selina's mouth. 'It's your fault for being so divinely hairy.'

Selina had to keep her mouth shut, so as not to swallow her own hairs, save when Belinda ordered her to open up, as the pubic plucking continued, and take another tuft into her mouth. Gradually, her mouth filled with cunt hairs, as tears streamed down her face. She groaned, as Belinda's fingers penetrated her pouch, with loud squelching sounds; the come-slopped fingers were thrust in her face.

'No need for lather,' Belinda said. 'You're sopping wet. A proper perverted swanky bum, aren't we? Excited by pain? You're lucky it is I who shave you, for I won't tell of your depravity . . . *perhaps.*'

Her fingers vigorously rubbed Selina's come into her pubic thatch, and then the shaving proper began. The blade slid across Selina's cunt hillock, with Belinda holding the metal under a dribbling shower, after each stroke. A clump of golden curls were sluiced off, into Belinda's palm, then stuffed into Selina's mouth. The blade descended to the lips of the cunt, shaving each side of the outer vulval walls, then slipped to the perineum, raking across the taut skin around Selina's anus bud. A tingling, itchy pain suffused Selina's cunt basin, at each stroke of the razor.

This isn't like shaving my legs, or pits. Jane used to soap me all over, and shave me, but it was never such a shivery thrill. Stuffing my mouth full of my own pube hairs is shamefully exciting! Belinda is so powerful, so aggressive, it makes my cunny wet.

150

Selina opened her thighs wider, thrusting up her cunt basin, to meet the razor. She felt the cool air blowing on her naked hillock, and gasped to herself, submitting to the dominant girl, and presenting her naked body to be shorn. Her gash dripped come.

Oh! I can't wait to see my naked slice. It's so thrilling, as if I'm defenceless. Pube hair is a defence, after all, keeping the real me, the soft wet pink of my pouch, a secret from strangers. Now, all these gels will see me, and know me. A girl shorn is just meat, to be spanked, fucked in the bumhole, humiliated, cleansed by harsh sluicing. That enema was the loveliest I've ever had, so hard and cruel, like hot cream stroking my belly from the inside, tickling me, hurting me, owning me. And I'm so clean . . . clean for any cock or tongue to penetrate me. Oh! Why do I think thus?

Bethany and Hardast were already sitting, rubbing their shaven hillocks, and gazing at Selina, writhing under the blade. She jerked, moaning, as something sharp and hard pushed against her throbbing clitoris.

'Oh, yes . . .' she whimpered, her mass of golden pubic hairs gushing from her mouth. 'I'm helpless. Take me . . .'

Her cunt spurted hot come.

'That wasn't the blade, gel,' whispered Belinda. 'It was my thumbnail. You really *are* a submissive, aren't you?'

10

Naked Squelching

'Dear Harriet,

I've been here about a week, I think, and I'm sorry I haven't written sooner. I'm writing to you, because we're jolly good chums, and you're at ease with corporal punishment; some of this might upset Claire, even though I know she's been to boarding school like us. The censorship is very strict. You can't say what this place is really like, but I've found a way to sneak a letter out – it's *awfully* naughty – more of that in a mo.

'Really, I don't think a week is enough for me to get the real grasp of all the strange things going on. This could be a real scoop! That's all you need tell Claire. It's weird, the regime is ultra-tough, but I feel not at all unhappy. There are weird rules and punishments – *lots* of punishments – but it's a challenge to outwit them, a bit like school, I suppose. I've changed a bit in just a short time, and come to understand more about the "real me". The governess, Miss Gurdell, is rather delightful, head in the clouds, and fancies herself a sort of modern-day Sappho, with a coterie of favoured girls who attend her in the nude, recite poems, put on plays, and play the lyre and suchlike. She likes to go around topless, with the most adorable golden nipple rings – she's blonde, like me, and has *scrumptious* big bubbies, though not as scrumptious as mine, swank, swank – and her most favoured girls get to wear nipple rings, too. It sounds lesbo, I know, but it's quite innocent really – there are fearful penalties for "unchastity".

152

'Some stuff might seem lesbo – wanking games, mostly – but no more than at school, and it's mostly harmless fun, although we are thrashed, if caught. Bare-bum, naturally! It's funny, on a desolate, seagirt rock, all heather and thistles and moss, and – you know, Scottishy things – you get to value the touch and the scent of soft bare flesh, even – in fact, especially – another girl's. A simple caress, the touching of two naked breasts, or the stroking of one another's bare bum – or quim – is awfully cheering, somehow. There are plenty of times girls can be together, away from the strappers. We are sent out on really horrid cross-country runs, in the nude – we get *so* muddy and scratched! – and the strappers are so dashed lazy, they let us do it pretty well unsupervised. They inspect our bodies for scratches, and if we have enough, they assume we've run the course. Of course it's easy to give yourself the necessary scratches, with thistles and brambles and things, although it hurts a bit. The old slags know the short cuts, so two or three of us – or more – can always take time off for a lovely juicy wank. Yes, I said 'we' – if I'm going to be properly undercover, I have to join in all the games and intrigues, and anyway, what healthy girl, who is temporarily [I hope] sex-starved, doesn't enjoy some yummy mutual diddling? We all have our own techniques for wanking off, of course, but some of the girls here are so practised that they can make me wet with just the slightest flick of a thumb!!! Miss Gurdell is quite a softy, thinks a bare-bum spanking is absolutely the worst punishment imaginable, and doesn't know half of what really happens. The prison is run by the discipline mistress, Miss Kew, a very hard bitch, but with an adorable figure, very lithe and muscly, and with a wicked caning arm. She has her own clique of favourites. There is a rumour that she is descended from William the Conqueror, and her real name is Norman French – "cul".

'She also has rivals – there's Phryne Wuldingdoune, the pilot, who is quite sadistic, watching girls lashed, but likes to bare up herself, in expiation I suppose. We were flown here in the prison's own air taxi, called "Air Bare" and our

153

in-flight entertainment was quite wild. Suffice to say, there was a lot of bare spanking, *and more.* Well, I might as well confess, I made friends with Hardast Bratt, who is my best chum, though she's an absolute *slut.* I think she's what they call a "submissive". She actually gets off on being caned or spanked, the harder the better, and preferably when she's tied up in bondage, with cords or straps. She likes me because I'm not jealous – she has sex with anyone who'll do it to her. I don't mind doing really far-out lesbo things with her, because she likes it so much, and has such a fabulous bod. I mean, one has to adapt to prison *mores.* Girls are fond of tonguing each other, that is, licking each other's clitties till we spend, and it's surprising how soon it seems healthy and normal.

'As well as caresses, Hardast likes 'fisting' and being tupped in the bumhole, with a stiff rubber strap-on thingie, and of course she isn't happy unless her bare is lashed. The strappers like to let off steam, like any girl, and one of them, Jasmine Wadd, has an adorable pash for me, which I do my best to exploit. The other new entrant, Bethany Knowte, is a queer one. She has these incredible big breasts, firm and round as footballs, and a gorgeous bum, which gets more than its fair share of floggings. Unlike Hardast, she bursts into tears, and wails, the moment a cane or strap touches her naked bottom, and pretends she loathes it – of course, that encourages the strappers to lash her all the harder and more frequently. Nor is she averse to beating another girl's bottom, in one of our spanking games – and she lays it on hard, with a strange vengeful gleam in her eyes. I saw her whip Phryne, on the flight up, after our own bottoms were well ribbed, and I hope she never flogs *my* bum.

'Then there's nurse Belinda Cream, a Somalian, gorgeous skin and a figure to die for. I'm not sure I'm not rather in love with her, or maybe Jasmine Wadd, the strapper. Being a girl is just as confusing in prison! Nurses can get away with anything – once in surgery, you're off the normal "punishment book". I suspect Belinda is a nympho – so many nurses are, aren't they? She gives me a lovely wank with my enema – wanking's forbidden, but universal – but I know she wanks lots of other girls. We have to take gut-wrenching enemas, and the nurse wields her cane like any other strapper. You've no idea what it's like to take a caning on the bare, with two litres of ice-cold water up your bum, and an anal plug holding it in! Or maybe you do. Belinda says the female waterworks can hold *six* litres – just imagine! It makes me shiver, not too unpleasurably. There's a really yummy feeling about being sluiced, when you get used to it, and – confessions again – it makes my cooze wet, as if a big tool is poking deep in your innards. The main items of discipline here are "thwangs", which is the fearsome Scots tawse, two tongues of hard leather; a cane, like an English school cane; and the quirt, a sort of cat-o'-nine-tails, of hard rubber thongs. I don't know which is worse. Punishments are always on the bare bottom, of course, except when girls are fastened in the pillory, to be whipped on the naked back.

'I hope I don't sound awfully pervy! In here, you get a different idea of what is "normal", or desirable. I'm determined to find out *all* the secrets of this place. I've always recommended cold showers and spankings to my readers, slightly ironically, but now I believe that's not enough. Girls are shameless creatures, and need far stricter discipline, both for their training, and, dare I say it, their secret pleasure. Girls are *made* to have their bare bottoms beaten. I hope that doesn't sound too awful. Prisoners are assigned here on the 'excellence and receptivity of derrière', which is Miss Gurdell's way of saying we are chosen for our big bottoms. What a strange way to assign felons, you might think, yet Miss Gurdell teaches that girls with big bottoms are more feminine, hence more sensitive, and even more intelligent, than other girls, and certainly more than males, who she holds in low esteem. It follows that our bottoms, our most sensitive areas, are most receptive to "moral stimulus", and that means spanking, or more.

'I might as well tell you everything, hoping you'll understand. Yes, I *have* been whipped on the bare, by all three disciplinary instruments, and hand-spanking, too –

oodles of bare-bum spanks. It was scary at first, but now I don't mind so much, and even look forward to it, for I know it's doing me good to be beaten. Me, the prim and proper "Miss Etiquette"! I remember advising that girl from Pangbourne to whop her hubby, and you said she should take a spanking herself, and there was some dreadful girl from Essex, who really did need spanking, so now I can't complain at getting my own advice back. I'll have to tell you about it, now I've started, won't I? I've sneaked away to a cave, having picked my quota of *Fucus aromaticus* – that's this peculiar seaweed with a pungent scent, used in the best restaurants as a condiment, rather like truffles, only vastly more expensive! It only grows on this island, thanks to this geyser beneath us. We have to work in the nude, and the strappers sniff our cunnies, to make sure we haven't secreted any of the precious pods. Although I'm positive smuggling does go on, there is a dreadful punishment for smuggling out the fucus pods – girls whisper of it with dread, and call it 'the works'.

'Auchterhuish is mostly quite warm, with a salty breeze, and being in the nude is very comfortable – even lying in this cave, with warmish rock under my tummy – and I pretend I'm on my favourite nudist beach in Porquerolles or Mykonos. All round the island there are fumaroles, or little steam holes, and the strappers like holding an errant girl with her bare quim held open over a fumarole, so that she gets a real basting – that's when they are too lazy to flog her. Hardast is going to give this letter to one of the blokes from the mainland, who visit secretly, and exchange tuck for favours. I haven't steeled myself to that yet, for Hardast lets me know in graphic detail what sort of favours Scots fishermen require – a lady's *smaller* hole is favoured – but I know I'll have to, for lack of cock is driving me absolutely spare. I wank off I don't know how many times a day, dreaming of a big hot tool splitting me and pounding me ... *you* know. All the girls do – masturbate, I mean, dreaming of men with lovely big pegos. That's why we're whipped so much. Most beatings seem to be for wanking off, although there are a host of other misdemeanours that merit the cane, or thwangs. Not to mention the pillory, or being hanged and whipped – ugh! It makes me shiver, but I sense I shan't be able to avoid it. I just need a male body, penetrating me, in whatever hole, and I'll risk any punishment to get it.

'Did I mention I've *been* buggered, already? How easy it is to write those awful words! Not properly, by a man, but with a strap-on, or *godemiché,* which hurt like the dickens at first, but then brought me to a super come. It was Phryne who buggered me. We call it "full bung". I'm quite giddy, thinking of my turn with the real thing, but that will have to wait till my next letter. Hamish, his name is, the island's premier stud. He's fucked or, more usually, buggered, an awful lot of the girls here, and there is quite a pecking order, with the usual cat spats and jealousies. Vicious tongues even accuse Miss Gurdell of bending over for his tarse in her bumhole, but that's just nasty gossip, she sets such store by chastity. Hardast promises she'll recommend me, and he might do me on his next visit. My bumhole's tingling already! I can hardly wait, especially now I've been 'broken in" by a *godemiché*, and in fact I'm rather itching to feel a hot stiff pego in there. I wonder if his tarse is as big as Henry's? You know, Henry Addercop?

'No point in keeping secrets up here. Henry was one of my studs in London – terrifically well hung, a better than average poke. He'd give *anything* to do me in the bumhole, the cad. You won't be shocked to hear I like my cocks big. Well, we all do, don't we? At my hearing, in Saltdean, one of the judges was Gawain Breasted, a friend of Henry's, and he was big! It proved to be a hearing *in depth,* and I left with a right sore bottom, though, thankfully, nothing else. Gawain bummed the two lady judges! They were turned on by my bare bum getting its first proper thrashing. Ouch! He thought I wouldn't see, or that, if I did, a felon's word counts for nothing. It's somehow thrilling to be so abased! Anyway, a girl who claims to be satisfied with a mere seven-incher is bonkers. Hamish is reputed to possess an absolute *monster.* Even though, with my luck, I'll probably be whipped in the pillory, it'll still be worth it. Harriet, I know you play spanking games with your boyfriend, and he beats you on the bare with a riding crop, doesn't he? So I'll just tell you about some of my whippings, and how . . . I can't find any other way to say it, I've come to – not exactly crave beating, but I get itchy when my bum's left unthrashed. Naked caning or spanking gives you a feeling of wholeness and serenity. Most of the girls feel the same! I feel *sure* you'll understand. You will, won't you?

'After our vigorous airborne fun, my bum was pretty well marked . . . then, we had to take our first enemas from Belinda Cream. Real enemas, that make your tummy swell up, with all sorts of lumps, quite horrid, but rather exciting, when you look in the mirror. She gave my bubbies and tummy a right old prodding, even though I'd been lashed on the bare breasts – just a few strokes by a really dominant, gorgeous strapper, but enough to leave a few weals. Sounds awful, and it is, but there is something thrillingly *submissive* about having your bare bubbies lightly whipped. I'd hate to be a real submissive, like Hardast, but there is no denying the excitement in briefly playing the role. Isn't all corporal punishment about playing roles? All sex, if you think of it.

'Anyway, after our enemas, we had our quims shaved. I dare say you've tried it, Harriet? Being quimstark seems awfully clean and sweet, and somehow wicked. It's supposed to be a mark of felon's shame. Then, in Belinda's surgery, we lay on our tummies, and Belinda put this monstrous thing inside our cunnies, and then our bum-holes – it's called a speculum, a bit like a corkscrew, with a round thingy, to hold your hole wide open, so the examiner can poke around. She seemed more interested in my bumhole than my quim, and reamed my insides quite shamelessly, making me squeeze her fingers with my sphincter. Then, I got a real shock, when she greased a horrid-looking rubber cylinder, that she called a 'phallos', and shoved it into my bum – all the way! She did warn me to relax, I admit. She pressed a little felt pad to my clitty, and held it there, telling me to use my sphincter, and squeeze on the beastly tube that was quite filling my rectum. The pad had wires attached to some whirring machine, and she said it was a clitoral plethysmograph, to measure the erection or stimulation of my nubbin, with that horrid phallos inside me. Really! I writhed around, squeezing the phallos, for several minutes, and, truth to tell, I did get a bit excited – I could feel my cunny juicing, as I imagined myself buggered by a live tarse. Well, you would, wouldn't you?

'All three of us took a phallos, and from Hardast's writhing, I saw she was absolutely eating it up. When matron took mine out, with a big tickly plop, just like a huge dung, she said that, according to my anal test, I was quite pure, but the clitoral thingy had me registered as most stimulated of the three of us! I couldn't disagree, for my clitty was stiff and really throbbing from that gorgeous full bung in my rectum. Bethany was moderately pure, while Hardast's rectum had obviously been stretched by numerous cocks, although she had developed superb sphincter control to compensate. She explained that males liked fucking girls in the bottom, as it squeezed their pegos more pleasurably, and warned us against even thinking of such practices while we were prisoners.

'We had tea in the refectory, absolutely awful – bashed neeps and mutton, ugh! – then went to the library for "homework" – the girls here must attend classes, as well as do hard labour. Of course we had no homework, so any book would do, when the strappers inspected. I found quite an interesting one, about the ancient history of the Hebrides, from neolithic up to Roman times. The pages were brand new, so I don't suppose anyone had looked at it much, and it seems that Auchterhuish was a health hydro way back in the Stone Age! Furthermore, the island was a big centre for druids, with lots of strange magic rites, that the book only hinted at, but it seems they performed ceremonial scourgings of naked girls, using dried and pickled thongs of the *Fucus aromaticus*. Naughty old druids!

'The Romans never conquered the Picts of Caledonia, who were called Picts because they painted their bodies with woad, [Scotland came later, after conquest by the Scots, who were really Irish. Confusing!], but troops from the Carlisle garrison, and Hadrian's Wall and so on, used to visit Auchterhuish, on weekend leave, I suppose. They had lots of steam baths, and used to birch each other, or be birched, like people in the sauna, and it seems the local girls were adept at that!!! Also, being gourmets, they bought fucus pods for export to Rome. Miss Kew was looking at me a bit oddly, and when we had to go to bed, I saw her examining my book, and I've never found it again, in the library. Hmm . . .

'We were put in a hut, grandly named a "dormitory", with half a dozen other girls. We three newcomers were issued with short nighties in lime green nylon, surprisingly tasteful, and quite comfortable, as we were nude underneath. We had straw palliasses, covered in a sort of itchy hemp sackcloth, on the floor. There are six dorm huts, then a hut for maids, who fancy themselves, in their French frillies, and a hut for girls on temporary guesthouse duty, who are forbidden to mix with the rest of us. The guesthouse, down by the harbour, is actually an old Martello tower, built in Napoleonic times. Lucky girls are promoted, to serve permanently in the guesthouse, run by Miss Wapping, whom everyone seems to adore. They never reappear amongst the "low girls". I thought at first that the guesthouse was a sort of halfway stage to becoming one of Miss Gurdell's disciples, but they have to be terrifically pure, with their bums not beaten at all, or just spanked, so I can't see how the guesthouse would help them. The "GGs" have to entertain visitors, and I suspect that includes bending over, in every sense. When you do see a guesthouse girl, she is terrifically snooty, and mustn't talk to us lower slags, not that the toffee-nosed bitches want to.

'The strapper at one end of our hut was supposed to keep us quiet. But she wasn't there half the time – kept popping out for a smoke [everyone smokes here, and it's absolutely forbidden, on pain of thrashing] – so the girls fell to chattering, and then drifted off into moans and gasps, so I could tell they were wanking. Some of them even lit up a cig, as I could smell the smoke. They stared briefly at me, Hardast and Bethany, but were cautious about approaching us – Miss Kew sometimes introduces new bums who are actually spies. I began to dream of those hunky Roman legionaries in the nude, their muscly bare bottoms birched by equally naked Pictish slave girls, painted with woad, and started playing with myself. Of course, one thing led to another, in my fantasy, and the birched legionaries got monstrous stiffies, grabbed the naked girls, held them down, and fucked them in their bumholes, with lots of slapped breasts and shrieking and yelping as they spurted spunk in their rectums, like a super hot enema! It was a really good wank, and I frigged myself to a super come with that fantasy, and then I wanted a fag awfully. You do, here. Surprised?

'So I slipped over to a girl who was smoking – her name was Kristel Gummi – and asked her for a few drags. She was surly, because Miss Kew had bare-caned her that very day, for no reason, so she said. Apparently it was something Miss Gurdell's maid Susan, the little madam, had let slip about Kristel, and Miss Kew overheard. Miss Kew overhears everything. So Kristel was hauled off for twelve on the bare. She said that if I wanted a smoke, I'd have to lick the weals – on her bottom! Well I did, so I did. She turned over, and I began to lick her stripes, very hard and ridged and the bumflesh puffed up, like corrugated cardboard. I admit it turned me on! She had such a lovely bum, firm and velvety, and she wiggled and twitched when I licked her, so I let my tongue go into her bum cleft, and she wiggled some more, and began to pant.

'I got to her anus bud, and – taking a deep breath – began to lick her pucker, and she gasped and squirmed as if electrified. "Don't stop," she moaned. "It's so good" and things like that. Her thighs parted, and I could see her swollen quim lips, glazed with juice – she was oozing come, as I tongued her. My mouth went down her perineum, with my nose between her buttocks, and I began to lick her cooze. It tasted lovely and fresh and salty, like a sea breeze.

My tongue went between her lips, and a flood of come spurted into my mouth. She was so hot, groaning, and flopping her belly up and down, with me kneeling by her bed.

'She raised her hips, and my tongue went all the way into her slit, and I was positively drinking her lovely hot come, while I wiggled my tongue inside her pouch, then withdrew, to tickle her nubbin, which was all stiff and hard, and very big. That made her jerk, gasping, so I continued to tongue her clitty, and now I climbed on the bed, and lifted my nightie, baring my own cunny and bottom. I turned her body over, sort of squelchily, because the palliasse was soaking with her sweat and come, and pressed my quim right on top of her lovely big bubbies – they were conic, with huge hard nips, like kiwi fruits – and started to rub my quim and anus against her nips, squashing her titties flat. I was juicing quite a lot myself by this time, you see.

'She thrust her breasts up in the rhythm of my squirms, and gave my quim a lovely nipple-fuck, while I continued to snuffle at her pouch, with my nose dipping in, between chews of her ginormous clitty, absolutely bathing in her oozed come. The position wasn't too comfortable, as I had to bunch up to get my quim on her nips, so I slid down, and straddled her face with my freshly-shaved cunny. She liked my smooth mons, and began to lick and chew it, before getting her own tongue into my gushing slit. I really was gushing, all lovely and wet and flowing, and I heard her throat gargle as she swallowed my come. That was quite a turn-on; both our nighties were round our necks, and we rubbed our slippery nude bodies together in a proper gamahuche, like real lesbos – the playacting made it all the more thrilling. "Squelching! This is what lesbos do," I thought. "At school, I used to cane depraved girls on the bare, for naked squelching, not that it dissuaded them – and now I'm loving it! Time is not so bad in prison, with dozens of juicy girls' bodies to enjoy."

'She began to gurgle, "Ooh ... ooh ..." sending vibrations through my cunny, "I'm going to come, don't

162

stop, oh, yes, yes, ooh . . ." and more like that. I suppose
I must have been moaning just the same, for I was far gone
in desire, and my pouch was absolutely slopping with come
– I could feel myself gushing, and was helpless to stop it,
which is that yummiest of feelings, isn't it? When a girl is
so helpless with lust, she can't stop wetting herself. I began
to chew her clitty quite hard, giving it little bites, and that
drove her wild. "Ooh! Ooh!" she began to howl, and a
geyser of come spurted into my mouth. I had to hold her
down, pinioning her with my arms and legs, she was
squirming so much. I couldn't hold back. Her writhing in
orgasm brought me to my own spend, and I just gave way,
as the my whole body dissolved in electric pleasure.

'It was a super intro to the dorm, because when I looked
up, I saw that all the others were watching me, and
wanking off as they watched us gamahuche. Hardast and
Bethany were sitting up, Bethany on Hardast's lap, and
their fingers in each other's cunny, wanking furiously, with
streams of come shining on their bare thighs. Kristel's
straight had long gone out, but she gave me a whole ciggie,
and two matches, and I crept back to my palliasse with my
prize. I had taken three or four drags, when the strapper
came in. "Who's been smoking?" she rasped. Well, it was
too late to put out my gasper, so I waited for the inevitable.
"You are to report to Miss Gurdell first thing in the
morning, after quim-shave [see below], for your prelimi-
nary interview, and your offence is noted," she said, taking
my smoke. Her hand dived between my legs, and she felt
how wet my cooze was. "Have you been masturbating?"
she demanded. Goose that I was, I admitted it, but said I
had only been wanking off alone. "Another offence on
your sheet!" she chortled, and promptly left the hut to
finish the ciggie herself! It's like that in the prison system,
you get used to it. Girls will do anything for a smoke, even
the strappers. Wanks are currency. In fact, I'm feeling
rather fruity just now, with the breeze playing on my titties
and naked quim, so I must pause, for you know what . . .

'That's better! I've just had a lovely wank, reading over
my saucy outpourings . . . Pretty shameless? Lying here in

163

the nude, with the steam hissing from the fumaroles, and the beautiful whitecaps spurting on the ocean, and the scent of heather and moss in the air, with my legs wide apart, and the wind tickling my spread quim, and shivers of pleasure, when I touch my stiff clitty – it's enough to make a girl wank off just for the sheer pleasure of being at one with nature. I'm sure you've sometimes felt the same, Harriet? Swimming naked in the turquoise Aegean, didn't you ever feel that life was so gorgeous, you simply had to masturbate? I know I did – one day this dishy Greek boy was watching me, it was on Kos, I think, or maybe Skiathos, and I was floating on my back, legs spread, and just wanking away, and when I got back to the beach he was standing there, smiling, with an absolutely huge erection, like a pine tree – one of those yummy ones that goes straight up, you know? I couldn't resist – he knew what I wanted. I knelt, and took his cock in my mouth, right to the back of my throat, and sucked him for a few minutes, then he lifted me by the hair, all wet and seaweedy, and took me standing up, with my ankles round his neck, holding my bum like a basket of grapes as he fucked my cunny. The feel of his powerful bare buttocks under my soles, as he pumped me! I felt like a goddess. And that massive pego, just pounding my pouch! I was so wet, spurting come all over his balls, and it sprayed into the sand, making little patterns, like peeing [which I did later of course, squatting as he watched me, and licking my come and his spunk from his turgescent cock!]. He was cupping my bottom with his palms, and at each thrust of his cock, he half let go of me, then slapped me back against his balls, so that it was like being spanked as he fucked me, with his cock slamming my wombneck, and my pube bone thudding against his. Gosh, Harriet, I just came and came! I knew other nudists could see us, and that made it even more of a turn-on ... [Oops! Sorry! Got to pause for another wank!] That's better! Just thinking of that Greek boy's cock, and everything, made me absolutely gush with come, and my clitty is stiff as a brick! Perhaps it's the island air that makes us randy for cock and wanks.

Anyway, that night, I masturbated to sleep, knowing that next morning I would have to pay for it.

'After the wakey whistle, the strappers herd us into our hut bathroom, where we have to squat in a row, for dungs and pees, followed by a communal ice cold shower. Then, each girl is given a razor, and must shave herself – armpits, legs, arms, and, most important, her cooze mound. Bum clefts too, everywhere must be satin smooth, and the strappers make us part our thighs for close inspection. It's very difficult to shave your quim hillock accurately, when you are shivering with cold, and it's easy to nick yourself in a painful place – which is a spanking offence. So the bathroom echoes with the sound of spanks on wet bare bottoms, which is most painful! The strappers wear their swimsuits for bathroom patrol, and I've been over a thigh many a time for a walloping on my wet bare, but that first morning, my bum was unspanked – in the bathroom, I mean . . .'

11

Thwangs

'After shower, we run at the double, knees-up, to the refectory, for a breakfast of tea and porage, taken standing up, and in the nude. Then we return to our huts to dress. The prison garb is very short shorts [too tight, and really pinching at the cunt, on purpose] fluffy socks, a tight blouse, no stockings or sussies, and thong panties which itch abominably – made of hemp, or something. Bras are optional, and the standard issue is hempen also, so, like many girls, I choose not to wear one. For so many of our penal duties we have to be in the nude anyway, apart from our socks and shoes. It's easier for the strappers to whop us. Some errant girls wear "disgrace dress" – a sack, much too small, clinging to the bare body, and no shoes or socks. It makes it easy to bear up for thwangs, by simply lifting the sack dress. I've had thwangs, as you'll see – the most horrid, vicious leather tawse, whipping the bare bottom. You can't imagine! Or can you?

'Well, that first morning, the strapper took me to Miss Kew's office, directly below Miss Gurdell's, in the administration tower, made of grey granite, like the guesthouse. Miss Kew looks very striking, sort of Mediterranean, with a beautiful big bum and balcony, and her black uniform rather sinister. She looked at me a bit oddly, and said, "so you're Selina Rawe, eh?" in a sort of *acquisitive* tone. She looked at me like a piece of meat, and I felt embarrassed by my prison garb, like girly gym kit, when she had black seamed nylons, shiny jackboots, and firm breasts jutting,

166

with, I imagined, the tiniest scalloped bra. I was sure she was corsed, her waist was so slender. Though braless, my own titties stood as firmly as hers, but I suppose a bra does give a girl that extra confidence. I was to go straight to Miss Gurdell's for my induction, alone, since I already had a punishment file. Afterwards, I was to return to her, for my judicial punishment. I shivered – punishment obviously meant something else than mere discipline. On Miss Kew's wall hung a row of instruments – vicious thwangs, quirts and canes – all worn from use.

'The strapper escorted me up a spiral stone staircase, into Miss Gurdell's anteroom. From the window, I could see the whole island, scarcely two miles long, with the frothy grey sea, and gulls wheeling in the blue sky, and I cheered up. From Miss Gurdell's office, I heard a rhythmic whack-whack, and I shivered some more. A bare-bum spanking has a sound like no other, but it didn't sound vicious, which cheered me again. Then, a girl entered, in a frilly French maid's outfit, very revealing – I could see most of her big bare bubbies, squeezed together by a push-up bra, and her long nyloned legs were scarcely covered by her frilly black tutu, so that I glimpsed her creamy panties and sussies. She balanced ably on astonishingly high stilettos, as she led me to Miss Gurdell's chamber. Her face was flushed, and she walked with her thighs well parted, rubbing her bottom, through her panties.

'Miss Gurdell sat on her desk, wearing cream skirt and shoes, shiny crimson nylons, and a crimson blouse, very tight over her big bubbies. Her long blonde tresses hung, shiny and flattened, over her shoulders. I thought her quite regal. Her legs were crossed, lifting her skirt high, so that I glimpsed her crimson silk panties gusset, and cream garter straps. I was sure her panties were shiny with moisture, over and above the natural sheen of the silk. "Thank you, Susan," she said to her maid. "You may go about your cleaning duties." Susan, cheeky minx, gave me a leer, and went into an adjoining room, where I heard bangs and clatters. Miss Gurdell leafed through some papers, then put them down, and stared at me, with her

167

hands clasped under her chin. "It is customary for me to greet each lower girl, on her arrival, and explain our system. If a gel maintains a pure bottom, she may win promotion to the ranks of my disciples," she said, sighing. "However, you seem to have offended already, gel. So, your introductory bare-bottom spanking – which all gels must take – shall be a disciplinary one. Your dossier mentions wilful destruction of a flowerpot, in Saltdean, on top of which, you were caught *masturbating* – on your very first night in our custody. Have you anything to say, before I invite you to bare up, and bend over my knee?"

'I shook my head. She'd see my bottom, still generously wealed, and know that a spanking was easy-peasy, so I'd have to act up. "I'm awfully sorry, Miss," I said, curtsying, and started to lower my shorts and panties. She moved to a sofa, and pressed her knees together, with her skirt pulled up fully, so that I would be spanked on her nylons. With my panties at my knees, I hobbled to her, and knelt down, then completed my baring. My belly fitted snugly on her thighs, with my bum high in the air. I had a lovely view of Auchterhuish through her window. Down below, in the courtyard, a naked girl wriggled in the pillory, under caning by a strapper. It made me shiver. I spread my cheeks wide, feeling cool air on my exposed quim and arse pucker. My bottom shivered, as Miss Gurdell stroked me. "Such cruel weals," she murmured. "I shan't ask whence they came to such a noble bottom, but hope that my spanking will dissuade you from further miscreance." I gulped, and told her that I was the victim of several misunderstandings, which made her sigh again, and say "It is so often the case. Now, instead of a new gel's cautionary spanking of a dozen, I propose to punish you, with four dozen." "I understand, Miss," I murmured, wiggling my bum, and spreading the cheeks, with a squeeze of both sphincters, to wrinkle my quim and anal pucker. I felt her thighs tense and shiver.

'I jumped, and my bum clenched, her first spank was so surprisingly hard. I knew four dozen was going to be a long set. I felt a warm smarting in my fesses, and then she

168

smacked again, and again, the spanks coming on the three seconds, which is a bit diabolical – it lets your arse flesh take the sting, then, just as the smart is calming, you get another. Quick passionate spanks are sometimes better than slow, methodical ones. Also, whopping *on the bare* is most efficient. Bare-beating means the thrasher can observe how the bum colours, where precisely it squirms most, and can pattern the strokes accordingly, to give maximum pain. Miss Gurdell did so.

'By the tenth spank, I had tears in my eyes, my gorge was rising, and my bottom clenching hard. I felt my shaven cunt slithering on her nyloned thighs, which were tense, the muscles jerking with each spank. I felt alarm, for, to my horror, my quim was beginning to seep come, at the lovely glow in my buttocks, and I knew it would slime her nylons – a dead giveaway. I wasn't sure whether juicing under spanks was an offence. [It is.] Her breath came in pants, as she spanked me. I managed to bite my lip, and keep from blubbing, but by the twentieth spank, my bare was on fire, and hurt so much, I gasped, "Oh, Miss! Ouch!" as her palm slapped me a real stinger right at the cleft, on the lower fesses. "Good gel," she panted. "Do try not to cry." *Wap! Wap!* She didn't lessen the force of her spanks, and soon I was blubbing. The total impact of a beating isn't just in the force of the strokes, nor even taking them on naked skin. It's the shame and submission, head down, over the knee, bum up, exposed and vulnerable; the attitude of the spanker, the feeling of helplessness and dread. Also, the knowledge that your pain isn't private – I couldn't hear any clanking from Susan's room, and deduced correctly that the minx was peeking at my punishment through the keyhole, and probably masturbating, at the sight of my spanked bare. [She was.] When I was a prefect at school and had to cane a girl's bare, I'd practise on myself, with a hairbrush – certainly uncomfortable, but a girl cannot make her gorge rise, or beat herself to tears, no matter how hard she whops.

'By the fourth dozen, I certainly had tears in mine! It's that feeling of guilt an accomplished spanker can instil.

Miss Gurdell said masturbation was a beastly thing, which a good English girl must resist, and that I was letting the side down. That hurt – no proper English girl wishes to let the side down. Yet I was panting with excitement, as my bum bruises throbbed and smarted, all lovely and hot – *you* know, Harriet. I groaned, as she let me rise; to my horror, her thighs were glistening with my seeped come! It's one thing for a girl to relish her smarting bare, quite another to make a mess from her cunny. Miss Gurdell's eyes fell to her come-slimed thighs, then met mine – and she blushed! She'd noticed.

'In a shaky voice, she ordered me to stand by the window, to cool off. I was to cup my hands in front of my quim, and stand with my pants down, to let the air heal my spanked bum. I shuffled to the window, and stood as she had ordered, enjoying the view, including the nude girl still flogged at the pillory, only now, with her bare back striped by a leather whip. She wriggled like a puppet. Her cries echoed faintly – I felt sorry for her, but the spectacle was somehow *exciting*. Suddenly, I saw, by her huge bubbies, it was that whinger Bethany Knowte, just arrived with me – what *had* the silly girl done? Then I saw the strapper was bare-breasted, in a red skirt, with a pretty big bum, wiggling, as she flogged, and I recognised Phryne Wulding-doune, so, who knows? Miss Gurdell told me to look to the horizon. "You are free to rub your bottom, if it's sore." she murmured. I rubbed my hot, spanked bum, puffing up after my walloping. It felt awfully nice.

'I heard Miss Gurdell breathing heavily, as she told me that well-behaved girls had freedom to roam the island, within limits. "Over there," she said, "you will see a work party at the strand. They are picking *Fucus aromaticus*, a valuable seaweed delicacy which helps our budget. They work in the nude, for security, and their orifices are checked by the strappers, to prevent smuggling, for which the penalties must regrettably be severe." The girls looked like tiny pale crabs, grubbing in the shingle. "Over there are the caves. Entry is sternly forbidden. Amongst them are fumaroles, spouts of steam from our underground spring. Strappers may use them for punishment of miscreants, in preference to the cane, or else Miss Cream may use them for colonic irrigation." Sure enough, I saw a couple of girls, nude and writhing in agony, with uniformed strappers holding their thighs over slits in the ground, from which emerged gusts of steam. "Furthest away, is a neolithic circle, enclosing the sacred megalith. It is strictly out of bounds." It didn't look very exciting in daylight, and my attention was drawn to a posse of nude, barefoot girls, struggling to run across a field of heather and thistles, with their arms up, balancing rocks on their heads. Obviously a punishment drill. The girl curiously suspended against a low clifftop, beneath the neolithic mound, was also undergoing punishment. Her nude body, splayed in a cross, was pressed to the cliff face, with ropes at her wrists and ankles, and it was all blue and dripping, as if she'd been painted with woad! Even so, I could see her body was bruised with whipmarks. The tide was creeping in, and I shuddered to think how far the sea must rise, before her release.

'Miss Gurdell said merely that the miscreant was being "whipped and dangled", She pointed out the Martello tower, the guesthouse, where important visitors lodged, and where virtuous gels were privileged to serve. I said I'd love that, if it meant I'd get one of those yummy French maid's uniforms, and Miss Gurdell said rather drily that Miss Wapping, the hospitaller, provided all necessary apparel. There was a little fishing boat at the harbour, with a muscular, bare-chested young man unloading boxes, and Miss Gurdell told me that the harbour was out of bounds, too, except on official, supervised duty. A troop of inmates in uniform was loading the boxes into a cart, under the unfurled whips of the strappers, but I could see from their body language that there was mimed or whispered dialogue between them and the topless hunk. I was so jealous, and frankly randy – even at that distance, I could see his muscles rippling, and persuaded myself I could see a whopper bulging in his jeans – though that was just my imagination. There were two other dishy bare-chesters, hidden in the deckhouse of the boat, and I just knew the hung stud had to be Hamish.

'Miss Gurdell went on, about the prison regime, and corporal punishment. She said that a virtuous girl could avoid CP, eventually winning the coveted nipple rings, like Phryne, or the governess herself, with the right to go bare-breasted. Winning my nip rings is my ambition! Lovely gold, pierced through my nips, and caressing my bare titties, while the other girls drool with envy! But the governess recited so many prohibitions – smokes, wanking, illicit foodstuffs, and men – I didn't see how I could possibly remain virtuous. Some of the girls at the jetty noticed me, and were pointing; I couldn't help rubbing my cunt, and parting my thighs, in a sort of striptease. I rubbed my bum, too, and heard Miss Gurdell panting. My reflection swayed in the glass, and behind me was another reflection, that of Miss Gurdell herself. She had her skirt up, and her fingers twitching inside her panties, as she ogled my bare bottom. The governess was wanking off! I began to wriggle and jerk my buttocks, rubbing my finger up and down my cleft, provocatively; her breathing rasped harsher, and my own fingers really were wanking my cunt, wet with come, for I was enjoying my exhibitionism, as girls do. I didn't spasm, though – Miss Gurdell did. Streams of come were wetting her nylons, and her hips writhed, as she masturbated. Soon, she whinnied, gasping, and I knew she had brought herself off. She ordered me to pull my pants up, and when I turned, she was smoothing down her dress, and quite red in the face. I was to return to Miss Kew, for my next "treatment", which I rather dreaded. Susan entered, with her skirt and undies in obvious disarray, and wearing a sly grin on her flushed face. I guessed the minx had had quite a few wanks, watching me spanked. The strapper, immobile throughout our proceeding, came to life, flicked her cane on my bum, and drove me down the spiral staircase to Miss Kew's lair. I heard the unmistakable tap-tap-tap of a bare-bum spanking, and supposed Susan was being whopped for her malfeisance. I discovered I was wrong, when I heard Miss

G whimpering "Oh, Susan, it hurts!" She wanks, then begs to be punished for it – corses herself fearfully tight, for the same reason!

'But CP is no giggle under Miss Kew. How I envied her, so tight and smooth in her immaculate strapper's black, with her gorgeous sheeny stockings and boots so shiny, you could see her panties reflected in the toecaps! Her skin was a lovely tan, all over, by the looks, and I felt jealous! She didn't beat about the bush – told me to get my panties totally off, and lie down on her whipping table, with straps and cuffs, and a hummock in the middle, to push the miscreant's buttocks up. Trembling, I pushed my knickers and shorts down over my thighs, quite slimy with my seeped come, which she noticed, smiling. I blushed! I stood there, nude but for blouse, socks and shoes, and she ordered me to knot my blouse below my breasts. "Miss Gurdell has spanked you for masturbating," she said, "but I know you were smoking, too. I'm going to whip you with thwangs, till you say who gave you the smokes."

'I lay down on the table, on my tummy, with the hummock pushing my bum up in the air. She gestured at her rack of instruments, and took down a tawse, of black leather, three feet long, with the end split into two tongues of six inches. "I control this prison," she said. "There is nowhere my writ does not run. At spanking, I overheard Susan and Miss Gurdell mention a misdemeanour by Kristel Gummi, thinking they were unheard. Why, I thrashed Kristel straight away. You've been caned, of course –" she caressed my bare "– but I favour thwangs, because the tongues can lick for such a deliciously long time." She dangled the tongues at my eyes, then drew the leather gently over my face. "You may lick the thwangs," she murmured. Petrified, I licked the hard black leather, shuddering at its weight and power. It tasted beastly and sort of acrid. She forced my legs apart, until my ankles were at the table corners, then I groaned, as she tightened the horrid rubber cuffs around my ankles, pushing my socks down. My wrists were cuffed too. I was helpless, and shivering, yet my quim was juicing! My naked body was at the mercy of her whip, and there was something thrilling in my total submission. I had no choice, and that was part of the thrill – like when a man has you naked, with his stiff cock throbbing against your belly, and you are just flowing with wet, and there is no way you can resist his penetration, you simply must have that cock inside you. It was the same with those evil leather tongues – I just had to feel them lashing my bare bottom, had to be beaten by this strong beauty, knowing she despised my tears and wriggles! I realised my maid Jane must have felt the same, when I spanked her naked, and that was also thrilling.

'Miss Kew loosened the top of her blouse, so that I could see her bare bubbies, the top half, very firm, with scarcely any uplift from her single band scallop brassiere. "An all-over tan, eh?" she said, and I told her about nudist beaches. "Depraved sensualism," she snorted. "We'll soon whip *that* out of you." She began to caress my bare with the leather thwangs, stroking me, until their soft slithery touch made my come seep. I knew she was teasing me, but couldn't help getting wet. "You want it, don't you?" she whispered. "You submissives are all alike." I gasped, as something hard and metallic slid between the wet lips of my quim – a speculum, bigger than the anal speculum used by Belinda. She jacked open my quim lips, forcing them to stretch horridly, then I felt the sensor pads pressed to my clitty, which was already stiff and throbbing. "The clitoral plethysmograph will test your excitement under a beating," she explained. She stepped back, lifted her arm, and began to flog my naked buttocks.

'The first stroke landed, slamming my cooze bone against the hummock, and made me gasp. The leather tongues were so heavy! I felt all my breath knocked from me, even though they only whipped my bottom. I'd never dreamed anything could hurt so much. I'd tensed my cheeks as if for the cane, with its short, sharp sting, and a single, smarting welt, but the thwangs seemed to lash the whole breadth of my bumflesh, like a kiss, with a slow, insidious afterburn, so that I didn't feel the full force of the stroke, until the next one was already whistling towards my bare. I bit my lip, to stop myself crying, it was so horrid; my gorge rose, and my eyes were wet with tears. The strokes came on the four seconds, with the awful whistle of the leather before each crack on my bare. I was clenching and churning, and could feel my buttocks squirming, with my wrists and ankles jerking in their cuffs, but I was glad to be restrained, since I couldn't have taken it otherwise, not lying still. The leather cracked again and again on my naked bum, and my shaven cooze mound began to slither, as it slammed against the hummock, for, to my shock, my cunny was juicing copiously.

'I could feel the sensor pads pressing, as my stiffening clitty pushed them wider. I lost count of the strokes, after the twentieth, bitterly ashamed that Miss Kew would see my excitement from her beating. She paused, and I turned – to show her my pain-wracked face, really – and I saw her strip off her blouse and bra, although she was only sweating a little. Her titties thrust up, beautifully tan, with big dark nipples like little brown apples, perched on the creamy swelling teat flesh. "No nip rings, Miss?" I heard myself say. "Cheeky bitch!" she snarled, and began to flog me on the two seconds, the tawse whirring with no pause between lashes. *Vap-vap-vap-vap!* It sounded like a bicycle, when you stick a plug of cardboard between the spokes, only much much louder. And I could hear those big bare titties slapping together, as she whipped me. "Where did you get the smokes?' she rasped. "From Hamish?" *Vap! Vap! Vap!* "No, Miss, I swear!" I whimpered. Foolish, not to deny the smokes altogether. "From Roddy, then?" – "No, Miss!" – "Denis?" – "Please, Miss, I swear I don't know! Oh, please stop, it hurts so!" I burbled, drooling from my lips, and my titties and cooze thudding against the table at each stroke. "Liar," she snapped. "I'll flog you till you blab, even if I have to send you to Miss Cream in a basket." – "Miss, I'm a new slag, I've only seen Hamish through Miss Gurdell's window." – "Then how do you know who he is?" she snarled. "The lustful cur likes new slags best." All the time, I knew I mustn't give away Kristel, my wanking chum in dorm, for sneaking is unspeakable. "He had you last night, didn't he?" she blurted. "That monstrous organ has tupped your bumhole at the stone circle."

I could hardly think, for my bum was wriggling so much, I thought I'd topple the table. *Vap! Vap! Vap!* I felt my clit throbbing so hard, and my come flowing so much, that the smart of the leather on my bare seemed a caress, almost a tickle. "The nympho Belinda Cream took you there, didn't she?' she gasped, her titties slapping together very loud. "Hamish had you – Roddy and Denis too – then they buggered Miss Cream, while the witch Phryne and her gang sucked and gamahuched, like the lesbo slags they are, while cheering your shame. Admit it! And when you came back to dorm, you smoked the cigarettes they'd paid you with, and had to wank off, they'd made you so hot, with bum-fucking." My cooze gushed come! My clitty was so huge and throbbing, there was a ping – it had blown the sensors clean off! She went on whipping me, I reckoned over the hundredth, though I couldn't imagine my bottom could take that many strokes without bursting. I was going to give Kristel away – I'd give anything for the pain to stop. I looked round at my whipper, her lips curled in a steely grin. Her nipples were very swollen, and quite rigid.

'Suddenly I saw a way out. "All right, miss, I admit it," I groaned. "Miss Cream took me to the stone circle. We were in the nude – she put my head in a cloth bag, so that I couldn't see the other girls, though there were several. They painted themselves in blue woad, Miss Cream said, and I could hear the slopping. I was very frightened – they laid me on the megalith, and I was fucked by three boys, while the girls chanted." – "Fucked in cunt?" she demanded. "Yes, Miss," I sobbed, "and in my bumhole." – "Was there a cock that made you shriek, as it penetrated your rectum?" – "Oh, yes, Miss." – "More than the others?" – "Certainly, Miss. One cock was so big, I thought it would burst me." – "That was Hamish," she grunted. "You had a full packet of cigarettes?" – "No, Miss, just three. I smoked them all," I moaned. "Honestly, that's the truth." She ceased my flogging, and I felt the speculum taken out of my cunt, to be replaced by her fingers, at least three, bunched together.

'Suddenly, the bitch was all sweetness and light. She purred that I wasn't a wicked girl, just simple, and must have nothing more to do with these orgiasts and their obscene rites. "I am your friend," she cooed. "I understand you, Selina. If I thrash your bottom, know that it's for your own good." All the time, she was reaming my pouch, and pressing on my clitty with her thumb. "You went off the plethysmograph," she murmured. "Your clit was the stiffest I've ever witnessed, under tawsing. You really are a submissive, aren't you? Your glowing bottom makes you long to come." She got all her fingers inside my pouch, stretching me like the dickens, and balled them into a fist. She began to pound my wombneck with her knuckles, fisting me. I was so turned on – it was animal, brutal, pure lustful force. My cunt flowed with juice, and I writhed as much as under the thwangs. "Oh, yes, Miss," I sobbed, "I so want to come. I'm so wet, my bum smarts so." It was the truth! She said nothing, but panted, and when I looked round, she slapped my face away. However, I saw the strapper, previously standing to attention, kneeling behind Miss Kew, and with her head under her skirt. Miss Kew's panties, stained at the gusset, were down her thighs, and the strapper's hair bobbed up and down behind her naked bottom, as she licked her anus. From the angle of her head, it was definitely the anus she tongued. I didn't observe Miss Kew masturbating, or the kneeling girl wanking her off, although it may well have happened. Miss Kew leaned over, and pressed her lips to my bare, licking my weals, and tonguing my bum cleft, all the time with my cunt filled by her slamming fist. "Oh . . . Oh . . . Oh!" I heard myself yelp, exploding in a super orgasm, and I think Miss Kew came too, just from the tonguing of her anus, for her teeth bit my bum quite hard, and she trembled, drooling over my skin. By the time I'd finished gasping and oozing come, she was smartly dressed, as if nothing had taken place. She released me, and sent me on my way to lunch, with more platitudes about behaving – and the promise that, if I sneaked on any gels I found smoking, I could become one of

Miss Kew's favourites, far better rewarded than any disciple of Miss Gurdell! Piously, I agreed.

'The funny thing, at luncheon, I was sitting beside Kristel Gummi, and told her everything, and how Miss Kew had wanted me to grass her up, but I wouldn't. "You're solid," she said, squeezing my cunt, which I took as a compliment. I asked her if there really were sexy rites at the stone circle, and she went all coy. "In Miss Kew's dreams," she said, "just like she dreams of winning her nip rings." I was persistent. "A slow, slippery squelch in dorm or sauna, or a flick-diddle in the heather, are one thing, boys quite another, and Hamish is a ritual in himself," she said mysteriously. "Believe me, you don't want to go near the stone circle. It's the last place for a girl." I said I was keen to earn my own tobacco, and she smiled crookedly. "Your tongue and cunt can always earn smokes from me," she said. "The way you earn them from Hamish?" I blurted. My big mouth! She pushed down the waistband of her shorts, showing a bit of bare bottom. There was a blue smudge, like paint, imperfectly washed off.

'Since then, Kristel's my regular wanking chum, in dorm, but I've wanked with oodles of girls, outdoors, where we aren't so possessive. Jasmine Wadd has rather a pash for me, unbeknownst to Phryne, who is awfully jealous, and would give me a whipping, followed by a strap-on buggery, if she knew. I'm pretty sure Belinda Cream suspects, and is jealous too – she gave me an absolutely corking enema the other day, which nearly had me shrieking, with my tummy swollen like a balloon, and all lumpy. So nice to look at your lumps in the glass, with your enemist rubbing your clitty! There is so much intrigue, not just about tobacco, as in any nick, but about caned bottoms and clit-slurping tongues and tight wet cunnies. A girl has to prize her assets. I know a lot more now, about skiving, dodging, and scrounging, and all the tricks of a con, although it hasn't saved my bare from the strappers' canes, rarely more than three dozen, thank goodness – and I've had to run under whip, while clutching a boulder on my head, and holding in a mouthful of yucky pebbles! As yet, I haven't been pilloried. Shudder! But I'm still itching for cock in my cunny, or in my . . . no, *and* in my bumhole. I *do* want to be bummed, by the biggest, hardest cock imaginable! There, I've admitted it. Hamish will surely have me, one day soon! I'll have to stop, because Hardast is coming to fetch this letter. I know she'll want a wank, the randy slut [so do I]!

hugs and kisses
Selina'

'Selina's coming along nicely,' gasped Harriet, throwing aside the letter.

'An impressive slut,' said Henry Addercop. 'She's gagging for it.'

'Hamish's cock up the bum,' said Harriet, with a shiver. 'Gosh! How wet-making.'

'Useful, her love of enema,' Henry said. 'She'll be handy in the guesthouse. Just as well, since she won't have a job to come back to. You *are* a ruthless bitch, annexing her column like that.'

'Why, thank you.'

Henry slapped Harriet's wealed bare bottom.

'Ouch! I'm still smarting, you know. A hundred with that horrid crop is rather wriggly-bum. Maybe Selina will opt to prolong her sentence – if she isn't cross, when she realises how she's been set up.'

'Cross! She'll be grateful. Anyway, with such a glorious arse, what can a gel expect? She's even dirtier than you, Harriet, as she is finding out, so she won't take much persuading. Such a filthy submissive, deep down – I knew she'd be a voluptuous addition to the guesthouse!'

'I say, Henry,' Harriet panted, 'aren't you going to spurt? I've wanked off twice, writhing around on top of you, while you smoke your beastly cigar. My arsehole's jolly sore.'

'Not just yet. I enjoy the feeling of power.'

'You absolute bugger.'

Henry blew smoke over her nude, blue-painted body, as his cock squelched in and out of her anus.

'You've noticed,' he said.

179

12

Squirmbottom

The moon glinted above the placid Hebridean waters, lapping the shingle beach; silhouetted against the velvet, starry sky, a small ketch rocked at anchor. Hamish Weels, clad in blue oilskins, scanned the shoreline through his binoculars. A single girl, in prison uniform, approached the beach, her rippling bare legs gleaming in the moonlight. Hamish watched, licking his teeth, as the girl stooped to remove her footwear, unbuttoned her blouse, to reveal her glinting bare breasts, then slid down her shorts and panties. Nude, she folded her clothing, and concealed it under a rock. She padded into the water, until the wavelets lapped her shining, hairless pubic hillock, and plunged, to surface several feet ahead, propelling herself at a brisk crawl stroke. Her bobbing bare buttocks and blonde mane, piled in the lush coils of a beehive, approached the boat. Hamish stepped inside the steamy bridge, heated by an oil stove.

'She's coming,' he said to his companions, Roddy Troon and Denis Acart.

'Is it Susan?' Denis said.

'Don't think so.'

'Arioma? She's hot,' Said Roddy. 'Or maybe Kristel?'

'What about that scrumptious Gwendoline Gurdell?'

'That's enough!' snapped Hamish. 'I think this is a new gel. It's a very blonde blonde, with a tasty arse.'

The two young males leered.

'A new bum, eh?' said Roddy. 'Just the ticket.'

'Remember the fuss we had, though, breaking Dawn in?' said Denis. 'Or Jasmine, before she turned snobbish, with her red uniform. It was jolly hard work, making those gashes compliant.'

'But pleasant,' said Hamish, lighting a cigarette, and passing smokes to the other two. 'Even better, Hardast – that bitch is a hundred octane compliance.'

'Not like Bethany,' said Roddy. ' "Tie me tighter, fuck me harder, whip me raw" – then, "you beasts, all you want is to abuse me!" What a madam.'

All puffed smoke, and laughed.

Selina clambered onto the deck, shyly accepting the hand of the dishy, sandy-haired stud in blue oilskins. Panting and spluttering, she shook water from her hair, while Hamish eyed her titties, bouncing wetly in the moonlight. He laughed, as her arms assumed an automatic, futile pose, to shield her breasts and quim.

'No need for modesty, miss,' he said. 'You know why you're here – with the biggest, firmest bottom I've ever clapped eyes on.'

Selina blushed.

'Yes,' she murmured. 'I'm here willingly.'

'Your first time, eh? With magnificent globes like that, I'm surprised you haven't been before. Name of . . .?'

'Selina Rawe,' blurted Selina.

'And you know the drill.'

'Yes, I do. Susan briefed me.'

'But didn't come with you?'

Selina smiled coyly.

'She owes me a favour,' she whispered. 'I'm a bit nervous. I . . . I didn't want another gel to watch me . . . *you* know . . .'

She blushed crimson. Hamish led her onto the warmth of the bridge, and invited her to get comfortable. Selina looked nervously at the two seated males, with a glance at the steps leading down to the faint glow of the sleeping quarters.

'Surprised?' Hamish said, handing her a mug of hot tea. 'Four sugars all right?'

She nodded gratefully, and stood, gulping tea, with her bottom next to the stove. The males stared at the steam rising from her wet bum cleft.

'It's just . . . I didn't know there would be *three* of you,' she said.

'That's the good news, miss,' drawled Roddy, stretching, to show the blatant bulge of his erection.

Selina flushed, still eyeing his crotch.

'I suppose so,' she murmured. 'You do have the merchandise? I'm awfully sorry, but I suppose I ought to see it, before we . . . you know.'

'A case of potato crisps, and a carton of smokes,' Hamish said. 'Suppose we didn't have them, what would you do?'

'I . . . I don't know,' Selina stammered. 'I imagine I'd have to, um, refuse my services.'

The males laughed.

'What if we raised anchor, and sailed back for Oban?' Denis sneered. 'We could dump you ashore, as an escaped convict. In the nude!'

'Oh, don't tease,' Selina said, blushing.

'Come below, then, miss,' said Hamish, 'and inspect the merchandise.'

Selina went before him, into the crew's quarters. There were bunks, stools, a wooden table, various ropes, chains, hooks and grappling irons, as well as a large oaken armoire. On its doors, a carved satyr thrashed a cowering nude maiden, using his monstrous erection as a whip. The girl's body bore deep welts, with her face contorted in pain.

'Like it?' Hamish said. 'That's medieval, actually. It would fetch a fortune at auction in London, but I couldn't bear to see it go to some sassenach.'

'I say, I'm a sassenach, you know – ooh!' Selina gasped, turning, to see that Hamish stood naked before her, with his legs apart, and his cock massively erect, almost vertical, with the huge shiny bell end almost touching his navel. 'Oh, gosh . . .'

Selina's voice trailed off, as her hand clutched her lips.

'Never seen a straight-upper before?' murmured Hamish.

'No . . .' she blurted, 'I mean yes . . . it's just awfully big.'

Roddy and Denis joined them. They, too, were nude and erect.

'Oh, gosh,' blurted Selina.

'That's best Scottish cock,' said Denis, stroking his balls.

'You chaps don't sound awfully Scottish,' said Selina, shyly.

'Why, the best English is spoken in Oban,' said Hamish. 'And we have the biggest danglers.'

'Not exactly danglers, gentlemen,' she murmured. 'They're so big and stiff! I suppose I may take that as a compliment.'

Hamish drew back a tarpaulin, and showed Selina the merchandise, wrapped in plastic, with a tow rope attached. Selina knelt to look.

'Oh,' she said, frowning, 'prawn cocktail flavour. We expected sour cream and chives. And the ciggies, Embassy instead of B and H. Never mind, I suppose they'll have to do.'

'A bold lassie,' drawled Denis, stroking his massive cockshaft. 'I wonder what bold lassies deserve?'

'Where are you from, miss?' Roddy asked.

'London,' Selina replied.

'What part?'

She hesitated, before replying, 'Um, Manor Park.'

'And what got you banged up?'

'Oh, I . . .' Selina bit her tongue. 'I was convicted of dole fraud.'

'Really?' Denis said. 'Where were you signing on?'

'Why, er, Manor Park, of course.'

She stood up, slowly parting her thighs.

'Well, gentlemen,' she said, with a self-conscious giggle, 'I suppose we ought to . . . get down to business.'

Hamish stroked his swollen bell end.

'You are pleasingly direct, miss,' he said. 'You *do* know the drill?'

'I think so,' Selina said, blushing, and wiping a trickle of drool from her mouth.

Her nipples were stiffening to erection; a smear of come glistened under the swollen crimson lips of her gash.

'You may each give me a portion,' Selina gulped, 'in . . . in the place of your choice. My body is yours, until you have all spunked in me. Shall I lie on a bunk? Face up or face down? Oh, gosh . . . I feel so helpless. Yet it's rather thrilling. Please do me, chaps. I'm . . . I'm getting awfully wet.'

She blushed furiously, baring her teeth in a smile. Her fingers strayed languidly down her quivering bare tummy, to her quim, where she parted the cunt flaps, showing pink wet pouch meat. Come glistened, trickling from her open cunt, to slime her upper thighs. Her eyes were hooded, and she breathed through flared nostrils.

'In truth, I've been rather looking forward to this,' she murmured hoarsely, licking her lips at Hamish. 'Such huge sex organs! As you are the captain, sir, I suppose you'll take me first?'

'We Scots are rather democratic,' Hamish drawled. 'Perhaps we'll take you all at once.'

Selina frowned, then blushed, and bit her lip.

'Oh . . .' she blurted. 'You mean . . .'

Hamish nodded.

'Three up,' he said, gesturing to the widest bunk. 'One for'ard, in your mouth, one astern, bumming you, and one below, fucking your cunt.'

'You are familiar with bumming?' Denis said.

'Why yes . . . that is, I haven't had . . . I mean yes, I've been buggered. It hurt dreadfully. You won't hurt me, will you?'

Her eyes pleaded with each male in turn. Hamish rippled his belly, making his cock buck. She gazed at his dancing bell end.

'It's rather a surprise,' she blurted. 'Three sex organs penetrating me at once! But I'm excited – there's something so lust-making about being at sea.'

The mariners pulled back their prepuces, revealing their shiny crimson bell ends.

'Gosh! So hard,' she gasped. 'You beasts, you *know* a gel can't refuse. Yes, take me in the cunny and bumhole, while I suck. Oh, I feel giddy! I begged Susan for this job. She owed me a wank, you see. I'm so wet! Come on, come on, don't make me wank off, in frustration.'

Her fingers tweaked her stiff wet clit. The three nude males stood, hands on hips, and cocks throbbing, watching her masturbate, while Hamish swung the armoire door half open. Selina brushed a stray strand of hair back to her towering blonde beehive, while continuing to wank her clitty, with her fingers teasing her nipples to full stiffness. Her come cascaded down her rippling inner thighs, sliming her skin with its oily wetness.

'Let's have *your* merchandise, then, miss,' Hamish said pleasantly. 'Just stick your fingers further up that hot slit – unless you'd like a fingerfuck, while I get it. *Susan* likes that.'

'I . . . I'm sorry?' Selina said.

'The fucus, miss,' Hamish said. 'Don't you have it in a plastic bag up your cunt?'

'Why, no. Susan said nothing about any fucus. That would be illegal. We're not allowed to . . . ooh!'

Hamish slapped her hard, on the nipples. Her breasts wobbled, reddened with his fingermarks.

'Don't play games, miss,' he snarled. 'You've fenced our delivery somewhere else. Skye? Fort William?'

'No! Honestly, I had no idea . . . oh, that bitch Susan!'

Hamish opened the armoire door fully. Selina gasped; inside hung whips, canes and gleaming leather tawses.

'There's something dodgy about you, miss,' he said tersely, 'and we'll find out what it is.'

'No,' she blurted. 'I . . . I think it's best if I leave. Let me through, please.'

She tried to force her way past the naked males, who stood motionless, blocking her.

'There *isn't* a dole office in Manor Park, miss,' Denis drawled. 'Few Scots have a less than perfect knowledge of London, you know. You'd have signed on at Stratford.'

'Didn't I say Stratford?' blurted Selina.

Hamish slapped her naked breasts hard, backhand and forehand. Her bare teats trembled, flushed with angry bruises.

'Liar,' he hissed. 'Seize her, boys. She thinks she's had thwangs, in her girly jail. Now the bent bitch will *really* learn to squirm.'

'No! Please!' Selina whimpered, struggling in their grip.

Her thighs wriggled, spraying come over their balls and cocks.

'*Ooh . . .*' she wailed, as Hamish slapped her face. 'Ooh, no, please, *please* don't hurt me, I beg you. I'll do anything you want, anything.'

'But of *course* you will,' said Hamish pleasantly. 'Susan didn't tell you very much, eh? We mariners like a gel who'll take cunt-fuck, throat-fuck, and full bung, but most of all, we love a squirmbottom. You'll be wriggling in agony, with your bare arse lashed like the briny in a force nine gale, *before* we go three up on you, miss.'

Roddy and Denis forced her to kneel on the deck, bending over a wooden stool, with her breasts hanging, her cunt bitten by the stool's sharp rim, and her ankles and wrists tightly roped to bolts in the deck. Hamish took a long, shiny tawse from the armoire, stroked it, and flicked its splayed tongues against her bare breasts. Selina shivered.

'A tawsing,' said Hamish, 'just to warm you up.'

'No,' whimpered Selina, wrenching at her ropes. 'Please don't whip me. *Please.*'

'I expect you are accustomed to being flogged at the upright,' he said. 'I find the kneeling position more humiliating, especially as you cannot stretch your legs, or back, to ease the pain.'

'Please, no,' Selina sobbed, tears trickling down her cheeks. 'Don't flog me . . . don't . . .'

'Would you like a cigarette before we begin?' Hamish said.

'Yes, please,' Selina gasped.

Hamish lit one, and pressed it between her lips. She sucked hungrily, and blew a thick plume of smoke.

'Ready?' Hamish said.

Selina nodded.

'Please spread your arse cheeks wider, and a little higher. I want to see your open cunt and bumhole.'

186

Clutching the glowing fumable between her lips, she shut her eyes, spread her bare bum wide, with her arse cleft and perineum a taut drumskin.

'Much better,' murmured Hamish. 'Scots thwangs like stroking a gel's private parts.'

'Oh, no. Please, at least tell me how many I'm to take,' she whimpered.

'Fifty,' Hamish replied.

'Surely not all on my cunny and hole?'

Hamish laughed.

'Only when you aren't squirming satisfactorily.'

Selina puffed furiously on her cigarette, and tensed herself. A cylinder of ash fell from her cigarette, landing on her left breast, and lodging at the nipple. The twin tawse thongs took her squarely across the mid-fesse, wrapping the leather around her naked bottom, from haunch to haunch.

'Ooh,' Selina gasped.

Her buttocks clenched, and the ash dropped from her nipple. Hamish withdrew the leather, revealing a livid red welt across her bare croup. A second stroke followed the first, and the third made three lashes to the same weal. Selina's bottom glowed crimson, in the wide ridge where the thwangs had whopped her. Tears streamed from her eyes, as her flogged bare clenched furiously. She sucked at her cigarette, blowing smoke over her smiling spectators, until the third stroke whipped her on top buttock.

'Ahh,' she gasped, dropping the cigarette onto her left breast.

'Ooh! Oh!' she shrieked, wiggling her heaving titties, to disodge the glowing ember.

Three rapid strokes coloured her bare bottom from top to thigh, the bruises already puffing up to blotchy ridges.

'Urrgh . . .' Selina groaned, her face red and glazed with tears, while her flogged buttocks clenched, squirming and slamming her pubic hillock against the stool's rim.

The tawsing continued, with Hamish pausing to light up, and striping her whole fesses, thighs and haunches. As her bumflesh reddened, Selina wailed, squirming and panting hoarsely.

187

'*Ahh!*'

'That's twenty-five,' Hamish said eventually. 'Smarting much?'

'Need you ask?' sobbed Selina. 'You know it hurts. My bum's on fire. And those thigh strokes – why, that's scarcely fair.'

'Wait till I whip your cunt,' Hamish said. 'Which, by the way, is juicing quite heavily. Do you always ooze come when you're whipped?'

'No!' Selina protested.

Whap!

'*Ohh!*'

The tawse cracked on her naked bumhole and gash, from whose lips, squashed by the whipping leather, a jet of oily come spurted. Her buttocks clenched frantically, hiding and showing the livid crimson welt, searing her bum cleft, while her head jerked from side to side, her face a wrinkled mask of anguish, and her beehive tresses bobbing. Hamish flogged her wriggling bare buttocks to the full fifty lashes, while Selina squirmed, sobbed and whimpered, her cunt gushing come.

'You love it, miss,' Hamish drawled.

'Certainly not! You beast!'

'Liar,' said Hamish drily. 'You're a submissive, like most gels.'

'No! How dare you . . .' she wailed.

He caressed her inflamed bumskin, getting his finger into the cleft, and allowing her cheeks to squeeze it, as they clenched. Selina moaned, a long ululation, while drool dripped from her gaping lips. Hamish withdrew his fingers, slimed with her come, and put them into her mouth, ordering her to lick them dry. Sobbing, she obeyed, swallowing her own come. Beside her face, Roddy's and Denis's stiff cocks quivered. Selina's tongue hung out, as she panted. Roddy was elected to service her mouth, and his throbbing crimson bell end approached Selina's gaping lips.

'Noo . . .' she moaned. 'Urrgh!'

The entire helmet of his cock sank into her mouth. He clasped her head, and pulled her gently towards him, thrusting his loins, until her lips enclosed his balls, and the cockshaft filled her mouth and throat. Selina began to suck, with little bobbing movements of her neck, while Hamish and Denis strapped thin, two foot canes to their erect cocks, with sticking plaster. Hamish twirled, cane whistling towards Selina's bare. It striped her upper thigh, just below the folds of the buttocks. At once, Denis spun, and his cock-cane lashed her full on the mid-fesse.

'Mm!' groaned Selina, shuddering, with her cry muffled by Roddy's cock.

Her fesses squirmed, the wealed bare flesh wriggling in time with her lips, sliding up and down the drool-slimed cockshaft, and the cock sinking right to her throat, at the end of every suck.

'*Ah! Yes*,' gasped Roddy. 'She's guesthouse material.'

Selina's twirlcaning continued, her body shuddering, and crimson arse clenching, while her lips feverishly tongued Roddy's trembling stiff cock. A hoarse, gurgling moan rumbled deep in her throat; her eyes, screwed shut, flowed with tears, while between her churning thighs, her swollen gash flaps squirted copious slimy come, at each lash of the canes to her naked buttocks. Her naked bum squirmed, as her tears dripped on Roddy's balls. He clutched her head to his belly.

'Uhh,' he gasped. 'I'm there. Swallow it, bitch, swallow it all . . . oh, *yes!*'

Her cheeks bulged, as he spurted; her throat gulped convulsively, swallowing the hot spunk, yet unable to prevent copious ejaculate from escaping her lips, and dribbling down her chin, onto her breasts, as Roddy rammed his cock deep in her throat. Denis and Hamish lashed final strokes, whipping her exposed cunt and anus, before lowering their canes.

'*Urrgh!*' Selina squealed, her whipped cunt writhing.

Her body arched, shuddering; Roddy's buttocks pumped, as he fucked her in the throat, and she gurgled, crimson in the face, convulsively swallowing the spunk, with bubbles of sperm erupting from her mouth. Streams of come glistened on her quivering thighs, as her gash gushed copious cunt-slime. Panting, Roddy withdrew, leaving her mouth agape, drooling sperm and saliva, and quivering in convulsive, gagging sobs.

'The filthy little beast didn't swallow it all,' he said. 'She needs punishing.'

'I'm sorry . . .' Selina wailed. 'I tried my best . . . oh, my bare! How it smarts! *Please*, no more punishment.'

'A bum like that, and you expect *less* punishment?' said Hamish. 'We only caned you thirty.'

He pinched the swollen pink gland of her nubbin.

'Ooh,' Selina gasped. 'Oh, damn you, yes, touch me. Do me, I'm going to come, please touch me there, stroke my clitty, please . . .'

Hamish pushed a lit cigarette between her lips, and she sucked smoke.

'*You* come?' he drawled. 'First, something to make your filthy submissive cunt even wetter.'

Selina moaned, rubbing her shaven mons against the stool, while puffing deeply at her cigarette. She did not resist, when the males unbound her. Roddy and Denis lifted her, whimpering in pain: Roddy clasped her between the thighs, using her quim as a handle, while Denis cradled her back, with his hands pulling at her nipples, stretching the titties tight. They carried her to an athlete's hurdle, consisting of two poles, four feet apart, supporting a narrow circular rail as a crossbeam. Selina paled.

'No! Not the rail! I'll tell you anything you want!' bleated Selina, as they hoisted her onto the rail, so that her weight was taken by her naked cunt, poised at the end of the crossbeam, and her buttocks presented an unhindered target. 'You've only to ask.'

'No, you tell us what *you* want,' Hamish replied.

'Gosh, this hurts,' she wailed. 'The rail is wedged right in my cunny. Hamish, you beast!'

They bound her ankles with fresh ropes, looped through rings in the deck, and stretching her legs wide, in a vee shape. Her arms were stretched likewise, raised above her head by two chains, hanging taut from the overhead. Selina whimpered, as Roddy fastened clothes pegs to her nipples, with the pegs attached to ceiling cords, and

190

wrenching her breasts to pale envelopes of distended white flesh. Denis fetched a section of tubular rubber cladding which stank of oil. He wrapped it round her waist, tightening its straps, until she gasped, groaning that she could hardly breathe. Hamish said, laughing, that a waist like hers could easily take a seventeen-inch corset.

'Oh, please . . .' Selina moaned. 'It hurts so much.'

Hamish took a three-foot cane from the armoire, grasping it by its crook handle. Selina gaped, eyes wide, and her tongue dangling from her drool-slimed lips. The cane resembled the normal girls' school implement, save that the tip was cut into a snake's tongue, each half two inches long. Hamish stroked her bare bum, inflamed with sullen crimson and purple bruises from her tawsing, and Selina wriggled, sobbing.

'A caning on the rail must perforce be harder than one taken bending over,' he purred, 'as compacted buttocks are less sensitive. However, a wet bum smarts more.'

He pressed his cock against Selina's naked bottom, with his balls nestling in her arse cleft. He bent slightly back, legs apart, and a fountain of piss erupted from his peehole, spraying vertically, and inundating Selina's back, whence it flowed down to drench her buttocks. Selina began to cry.

'Why must you humiliate me so?' she sobbed.

'Because you want it,' answered Hamish, lifting his cane. The wood whistled, to slap wetly across Selina's fleshy bare mid-fesse.

'Oh!' Selina squealed, her buttocks shifting, and her face wrinkling, as she jerked again, at the pain of the rail slicing her gash.

'Ooh . . .'

Her legs straightened, rigid on either side of her clenched buttocks, as her rubber corset heaved.

'Ahh! Please stop . . .' she whimpered. 'Ooh! Ahh! Enough!'

Her nude body wriggled frantically, with the rail burrowing deeper into her slit, her rubber-corsed belly and clamped breasts heaving, and her thighs rippling, while her feet twitched in their ropes, making the deck rings rattle.

Hamish caned every visible inch of her buttocks and haunches, laying an intricate pattern of crossed strokes on the quivering bare fesses, and raising sharp crimson weals atop the purplish blotch of her tawse bruises, with especially livid stripes on on the tender skin of haunch and top buttock. He began to cane the backs of her stretched thighs, to Selina's gasps of distress.

'*Ohh!* Gosh! That's not fair. Not my legs, oh, *please.*'

Her head lolled forward, drool seeping from the corner of her slack lips, to be jerked up, at each stroke of the cane. The rail, under Selina's writhing thighs and buttocks, gleamed with come, seeping from her bitten cunt.

'Who gets our merchandise, miss?' Hamish asked. 'Who is tuck mistress? Phryne? Belinda? Miss Kew? Miss Gurdell, perhaps?'

'Ooh! Oh! I don't know . . . I'm allowed to keep a packet of crisps and ciggies for myself, and the rest I must bury under a secret stone. It's not always the same one – I don't know who's in charge, honestly.'

Vip!

'Ahh! Cripes . . .'

'Never thought of keeping it, and running the racket yourself?'

'I wouldn't dare. No gel would, not even Susan.'

Vip! Vip!

'Ahh . . .'

Selina wriggled, stretched on her rail, with tears streaming down her cheeks and wetting her stretched breasts. Her glowing bottom wriggled frantically.

'There are punishments you can't imagine . . .' she moaned. 'Every gel dreads them.'

'Don't you dread fifty with the cane?' Hamish purred.

'Fifty! Oh, no . . .' Selina wailed, squirming on the rail, now heavily soaked with her come.

'Why not?' sneered Hamish. 'Your cunt's dripping – and you never even asked for your tariff. You spank and wank with all the other cons, don't you, submissive slag?'

'No,' whimpered Selina, 'just Hardast, and Bethany, Susan of course, sometimes Belinda, under enema, and

192

Kristel's my wank chum in dorm, Jasmine – well, she has a crush on me, and then – hardly anyone, really.'

Vip! Vip!

'*Oww!*' Selina squealed, clenching her striped bare bum, 'you . . . you have no right to treat me this way,'

'Your cunt is wet under punishment – proof that punishment is what you want. And at Royal Hebridean, our old school, we were taught that a gentleman's duty . . .'

Vip!

'Ooh!'

'. . . is to give a lady . . .'

Vip!

'Ahh!'

'. . . exactly what she wants.'

The cane sliced three livid welts on the back of Selina's right thigh, just below the buttocks.

'Ooh!' she whimpered. 'Oh, gosh, that's tight. It's awful. Why do you wish to hurt me so? You've never suffered such shame.'

'Haven't I?' snarled Hamish, his face close to hers.

He sank his teeth into her left breast, and bit hard.

'Ahh!' Selina shrieked.

Hamish withdrew, leaving crimson teeth marks on the distended teat flesh.

'At school, we were beaten,' he said.

'But that's normal,' replied Selina. 'Schoolboys are supposed to be beaten.'

'On the bare buttocks,' he continued.

'Isn't it always on the bare, at boys' schools?'

'By a lady!' he growled. 'Two dozen, with the deadliest whippy cane – not a twig like this – and in the full nude, delivered by matron, for the slightest infraction. She loved the ceremony of ritual humiliation: the shy stripping – everything off – then the tongue-lashing, while I quivered in the nude, watching her flex her cane, and slithering her nylon stockings together, so I could peek at her panties, trying to stop myself getting stiff. She'd tell me how she would gloat, watching my naked bottom redden, and I mustn't cry out, for that would be unmanly, even when my

193

bare was squirming terribly, and covered all over in vicious weals. Then, she'd see my erection – I always got one – and decree extra strokes for my beastliness. Bending over, touching my toes, and biting my lip, as that dreadful rattan swished my bare arse, two dozen times – three whole dozen, if my erection hadn't softened. She'd rub zinc ointment into my weals, quite gently, and purr that I mustn't be a naughty boy, and that caress would make me stiff again! She'd pretend not to be angry, but would stroke my balls, and tickle my bell end, before dismissing me, with a smarting bottom and a throbbing cock! The teasing bitch – when I was in the upper sixth, I got yet another beating for smoking, and this time, I knew what she wanted, and gave it to her. I stripped, and bent over, making no attempt to hide my erection. After a dozen stingers, I rose, and grabbed the cane from her. I said I was going to give her what she really wanted. I ordered her to strip off her skirt and petticoat, then her knickers and sussies, but keeping her stockings. I pushed her down over her desk, and gagged her with her stethoscope, then caned her two dozen on the bare, making sure to whip her thighs, and shred her frilly stocking tops. She was flowing with come, just like you, miss, and when her bare buttocks were well squirm-ing, and all striped with really bright weals, I pushed my fingers in her cunt, and got a palmful of her love juice, to oil my cock. Then I forced her cheeks apart, nuzzled her wriggling little pucker with my bell end, and penetrated. Two thrusts, and my cock was filling her rectum, and I began to arse-fuck her. She was screaming and wriggling, but I held her down. Her arms were free – she slipped her hand to her cunt and masturbated as I fucked her. When I'd buggered her for about a minute, I spunked inside her, filling her rectum with my cream, and spanking her wealed bum all the time. When I'd finished, she burst into tears, and began to lick and suck my cock and balls, begging for more. I pissed in her mouth, and she swallowed it. That's how I know what women want, miss. Revenge is sweet.'

He took her writhing bum to fifty, the wet slashes of the cane, on the piss-glazed nates, muffled by her shrieks and sobs, as her fesses gyrated on the rail, with come sluicing from her squashed cunt flaps. Her hard, swollen clitty peeked wetly through the gash folds, and she leaned forward, wrenching her clamped titties, to masturbate, by rubbing her gland on the wood, as she sobbed and moaned. Snarling, Hamish ripped her cunt basin from the rail, while Roddy and Denis unstrapped her from her bonds. Cocks erect, the males positioned themselves: Roddy lying on the wide bunk, and Denis waiting by its pillow. Hamish threw Selina, belly down, onto Roddy's cock, pushing her face into the pillow, to muffle her cries. Roddy lunged upward, his cock penetrating her dripping, come-slimed gash in a single thrust. Hamish prised apart her buttocks, and rammed his bell end into her anus pucker. Selina squealed, her flogged bottom squirming, as Hamish pushed his entire cockshaft into her rectum, and began to bugger her, while Roddy fucked her from below.

'Oh, no! No! Hamish, you're too big!' she wailed. 'You'll burst my bumhole! Please don't fuck me there! *Ahh* . . .'

Denis lifted her chin. Her mouth hung open, slack with drool, and he slammed his stiff cock against her palate, while she gagged, then thrust it to the uvula, and began a vigorous throat-fucking. Selina's lips fastened round the cockshaft, wet with her drool, and sucked hard. `

'Urrgh! Urrgh!' Selina groaned.

Her body wriggled, impaled on the two cocks, as she fellated the third.

'Hurting, miss?' gasped Roddy, and Selina gurgled in distress. 'I love the squishy feeling of a shaven cunt.'

'You're tight, bitch,' grunted Hamish, hips slapping her bum, as he pounded her anus. 'Squeeze my cock, slut. Milk all my spunk from my balls, I'm going to shoot the full load right up your guts.'

Selina's buttocks clenched, squelching with her spurted come, as her sphincter squeezed his cock.

'Urrgh! Urrgh!' she whinnied, gagging on Denis's throat-fucking; come spewed from her fucked cunt, over Roddy's balls.

Her anus wriggled, tightening on Hamish's arse-greased cock. Denis groaned, and spunk frothed from Selina's slapping lips, as she sucked him to his spurt, with the ejaculate squirting deep in her throat, so powerfully, that it bubbled at her mouth. Roddy gasped, sperming in her squelching wet cunt; Hamish, pulling her bum against his balls, grunted, spunking at the root of her anus, with spurts of sperm frothing over her anal lips, to drip down her pumping arse-globes.

'Mm . . . mm . . . *mm!*' Selina squealed, '*mm . . . mm!*'

Her back arched, and her belly convulsed in its rubber sheath, as her body bucked in orgasm. Sperm covered her face, buttocks and cunt, mingled with her torrent of come, as she continued to writhe in her spasm, while the males ceased their flow. They withdrew their softening cocks, and turned her on her back; each pissed on her, soaking her cunt and teats, with Hamish spraying her face.

'Urrgh! Ooh!' she spluttered, swallowing her bugger's piss, then, gasping, smiled in gratitude, as he pushed a lit cigarette between her lips.

When she had finished smoking, Denis and Roddy held her by the hair and cunt, while Hamish painted her body in blue woad. His decorator's paintbrush slopped the shiny muck into her every crevice, while she moaned. He ordered her to lick the dripping woad from her nipples; sobbing, she bunched her titties, squashing them up into her mouth, and licked her whole teats clean; then, her feet and legs, contorting herself, until every part of her was licked clean, except her belly, gash, elbows and bum. All three Royal Hebs were erect again; Hamish lifted a nine-thonged rubber quirt.

'That muck must be whipped off,' he purred.

'No! Please! Haven't you humiliated me enough?' Selina whimpered.

Hamish put a lit cigarette between her dripping blue lips.

'Go on, then,' blurted Selina, puffing gratefully.

Dawn was breaking, when Hamish finally said she could return to prison. Her welted nude body dripping with sperm, girl come, and piss, Selina fastened the wrapped merchandise to her waist, and went on deck.

'I've never had real cock in my bum before. Thank you,' she murmured to Hamish.

Grimacing, she rubbed her swollen, bruised anus bud, and wealed bottom. Lowering herself into the sea, she looked up to Hamish, and tugged at her beehive hair, until her tresses cascaded around her breasts.

'Silly me, I forgot something,' she said. 'Susan *did* tell me to give you this.'

Pulling a plastic bag, filled with fucus pods, from her hair, she handed it to her ravisher.

13

Hot Weals

'Would you like me to birch you?' said Jasmine Wadd.

'Birch me?' gasped Selina. 'But I haven't done anything wrong.'

Jasmine laughed.

'Of course not, but in the sauna, gels always tickle each other with birch twigs, for the pores, you know.'

She picked up two sheafs of birch rods from the empty water bucket, and Selina eyed them warily.

'They look vicious,' she said. 'I've never been birched, and it sounds horrid, much worse than the cane.'

'Silly! It's not a birching for punishment. Here, I'll show you.'

Jasmine began to lash Selina's thighs, very gently, with the bushy sheaf of full-sized birch rods, and Selina shivered. She responded by swishing her own birch on Jasmine's back.

'Ooh, that's nice,' Jasmine cooed.

The girls laced their nude bodies for several minutes, the twigs crackling softly on their skins, with strokes to the titties and buttocks, as they twisted, to allow the tips access. Selina impishly swished her birch on Jasmine's unguarded gash flaps, and Jasmine squealed.

'Naughty gel! But so invigorating . . .'

She responded with a generous swish to Selina's spread buttocks, the twigs covering the whole fesses.

'Mm . . .' Selina said, panting, and lashing Selina's breasts. 'It's hot work.'

Their naked bodies shone, dripping with sweat, and they laid the birches down.

'I say, you've grown your lawn,' Selina said. 'May I feel it?'

'That would be nice.'

Jasmine parted her thighs, to reveal her cunt lips, shrouded in a massive curly fleece, whose tendrils dangled in her perineum, tickling her anus bud.

'It's awfully hairy.'

'Do you like it?'

'It's super. Quite jealous-making.'

As both nude girls dripped with sweat in the sauna, Selina stroked Jasmine's luxuriant pubic thatch.

'More a forest than a lawn, and awfully tempting,' Selina murmured.

'Oh, don't tease,' trilled Jasmine. 'Miss Gurdell's mannerisms catch on – Phryne says her lawn is beautifully trimmed.'

'The slags say Miss Gurdell has a spanking pash for Phryne,' Selina murmured, 'and Miss Kew is jealous.'

'Ssh,' hissed Jasmine. 'It's cheeky, telling me slags' gossip. Remember what a privilege it is, to sauna with a strapper.'

'Aren't you taking rather a risk, then?' asked Selina, her fingers nearing the apex of Jasmine's open bare slit.

'Not at all,' pouted Jasmine, wriggling, and parting her thighs further; her breasts wobbled, dripping sweat from the points of her nipples. 'Mm . . . that *is* nice. I like to show my rank, occasionally. The other strappers call us air gels horrid names. They think we are just glorified air hostesses.'

'What sort of names?' Selina asked impishly, still ruffling Jasmine's sweat-soaked fleece, but with her little finger prising the lips of her gash apart, to reveal her gland, slightly swollen.

'Flying fannies is one,' Jasmine said. 'Or, airborne arseholes.'

'That *is* horrid,' Selina agreed.

Jasmine wriggled, clamping Selina's probing fingers between her thighs. She sighed deeply.

'Is something wrong?' Selina said.

Jasmine clasped Selina's shoulders, and stared her in the eye.

'Not wrong,' she gasped. 'But you are exciting me, Selina, and it's wrong to tease. You ... you are very special to me. You aren't like the other slags, and I don't just mean your adorable body. How many sleepless nights I've had, tossing and turning – yes, masturbating – as I think of your lovely bottom! I've rather a pash for you. If I thought my feeling was returned, then –' she pressed a hand to her breast '– I'd ... I'd look after you. I want us to be special friends.'

'I'm not teasing you, Jasmine,' murmured Selina.

She put a hand on Jasmine's knee, and slowly prised her thighs apart. Selina's fingers slipped lower, cupping Jasmine's wet cunt lips, and Jasmine moaned, closing her eyes. Selina touched the clitty; Jasmine jerked, gasping, and opened her thighs fully, as Selina began to caress the nubbin, with fingertips inside the girl's juicing slit.

'Ohh ... that's so nice,' breathed Jasmine. 'Feel how wet I am – my nips are all tingly, and my clitty so stiff ... oh, yes, you know how to turn a gel on. You must have frigged hundreds of gels. That's why I'm so frightened of you. I know slags play naughty diddling games, and ... and squelch each other. But I'm so afraid of ... of getting hurt again. I don't think I could bear it, if you hurt me.'

Her moist eyes shone, pleading.

'You mustn't believe beastly rumours,' Selina murmured, coolly masturbating her trembling companion. 'Don't you think *I've* been hurt? I don't mean caned – why, that's nothing. Slags have feelings too, you know. I must be careful, before committing myself. But, Jasmine, I ... I so want to.'

She parted her thighs, and placed Jasmine's fingers between her gash flaps.

'Oh, Selina,' she gasped. 'You're wet.'

'Wet for you, Jasmine. But slag-strapper love is risky. We think of all strappers as brutes with canes. My bum has the weals to show for it.'

200

'Selina, we're not all like that,' cried Jasmine. 'I have to join in the games on Air Bare, because Phryne would be cross, otherwise, and the thought of buggery with her strap-on –' she shivered '– well, *you* know. I'll show you the real, *gentle* me.'

'Very well,' Selina said, 'although I'm not sure I want *too* gentle.'

She bit Jasmine's right nipple, and Jasmine squealed; then, began to tease Jasmine's breasts, flicking and squeezing the erect nipples.

'Mm!' Jasmine panted. 'That's so lovely ... but *do* you wank off with the other slags? Tell me the truth, Selina.'

There was silence, as the girls masturbated each other.

'It is hard to avoid relationships in here,' Selina said. 'Wanking is currency, like tobacco, and nobody likes a meanie. Understand, Jasmine?'

She pressed three fingers deep into Jasmine's soaking slit, and began to ream her wombneck. Jasmine wriggled, gasping, as come spurted from her cunt flaps.

'Yes ... but who?' she pleaded, as Selina's fingers caressed her soaking slit. 'I promise I shan't be jealous, but we must be truthful with each other.'

'That works both ways.'

'Of course.'

Selina suddenly withdrew from Jasmine's quim, and flung her arm at the sauna stove. A handful of come sprayed the stove, which hissed, with a fierce eruption of steam. The heat leapt in the sauna, and fresh sweat bubbled from the girls' pores.

'Oh, you minx!' Jasmine cried. 'I so adore you. Don't stop wanking me, please, please.'

Selina put her finger and thumb inside Jasmine's inner lips, and stretched them wide. The girl's fleshy cunt gaped, pink and wet, with the hard shiny clit standing free of its quimfolds. Selina barrelled all four fingers and thumb, and rammed them right to her wrist, inside the cunt. Jasmine moaned, gasping; Selina balled her fingers, and began to fist the squirming girl.

'Ooh, Selina,' Jasmine panted, 'no one's ever done that

to me! It's better than any man's sex organ. Is that what you slags do to each other?'

Her fingers slipped in and out of Selina's gash, with her thumb on the stiffening clitty. Come poured over each girl's wrist, as she masturbated the other, their bare bellies heaving, and breasts trembling, with nipples swollen and erect.

'One of the things,' Selina said.

Tweaking and pinching Jasmine's nipples, she lifted her bottom, so that Jasmine's free hand could squeeze under the bare, sweating buttocks. Selina clamped Jasmine's forefinger at her pucker, gasping, as Jasmine's finger penetrated her anal elastic.

'Go on,' Selina murmured. 'I like that.'

She wriggled, allowing Jasmine to poke all the way into her rectum, and squeezed her sphincter over her finger, as Jasmine began to ream her arse root. Selina slid her fingers from Jasmine's breasts, clawing all the way down her belly and thighs with her fingernails, and Jasmine moaned. Selina's hand slipped under the girl's thigh, and found the anus; she penetrated Jasmine's bumhole with a single finger, working it to the root of the rectum, and reaming hard, to stretch the anal walls; then, joined a second finger, and a third. Jasmine squealed, as three fingers stretched her anal elastic wide, with the fingernails jabbing at the rectal root. Fingers buried in each other's holes, and thighs enlaced, the two naked girls pressed their upper bodies together, as they poked each other. Jasmine's tongue hung between slack, drooling lips.

'It's so good, so special,' she gasped. 'Mm!'

Selina's lips pressed hers in a deep tongue-kiss, and their faces writhed together for over a minute.

'Let's kiss deeper,' murmured Selina, removing fist and fingers from Jasmine's holes, with a wet, plopping sound, and disengaging her anus from Jasmine's caress.

She held her fingers to her face, sniffed, then licked them.

'Mm . . .' she said. 'You taste nice, for a strapper.'

Jasmine sucked her own fingers, slimed with Selina's come and arse grease.

'Tease,' she panted.

Selina made Jasmine lie on her back, and straddled her, upended, with her shaven pubic hillock at Jasmine's face, and her own mouth poised over the glistening folds of Jasmine's cunt, wreathed in a lush tangle of sweaty pubic curls.

'You have the better bargain,' Selina murmured, parting Jasmine's buttocks, to plunge three fingers anew into her stretched anus. 'They say shaven gels taste nicer.'

'Who say?' Jasmine moaned, gasping, as Selina's full weight pressed her teats and belly.

'Boyfriends,' whispered Selina.

She stifled Jasmine's squeak of outrage, by chewing hard on her erect clitoris, then fastening her mouth over the whole cup of Jasmine's cunt lips, and sucking the clitoris and entire vulva into her mouth. Jasmine's hips wriggled, pinioned by Selina's weight, as Selina sucked come from her cunt, while jabbing her rectum with her three fingers. Selina herself gasped, as Jasmine's lips found her clitty, and began to suck; Selina parted her arse cheeks wide, and Jasmine's finger penetrated her anus, plunging deep into the rectum, followed by a second, then a third, finger. Wriggling, the two slippery bodies gahamuched, the silence broken by whimpers and moans, as come gushed from their sucked cunts, to flow down their squashed lower buttocks and perineums, mingling with their dripping sweat. After minutes, Selina changed her powerful cunt-sucking to a delicate, teasing nibble of Jasmine's clit,

'Ooh,' Jasmine gasped, 'you're so fabulous, I'm going to come any second . . . Oh, gosh, *yes*! Is this what you do to all your wanking chums?'

'Only a few,' said Selina, her lips slurping Jasmine's gushing come, and making little gulps with her throat, as she swallowed the love juice. 'There's Hardast – she's my best chum, but then, she's everybody's best chum. Kristel Gummi was my wank partner in dorm, but she went to the guesthouse last week – Dawn, Janet, Susan, of course. Well, Susan does everyone. I try and avoid Bethany, honestly, you have to spank her so hard, and then she snivels so much, as if that's her real pleasure. I miss Kristel – she has such a lovely, squelchy cooze, and a bottom to die for, but when a gel goes to be a guesthouse maid, we never see her again.'

'No strappers?'

'Not unless you count Miss Kew, and Phryne – *they* wank off, while thrashing me, knowing I'm a . . . I'm one of those gels who can orgasm just from a bare-bottom caning. With Phryne, it's the strap-on. She's buggered me quite a few times, after whipping me, then made me wank or tongue her cunny. They sneer that I'm a submissive, just because my bottom can take the cane, to orgasm. Surely other gels are the same?'

'The beasts! Just as long as you haven't wanked with that bitch Belinda Cream. I hate her. She is a ruthless nymphomaniac, and likes to make gels suffer, with her beastly enemas, before she . . . you know, diddles them.'

'Jasmine, don't tell me that you are chaste. You are free to have boyfriends, after all.'

'Never! I've been hurt too much. I admit that Avril, Tuppi and Kim and I sometimes pleasure ourselves – just wanking off, really, although we do practise bare-bum spanking while we wank. Bethany freely offers her bottom for weals, but she's *so* demanding. As for boys, who? That horrid oaf Hamish and his crew? I . . . I shouldn't tell you this, but there are rumours that Miss Gurdell has a pash for Hamish. Unrequited, I'm sure – what gel could stand penetration by that enormous sex organ, that he flaunts so impudently?'

The fingers of her free hand raked Selina's arse weals.

'You have been thrashed! Oh, you poor gel. These weals feel dreadfully fresh. Whoever gave you such a dreadful whipping?'

Selina did not answer, but renewed her sucking of Jasmine's whole cunt, with her tongue flicking the clitty against her teeth, inside her mouth.

'Oh . . . oh . . . yes . . .' Jasmine gasped, drinking Selina's come, as her tongue flickered on the girl's throbbing stiff clit. 'Your bumhole is so smooth, so elastic. You must have taken Phryne's strap-on a horrid number of times. Oh, I'm almost there ... suck me, Selina sweet, poke me and tongue me and squelch my cooze, drink my juice ...'

'Yes ... yes ...' Selina panted, her come gushing into Jasmine's lapping mouth. 'Oh, fuck my arse, please fuck my arse hard, split me open ...'

'Oh, oh, *ooh!*' squealed Jasmine. 'Ah ... ah ... I'm coming!'

Her belly heaved, and hips writhed, as come spurted from her cunt, in her groaning, shrieking orgasm.

'Bugger me Hamish, bugger me!' Selina moaned, her own belly shuddering, as her cunt spewed come. 'Split my bum with your cock! Fuck my arse, burst me, Hamish! Oh! Yes ...'

The two girls writhed, yelping, in their comes.

'*Hamish* buggered you? No!' whimpered Jasmine.

'Yes ... yes ... *yes!*' Selina shrilled, as she climaxed.

The girls did not move. Straddling Jasmine, Selina plopped her fingers from her anus, extended her arms, and clasped Jasmine's feet.

'Is it true that Hamish fucked you?' asked Jasmine, in a small voice.

'Yes,' said Selina. 'On his boat.'

'You filthy, depraved beast.'

'We promised to be honest with each other,' Selina murmured.

'Yes, but *that?*' whimpered Jasmine bitterly. 'I suppose you enjoyed it. That monstrous tool, gouging your rectum, filling your belly with his spunk – lots of it, I'll bet. He tawsed you, then? Made your naked bottom squirm under a savage lashing with the tongues?'

'I was caned, too,' Selina replied, 'and I took three cocks at once, I was fucked in my cunny and bumhole, while I sucked a third, and swallowed all his spunk. I was nude and helpless, whipped and fucked by three studs. I loved it, Jasmine.'

'Oh!' shrilled Jasmine. 'I suppose you concealed the truth about your wanks in prison, too. I'll bet you've diddled that beastly Belinda – how could a slut like you resist her luscious chocolate bum, those fabulous firm titties, that flat belly, and rippling thighs? Did she wank you off, with your belly full of her enema fluid? Did you drink her juice, from that silky wet pouch, the slit meat all pink inside and spurting come?'

'Don't be cross, Jasmine,' Selina pleaded, kissing her wet cunt.

'Oh ... I'm not cross,' sighed Jasmine. 'I'll have to report you, that's all.'

'But we are supposed to trust each other.'

'Not where absconding from prison is concerned. You went to Hamish's boat. You said so.'

'Oh, Jasmine, come off it.'

The door flew open.

'Come off what?' purred Belinda Cream. 'You, Selina? I'd know that bottom anywhere! And with some depraved slag, using surgery property for your vile pleasures? You disappoint me. No – don't look up, I don't want to see the lies in your face. That juicy arse has earned a juicy whopping.'

Behind the swimsuited nurse stood Hardast Bratt, in the nude, head bowed, and hands behind her back. Belinda picked up a birch sheaf.

'Take that, Selina, you dirty gel.'

Belinda's birch descended smartly on Selina's wet bare buttocks.

'Ooh ...' Selina moaned, her teeth fastening on Jasmine's cunt.

Jasmine shrilled, and her body bucked, but Selina's weight pinioned her helpless to the bench. *Swish! Swish!* Reddening, Selina's bottom began to clench, her cunt churning Jasmine's trapped face. *Swish! Swish!*

'Ohh!' Selina gasped.

Her naked buttocks squirmed, spraying droplets of mingled sweat and come. Belinda's body, teats and bottom bursting from her clinging one-piece white swimsuit, twirled on tiptoe, as she birched the naked girl. Selina's hands clutched Jasmine's feet, her fingernails clawing her soles, and her cunt basin slamming Jasmine's face, at each birch cut to the quivering bare nates, so that Jasmine moaned, writhing under her body. The birch lashed Selina's cunt and anus bud.

'Ahh!' Selina howled, smashing her chin against Jasmine's clitty.

Two strokes took her on the haunches. Belinda settled to a methodical flogging, lashing every inch of Selina's exposed bare, from underfesse to top buttock. The birch slapped with a wet hiss on the squirming buttocks, and a blotchy patchwork of delicate weals soon mottled Selina's wriggling bare fesses. Behind Belinda, Hardast watched with bright eyes, and her fingers rubbing at her naked vulva, which seeped come over her thighs. She licked her teeth, as she masturbated.

'Ouch! Oh,' Selina squealed, drooling into Jasmine's gash. 'Miss, mayn't I know my tariff?'

'Same as when we last squelched, Selina,' spat Belinda.

'No,' moaned Jasmine. 'You lied to me.'

Two strokes lashed Selina's bare back.

'Ahh,' she gasped. 'Not fair.'

Belinda birched buttocks, shoulders and mid-back, until Selina's body was a mass of red weals. Selina's head hung, buried in Jasmine's cunt, and her gasps became shriller and hoarser, as her body darkened with birch blossoms. The flogging continued to thirty-six strokes, until a cut to the perineum and cunt flaps made Selina double up in agony, and fall from the bench, to squirm on the floor, sobbing and clutching her birched cunt. Jasmine opened her eyes, misted with tears, and covered her quim with her hand, not enough to conceal the trickle of come oozing from her gash lips.

'A strapper!' Belinda gasped. 'What an ugly hairy minge! Why, Miss Wadd, you are in serious trouble – diddling with a felon on surgery property.'

Jasmine rose on her elbows.

'You filthy beast,' she hissed. 'You've wanked my Selina!'

She leapt from the bench, and flung herself on the African girl, with claws at her face. Belinda staggered, and went down; Jasmine straddled her, ripping off her swim-suit, to reveal the bare chocolate breasts, and bending, to bite savagely at the big brown nipples, while kneeing the nurse in the groin. Belinda groaned, flailing, and punching Jasmine's face. Jasmine's thighs were spread, over Be-linda's belly, and Belinda's fist snaked down to Jasmine's exposed gash, where she began to claw the vulva with fierce raking strokes of her fingernails. Jasmine howled, faltered, and Belinda was able to topple her. Her white swimsuit was ripped to shreds.

Belinda stood with her foot crushing Jasmine's face, while she methodically kicked the squirming, wailing girl in the cunt, and on her titties, which soon bruised purple. She ripped off the shreds of her swimsuit, and the two girls fought in the nude. They streamed with sweat, kicking, gouging, and biting, the naked combat interspersed with squeals of anguish. Belinda whirled back, and aimed savage kicks at the cunt of her opponent, her foot landing between the gash flaps with loud, squelching slaps, that had Jasmine shrieking and tottering, clutching herself. When Belinda moved close, Jasmine butted her, and bit hard on the black girl's nipples, shaking her head, with the stretched nipple between her teeth, and making Belinda squeal in agony. As their slippery nude bodies grappled, drops of sweat sprayed the stove, filling the sauna with the hiss of steam.

'You filthy bitch . . .'

'Slut . . .'

'Her bottom's mine, you bitch . . .'

'Mine, whore!'

Selina and Hardast caressed each other's bottom, while Hardast wanked off at the naked spectacle.

'She gave me three litres, the cow,' Hardast complained, casually diddling her clit. 'My arsehole and belly hurt like the dickens. And I had to tongue her clitty, while I held it in – I couldn't release the fluid until I had brought her off. She's so selfish!'

'Jasmine was going to put me on punishment,' Selina said bitterly. 'She's jealous of me wanking off Belinda.

Then I admitted Hamish had had me, you know, up the bum, and she went berserk.'

'Hamish is the best fuck I know,' said Hardast, 'and his cock has enough spunk for the whole prison. Jealousy is so lower class. Let's sort the bitches.'

She ceased diddling, and patted her cunt closed, then scampered naked towards the surgery, returning, moments later, with an armful of equipment. Both combatants were dripping with sweat, exhausted, and on their knees, titties pressing, as they took feeble swings at each other's cooze. Belinda's creamy chocolate quim hillock, shaven satin smooth, rubbed against Jasmine's ripe bush of hairs, as each girl's loins bucked, butting her opponent's pubic bone with a loud smack.

'They fancy each other,' sneered Hardast. 'Come on . . .'

Both naked combatants panted raucously, bare breasts heaving, come dripping from their bruised cunts, and slack mouths drooling, as Hardast and Selina hoisted them to the bench of the sauna, still damp and perfumed with Selina's and Jasmine's wanked come. Jasmine slumped in her former position, with the nude black girl on top of her, nose between Jasmine's thighs, and her shaven cunt on Jasmine's face. Hardast scooped come from their wet slits, and hurled it on the stove, jumping at the roar of steam. Jasmine's arms were stretched behind her head, and her wrists bound with layers of twine, while Belinda's hands were similarly bound, at the small of her back. Feeble moans of protest earned slaps to the buttock or face, although Belinda moaned but little, most of the protest coming from the oppressed Jasmine, crushed beneath the black girl's naked body. Quickly, Hardast cupped Belinda's massive, silky croup, binding each thigh in a girdle of thin steel strips, widening to a flange, which she passed beneath Jasmine's lolling neck. The girdle locked shut, Hardast began to tighten its screw, until Belinda's cunt basin was pressed against Jasmine's face, and she was helpless to move.

Selina did the same for Jasmine, strapping her thighs in the steel girdles, then looping the flange around Belinda's neck, so that the strapper's cunt and the African girl's head were locked immovably together. Hardast slipped her hand between cooze and mouth, and ordered each girl to put out her tongue. She clamped each fully-extended tongue in a tongue brank, obliging the tongue to remain rigidly extended. Hardast and Selina tightened the steel strips the remaining few notches, pressing the faces tightly into the open cunts, with each girl's tongue trapped inside the other's pouch, and her chin pressing her enemy's clitoris. Hardast propped two enema jars above the trapped victims, sucked on the tubes, and, with a powerful flow started, plunged a tube into each girl's anus, beside her opponent's mouth and nose, trapped in the gash.

'Ooh . . .'

'Nnnh . . .'

Belinda and Jasmine moaned, wriggling helplessly, as gravity forced the fluid into their rectums and bellies. At each jerk of their bodies, tongues probed slits, with a slop of gurgling come, and the girls gasped with pleasure. Hardast delved in her bundle, and withdrew a packet of cigarettes. She extracted two, lit them, and passed one to Selina. The two girls sucked smoke. With her cigarette dangling at the corner of her mouth, Hardast put her fingers to her cooze, and reopened her wet cunt flaps.

'My last gaspers – I've been saving these. Now I can have a really good wank, while you birch that strumpet Belinda,' Hardast said, thumbing her swollen red clitty.

She began to masturbate, with come spurting down her rippling bare thighs. Her own smoke dangling from her lips, Selina took Belinda's birch, with shaky fingers.

'I'm not sure I can . . .' she murmured, rubbing her glowing buttocks. 'Birching hurts so awfully . . . a strange, wonderful kind of pain, and my bottom ribbed with a thousand smarting weals, yet my cunny is wet. I'm not sure I don't need to masturbate.'

'Wank off, while you whop,' said Hardast. '*They* won't report us.'

Belinda was tongue-fucking Jasmine's cunt, and sucking her come, while Jasmine's crushed face gamahuched her oppressor's smooth bare quim and gushing slit. The bellies of both girls wriggled, as the enema jar seeped its contents into their rectums.

'Her bottom is so lovely,' said Selina. 'It would almost be sacrilege to mark her.'

'She's just birched you three dozen on the wet bare,' snorted Hardast.

'I rather deserved them.'

'Think how you've suffered, under her beastly enemas.'

'That's just it ... I've rather come to like it,' Selina replied, blushing. 'I love the full sensation, as the fluid fills my colon and caecum, and the lumps on my swollen belly. And she wanks me off so beautifully.'

'She's a nympho whore,' spat Hardast, smoking angrily. 'Look at her drink Jasmine's come. I bet it's *she* who runs the fags and crisps racket. *She* keeps us short, and exacts her price in wanks.'

'How interesting,' hissed Selina. 'I never have a smoke when I need one. Is it true, Miss Cream?'

'Mm! Mm!' Belinda squealed, waggling her head to say no; Jasmine gasped, as the black girl's tongue frotted her clitty.

'Fibber,' murmured Selina, wiping the sweat that poured from her brow and breasts, as she raised her birch over Belinda's bare chocolate buttocks.

She sliced the black girl squarely on mid-fesses, following the first stroke with three more, in hard succession, on the same weal, which flared rapidly to a glowing puce colour.

'Uhh ... uh ...' Belinda gasped, her birched bottom wriggling over Jasmine's trapped face. Selina thrashed Belinda's haunches.

'*Mm! Mm!*' gurgled the flogged nurse, her naked buttocks quivering like dark velvet jellies.

Belinda's bottom clenched, and began to squirm, the livid fesses pressed together in a hair line. Selina stood with legs parted in a fencer's stance, her breasts quivering, as she birched the squirming black bare, glistening with sweat.

211

'Mm! Uhh . . .'

Belinda's bottom was striping vividly with the vein-like weals of birching, and Selina applied strokes to the meaty thigh backs, then to her back, on the rippling dark flesh, framed by Belinda's bound arms.

'Make the bitch wriggle,' murmured Hardast, masturbating vigorously, and licking her bared teeth.

'Urrgh . . .' Belinda groaned.

At each birch cut, her head, wrenching against its metal brank, slammed Jasmine's cunt, and her mouth twitched, as her embedded tongue frotted the girl's slit. Come dripped from Jasmine's tongued pouch, sliming her haunches and buttocks, and pooling on the bench beneath her jerking bum, while copious come dripped from Belinda's bright pink gash meat, into Jasmine's mouth, with the crushed girl working desperately to swallow the oily cooze juice.

'How many?' Selina asked Hardast.

'Until I've come, of course.'

Hardast fetched the empty water bucket, and placed it under Belinda's buttocks; at once, the bucket began to fill, with a steady drip of girl come.

'It's so hot,' Selina said.

'That's the fun,' replied Hardast. 'Your nude body all lovely and slippery. Here . . .'

As Selina raised her birch, Hardast's free hand entered Selina's wet gash, and she gasped, as the girl's fingers began to rub her throbbing clitty. The birch lashed Belinda's bare twice.

'Uhh!' the girl sobbed, bottom wriggling, and her face working between Jasmine's twitching cunt flaps.

As Hardast masturbated her, Selina continued to birch Belinda across the entire buttock flesh, with sideswipes to her back and shoulders, and every fifth cut at the vertical, lashing her on perineum and anal pucker, the tip of the birch striking just short of Jasmine's tongue, locked in the black girl's cunt. Both victims squirmed, squealing, with their come dripping copiously into the pail, until Hardast swooped to grab it, and spray the contents over the stove.

There was a fierce hiss, and a jet of steam, and heat washed their sweating bodies. Hardast's fingers penetrated Selina's cooze, right to the wombneck, and began a vigorous fingerfuck, with her thumb tweaking Selina's stiff clitty.

'Ooh . . .' Selina moaned, sinking her fingers between the folds of Hardast's own hot soaking cunt.

The two girls masturbated, while Selina birched the writhing Belinda, whose groans became shriller.

'I do believe the cow's going to come,' Hardast panted.

The girls wanked hard, as birchstrokes rained on the squirming black bare of the African. Jasmine, too, groaned shrilly and repeatedly, until both she and Belinda erupted in staccato squeals.

'Mm! Mm! Mm . . . *uhh!*' Belinda gurgled.

Come gushed from their cunts, and their slippery bodies writhed, pressing flesh to flesh, as they orgasmed. Selina laid two strokes on Belinda's top buttock, as the black girl shook in orgasm.

'Oh, yes, Hardast, do me, I'm coming . . .' gasped Selina.

'*Yes* . . .' Hardast squealed.

Selina dropped the birch, and turned, to clasp Hardast's wet bottom, clawing and stroking it, with her fingernails at Hardast's twitching bum pucker. Hardast's palm cupped Selina's buttocks, brushing over her birch weals, then getting her nails into the puffy ridges of her welts, and stabbing Selina's bruised red bumflesh.

'Oh! *Yes* . . .' Selina gasped, as come poured from her cooze, over Hardast's wanking fingers.

'*Mm* . . .' groaned Hardast, her belly fluttering, as her cunt clamped Selina's fist. '*Ooh* . . .'

Their lips met, with Hardast's tongue deep in Selina's throat, as the girls shuddered together in orgasm. Panting and heaving, they let their comes ebb, and withdrew fingers from cunts with a squelchy plop, while surveying their squirming prisoners. Hardast released the girls from their branks, and lifted Belinda, squealing, by her hair, to a sitting position, while Selina released Jasmine.

'Oh! I hate you!' Jasmine hissed at Selina.

'I'll have my revenge on you, slut,' spat Belinda.

The two girls' eyes met. Belinda smiled, then flung her arm around Jasmine's shoulders, pulling the blonde towards her, and pressed her lips to hers, in a deep French kiss. Their naked breasts quivered, pressing and rubbing, and hands caressed bare croups. Both cunts dripped copious come, filling the bucket. Suddenly, Jasmine broke the clench, and sprang on Belinda, toppling her to the floor, with her face down. Jasmine sat on the small of her back and, holding Belinda's head down by the neck, began to furiously spank the naked black buttocks.

'You bitch, you absolute rotter . . .' she drooled, spittle spraying from her slack lips, as come spurted from her cunt, to trickle down Belinda's quivering flanks. 'You . . . the tuck mistress. I suspected Phryne, but never a nurse.'

'It's a lie,' wailed Belinda, her bare bum squirming, and her cunt slapping the floor, as spanks mottled her birch-wealed buttocks. 'Miss Kew is the tuck mistress. Who else could it be, but that scheming bitch?'

Selina stooped, to throw the bucket's contents on the stove, obscuring the sauna in a cloud of steam. Hardast and Selina tiptoed out, with Hardast giggling, as she locked the pair inside, with a wooden bar stuck through the handle. They padded to the changing room, to retrieve their uniforms.

'Who *is* the tuck mistress?' asked Selina, grimacing, as she carefully pulled her panties over her brightly wealed bottom.

'Who cares?' said Hardast. 'It's nearly time for tea. Have one?'

From her shirt pocket, she pulled a soggy packet of prawn cocktail flavoured crisps. As the whack-whack-whack of bare-bottom spanking made the sauna's walls vibrate, Belinda's voice cooed:

'Come on, Jasmine, do me properly. You can spank harder than that . . . mm, I love how your pube hairs tickle. Your cunt is so wet and chewy, sweeter than any other gel's, and your bottom is a dream.'

'You mean that? I'm so glad,' Jasmine panted. 'You've always been special to me, Belinda. I've longed to be your best friend, as I masturbate, dreaming of your lovely bare bum, only I'm . . . I'm so afraid of getting hurt . . .'

14

The Birch Bucket

Gwendoline reclined on her couch, sipping from a glass of orange juice, proffered by her maid Susan. The girl was barefoot and nude, save for a filmy gauze wrap around her naked breasts. Her bottom, brightly-painted in blue woad, swayed, as she served her mistress. Gwendoline perched on her elbows, nipple rings dangling from her breasts, while another painted, bare-bottomed disciple, Arioma, rubbed scented cream into her buttocks and thighs. Two more bare-bottomed wenches, Hardast and a pouting Bethany, escorted Selina Rawe before the governess. They made Selina kneel in obeisance, then curtsied, and resumed attendance, bottoms facing the governess.

'Rise, Selina,' Gwendoline purred. 'You may divest yourself of clothing.'

'Strip, Miss?' said Selina.

'Of course. Don't be shy, gel. Bare your bottom and balcony, please.'

Selina began to undress, first removing her shoes and socks, then her blouse, from which her braless teats sprang firm. Finally, she slid from her shorts, with a slow, sticky peeling of her panties thong. She stood nude, cunt facing Gwendoline, with hands on hips.

'Turn around,' Gwendoline commanded.

With a moue, Selina did so, and the governess gasped.

'Are those birch marks, Selina?' said Miss Gurdell.

'Do they still show, Miss?' gulped Selina. 'Why . . . Miss Kew whips very hard, Miss.'

'Miss Kew does not use the birch,' said Gwendoline. 'I know birch marks – I was birched once, on the bare, at school.'

She shivered.

'I'm sorry, governess,' Selina blurted. 'Sometimes you don't see, when bending over, and a bare-bum whopping hurts so much, a gel gets confused.'

'Come here, let me touch.'

Her fingers stroked Selina's proffered bottom.

'Birch marks fade slowly,' she murmured, 'yet leave a delicious mottled pattern, quite unmistakable. Such deep weals! How it must have hurt.'

'Yes, Miss,' blurted Selina, 'but my bottom is thrashed so much, that I can't be sure who administered that particular punishment. Sometimes I'm hooded, and several strappers have a go.'

'How barbaric,' said Gwendoline. 'Does Miss Kew know?'

'Miss Kew orders it, Miss,' replied Selina.

'Well, we must keep the lower gels in order. Arioma, relinquish the ointment to Selina, so that she may massage me.'

Selina took the jar and, straddling Gwendoline's buttocks, began to rub unguent into her shoulders.

'Mm . . . that's good,' Gwendoline sighed. 'I have invited you, Selina, because your magnificent bottom is not truly that of a lower gel. As my disciple, you would enjoy bounteous privilege. Susan, Arioma, Hardast – even dear, oppressed Bethany – have acceded. Bethany burst into tears, until I would accept her, and I cannot stand a gel crying. If your bottom pleases me, during your visit, I shall consider the matter.'

'Permit me to prove my bottom, Miss,' Selina murmured.

Selina climbed onto Gwendoline's couch. She plunged her fingers in the jar, and smeared large gobbets of cream across her bare bottom. Then, bending backwards, she positioned herself in a crab, her body supported by hands and feet, and lowered her croup onto Gwendoline's

216

buttocks. Hips writhing, in a wide arc, Selina massaged the governess's bare bottom with her own, her cheeks clenching, to rub the cream into Gwendoline's bum cleft, which opened, spreading her perineum wide, while her disciples stared, blushing, at Selina's open gash flaps, and pink slit meat. Selina's cunt basin pumped up and down, as her buttocks slimed Gwendoline's croup with unguent. Gwendoline's face flushed, and she shifted on her couch, pressing her breasts against her nipple rings, with the pierced nipples stiffening, as she squirmed under Selina.

'Mm,' Gwendoline murmured, 'how cool and fresh your buttocks feel, despite their basting by a cruel birch! I well remember the shame of my own birching, before the whole school – so dreadful to relate, but I feel I must, if you would like me to.'

Her disciples begged her to relate the dreadful story.

'I had to mount the headmistress's dais,' said Gwendoline, sighing, 'and kneel at the flogging block, then lift my pleated grey skirt, and show my knickers. That's what worried me, for instead of the regulation navy blue undies, to match our stockings, I was wearing a lovely pink set, with a floral pattern. "Unseemly costume!" said the head. "That will double your punishment, miss. You shall now receive twenty-four strokes, on the bare. You have let the school down – you have let down every gel in school." I was quaking, and close to tears, ashamed of letting the gels down, and I knew I deserved my punishment. The head prefect ripped my knickers off, tearing them in two, and ordered me to unfasten my garter straps, and fully remove my suspender belt. My bottom and thighs were completely naked, above my stocking tops, exposed to the whole school. I could feel goose pimples on my bared buttocks. "Gwendoline, you have been caught with illicit tuck – a pound of quails' eggs – with the further offence of wearing unseemly underthings, and have earned twenty-four strokes of the birch, on your bare bottom," the headmistress said. "Have you anything to say, before the head of school carries out sentence?" I was trying not to sob, and shook my head – the birch was pressed to my lips, and

I had to kiss it – and my birching began. Oh! The pain was so horrid, I thought I should wet myself. The tongues of the birch spread across my fesses like worms of white-hot metal, and at each kiss of the birch, my bottom wriggled horribly, slamming my tummy against the wooden block.'

Selina summoned another cream pot. The governess lay on her back, to watch the sweating Selina daub the whole potful of cream onto her bare breasts. Selina lowered herself over the governess, and pressed her breasts against her nipple rings, beginning a firm, slow massage of Gwendoline's naked breasts with her own.

'Ohh ... mm ...' Gwendoline panted. 'That birching was so horrid! I counted the strokes, up to twelve, then gave up. It seemed as if the dreadful swish of the twigs, and the awful pain, as they crackled on my naked bottom, would never end. The birch! I was used to bare-bottom caning, a quick swishing of six, or a dozen, but the smarting *vip-vip* of the cane is nothing compared to the horror of the birch on the naked buttocks. It seems to creep and crawl into every crevice of pain imaginable, and after the first shock of smarting, just when you think it is ebbing, a second wave of throbbing, smarting agony washes over the bare. The school was quite hushed, in awe. Tears streamed down my cheeks, and I couldn't help crying out, with a gasping wail, every time the wood streaked my bare bottom. The hall was silent, save for the swish of the birch, its crack on my bare, and my gasps of agony. As they lashed my flesh, birch twigs splintered from the stock, and cascaded over my squirming bottom. At last, it was over, and I had to kiss the birch once more, the twigs half denuded, and pull down my skirt, remaining knickerless, with my unstrapped stockings sagging, for extra shame. How it hurt, the slightest touch of cloth on my flaming bottom, whose weals were so fierce and ribbed, I could feel them through the pleats of my skirt. I hobbled back to my seat, naked under my skirt, my face scarlet and wrinkled in agony, and with my tears streaming, although I have to say it was quite thrilling to be bare-bum, without panties – that lovely feeling of air on your bare cunny and bottom.'

Selina wriggled down Gwendoline's belly, smearing it with cream. Gwendoline parted her thighs, revealing her gash, pink and moist. Selina began to massage her open quim lips, and her trimmed pubic lawn, with the erect, cream-topped tips of her nipples. Her left teat delved between Gwendoline's spread cunt flaps, and the nipple touched the stiffening pink clitoris; Gwendoline gasped, wriggling her buttocks.

'Ooh ... when we were dismissed, I rushed to the lavatory, and tore off my skirt, to douse my bottom in cold water. A throng of gels followed me, and wouldn't stop touching my bottom, and at their gasps of admiration, I let them do it, enjoying the feel of gels' fingers caressing my horrid red welts, all ribbed and crusty. I saw that the gels touching me had their skirts up, and were also touching themselves, down there, with their fingers inside their panties. I was excited to be bare-bum, while they touched me there, on my secret place, and stroked my birched bottom, and I became very wet, and, well, the gels' fingers in my wet cunny brought me to a ... a lovely experience!'

Selina's bare breasts rubbed cream into Gwendoline's wet slit, kneading her fully erect clitoris.

'So, no matter how harsh or merited the punishment of a bare bottom, there is always joy at the end of it,' Gwendoline panted. 'Oh, yes, Selina ...'

Selina switched position, and placed her naked spread gash, and parted bum cheeks, before Gwendoline's face, so that her shaven quim was inches from the governess's face, while her shaven breasts continued their kneading of Gwendoline's gushing bare slit.

'How full your shaven cunny is,' gasped the governess, 'so smooth and shiny, like porcelain, with those lovely juicy lips winking at me, all moist and glistening ... and your perfect curving peach – oh, I must taste you, Selina.'

Her hands caressed Selina's bare bum, drawing the buttocks closer to her face. Selina lowered her bottom, straddling the governess, until Gwendoline's mouth was on her cunt, and her nose penetrated Selina's anus. Selina's breasts were washed in come, from the governess's gushing slit, as she flicked the erect clitty with one nipple, then the other, pausing to press hard, and squash Gwendoline's gash flaps with both cream-slimed breasts. The unguent soaked into Gwendoline's cunt, making her wet slit lips glisten, as her juice spurted from her pouch, over Selina's breasts. Gwendoline moaned, as her tongue began to lick Selina's quim lips, pressing the clitty, which made Selina gasp in response, with a shiver of her buttocks, her come-slimed bum cleft writhing on Gwendoline's face. She arched her back, sliding her breasts up onto Gwendoline's squirming belly, and began to tongue the governess's wet quim. Selina chewed Gwendoline's swollen slit lips, then sucked, with the whole vulva in her mouth, flicking the clit with her tongue. Her throat fluttered, swallowing the come she sucked from Gwendoline's writhing cunt.

'Mm ...' gasped Gwendoline, her lips squelching on Selina's swollen wet gash, as her nose reamed the anus pucker, and her palms clamped Selina's quivering bare bum; her teeth brushed Selina's erect nubbin.

'Ooh ...' Selina groaned, mashing Gwendoline's cunt between her lips.

'Wank me, wank me,' whispered Gwendoline. 'Oh, my disciples, let me worship your bottoms.'

Arioma, Hardast, Bethany and Susan proffered their bares, inches from Gwendoline's crushed face. Her hands played over each bottom in turn, caressing and stroking, with fingers delving between the girl's thighs, into their pouches and anal crevices. The girls waggled their bums, teasing their governess, and trapping her fingers with their cunt lips or arse clefts. Their own fingers played over the squirming bare orbs of Selina's bottom, clawing and pinching her fading birch welts into new, puffy redness. Selina groaned, squirming, as come gushed from her cunt, slopping over Gwendoline's face. Giggling, and red-faced, the girls began to masturbate, as they played with Selina's glowing bottom: their free hands parting their quim lips, to reveal glistening pink flesh, and tweaking the stiffening bulbs of their clitties. Susan grasped an empty cream pot, and flicked her clitoris against its rim, so that the jar rapidly filled with her spurted come. The chamber filled with the coos and panting of the naked, masturbating girls. Gwendoline's gurgles, as she swallowed the come streaming from Selina's cunt, grew shriller.

'Ooh . . . mm . . . yes . . .' she groaned.

Her belly fluttered against Selina's breasts, as come spurted from her pouch.

'Oh! Oh! *Yes* . . .'

Gwendoline clawed Arioma's and Hardast's bums. Her cunt and belly heaved, as she gushed come, in a long, twitching orgasm, accompanied by shrill yelps, muffled by Selina's buttocks, pumping on her face. Arioma and Hardast winced at the long weals scratched by the governess's fingernails in their buttocks.

'Ooh . . . ahh . . . ooh . . .' Gwendoline's shrieks ebbed, and she removed her hands from the girls' bottoms, gently prising Selina's arse off her face. She wriggled from Selina's cunt, and peeked, scarlet-faced, from under her belly.

'We've been naughty, gels,' she gasped, through lips slack with come and drool, dripping down her glazed chin. 'We must all be spanked for our naughtiness, and none more so than I. I'm so ashamed. I've let the school down.'

The girls lined up, bending over Gwendoline's couch, and each took her turn at spanking the others, their bare bottoms upthrust, fluttering like petals, as they reddened under slapping palms. Each girl masturbated, as she was spanked. Gwendoline sat on her couch, knees primly together, and her hand under the seat of Selina's bare bottom, fingering her anus and pendant, hairless cunt flaps. Lazily, she overturned Selina, and began to spank her bare bottom. Her thighs were parted, with her fingers at her quim, tweaking her swollen clit, with come wetting the couch, beneath her gash. Her spanking of Selina's bare was rapturous, as she masturbated. At her murmured command, the girls ceased spanking; they knelt, each displaying her glowing bare bum, reddened by over a hundred spanks. When she had spanked Selina to a glow, while frotting herself to overflowing wetness, Gwendoline ordered them to rise.

'Now you must spank *me*,' she gasped.

She knelt before each girl's naked cunt, in turn, kissing the shaven pubes and cooze lips, and cupping the buttocks in her hand, while she masturbated.

'Bottoms,' she whispered, 'so pure and smooth ... I know you all. Bethany, like firm young apples; Hardast, apricots; Arioma, a ripe peach; Susan, twin plums ...'

Her tongue flickered between their thighs, licking the dew from the fresh bare cunts of the trembling maids. Their bottoms shivered, as she tickled their spanked arse meat, probing cleft, anus and cooze.

'You, Selina, have the finest, ripest melons,' Gwendoline purred, through come-glazed lips.

She stroked Selina's bare, pressing her nose into the wet slit flesh, until her face dripped with Selina's come. Rising, Gwendoline lay face down on her long, low coffee table, her naked buttocks thrust upwards, with an inch between her pubic lawn and the glass tabletop.

'Like every gel, I need spanking,' she murmured. 'Hold me down, my disciples, crush me with your bottoms, while my fesses pay the price of my naughtiness.'

The girls squatted on Gwendoline, their bottoms pinioning her to the glass tabletop. Selina sat on her fanned hair, while Susan rose, to commence the spanking of her mistress. She stood over Gwendoline's trembling bare fesses, cheeks parted, and her hand fell, smartly cracking on the naked bum. *Slap!* Gwendoline gasped, then gasped again, as the second spank took her, then the third. *Slap! Slap! Slap!* Susan quickened her spanking, her breasts swaying and heaving, as she chastised the wriggling bare buttocks, and Gwendoline's breath became short, rasping pants.

'Ooh! Yes ...' she moaned. 'It tickles so!'

Her head shook from side to side, pulling her hair beneath Selina's quim. Susan panted hard, as she spanked; her free hand touched her own bottom. Slap! Slap! Susan's face was crimson, as she spanked her own bare buttocks. She continued spanking both her own arse and Gwendoline's, until her bare glowed as red as her blonde victim's, and her place was taken by Hardast, who commenced the same double spanking, slapping her own bare, as well as the squirming governess's. Gwendoline writhed, panting hoarsely, as her bum darkened from crimson to puce, and Bethany sulkily took over her spanking, with her spanks to her own bare louder than those to Gwendoline's; then, it was Arioma's turn.

Gwendoline gasped, squirming, for over an hour, tongue lolling from slack, drooling lips, and her bum blotched with dark palm prints. Her cunt slithered, in the come spurting from her gash. The girls, sitting on her to pinion her to the table, raised their bums, to spank themselves. Selina rubbed her quim and clitty on Gwendoline's blonde tresses, while spanking herself hard, on her own naked buttocks. As her bum reddened with slaps, her cunt soaked Gwendoline's hair in come.

'Now, you, Selina . . .' Gwendoline panted.

Selina rose, wrenching away Gwendoline's thick tresses, gummed to her cunt. Blushing, with come trickling down her rippling thighs, she took up her spanker's stance, at Gwendoline's bottom.

'You must really spank me, really punish me,' whimpered the governess. 'A naughty gel deserves it.'

She began a fierce spanking, making the bum quiver and clench at each impact, with Gwendoline gasping. Selina's hard spanks slammed Gwendoline's vulva to the glass tabletop, where it slithered in a pool of her oily come, with the nipple rings clanking, as they bit into her squashed titties. Selina's breasts trembled, swaying, as her palm smacked the glowing bare orbs, and her mouth opened wide, with her eyes briefly shutting, as she spanked her own bottom. Come sprayed from her quivering cunt flaps. She took Gwendoline past fifty, the squirming naked bottom glowing in its dark patchwork of bruises; past a hundred, and a hundred and fifty. Gwendoline's glowing bare wriggled furiously, as the girls, spanking their own nates, struggled to hold her down on the come-slimed tabletop. Selina's wet slit gushed an oily torrent of come, dripping down her thighs and calves, to squelch beneath her bare feet. She paused only to wipe the sweat from her eyes, as the other girls masturbated vigorously, their bums crimson from self-spanking.

'Oh, yes, Harriet Purse said you were the best,' Gwendoline gasped. 'She said your magnificent bottom meant you were the cruellest of wenches.'

'What? You know *Harriet*, Miss?'

'Did I say . . .?'

Selina stooped, and tugged Gwendoline's left nipple ring, wrenching her breast. Gwendoline's face crinkled in pain.

'Ouch! Oh! Stop it! That hurts!' she squealed.

'Tell me the truth, Miss,' panted Selina, twisting both nipple rings hard. 'You, Harriet – what's going on?'

'Oh, stop,' sobbed Gwendoline, writhing, with her nipples stretched to white strips. 'Harriet and I are old school chums. We were at Royal Saltdean Girls' Academical together, with Auntie Ros, and that's where we learned to bare up for caning, actually. Well, Harriet told me you'd been banged up, for your naughty games as Miss Whippham, and Gawain Breasted told me about your super bottom, and Pippa and Leofra said you were the nicest bum they'd ever spanked, and I must keep you here, on any pretext, after your sentence, if I wanted Home Office promotion, and . . . oh, Selina, don't be cross with me.'

Faces red as their spanked bottoms, the girls glowered at her.

'I rather think I *am* a bit cross,' Selina said.

'Spanking's too good for her,' murmured Hardast.

'She needs the cane,' added Bethany.

'Or a lovely birching,' Arioma purred. 'But where to find a birch?'

'From the governess's secret birch bucket, of course,' said Susan, opening Gwendoline's armoire.

From a bucket of water in the lower part of the armoire, she withdrew a long, thick sheaf of birch rods, and handed it to Selina.

'You've been set up, gel,' she said. 'I dare say we all have.'

'Surely not the birch . . .' Gwendoline whimpered, as Selina swished the rods above her bottom. 'Why, birching is illegal. Haven't I been punished enough?'

'You have disrespected us, Miss,' Selina said gravely. 'You deserve birching.'

'Yes, I suppose I do,' Gwendoline purred, licking her lips. 'It'll hurt my poor bare quite awfully.'

Hardast pushed a broom handle through Gwendoline's nipple rings and, fastening ropes to each end, drew her up to vertical, the bare breasts wrenched white, and Gwendoline whimpering with pain. Arioma and Bethany each grasped an ankle, stretching her legs in the splits, while Susan thrust a heavy bolster under Gwendoline's quim, pushing her buttocks up for the birch. Her cunt pressed the edge of the table, with her legs splayed on either side, and her buttocks completely spread, showing her full quim and anus cleft, while the teat-hobble raised her high enough to perch on her fingertips, and support her weight thus, although the naked bubbies remained stretched.

'Oh, I'm so uncomfortable . . .' moaned the governess. 'You will birch me gently, Selina?'

'Certainly not,' Selina spat.

'Thank you,' she murmured.

Selina lifted her birch. The twigs lashed the upthrust naked buttocks, which clenched, as Gwendoline shuddered.

'Ouch,' she gasped. 'Ooh, it hurts!' Gwendoline's thrashed bottom squirmed and wriggled, as pink blotches began to etch themselves across the taut bare fesse meat. Selina panted, titties bouncing, as she birched, taking the strokes past a dozen, then past a second dozen, with Gwendoline's bottom striping darker and redder, the tiny imprints of the birch twigs forming a livid mosaic on her pink satin bum flesh. Gwendoline's face was bright red, and her titties wrenched on their nipple rings, as her stretched torso shuddered under the flogging to the bare buttocks. Come dripped from her spread gash, into a shiny pool on the glass tabletop.

'Pity it's not done to birch on the back,' said Selina, 'for you deserve it.'

Swish! The blotched fesses writhed.

'Ohh!' Gwendoline gasped. 'It hurts so much on my bare! Flog my back if you must . . . if only I could watch my bottom, as you birch me! The full roundness of my fesses, quivering in torment, as the sweet blossoms swell on my whipped nates, and colour my skin with delicious red petals. No sight in the world is so beautiful as a gel's naked buttocks well thrashed, her most private, loveliest secret swellings exposed, shamed and tickled by a stern rod, conducting her symphony of tears. And the birch . . . oh, sublime torture, its crackling twigs the cruellest and most superb lover – under its deadly, knowing swish, a gel's buttocks clench and shiver, each fesse wickedly pocked by the cruellest of twigs. Birch me . . . birch me!'

Gwendoline's bare nates shuddered. As Selina flogged the girl's squirming arse globes, the four disciples masturbated openly, cooing with pleasure, as they wanked their open, dripping cunts.

'Oh!' whimpered Gwendoline. 'Thank you, Selina . . . Harriet was too squeamish to birch me, and said that *you* would, that you were cruel . . .'

Come gushed from her writhing gash, with Susan holding a cream pot below the lips, collecting the rapid plink-plink of come drops. She raised the filled pot, drank, and offered it to the others. Wiping the sweat from her face and breasts, Selina drank briefly from the pot, then raised the birch over Gwendoline's buttocks, spread and thrusting upwards, inviting the kiss of the rods.

'Ohh! Yes . . . it hurts like fire. Hamish's cane and Miss Kew's thwangs can never raise welts like these. Pippa and Leofra and Harriet were so right – you are an utter bitch, dearest Selina!'

Selina's face paled.

'*No one* says that to me,' she blurted, lifting her birch in both hands, and lashing Gwendoline's bum cleft, with the tips crackling on the dripping bare lips of her gash.

'*Ahh!*' Gwendoline shrieked. 'Oh . . . oh . . .'

With an upender, Selina whipped her between the cooze flaps, the rods sizzling on the wet pink gash meat.

'*Ohh!* Uh . . . uh . . .' Gwendoline drooled, her arse wriggling frantically, and come spurting from her birched cunt.

Selina returned to the wriggling buttocks, birching so savagely, that twigs began to split and crack from the birch sheaf. All four disciples wanked off, spanking themselves, with resounding slaps to their waggling bare bums, cooing in delight, as they watched the squirming buttocks darken to a blotchy, wriggling mass of purple weals, like insects crawling over the flogged skin. After seventy lashes of the birch, the instrument was denuded and unusable. Selina stood, panting, while Susan fetched from the armoire a strap-on dildo, its shaft sculpted in black rubber, to resemble an erect cock, two hands long, and a wrist thick.

'Miss Gurdell uses it when Hamish isn't available,' she murmured. 'She likes cock in gash.'

'I'll give the slut Hamish,' Selina snarled. '*Full bung.*'

'Ohh . . .' Gwendoline moaned.

Bethany and Hardast strapped the dildo to Selina's loins, while Susan oiled it with come from their victim's cooze. Selina squatted, bringing the dildo's tip to the pucker of Gwendoline's wriggling anus bud.

'No, please, not in my bumhole,' gasped the governess, writhing in her bonds, with her breasts jerked savagely by her nipple hobble.

With one thrust, Selina plunged the come-slimed dildo into Gwendoline's anus.

'Ahh! It hurts!'

A second thrust, and the tool penetrated Gwendoline to her rectum's root, the black rubber disappearing into the anus, save for its ball globes. Selina began to bugger the girl, slamming the dildo at each stroke of her loins, and drawing shrill cries from the wriggling victim, impaled on the giant rubber shaft, dripping with her own arse grease.

'You're splitting me in two. I'm bursting. Oh, no . . .' Gwendoline wailed, her buttocks pumping in the rhythm of Selina's thrusts, as the rubber balls slapped her bottom.

Come sprayed from her writhing cunt, as Selina continued the brutal arse-fucking for over six minutes.

'Ah . . . ah . . .' Gwendoline whimpered. 'My bumhole's raw . . . harder . . . bugger me, fuck me till I burst, split me . . . oh, yes, yes!'

Come spurted from her cunt, as she gasped, then yelped, in a shuddering orgasm, that made her nipple rings clash.

'Ooh . . . uhh . . . spank me . . .' Gwendoline drooled. 'My bottom wants more . . .'

The chamber resounded to cracks, as the girls spanked her birched bottom, which wriggled, until her orgasm ebbed, and she drooped in her nipple hobble, gasping and sighing. The four disciples masturbated in a huddle, quims and bubbies pressed close, while they wanked each other off, with eager, slimy fingers. The air filled with their shrieks of climax, as come spurted thickly over their shivering bare thighs. Selina pressed her dildo deeper into Gwendoline's rectum, leaning on the girl's buttocks, while she flicked her clitty with the ball globes, and masturbated herself. At only three touches of her clitty, she came. Her gasps joined those of the wanking girls; in the throes of her climax, Selina jerked her hips, and recommenced buggering Gwendoline's bum. As she buggered, she picked up her birch, and began to flog Gwendoline's quivering haunches. There was a thunderous knocking; the disciples separated, and crouched in the corners of the room, while the door flew open, and Miss Kew stood, stroking one palm with the shiny leather thwangs of her Scots tawse. Her birch caressing Gwendoline's haunch, and dildo plunged in her bumhole, Selina looked round, brushing stray tresses from her brow.

'Oh . . .' she said, 'Miss Kew.'

'Infamy,' hissed the discipline mistress.

'Please, Miss,' squealed Bethany. 'It wasn't us. She said she'd bash us in, if we tried to stop her.'

'She's vicious,' said Arioma.

'Absolutely feral,' added Hardast.

'I see,' snapped Miss Kew. 'You may seize the miscreant, gels. Birching – forbidden by Home Office regulations – buggery, ditto – assault on the person of the governess, ditto. Only one punishment is appropriate.'

'Miss Gurdell wanted –' Selina began, silenced, as Hardast clamped her lips.

'You are for *the works*, miss,' spat Miss Kew. 'Escort the slut to my office, gels.'

Selina was hustled out. Miss Kew thrust a cream pot under Gwendoline's dripping quim, and waited several seconds, as it filled. She flung it over Gwendoline's bare, rubbing the moisture into the glowing, wealed arse melons.

'Wet bum, you cheeky bitch,' she drawled.

Lifting her tawse, she dealt a single savage swish to Gwendoline's naked buttocks. The leather thongs cracked on Gwendoline's birched bare, and she squealed. Miss Kew paused, to rub the weal her thongs had raised. Then, tawse between her teeth, she stripped off her blouse, skirt and boots, unhooked her black scalloped bra, allowing her tan titties to sway bare. She rolled down her thong panties, and stood nude, but for her black stockings and sussies framing her shaven quim. She lifted the tawse high over her head. Gwendoline's arse melons clenched, quivering, as the leather tongues lashed her naked bumskin. She groaned.

'I believe you wanted *more*, trollop?' said Miss Kew, palm caressing her nut-brown nipples.

She squeezed each of her nipples between finger and thumb, until the brown berries were swollen stiff, then rubbed the tawse thongs across her cunt mound, the tongues passing between her olive gash flaps, caressing the pink wet slit flesh inside her winking pouch. Her extruded clitty nestled, hugely erect, between the upper folds of her cunt lips, and she gasped, with a little shiver, as the tawse thongs touched her there. She caressed her own bare arse melons with the tawse; licking her teeth, she raised the oily leather. Miss Kew whipped herself on the bare, for over two minutes, while Gwendoline's bare bum quivered below her. Come squirted from Miss Kew's naked cunt, as her bum clenched and reddened.

'See what you've made me do,' she hissed, showing her wealed buttocks.

'Oh, Miss,' whimpered Gwendoline, 'Please don't be cross . . .'

'I'm not cross, governess,' hissed Miss Kew. 'I'm going to tawse you to the bone.'

She stood, panting, for moments, masturbating her clitty with a finger, and stroking her wealed bumskin. She lifted the tawse. The tongues lashed Gwendoline's birch-raw buttocks.

'Oh! Thank you,' Gwendoline gasped.

'Sleep well, Selina?'

'I was too excited, Miss,' Selina murmured, biting her lip. 'It would be jolly hard to sleep, thinking of . . . you know.'

Morning sunbeams slanted through the windows of the surgery. Selina stood before Belinda Cream, the black girl in her nurse's uniform, dark satin thighs shiny in their nylons, under the short white slip of her skirt; her brown breasts, visible almost to the nipples, swelled bare, supported by the sheerest scalloped cups, with the top three buttons of her tunic coolly undone. The antiseptic fragrance of the surgery enveloped both girls, with bottles, clysters and speculums sparkling on their racks, beside the array of canes, and the pipes hissing and gurgling next door.

'You'd better strip, now,' said Belinda. 'I have to examine you, and pronounce you fit for punishment, and it's almost time. You aren't going to make a scene, are you?'

'N-no,' Selina blurted, undoing her blouse, and the waistband of her shorts.

She stripped off her top, rubbing her breasts, as they popped naked from the cloth's constraint, then rolled down her shorts, panties, and fluffy socks. Nude, she lay face down on the surgical table, her buttocks raised by its rubber cushion. She shivered, as Belinda's fingers touched the bare fesses.

'Oh, that lovely smooth bottom, so firm, yet so soft . . . I really must kiss it,' Belinda murmured. 'I'd love to spank it, but we haven't time . . .'

She pressed her nose into Selina's bum cleft.

'Mm . . .' moaned Belinda. 'You smell so good . . . and that ripe bottom's begging to be spanked. But you must be unmarked, ready for . . . the works.'

'Oh, Miss,' Selina cried, shivering, 'I'm ready, but please don't remind me.'

'I'm sorry,' said Belinda. 'I'm supposed to probe your bum and cunny and everything, and I'll try to make it not too painful. Gosh, you must hate me, after . . . you know.'

'No, Miss. How could I hate *you*?' Selina whispered.

'Hardast, and the other gels, then. They sneaked on you, to Miss Kew.'

'Not really. There's no loyalty in prison, Miss, only power. Ooh!'

She wriggled, as Belinda's finger entered her anus, then penetrated the rectum, and began to probe her arse root.

'Ooh, that tickles,' Selina whimpered.

Belinda sighed, and began to lick her quivering bare buttocks, in the cleft, and on the fesse meat.

'Gosh, I'm wetting,' she gasped. 'I've never seen such a gorgeous bottom, Selina. Forty inches! That's . . . that's why I've been picking on you, with heavy enemas, and wanks, and things. I'm jealous.'

Her bum squirming under the anal penetration, Selina panted, as Belinda inserted three fingers of her left hand into the lips of Selina's cunt, thrusting to the wombneck, and reaming the walls of her pouch. Come dripped from Selina's cooze flaps, onto Belinda's knuckles.

'You're wet, too, you minx,' gasped Belinda.

'Yes,' Selina panted. 'You are so powerful, Miss . . .'

'If you'll give me your lady's word that you are fit for chastisement,' Belinda panted, 'we can skip the doings, and have a proper wank.'

'Yes, please,' Selina whispered.

15

Selina Smarting

Belinda plopped her fingers from Selina's holes, then rose, and grasped Selina's hips, pulling her bum up to her face, and plunging her nose and lips between the buttocks. She gurgled, as her tongue darted into Selina's wet slit, and began a brisk tongue-fuck, licking the clitty bud, which made Selina moan, and wriggle her arse. The black girl's nose poked into her anus, parting the pucker, until her whole nose was inside the elastic channel. She began to bite the inner arse cheeks, rubbing her face across the quivering bum flans, and chewing Selina's buttock meat. Returning to Selina's cunt, she sucked the whole vulva into her mouth, biting the lips, and tonguing the stiff knob of the clitoris, with loud squelching gurgles, as Selina's slit gushed come. Belinda's throat shook, swallowing the cunt juice. Selina locked her legs around Belinda's neck, forcing her face hard against her flowing cooze.

'Mm . . . yes . . .' she whimpered. 'Do me . . .'

'Ahh . . .' Belinda gasped, slurping Selina's come, as she chewed and licked the stiff clitty, with her nose squashed in Selina's slimed anus. 'I want to eat those cunt lips, and that big nubbin, and swallow your gorgeous bum whole.'

'Ooh! Mmm . . . gosh, I'm so wet,' panted Selina, 'your tongue is so strong on my clit, but it's not fair, Miss, I want to taste *you.*'

Panting, and with Selina's come drooling on her chin, Belinda released the girl's buttocks, and turned her on her back. Skirt up, she leapt onto the table, her panties

232

straddling Selina's face, and slid her hands beneath Selina's buttocks, cupping them in her palms, to lift them to her lips. Selina found the waistband of the nurse's thong panties, and ripped them down, revealing the girl's bare buttocks, and pink cunt flesh, sparkling with come. Belinda's distended clitty throbbed stiff between the cunt folds.

'Oh, yes,' gasped Selina, pulling the girl's come-slimed slit onto her face.

Their bums and bellies squelched, as they drank each other's come. Belinda's nyloned legs clamped Selina's face, while Selina's calves were locked around the black girl's hair. She tore open her blouse, allowing her naked breasts to pop from their skimpy bra cups, and rub Selina's belly.

'Ah . . .'

'Ooh . . .'

The moans and gasps of the masturbatresses resounded above the creaking of the table, as their bodies writhed and squirmed. Selina's face bobbed, stroking the nurse's come-soaked nylon stocking tops. Selina's wriggling cunt squelched, as Belinda swallowed her copious come, the residue trickling down her belly, to slime Belinda's breasts, squashed on Selina's navel.

'Mm . . . yes . . . I'm coming . . .'

'Ooh! *I'm* coming . . .'

'Ahh!'

'Ohh!'

'Yes . . .!'

'Ah! *Ahh* . . .'

Both girls erupted in shrill gasping squeals, as their cunts spurted come on their faces, and their bellies slapped together, heaving in orgasm. The door burst open; Miss Kew, flanked by two uniformed strappers, stood, frowning, and stroking the thwangs of her tawse against her sheer black nylons.

'Is the prisoner fit for chastisement, nurse?' she rasped.

Belinda rose, panting. With a hank of Selina's hair, she coolly wiped her cooze, before drawing up her panties, tucking her bare bubbies inside her blouse, and smoothing her skirtlet.

233

'Why, yes,' she purred. 'I was obliged to subdue her, Miss – she was restive. Best bind the slag extra-tight.'

She wrenched Selina by the hair, tumbling her into a kneeling position, on the floor.

'Oww,' Selina squealed. 'How could you, Miss? After we've – *ooh*!'

Belinda silenced her, with a vicious kick to the anus pucker. Holding Selina by the hair, Belinda offered Miss Kew the use of the surgery's stock of straps and hobbles. Selina began to sob, shivering helplessly, as Miss Kew ordered the strappers to secure her in restraints; Belinda watched, with her hands casually under her skirtlet, rubbing her panties string, and bare buttocks. Her fingers crept to her cunt, pushing aside the thong, to stroke the naked gash flesh. Come began to trickle into her nylon stocking tops, as the strappers fastened Selina's face in a tight metal brank, with a tongue depressor. Mute, she let them strap her quivering body in a mesh flogging corset, consisting of thin steel wire, leaving two inch squares of bare skin, and boned and rimmed in steel strips, which they laced more and more tightly, as Selina gasped for breath. Her bare skin puffed white, amid the biting steel corset wires.

'Seventeen inches?' said Miss Kew. 'I think you can take the slut to sixteen.'

Selina groaned, as the holes were knotted tighter, with the upper metal rim of the corset biting and squeezing her titties, to make them jut, shivering, above her ribcage. The lower rim dug into her top buttocks, forcing her arse globes into stark, swelling relief; the pumped bubbies and buttocks seemed about to burst from her constricted middle, laced to pencil thinness. Selina's feet were clamped in a two-foot wooden hobble, with narrow apertures for the ankles. She squealed, as Miss Kew thrust a ten-inch bum plug into her rectum, the plug affixed to a cunt brank, a hoop of thin, sharp steel, which snapped tightly around her perineum and bum cleft, with a metal waistband strung to the lower rim of her corset. The clip on her cunt brank, and one on her anal plug, as well as the eyelets of her corset, were all fastened to long rubber reins, held by the discipline mistress. She ordered Selina to clasp her hands behind her neck; her wrists were cuffed in steel clamps, dangling from the neck of her face brank. Inside the brank, Selina gasped, with her hair stuffed against her mouth. Miss Kew flicked her tawse on Selina's bottom.

'Giddy-up, pony,' she commanded.

Selina hobbled, at a clumsy trot, through the prison, out into the yard, and past the pillory. The nude bodies of Janet Pummer and Dawn Tregarsh hung listlessly, like wet rag dolls, tongues lolling from drool-slimed gaping mouths, and their breasts and buttocks mottled with whip weals. A crowd of slags were assembled, to jeer Selina as she passed amidst them, and pelt her with clumps of mud. Tears blurred Selina's eyes; buttocks lashed by Miss Kew's tawse, she staggered across the moor, pursued by the gleeful shrill of slags, and tripping in moss and bog, until they came to the stone circle. The sun was high, in a bright blue sky, adorned by fleecy clouds. Gwendoline Gurdell and her disciples, bare-breasted, in flowing gauze robes, awaited them, holding wands. They stood, encircling the table-sized flogging stone, its surface worn smooth. Above the stone stood the scaffold – an arch of ancient megaliths, encrusted with hooks, straps and pulleys. Miss Kew curtsied to the governess.

'Prisoner malfeasant ready for smart treatment, Miss,' she said.

Gwendoline nodded.

'Is she to be . . . put to the torture, in addition to her chastisement?' she murmured.

'With your permission, yes, Miss,' said Miss Kew. 'I have reason to believe she is the ringleader of a prostitution gang, procuring inmates to serve the vile lusts of males, and smuggle Home Office property, fucus pods, in return for illicit foodstuffs and tobacco.'

'Very well,' said Gwendoline. 'Chastise her, then free her from her tongue restraint, so that she may confess under torture.'

Selina's heart thumped, and her knees buckled.

'Mm! Mm!' she squealed, shaking her head, and rolling her eyes at Gwendoline, as her hobble was removed.

No ... it can't be! Gagged, I can't shout my code words, to free me from my nightmare ... surely Miss Gurdell understands?

She was spread face down on the cold rock. Her cunt brank was removed, but the corset remained, pinching her skin to ribbons. Her wrists were freed from their neck cuffing, and stretched to the stone's rim, to be bound with ropes; her ankles were clamped in cuffs, at the foot of the stone, fully spreading her legs, with her cunt, anus, and perineum exposed. The bare-breasted Phryne Wulding-doune fastened clothes pegs to her inner and outer cunt lips, stretching her slit wide open, with the pegs held by wires from above. Selina's branked head lolled over the stone's edge. The slags peered from outside the stone circle.

'Lash her arse black!'

'Whip her cooze raw!'

Selina wept, as she heard the eager taunts. Inside the circle, the disciples lifted their three foot wands, over her bare buttocks. Miss Kew lifted Selina's brank, and stared her in the eyes.

'This is only the *first* part of the works, trollop,' she hissed, dropping Selina's head, making her brank bang on the rock.

'*Uhh ...*' moaned the bound girl, shuddering, as a stream of piss hissed from her cunt flaps, soaking the rock, and dripping to the mossy turf below.

At a word from Gwendoline, the disciples, wands raised, lined up with their robes lifted and thighs parted. From their befurred cunts jetted streams of piss, filling Selina's head brank, and soaking her face and hair. Then they spat, on her head, back, buttocks and thighs, ejecting long gobbets of saliva from their lips, until Selina's body was fleckled with spittle. Selina spluttered, swallowing desperately. Phryne stood over her croup; arching her back, she directed a spurt of piss to wash Selina's fesses, followed by Jasmine, Avril, Tuppy and Kim, until Selina's bare was soaking wet. Piss dripped from her quivering bum, as the thrashing wands descended. Each girl laid her stroke on the three seconds, without pause.

'*Mmm! Urrgh!*' Selina gurgled, clenching her buttocks, with her titties, belly and cunt slapping the rock.

In thirty seconds, her squirming bumflesh was bruised crimson, with the bruises puffing to raw, angry weals, darkening to purple, as the flogging continued. The cheers of the watching girls fell silent, as they watched Selina wriggle on the stone, her branked head and corsed belly banging the rock, as her fesses squirmed. Her arms and legs jerked rigid against their bonds, as the canestrokes sliced her bare, spraying drops of piss at each convulsion of the wet flesh. Her cunt, wrenched by the pinching clothes pegs, spurted a constant dribble of piss and come. At a nod from Gwendoline, the wands began to cane Selina directly on the exposed pink slit meat. They sliced wetly on Selina's glistening cunt, so hard, that they sent her clothes pegs spinning into the heather. Selina's cunt basin wriggled frantically, rising and falling, to slam her pubic bone on the rock.

'*Urrgh! Urrgh!*' she screamed, deep in her throat.

The wands lashed her quim and anus for several seconds, then return to the blotched, wriggling arse melons. After a total flogging of two minutes, the wands rested, and Selina lay, snuffling, sobbing and writhing, on the stone, with piss trickling from her bruised cunt. Miss Kew poked two fingers into Selina's gash, and withdrew, rubbing them together, to show a film of oily come.

'The submissive slut was juicing,' she hissed.

'Really!' snorted Miss Gurdell. 'Such a gel deserves *no* sympathy.'

Belinda Cream, barefoot, in her white swimsuit, stepped forward, bearing a six-litre enema jar filled with yellow fluid. She curtsied to Gwendoline, informing her she had freshly prepared a chilli pepper enema. She hung the jar three feet over Selina's anus, and penetrated her with a slim rubber tube, poking the tube until it had passed her rectum, and was deep inside the sigmoid colon. She opened the drip on the jar, and the liquid bubbled, as it began its descent into Selina's bowel. Selina moaned, gasping in loud, anguished bursts, and wriggling her buttocks higher, to ease the liquid's passage. Her moans grew louder, as the jar emptied; Belinda removed the tube, when Selina had taken the whole six litres, plugging her anus with a rubber stopper, banded around her waist and cunt. Phryne and her girls released Selina from her bonds, and held her sagging body straight, while they plastered her bottom with bog mud. The groaning girl's wire-corsed belly bulged with lumps at her sigmoid colon and caecum. The anointing continued, until Selina's whole body below her neck was coated in a thick layer of the slimy brown mud.

Head lolling in her brank, she moaned, in a low, despairing whimper, as she was strung up on the scaffold. Her wrists were hung from ropes, wrenching her arms; pincers on wire strands clamped her cunt lips, stretching them to white flaps, above her quaking belly, and similar pincers on wires pinched her nipples, wrenching them into taut slivers, suspended from the scaffold; her legs were stretched in the splits, with the ankles roped to opposite megaliths. Piss and come dripped from her cunt, onto the flogging stone, while her bulging belly undulated in a rolling swell, as the enema fluid struggled to find release from her stoppered anus. She hung, groaning, for minutes, until the slime had caked to a hard brown carapace. Miss Kew gave the order; Phryne and the disciples raised long leather stockwhips.

The air seethed, whistling, as the heavy leather thongs flogged Selina's naked shoulders and back, lashing the squares of bare skin under her flogging corset. Her gurgling screams filled the air; the whips lashed her legs, buttocks, and breasts, even her hugely distended belly, lumpy with fluid under the bursting corset, until the caked mud began to disintegrate, and fly in chunks from her whipped body. The wires fixed to her cunt and nipples twanged, as her body jerked, swaying in space. A constant dribble of piss sprayed from Selina's open cunt, splattering her whippers' robes, bare bubbies, and white-fanged grimaces of malice. When Selina was flogged bare of mud, her whole nude body glowing with weals, and her corset now pressing on raw red flesh, Gwendoline deemed the thrashing complete. Phryne lashed her buttocks with a final stroke, and Selina howled: the stopper shot from her bum, and a torrent of yellow liquid spurted from her anus, drenching Phryne's beringed titties. Selina jerked and wriggled, as the enema liquid jetted from her hole, so that it sprayed the faces and bare breasts of Gwendoline and her disciples.

'Oh . . .' said Gwendoline faintly, wiping her breasts, and smelling her fingers, 'the gel must be tortured.'

Unbound, Selina knelt on the stone slab, with her wrists roped behind her back, thighs wide apart, and her cunt lips and nipples still clamped. The cunt lips stretched open, exposing pink wet slit meat. The nipples were winched slowly upwards, with the cunt clamps affixed to binding cords, pulling towards bolts in the earth. At each jolt to her stretched nipples, Selina mewled, and raised her thighs, only to scream, as the clamps pulled her gash flaps down, causing her to shrink lower, until her winched nipples pulled her, groaning, up again. Branked, she could only drool and sob, into her piled hair. Frantically, she nodded her head to Miss Gurdell, indicating her willingness to confess, whatever it was they wanted. Gwendoline said, sagely, that the torture was not to force an unwilling confession, but to make her *want* to confess, in gratitude.

Jasmine Wadd fetched a bucket, and began to ram its contents into Selina's stretched cunt. Helpless, Selina squealed and sobbed, as the cargo of live clams and lugworms filled her pouch, with Jasmine smiling coldly, as she crammed the cunt full of the slimy sea things. She filled Selina to the brim, taunting her, that she'd surely taken bigger cocks than this. Selina's belly bulged, as she wriggled at the crawling things inside her slit. Jasmine sealed her cunt with sticky tapes, and left her, squirming, while Tuppi and Kim upended an earthen jar of molten wax, letting it drip, slowly, across Selina's distended nipples and belly, on her thighs, pubes, and bare soles. Selina whimpered; still, the winches creaked, stretching her

239

gash flaps and nipples, as her wealed body was covered in the steaming, congealing hot wax. A thistle was pressed face in to her anus bud and moulded with wax.

'Ah . . . ah . . . ah . . .' she moaned.

The torture lasted over two hours. Head drooping, Selina gave no sign at its end, as the strappers unleashed her, only to bind each wrist, singly, to a rope seven feet long. Miss Kew and Phryne took the ends of the wrist ropes, while the strappers carried Selina to the cliff top, then down to a tiny cove, where the ebb tide was turning. Water lapping their boots, they lifted Selina on their shoulders, allowing Miss Kew and Phryne to tighten their ropes, until Selina was dangling against the cliff, suspended above the sand by her splayed arms. The strappers roped her ankles, pulling her legs apart, and fastened the rope ends to heavy, immovable boulders, leaving Selina pressed to the rock, her toes three feet above the sand, with the tide rising fast. Selina looked up, to see Gwendoline and Miss Kew peering, six feet above her. She was stretched like a starfish, with her naked quim and titties scratching the jagged cliff face. The strappers slopped her with blue woad, and then her gash was unplastered and emptied, and a new cargo stuffed to the brim, of live crabs. Selina howled – no pouch-fastening was necessary for the pinching beasts to remain in the wet, salty shelter of her squirming cunt. A strapper leaned over from the ascending path, and unfastened her brank.

'Ooh! Oh!' Selina gasped, shaking her piss-sodden hair from her mouth. 'Oh, please! It's agony!'

'Ready to confess, gel?' said Gwendoline.

'I've nothing to confess, Miss,' blurted Selina, dangling helplessly on the cliff face.

'The tide rises fast, here,' drawled Miss Kew. 'Sometimes it rises to a foot below your chin, and sometimes to a foot above. In that case, your all-over tan won't protect you, miss. By the way, the crabs inside your pouch are tasty snacks for the eels, brought by the high tide, and eels like ladies' cunts. Well, governess, time for our tea.'

'No! no!' Selina shrieked. 'Oh, no, no, I can't take it any more, I've had enough!'

'Confess?' said Miss Kew, peeping over the clifftop.

'No ... no ...' Selina moaned. 'I've finished, do you hear? Please listen. *I've been dreadfully misunderstood.*'

'Every slag says that,' sneered miss Kew.

'No, no, they're my code words, you know? You must! I've played your game, but I ... just can't take any more. *I've been dreadfully misunderstood!*'

'Oh, yes, the code words,' said Gwendoline.

'Thank you, Miss!' Selina gasped.

'I haven't heard those for *such* a long time,' Gwendoline continued. 'I do think Gawain and Pippa might change them.'

'What ...? Miss, I'm not really a felon, I'm a journalist.' Selina pleaded, as the waters lapped her thighs. 'I arranged to come here. You *must* believe me.'

'Oh, I do believe you, gel,' said Gwendoline. 'Why, none of my gels is a felon – they *all* arranged to come here, with the same absurd code words. I myself had to use them, after a lot worse than a dangling. You silly thing! We are *all* here *because we want to be.*'

The two girls departed.

'*Nooo* ... don't leave me!' Selina wailed.

The water frothed blue and brown at her buttocks, as the woad dripped, and her anus squirted a powerful string of dungs into the rising sea. Selina broke down into frenzied sobbing, wrenching helplessly at the ropes, and squirming against the cliff, with the rocks scratching her squashed titties and pubes. Her bottom threshed violently, as a monstrous fishy presence slithered into her cunt, and she screamed, slamming her quim against the rock. The water rose rapidly, over her belly, her breasts, and collarbone. Her screams were no longer of pain.

Please, no, please let it all be a dream ... they'll come at the last minute. Of course they will. I'm Home Office property ...

The sea rose over Selina's eyes, and, breasts heaving, she saw her hair waving in tendrils about her face, like seaweed, amid the swirling of woad. Suddenly a shape flitted in the water beside her. It was a nude girl; Selina fell

241

backwards, as her ropes were sliced, and began to swim to the surface, where she gulped air. Huge breast melons pierced the surface, followed by a whip-wealed bare bottom, as the nude girl did a somersault.

'Bethany!' Selina cried.

Bethany put a finger to her lips.

'I expect you'd like some tuck,' she whispered. 'Then I'll take you to safety. Follow me.'

She dived, and Selina followed her twisting nude body, darting amongst fishes, with Bethany's pink cunt flesh winking at her like a beacon, through a labyrinth of underwater caves, until they broke surface, at a huge cavern, its stalagmites illumined by oil lamps. The cave was piled with cigarettes, lager, and potato crisps.

'You . . . the tuck mistress!' she gasped.

'Well, *somebody* has to be. There's only one thing,' Bethany said, with a moue. 'I'm out of prawn cocktail flavour. There's only cheese and onion, this week. They never listen!'

After a feast of lager and crisps, the girls smoked cigarettes. Bethany continued her litany of complaints.

'They always pick on me,' she moaned. 'I have to be the tuck mistress, and still get whipped. It's jolly unfair.'

'Bethany,' Selina murmured, lighting a fresh smoke from her stub, 'where exactly is safety?'

'Why, the guesthouse, of course,' said Bethany, eating, smoking and drinking at the same time. 'The entrance is right here, up the chimney. 'I think they are expecting you.'

'But I've nothing to wear.'

'That's just the point.'

Selina followed Bethany's agile bottom, up the spiralling rock chimney, to emerge within a courtyard. Through a spiked steel gate, the harbour sparkled in the moonlight, with Hamish's boat moored at the jetty. Bethany rapped on the door. It opened, in a pool of light, illumining a tall, full-breasted ash blonde, thirtyish, with shiny straight hair caressing her shoulders. She wore a long, flowing blue skirt, taut over her full bottom, and slit to the waist, to reveal a hint of stocking top; a white blouse, with a red bow; her long coltish legs shiny in grey nylons, above shiny grey leather boots. Pink tortoiseshell glasses perched impishly on her nose, above a broad, smiling mouth. The only thing distinguishing her from the editress of a ladies' fashion magazine was the smart wooden cane at her waistband.

'Bethany, darling!' she cried, embracing the nude, smutted girl, with a kiss to the cheek. 'Mwamph! Have you come to join us?'

'No, Auntie Ros, you know they work me so beastly hard,' sulked Bethany. '*You* would, too. And what thanks do I get? Whipped, and bummed, and absolutely *humiliated*. It's almost as bad as being Mr Breasted's slave, but at least *he* knew how to *cane* properly.'

'You are a minx, knowing how short-staffed I am. But this is Selina, at last! My, what a *ravishing* bottom – and such an *adorable* corset. Had the works, gel, eh? A good porage bath is what those buttocks need. Porage does wonders for weals! We've a full house this evening – the Royal Hebs' reunion. I dare say you know everybody. My, what a lot of bottoms to be whopped, and stiff pegos to be softened!'

'Miss Wapping?' Selina blurted.

'Call me Auntie Ros, gel. Everyone does, even the beastly Home Office.'

'I don't quite understand,' Selina said.

'Neither do I,' said Auntie Ros cheerfully. 'I've been trying to requisition you for absolutely yonks, but you know what bureaucrats are. Paperwork! A dozen on the bare would smarten them up. I suppose you have your pee forty-five, or whatever it's called? Oh, never mind, come in and have your bath.'

They passed the open door of a huge lounge, discreetly lit with candelabras, where costumed ladies and men in royal blue blazers quaffed drinks, served by naked maids, with thistles lodged in their bum clefts. On a small stage, a nude girl, touching toes, whimpered in pain, as another girl, wearing only black thigh boots, face mask and corset, tawsed her on the bare, to applause from the throng. Come sprayed from the slit of the whipper's gleaming, shaven cunt hillock, as her naked buttocks clenched in the sensuous rhythm of the tawsing. In the ornate bathroom adjoining, Selina and Bethany lowered themselves into a large round bath of hot porage.

'I expect you two minxes will want to play with yourselves, as gels will,' said Auntie Ros, 'so go ahead. And it's all right to, ah, relieve yourselves. Shan't be a jiffy.'

She left the girls alone, sighing luxuriantly.

'Shall we?' said Selina. 'I'm a bit . . . you know.'

'Oh, if we must,' Bethany replied.

The two girls peed, and were lazily frotting each other, as Ros returned, cracking her cane over a dozen sheepish, blue-blazered males, amongst them Hamish, Roddy and Denis.

'Right, you beastly oiks,' commanded Auntie Ros. 'This is your dinner dance – porage for dinner, while your beastly bums dance. Trousers down, and get licking.'

Selina gasped, as a dozen bare-bottomed males, grimacing at the swish of Ros's cane on their bottoms, slurped the porage from her naked body, with their tongues tickling her every crevice. She and Bethany continued to masturbate, come flowing copiously, until the diners, each stiff-cocked, had eaten every drop of the glutinous mixture. Hamish's tongue was on Selina's throbbing clitoris, when she exploded, wriggling, in a deep orgasm.

'Ah . . . yes . . .' she moaned. 'Do me, Hamish, it's so good . . .'

Auntie Ros's cane cracked bottom after bottom, until each had taken over three dozen.

'There is no end of naughty boys and gels,' she sighed. 'Saltdean or Auchterhuish, where there's whopping to be done, I must go.'

She surveyed the whipped men, rubbing their crimson bottoms, and frowned at their stiff tools.

'Well!' she said. 'I must be hostess. Let's hope those horrid erections are soon gone.'

Pointedly leaving her cane, she swirled from the bathroom. Selina climbed from her bath, nude body gleaming, and, grasping the cane, ordered Hamish to bend over.

'My arse is burning!' he wailed, red-faced.

'I'll have to test that,' Selina rapped.

'Ouch! I'll get even with you, miss.'

As Selina caned Hamish's squirming bare bum, Bethany began to suck Denis's cock, while the other canees lined up, cocks stiff in anticipation. Hamish was whimpering, his arse wealed crimson, when Selina abruptly knelt, plunged his stiff tool between her breasts, and gave him a tit-wank, until his cream spurted over her nipples. She rubbed the spunk into her breasts, then over the puffy weals on his bottom.

'Arse still burning?' she drawled; Hamish blushed.

Auntie Ros returned, half an hour later, to find every male's cock drooping, and Bethany licking her spunk-slimed lips.

'How many did Hamish take?' she demanded.

'Please, Miss, six dozen,' said Selina.

'Not enough for *that* insolent. Still, you've more than earned your nipple rings. Come, there are old friends you must meet.'

'Please, Miss, may I wear one of those thistles . . . you know, in my bottom?' murmured Selina.

Auntie Ros smiled.

'It means "total submissive". Do you mind?'

'No,' Selina whispered.

Selina mounted the stage, where the tawsing of the nude girl continued. Watching were Harriet, rubber-skirted, and bare-breasted, with chains piercing her nipples; Claire Boosey, crouching naked in a leather harness, with Henry Addercop holding her leash; Pippa Parkhurst and Leofra Wolliman, in catsuits of tight black rubber, holding whips. Behind them, Hardast and Arioma stood radiantly naked, with thistles at their bum clefts.

'Ooh, yes, Mr Breasted, harder, please. Fill my naughty bottom . . .' squealed Gwendoline Gurdell.

She leaned on a table, buttocks spread, wearing nothing but a tight rubber corset, with Gawain Breasted buggering her. She stroked her corsed belly, as her titties wobbled under his thrusts.

245

'Seventeen inches!' she drooled. 'I knew I could . . .'

The masked tawser completed the naked girl's flogging, knelt suddenly, and licked her anus. The girl cried out, shuddering almost at once in orgasm. Auntie Ros whispered orders to Selina, and the tawser, who curtsied. Selina, wincing, thrust out her bare breasts, as the masked girl pierced her nipples, and inserted golden hoops. She parted Selina's buttocks, and pushed a thistle stem into her anus, then removed her mask, and curtsied, to applause.

'Jane!' Selina gasped, her nip rings jangling.

'Hello, Miss,' said Jane. 'How pleased I am for you! It was I who recommended you to the SSS board. That's Harriet, Gawain, Henry, Pippa, amongst others, including Aunt Ros, of course. We of the SSS – the Saltdean Spanking Society – are a discreet group, funded by the Home Office, and dedicated to the honing and perfection of the English gel's bottom, Miss. Yours has proved supreme, as my report suggested. I . . . I suppose you'll want to slipper me, for my cheek.'

'Why, no . . .' blurted Selina.

Smiling, Jane fingered her thwangs.

'You'd rather I whipped *you* . . .?' she whispered, and Selina blushed crimson.

'Oh, do,' cried the tawsed girl, rubbing her blistered red bottom. 'She's the best I've met, ever since I found my true nature, thanks to Miss Etiquette's wonderful advice. You must know *her*.'

'I *am* Miss Etiquette,' Selina blurted.

'Well! I'm Valerie of Pangbourne.'

'You've left your beastly hubby, then?'

'Gracious, no! He's over there, enjoying himself.'

She pointed to an alcove, where a male, strapped to a stool, received a vigorous bare-bum birching, from Miss Kew, nude save for lemon yellow panties. Beneath Miss Kew's crushing bare foot groaned Phryne Wuldingdoune, her naked body bound in rubber cords, and belly swollen by a gurgling enema. Miss Kew smiled at Selina.

'First,' bustled Auntie Ros, 'Selina has to formally accept her new post, as governess of Auchterhuish.'

Selina's jaw dropped.

'Don't blame me, it's the Home Office,' said Ros. 'I don't choose the bums, I just whop them. Gwen Gurdell has turned a bit sub, and is transferred to Henry Addercop's staff. That leaves you, Selina – the perfect bottom, and a dominant personality. Your civil service number is on its way, at the usual snail's pace.'

'This was planned?' Selina blurted.

'Of course,' said Jane.

'But I don't feel awfully dominant, really. I rather like the thistle in my bum.'

Jane plucked it out.

'You beast!' Selina cried. 'I should thrash you.'

'Are those your orders, Miss?' said Jane, licking her teeth.

'Not yet,' said Selina, 'I'll do things my way ... *if you please, gentlemen!*'

Crouching, she snapped her fingers; the blue blazers of the Royal Hebs were quickly jettisoned, and a dozen nude, erect young men lined up, before Selina's proffered buttocks. Hamish, after fisting the writhing naked bum of Hardast, was last in line. Selina's arse flans shuddered, as the first cock penetrated her, spreadeagled on the stage. She squirmed, as cock after stiff cock buggered her quivering anus; her face contorted in pain, as her titties squelched on the boards. To enthusiastic applause, they spunked heavily at her arse root, until her thighs were slimed with sperm, mingled with the come, gushing copiously from her cunt.

'Yes,' she gasped. 'Fuck me, bugger me ... oh, I'm coming ...'

As Selina orgasmed for the third time, Ros whispered in her ear.

'This is all very well, governess, and quite within your rights. My duty is simply to ensure a steady supply of submissive pleasure girls for the VIP users of our guest-house. But, as governess, you must have just a *little* dominance. You will undoubtedly wish to punish Belinda, Miss Kew, all those who have reddened your bum.'

'Not really,' Selina gasped, her buttocks shuddering under rapid buggery. 'They are just doing their job, as civil servants. Oh, I'm so confused! I so love spanking gels, but I'm not the snob I was. I like being spanked, too, and – *you* know – *full bung submission*. I'm to be governess, I shall do things *my own* way. Ooh!'

Spunk bubbled from her bumhole, as her bugger spurted at her sigmoid colon. Panting, he withdrew, to be greeted by a frilly maid, with her skirt pinned up, to show her knickerless bottom, and the thistle peeping from her bum cleft. She carried a silver tray.

'Refreshments, sir? She said. 'Crisps, lager? And for you, Miss? Oh – Selina! How sweet your bottom looks. There's nothing like a good meat enema.'

'Kristel,' Selina gasped. 'How lovely. Yes, I'm waiting for someone rather important. Have you got a smoke?'

'Wish I could have your job,' said Kristel Gummi, placing a lit cigarette between Selina's lips. 'Must dash – I believe a gentleman wants to use my mouth.'

'A lady may seek her pleasure anywhere,' said Ros, as Selina puffed, stroking her bum cleft. 'Personally, I never tire of whopping naked bottoms. That's my job – I've forgotten my civil service number, it's awfully long. No matter, as long as there are lovely squirming miscreant bums for my cane to redden. Ah, the poetry of spanked bare buttocks . . .'

'Harder, bitch, harder,' groaned Henry Addercop, bent over a sofa back.

His bare arse wriggled, under Bethany's tawse, while he tongued the cunt of the maid Susan, squatting over him, with her frilly maid's tutu lifted, and come trickling on her flounced stocking tops.

'I'm whopping as hard as I can,' wailed Bethany. 'Why do I always get these rotten jobs?'

'Why, you cheeky slut – urrgh!' gurgled Henry, as Susan released a torrent of steaming piss into his mouth.

'Oh, auntie,' gasped Selina, 'I'd so like you to cane *me*.'

'Certainly, when your bottom is smooth,' murmured Ros. 'Your forty incher is indeed tasty. For the moment, try a tiny bit of dominance.'

'All staff are to shave their quims,' said Selina.

'Delightful. It's quite the fashion.'

'They must be jolly nice to me, and spank me, whenever I say so.'

'Hmm . . .'

'From now on, Belinda is to give six litre enemas. There is far too much blubbing and moaning with gels these days. They can easily take a sixer.'

'Well, *yes*, Selina . . . but how about something a teensy bit less submissive?'

'Very well. Bethany!'

'Yes?'

'Thrash my best friend Harriet within an inch of her life.'

'Oh, must I? Why do I have to do everything?' pouted Bethany.

'That is an order, slag!' snapped Selina.

Thwap! Thwap!

'Ouch! You rotten beast!'

The tawse lashed Harriet's bare nates, and she began to squirm.

'*That's* more like it,' said Auntie Ros, approvingly.

'*Yes!*' Selina gasped, as her buttocks parted, and Hamish's cock filled her rectum.

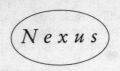

NEXUS NEW BOOKS

To be published in March

THE ANIMAL HOUSE
Cat Scarlett

The glamorous and self-possessed Violetta receives a chance invitation to stay at a dream French chateau. Following a casual, train-board encounter with a mysterious and self-assured man, it becomes apparent that her holiday opportunity is not as random as it seemed, and Violetta finds herself drawn into a community whose members take their pleasures disguised beneath animal masks. Behind the licentiousness of her holiday destination, however, she finds a dark tradition of Gallic libertinage and medieval torture she had not imagined, as the Sadean trappings of the chateau are revealed and used upon her in turn.

£6.99   ISBN 0 352 33877 6

HOT PURSUIT
Lisette Ashton

Lucy is Master Donald's second favourite. When she tries to ask him a favour, however, not only does he not hear her out but, in pique, he asks his favourite, Ginger, to discipline Lucy. When poor Lucy runs away, Donald and Ginger wonder if they've gone too far. But as they give chase, they realise that in their bizarre SM society it's really little Lucy who holds all the cards . . .

£6.99   ISBN 0 352 33878 4

EMMA'S SECRET WORLD
Hilary James

Becoming Ursula's slave was the most exciting thing that had ever happened to Emma. She is whisked away to the confines of an English country residence, where beautiful but cruel mistresses preside over a bevy of young and wayward girls. Their corrective regime demands ultimate sacrifice in return for absolute fulfilment, and Emma surrenders every dignity of adulthood to learn the discipline necessary for her training. A Nexus Classic.

£6.99   ISBN 0 352 33879 2

If you would like more information about Nexus titles, please visit our website at www.nexus-books.co.uk, or send a stamped addressed envelope to:

Nexus, Thames Wharf Studios,
Rainville Road, London W6 9HA